It's About Time

Dennis Patrick Treece

It's About Time

ISBN (Paperback): 978-1-989942-00-0

ISBN (Ebook): 978-1-989942-01-7

Printed in the United States of America

ELK PRESS
Chokecherry Lane SW,
Edmonton, Alberta, Canada
www.elkpress.ca
+1 888 410 0122

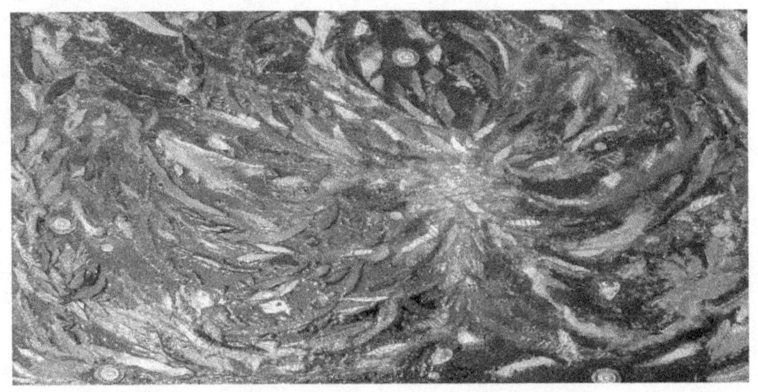

The background of the cover art is an originalglass shard painting by Eleanor Ruth Fisher, titled “Genesis.”

"Everything is energy, and that's all there is to it. Match the frequency of the reality you want and you cannot help but get that reality. This is not philosophy. This is physics."

Common Sense

Dedication

This book is dedicated to my beautiful and supportive wife, Dr. Eleanor Ruth Fisher, PsyD

TABLE OF CONTENT

Chapter One

Itself's Resonant "Correction"

It was a simple thing for Itself to do, almost trivial, really. He was just doing some vibrational housekeeping and thought little of it. "Putting my universes right" he might have explained it, if asked. Energy beings of this magnitude simply have different priorities and concerns than if they were in any way physical.

Itself took on the tasks of oversoul of the six Earth spaces early in their development, a very long time before the word "Earth" had been applied to any of them. Sufficient time had elapsed since the Big Bang for the planets there to form, and cool, and for spontaneous life to emerge. Like all physical plane situations chaos was the rule of their existence and out of that chaos came sufficient chemical and biological events on some of these six worlds to generate biological life which, while different in appearance in every case, were surprisingly similar in many other ways, especially given the random nature of their evolution in such different environments. Itself knew that whatever their form, intelligent life are to be cherished for their ability to Teach certain necessary things to immortal energy beings; things they can't Learn as an energy being without physical substance and all the conflicts which accrue to that life.

Itself was by this time in its own Journey a merged, super spirit of great magnitude. It had lived through every trial and circumstance of physical life and had eventually succeeded and then helped others succeed, too. It was well on its way to completing its endgame of reunification with the Divine Creator. It was therefore as familiar as any other conscious entity, except the Creator of course, with the various aspects of Creation and what it knew of the Divine Plan. His six vibrational variants of the same universe with all its suns and planets and other physical aspects, and whatever independently generated physical life forms, provided never ending lessons for Itself and for Itself's less developed colleagues as they pursued their journeys. The amount of time this took was not an issue for them, and indeed it was never considered. This is because for them Time does not exist. They find that it is often nothing more than a distraction when they deal with an Intelligent Physical Life Form and their obsessive interest with it. Itself's vast collection of merged spirits provided memories and experience that contributed to its great wisdom. Memories and the Learning from his many and varied IPLF partnerings on many planets that mortals are hyper-aware of Time. All mortals need some way to calculate and respond to the passage of time so they can measure the span of their days; important to them given their pitifully short lives. Even for Shonakians, who live more than fifteen hundred rotations of their planet around their star, time was extraordinarily important. But knowing this is not the same as sympathizing with this point of view. There are much more important things in pursuit of the Plan and time is really nothing but an artificial construct by IPLF on the physical planes and of no consequence to the ninety-five percent of Existence that is non-physical. Even on the physical planes it is of little consequence except in the minds of IPLF. Mountains eroding and shedding their mass onto the plains below them do so without concern for how long that takes. Water flowing downstream evaporating into the atmosphere only to be returned in the form of rain cares nothing and knows nothing of the passage of time. Plants and animals may care for the seasons and daylight and darkness but are unaware of any way to think of it as "time." People, however, create the notion of Time and then depend on it to define not only their own lives but also the various things they do. How much time to boil water? How long will it take to build the boat? Who crosses the finish line in the shortest time?

How long did she live and on what date did she die? Etc. ad infinitum. For mortals, therefore, time is as real as gravity, an inescapable aspect of life.

While this is, as noted, not true for energy beings, there are still aspects of time that can achieve notice by them. The different vibrational rates of each of the six universes causes slight differences in orbits and movement of Itself's six planets. Eventually the orbits lost perfect synch and Itself put that right. For Him it was not a time adjustment, just a synchronicity adjustment on the Physical Planes. "Putting the Physicals right" is how Itself would put it. This did, however, have some temporal impact, which Itself considered of little consequence since time was something of no real consequence, anyway. It was like an itch that had to be scratched. Nothing more. And he only had to think it as having happened in order to actually make it happen. And so he did. And so it did.

Chapter Two

Bon And Shonak

Bon emerged from his shell a thousand years, what they call on Shonak "Solar Rotations," before he became the Eldest of Plus-Five Base. It was the day he became a Gold, on his one thousandth birthday. He had so far had an exceptional career for a Shonakian, fitting in but only just, and in his long life doing what amounted to great things. He was normal as defined by Shonak social custom or he would not have been allowed to hatch, even, since they pre-test their young prior to emerging from their shell. So "normal," yes, but with a subtle difference between him and most of his fellows. He was not alone in this, but he was certainly part of a very small minority of people on his world who, while fitting the required social mold, only just managed to do so. And as always on Shonak, in a good way. No other way was acceptable.

Being in that cadre of "acceptably different" individuals stood him in good stead throughout his long life as it allowed him to see things others could not. In Bon's case, his almost uniquely different behavior, what set him apart from most others, was his inherent distrust of facts. This is odd and controversial on Shonak since facts support the core of Shonak's belief system. So, Bon tread lightly. And truth to tell, after five hundred thousand years of scientific inquiry, most known or "accepted" facts on Shonak were beyond question. While he did not take any special pride or satisfaction in disproving what had been considered a fact, he did feel a sense of accomplishment on the rare occasion when it happened. This was not out of spite or arrogance, He merely felt that his universe had been set right in some small way. Then he moved on with his vocations until he found another fact he could reasonably question, and then go after it with unwavering tenacity.

However, and of course, to survive in the collaborative, uncompetitive Team culture on Shonak he did his best not to disturb the established norms that make Shonak society so pleasant. The placid, age-dominated world culture on Shonak is one where the oldest person on any team or in any situation was automatically in charge and always right, no contest. And, in truth, most of the time older people were right. This is how their seniority system had survived for hundreds of thousands of years. Elders did not and do not just arbitrarily decide things. On this planet of mental titans all people trended to the correct side of any discussion and with the experience of age they got better and better at coming to the right conclusions or plans or best ideas faster than their juniors. And this is what made their system work. The fact that the final authority of the Eldest of any team was usually justified is what kept their culture on that track, liberating them from interpersonal conflicts or rivalries. Intellectual differences of opinion can and do exist and there is plenty of pre-decision discussion among team members whenever a decision is needed. Whenever a decision is made by the Eldest in any team or social situation that ends the discussion. This prevents the distraction of office politics and helps Shonak maintain their sedate march towards technology achievements and the life of immense satisfaction and the sense of comfort they enjoy. Interpersonal anxiety is virtually unknown on Shonak.

And because it is so important to their Team-based social structure, the age of any person must never be in dispute. This is achieved by tattooing the exact time of everyone's hatching on their right arm. This determines their placement in Teams, and society, for the duration of their lives. To assist with age recognition at a distance, they each have a colored age-dot on their forehead which corresponds to their age-range. They also wear a left-wrist badge in the same color. The color of the forehead dots and wrist badges are changed every 142 S-Rots (Earth years), by the Age Grand Team, culminating with gold at the age of one thousand. And however much longer they live, and they may live an additional five or six hundred years, their gold dot does not change.

Another feature of Shonak that differs from

Earth is the absence of gender relations. All Shonakians are the same gender and reproduce by regurgitating an egg at around age four hundred and then a second one, if they choose, at around seven hundred years of life. The second egg is often not produced but can be if their population numbers dictate it would be prudent to do so. They have quite happily maintained a world population of 142 million for tens of hundreds of Solar Rotations. These few millions on such a large planet are distributed throughout their 142 administrative Regions. Shonakians also do not have family conflicts because they do not have families. No Shonakian knows the identity of their parent and they don't care. Their eggs are anonymously dropped off at the nearest education center for hatching, and that's the end of the parent's involvement.

Free from interpersonal competition and other forms of social strife, and without any difficulties concerning health and welfare, Shonakians have been free to concentrate on improving their knowledge and mastery of all things in, on, and around their world. They continuously push the boundaries of science and technology through invention and exploration. If their mind can conceive it they do not stop until they have achieved it or proved it impossible. They discovered their five alternate-planet cousins in this way quite by accident. Their science and technology teams were experimenting with transport shuttles that could alter their inherent resonance, thus actively scrambling their molecular structure without losing identity. This allowed them to "fly" through solid matter without the need for digging tunnels. Like how water flows through sand. At one point in their advanced testing they were travelling through a mountain on their world and instead of coming out on the opposite side on Shonak, they emerged on another world, entirely! It was what they would later call "Plus-One" as it was one planetary frequency band above their own. Their exploration of that world showed it to be another version of Shonak but very different as it evolved in its own way and time. Through trial and error, they found all five of these planetary bandwidths above Shonak. Entire Universes, actually, since each of these planets had their own solar systems and galaxies just like theirs, but at different levels of vibration. As this science matured, they called their planet's resonance "Prime" since it was their own and because it lay at the bottom of the six planetary frequency bands. Only two of these worlds had intelligent life, that they could initially see anyway; theirs, at the bottom, and Plus-Five (eventually known as Earth) at the top. Their scientists thought there could be more levels above Plus-Five and they spent a great deal of time and effort trying to find out if this was true. The three scout ships they sent up to "Plus-Six" were never heard from again. They refused to give up on their crews or their desire to find a Plus-Six, so they established an outpost on Plus-Five to continue their search from closer to their objective. This was not an easy thing to do. In order to remain on Plus-Five, or any other of the worlds outside their own resonance, they needed to protect themselves by creating a protective Zone of Influence for their scout ships and crews. One of the hard facts that emerged from their efforts with frequency alteration was that everything in the physical realms of existence has a resonance that they were created or born into. This cannot be altered. A stone from Shonak set on the ground on Plus-Five will quickly disappear and reappear sometime later on Shonak because always remains at its native frequency. It will have appeared briefly on Plus-Four, Plus-Three, Plus-Two, and Plus-One before returning to its native vibration on Shonak. This is something the Shonakians call the Law of Nativity: the frequency something is created or born into is immutable and cannot be changed. He preferred not to, but Bon had seen enough proof of it to accept this as a fact.

The Shonak base on Plus-Five had been in operation for a little more than a thousand S-Rots. Over this time they had built a thriving outpost on Plus-Five out on a remote island on primitive Earth which contained a large headquarters facility maintained at the Prime resonance within a gigantic zone of influence. The base had been established with two main missions and a third had developed over time, eclipsing the first two. In the beginning of their quest to find a Plus-Six, they determined it was expedient to establish a base as close to it as they could. This put them on the "higher" planet in a serious way. Their mission on Plus-Five was to find out from the natives clues to two things. First, what happened to their scout ships, and second, to learn if there are any useful vibrations above Plus-Five. To facilitate these missions, they developed an extensive surveillance program to watch the natives on Plus-Five. The Shonakians were looking for evidence of the supreme beings all Earth cultures believed in. Shonak's thinkers reasoned that these beings, if they existed, likely did so at the Plus-Six resonance, or higher, and so were desperate to find one and talk to it. If, as many native stories insisted, they could appear among the natives on Plus-Five in any form they wished, then perhaps they could alter themselves with the power of thought, something only people from Plus-Six were thought to do. How marvelous it would be if Shonak could acquire the ability to achieve "thought-creation" like these deities supposedly can.

The gods and goddesses and spirits of Plus-Five lore may have been given different names, and the religious rites performed in their names may be different, but all Plus-Five native cultures believed in these beings in some form or other. Very early in their development, and all over the planet, natives of different cultures, ignorant of each other, believed in forces greater than themselves. They prayed to their various supernatural beings and offered gifts and sacrifices to them as payment or bribes for their help. Shonakians put no trust in stories of supernatural beings and this part of the mission was not taken very seriously by Shonak's leaders, but they felt it was an avenue of inquiry worth looking into. Shonakians have no religion, do not believe in anything supernatural, never even dream. There are no words in their language for such things. It simply does not occur to them that there may be forces in the Universe that can't be explained by any science they know of or can develop.

This effort on Plus-Five had as a result, over the many hundreds of S-Rots, put in place an ever-expanding network of surveillance devices disguised as both animate and inanimate objects. Prior to Bon's arrival, and despite all their surveillance, the base on Plus-Five did not definitively find a god or goddess, or Plus-Six, but they did find that Plus-Five watching was extremely popular back on Shonak. In order to maintain discrete surveillance of their favorite subjects, it was necessary for Shonak to construct devices made of native materials. This is because anything with the mechanism to establish a Zone of Influence to keep it from disappearing back to Shonak would be visible and give off the telltale "feeling" to it which makes them impossible to hide. So, they painstakingly constructed a manufacturing facility of native materials then manufactured native-material bots that could manufacture all their necessary collectors in the shape of rocks and trees, cockroaches and rodents, birds, and every other living thing, even people.

On his one-thousandth birthday, Bon arrived at Plus-Five Base to take command. He found that the Team he was inheriting was more focused on infotainment collection than on its original, stated mission, which they seemed to have lost faith in. He reckoned that Shonak's leadership wanted a change in direction, and chose him to make it happen, to put it right. These leaders thought if anyone could put the original mission back on track, and determine the truth of a Plus-Six, Bon could. This in spite of his relative lack of seniority as a brand-new gold. Where did their scout ships go and was it true, as some of their best minds speculated, that there was such a thing as "thought-creation" at the Plus-Six resonance of existence? How wonderful would it be to create something just by thinking it into being?

So, Bon set to work on his mission but, for most people of Shonak, when not caught up in their own team missions, Plus-Five watching was next highest on their lists of things to do. Essentially, Plus-Five had become something of a cultural theme park for their education and enjoyment. With little to do on Shonak but work in their teams, they greatly enjoyed the diversion of viewing the activities of these violent, hairy, sweaty, conflicted and contradictory people. When Bon was on Plus-Five, the planet was at a period in its social and technology development which saw tribes and a few small cities with no technology other than some metal smithing. The planet was mostly devoted to agriculture and tending animals. They were a violent people in a hostile, often violent world where there was frequently something hungry that would eat them or something poisonous to bite them or someone to fight for a mate or a drink or something to eat. As a consequence, the natives on Plus-Five developed very successful survival skills and had an inherent default to feeling threatened, especially by other people. Shonak was completely unlike that. There was no competition for food, or a mate, nothing was poisonous, and nothing ate meat. This allowed them to develop intellectually rather than physically in order to survive and manage the world around them. To be sure, however, compared to Plus-Five, Shonak was boring.

Bon had always showed an interest in all things Plus-Five, even in the education center before he got his red dot. He chose the Exploration Grand Team in an effort to get posted there but while he had many assignments which dealt with his favorite planet, he never managed an assignment "up there" on the planet itself. So after nearly a lifetime of study on everything related to Plus-Five Bon finally arrived there as its Eldest. During his time there he became even more familiar with native cultures on several continents and was able to connect with many of them on a more or less personal basis, by way of his various bots. He travelled extensively using his bots rather than his phase suit so he could mingle with the native population. With their technology, it was very much like being there in person.

The forty-four S-Rots/years Bon was Eldest of Plus Five Base, under the Grand Team Exploration, were perhaps the most eventful forty-four years in Shonakian history, up to that point. Understandably, for long-lived people, they tend to take the long view and see events in terms of centuries or millennia. But in this short time frame Bon achieved and did remarkable things while being watched by his countrymen back home. Vid-watch clubs were formed all over Shonak and following Bon's exploits was among the most popular vids. The people specializing in watching Bon were known as Bonners and were committed to catching his every move there, in the various guises he used and also his activities as Eldest of Plus-Five Base.

Bon is best known for cultivating a friendship with an Earther native in a primitive part of the world. They travelled together extensively. For his part, Bon was trying to leverage this very devout Earth native who claimed to have relationships with gods. The Earth native, who was called Atsa, was trying to leverage the "godlike" transportation and weapons capabilities of Bon, who Atsa thought must be a god himself. Bon wanted to find out if there was a Plus-Six and if so, could they use it? Atsa wanted to preach to the unconverted about Love and living life in an honorable way, the Fourth World way, respecting everything around them, animal, vegetable, and mineral. Both of them got their wish. A "god" came to address them and Atsa visited the population centers of the world in 975 BCE to spread his message of Love. After the lecture by the entity who the natives considered a god, Bon eventually closed down the Base, concluding there was no possibility of exploiting Plus-Six, that is, the energy layer above the physical planes of existence. Atsa returned home with a handful of enhanced corn seeds and memories even he would come to doubt.

In S-Rot 306102, five solar rotations after the lecture delivered by a "God" on Plus-five, Bon declared the mission of Plus-Five Base completed. The OE at the time, a Gold who had come up through the Agriculture Grand Team, had no interest in any notion of a Plus-Six, but was an avid "Plus-Five Watcher." He agreed with Bon's recommendations and that brought an end to the massive effort Shonak had in Plus-Five space. The base "up there" closed, but Shonak left behind sufficient collection bots of all types to continue the legacy of excellence and excitement for Shonak to appreciate on their live feeds of Plus-Five life. Their extensive surveillance network continued to send live feeds to Shonak of life on Plus-Five from every continent and every culture on the planet. It all went back to a very appreciative and attentive Shonak viewing public.

As our story begins it is Shonakian Solar Rotation 306107.210, five years after OE approved Bon closing Plus-Five Base. Bon 305058.141.61.05.01 is now aged 1049 S-Rots. As our story begins Bon is an under-occupied, unassigned Gold, waiting for his next team assignment. In the meantime, he is amusing himself by going over files from his past. Many people in his situation simply give up and self-terminate. But that is not Bon's style. Not even close. When Bon departed Plus-Five Base the Our Eldest at the time promised him an exciting new position devoted to exploring the possibility of time travel. But rapid turnover in that

Eldest position had steadily pushed the promise into a mostly forgotten memory.

Bon has waited now five Solar Rotations for that assignment, or any assignment, the OE thought he would be best suited for. No Grand Team Eldests had found a suitable job for him even though he was considered almost hyper-capable. This was not out of fear of competition, something unknown on Shonak, but rather they simply did not feel there were any missions within their teams worthy of his particular talents.

On Plus-Five, eventually known as Earth, where time is calculated differently, it would one day be seen as the year 940 BCE, and later -940 UAY, or Universally Accepted Year. That's how it would be referred to once the people of Earth adopted an agreed upon planet-wide system for calculating and keeping track of their time.

Chapter Three

Time Shift

The shrill comm alarms went off while he was sitting quietly in his home office reading some of his old entries from Plus-Five Base. Bon knew something was very wrong as the entirety of Shonak's senior leadership was suddenly in comms with each other, and with him, over what they all saw now on thez Plus-Five Home Screen. The live feeds, ubiquitous throughout Shonak, showed a sudden and dramatic change "up there." One instant the image showed a primitive, agrarian world and the next instant it showed advanced technology, huge modern cities, an extraordinarily large population, aviation, RF communications, etc. Bon turned to look at his own live feed and had the same shocking view they all did and instantly understood what all the commotion was about. What he did not understand, and neither did anyone else, was why it was suddenly so different up there! Had to be some sort of mistake . . . . perhaps a notional look at what that planet might look like in a few thousand years? Must have gotten mixed into the live feeds from Plus-Five?

Our Eldest came on the Gold comm link and called for an immediate, face-to-face meeting of all the Grand Team Eldests, all the Regional Councilors, and the Council of Twelve, and he added Gold Bon to the list, even though he was at present unassigned, and far younger. The call for a live meeting was highly unusual since most communications between the seniors of the planet, and everyone else, was achieved through comm link, not in person. Bon understood, though, that if the brain power of the most senior Shonakians could not immediately figure this out, then it would be, and apparently was, a mystery grabbing their complete attention. Shonakians are beyond brilliant, and if the senior golds of Shonak, who represent so many millennia of experience in all possible disciplines, don't understand something, then that something would be the most compelling problem of their lives, and they all craved a solution for it! Their cultural DNA demanded it.

Bon's private comm chimed, and Our Eldest appeared on his screen. Coincidentally, they knew each other personally from previous S&T teamwork and he told Bon he expected him to add meaningful comments during the discussion they would all shortly be having. He also hoped that Bon would be able to offer some explanation for what they were seeing. OE reasoned that Bon, as the most knowledgeable elder Shonakian on every aspect of Plus-Five, and with his well-known side interest into the nature of Time itself, might have the most informed opinion concerning what they were seeing. Bon, who was sitting transfixed at his own screen, told OE that he was just as mystified as they all were and had about as much idea as anyone else but he added that he would be pleased to discuss the matter during the conference, and make such guesses and recommendations as occurred to him with what additional data they might have by the time they all met. After the call, and as he made his way to the nearby OE Conference facility, he thought his five-year wait for an assignment might be over.

Many Shonakians would consider Bon something of a celebrity, but they lack a word for it and don't think in those terms. "Well known by everyone" is as close as they come to it and such recognition does not come with adulation, paparazzi, groupies, or fan clubs. A few People achieve some notoriety along with seniority and some measure of minor recognition within their Teams on Shonak simply by doing their best and staying alive in their age-dominated society. Bon, on the other hand, has achieved notoriety by his remarkable achievements in very noticeable, popular areas of work, most famously as Eldest of Plus-Five Base. This gave him Shonak-wide visibility in very popular areas of interest for his people. And he took the unusual step as an Eldest to participate directly in some of the most widely watched events in the history of their infotainment feeds from Plus-Five. His exploits with an Earth native called Atsa became the most followed live drama from a planet that already provided endless streams of fascinating native action. To further his mission, and the program of Plus-Five native watching, Bon continued to increase the extensive monitoring effort there, although his primary goal was far outside the infotainment collection everyone so enjoyed. While the people of Shonak cared more for the entertainment value of the surveillance gear and bot feeds, Bon was trying to find and interrogate a "god" so they could determine if there was a useful resonance at "Plus-Six," if there even was such a place. But on determining that yes, there was a level of vibration above Plus-Five, he also learned that it could not be exploited by anything physical. This was learned from something resembling their notion of a god during its visitation in 306097 but was not taken on board mentally by Shonak because they did not and do not believe in gods or supernatural beings of any kind. They thought it was a visitor to Plus-Five much as they were, using technology even more advanced than their own, attempting to dissuade them from staying on the planet. Bon was not so sure, but the decision by the OE at the time to ignore the entity's lecture was of course what they did.

There were a few portions after he arrived to chat with his old colleagues, the Eldests of Exploration and Science and Technology. They were just as mystified by the time discrepancy as he was and had nothing to offer by way of explanation. In this room of the most experienced brilliant minds in all of Shonak theories were virtually bouncing off the walls, but nobody had any useful insights. The fact of what happened was well observed by everyone there, but that fact was useless since it could not be reconciled with every other thing they knew or theorized about time and the flow of history. As observed this event made no sense whatsoever. In fact, they all considered it impossible even after witnessing it! Bon was reluctant to even call it a fact based solely on the projected image. He needed to be assured that the equipment was not malfunctioning or that some entertainment feed had not been misdirected.

Once everyone had arrived, some delay being caused by the unprecedented transport of Regional Counsellors and team Eldests from all 142 regions around the planet, the meeting opened with a short thanks by OE for taking the unusual trouble to meet in person to discuss this most unusual temporal event. This was followed by a briefing from Eldest Science and Technology Grand Team, to review the chronology of what happened. They showed the standard start page of the Plus-Five live feeds. It was familiar to everyone, all avid Plus-Five watchers. They observed an aerial shot of Plus-Five that showed a modest settlement on a river one segment and in an instant the scene changed to one of a giant city, clearly at the same bend on that river, with vast numbers of huge buildings, surrounded by ground and air traffic, and almost overwhelming communications traffic. The standard metadata at the bottom of the screen always displayed the date and time of the scene. This was expressed in both Prime and Plus-Five time. Because there was no native standard for reckoning time Shonak had always calculated Plus-Five time as beginning when they first discovered it, 2006 Solar Rotations earlier. When the scene showed the small town on the river it was 306107/2006 and after the image changed to a modern city, the time stamp showed 306107/2270 UAY! They had no idea what UAY meant, and they did not understand the change to 2270 from 2006. Eldest Exploration raised a hand to quiet the group, paused to listen to his Team comm, then said, "My team is reporting to me that there is data in our system that shows history for Plus-Five suddenly available to us that covers three thousand, two hundred and ten S-Rots. This means that the sudden appearance of modern technology on Plus-Five, which I am now told is now called "Earth" by its natives, has suddenly jumped 3210 S-Rots ahead while Shonak has remained the same. The date 2270 UAY refers to the native calendar which began 2270 S-Rots ago according to their Universally Accepted Year. Apparently, the natives call their Solar Rotation, "Years" in their accepted global language, "World Standard English." Apparently, we stopped using our year of discovery for them when they finally adopted their own calendar, although I certainly have no memory of this. Do any of you?" He paused to note anyone who did, and hearing nothing, continued. "This unprecedented time shift must have an explanation and I am grateful to OE for calling this extraordinary session for us to find it."

GT S&T-Eldest kept the image on the screen but turned off the volume and continued the conference discussion with the simple statement, addressed more to OE than the group, that at present they had no idea how this time shift happened or why. Nor did they understand why time had remained the same on Prime. Their own world was continuing as it had done since before this sudden change on Plus-Five. Perhaps the most amazing component of this event is that the Shonak records database for Plus-Five contained robust information on the entire three thousand two hundred and ten S-rots of activity that suddenly manifested themselves when the time shift occurred! And just as curiously, almost violently so, was the fact that none of them had any memory of those parts of the "new" Plus-Five history that would have existed during their own lifetimes! It was in their databases, but not in their minds! As smart as they were, they were all completely mystified by these things. People with IQs hovering around 500, as people on Plus-Five might someday calculate it, they were all accustomed to quickly "understanding" almost everything about anything. This is why OE called this extraordinary, in-person meeting and why all the rest of them were so frustrated. You could almost feel the tension in the room as every one of them wanted to get un-frustrated with answers to these questions! Their collective wisdom told them this thing was impossible. That should have been the end of it. Always has been. Until now, since this thing clearly happened.

OE spoke, then, thinking out loud, "The puzzle for us to solve is first, the time shift itself, then second, we need to know how our databases reflect the fact that we have been following their history for the last 3210 S-Rots, and third, we need to understand why none of us living Shonakians have any memory of this "new" history during our lifetimes." Then just to be sure, he added, "If any of you have any memory of a modern Plus-Five, please let me know now." No one spoke. He stopped speaking then, and they played the vid of the temporal shift several more times so everyone could grasp the entirety of this apparent, unexplained, and unprecedented temporal event. Everything they all knew about anything told them this simply was not possible – and yet they could not doubt their own eyes. Eldest S&T, thinking what they were thinking, said, "No, there are no equipment malfunctions. What we are seeing is exactly what our excellent equipment is showing us."

Eldest Exploration then took the floor and said that data coming in from space-borne survey ship on other business showed some sort of rift in the fabric of space at the Plus-Five vibration. They had heretofore not known of or thought of the vacuum of space having a "fabric" but there was clearly some sort of "ripple" through Plus-Five space that did not harm their ships or equipment but was definitely detected. The Eldest of Exploration then reported that except for the fact that they had clearly been collecting data during these three thousand-plus S-Rots, their own history showed no change. They remained in 306107. He said his highest priority in Exploration, working with Science and Technology, was to examine all the data and draw some conclusions for their collective consideration. Our Eldest then asked Bon to come forward to share his thoughts. Bon was well known to everyone there and indeed was expected by all of them to have some clearer insights on this thing than they had themselves. He had always been known for his unconventional mind and solutions-driven methods, and as the foremost expert on Plus-Five.

Bon advanced to the dais and said it was going to take some time to study this anomaly but as clearly as there must be an explanation it was equally clear that they did not have it at the moment. He speculated that this temporal event may have just given them some definitive clues as to how time really works, but it was too soon to formulate any opinions. He said, "Perhaps these temporal events happen all the time but are invisible to us as they occur for every location. Perhaps we simply had one that passed us by, in favor of Plus-Five, which makes it visible by way of comparison? We notice the change because it did not happen here. If it had also taken place here perhaps, we would have noticed nothing and would not be here talking about it? Food for thought, anyway." Bon then asked the Eldest Exploration if any changes had been noted on Plus-Four, Three, Two, and One. That Gold responded it was too early to say with precision. He did say initial checks found some changes, but they were harder to gauge since there are no civilizations there to monitor. He added that examination of such things as lava flow or glacial melt or growth seemed after quick review to show more change had taken place on Plus-Four than on Plus-Three and so on down to Prime where no temporal changes were evident at all. The few exploration ships out and about in their solar system and one or two visiting vibrations above their own indicated that their chronometers had not changed. They had also remained at Prime time, likely because their Zones of Influence kept their instruments at the Shonak vibration at all times. That told them it did not matter where they were, just at what vibration they were at, and of course all their spacecraft visiting other vibrations were maintained at Prime. The GT Exploration ships stationed at Plus-Five during the event reported seeing the same change they all witnessed there on Prime and reported they had no personal memories of a modern planet. Their ship's data reflected the "missing" history, but no conclusions could be drawn from that since their database feeds were from Shonak and not from onboard storage. Just like on Shonak itself, none of the crew had any memory of a modern Plus-Five but now that's all they could see and hear. GT-Exp Eldest said again that this needed more study, and they were working hard on it. Our Eldest then asked for any ideas from the assembly and, hearing none, said, "Gold Bon, 305058, I am directing you to stand up Grand Team Time, as its Eldest, and start finding answers. I am also naming you Eldest of Grand Team Plus-Five and am ordering all Plus-Five dedicated assets immediately transferred to you. I am setting two priorities for you. First, how and why did this temporal shift take place and second, what is the way forward for our relationship with the newly modern Plus-Five?" He paused then and continued, "Of course many sub tasks will be developed as your investigation continues and you are to proceed with everything as you see fit." OE then directed GTs Exploration and Science and Technology, as well as all other GTs, to provide Bon all the people and support to assist him in his tasks and said there was no higher priority than this effort to determine what happened on Plus-Five and especially what it meant for Shonak. People from all across Shonak had of course been deluging the comm system raising the issue of their live feeds suddenly showing modern societies up there instead of the largely agrarian culture they were used to. They also wondered why they were able to call up this suddenly robust "past" up there when that was not available before? OE put out a general statement that some sort of temporal event had taken place which they were trying to identify. He asked them to enjoy the new, modern Plus-Five as they had been enjoying the more primitive version. The "new" 3210 S-Rots were fully available so they could go back in time to their favorite characters and watch how they all progressed through the ages. Shonak's people, all busy with their Team missions, but who also enjoyed their Plus-Five infotainment feeds, took this onboard with the same intellectual curiosity as their leadership but were content to let OE and his Team handle it while they continued their own lives. They all trusted that eventually they would learn the particulars about this time shift. People who live over fifteen-hundred years are seldom in a hurry about anything, this included.

For all their intelligence, and perhaps because of it, and their long lives, they are a placid, emotionless, patient, and rational people.

Many things ran through Bon's mind including the obvious satisfaction at once again being "employed" in a meaningful way instead of sitting around waiting for his next assignment. He had not expected to be named as Eldest of two Grand Teams at the same time, a first in the history of Shonak. He also thought that Shonak would probably need immediate friendly relations with the newly modern Plus-Five. Earth technology was very possibly capable of detecting their presence in any event and he asked his team to look into that possibility. He wanted to know immediately if Shonak's vast surveillance network had been discovered. "What," he asked, "is the current state of affairs between our two planets? Did they know about Shonak, even?" He reminded them of the recent (to them) "god" event he and all Shonak experienced there, not that many S-Rots ago. "Has there been any development on Earth as a result of that manifestation and transport of all their collective leaders?" He was forming an opinion that perhaps this god (or whatever it was) had something to do with their sudden temporal shift. He knew this would be an unpopular theory to put forth on Shonak right now. It never ceased to amaze him how quickly that event had been put to the back of everyone's minds on Shonak and then seemingly forgotten in the public mind. He had expected more from Shonak's Elders than that. He even half expected the natural formation of a cult-following for this god who called himself "Itself" but nothing of the sort happened. Despite the live feed they all had access to, the god Itself was an entity no Shonakian really believed in, in spite of the official record of its appearance and lecture. It was only ten S-Rots earlier that all the leaders of Shonak and of Plus-Five were suddenly and instantly (not to mention safely) transported to the same place on Plus-Five and lectured on the realities of Creation. It was made quite clear that there could be no physical exploitation of the non-physical resonances above Plus-Five. When anything physical vibrates at that speed it just flies apart, losing all its physical cohesiveness. Curiously, to Bon, that event had quickly faded from memory and discussion on Shonak and he wondered if the same had happened on Earth. If so, Bon eventually reasoned, it was so many things, to so many people, all negative. No one on any world wanted to hear that some super being, all powerful, the agent of an even more all-powerful super being, was watching and listening and judging; everything, everywhere, all the time. So, Bon kept his thoughts on that to himself; thoughts which went contrary to public opinion.

He kept quiet, not out of fear of reprisal or a loss of faith in his judgment, but simply because he had no clue how to pitch it successfully. No, he reasoned, far better to proceed with his usual methodical approach, beginning with as much research into the "new" Plus-Five as he could find. He would not challenge the final analysis by the OE, who determined that there was nothing supernatural about it. This entity appearing as a "god" was simply from another vibration of reality, like they were themselves, with much more advanced technology, who was on Plus-Five for the same reasons they were up there, and its message was self-serving and highly suspect. Most elders took this popular view, expecting that someday Shonak would find this race of beings and meet them. Until then, the matter was closed. Bon did think it strange that no one offered this race as an explanation for the time shift.

When the extraordinary in-person session on the time shift was over and people returned to their own teams and places of work Bon quickly reassembled his former team from when he was Eldest of Plus-Five Base, in Grand Team Exploration. These people were the most qualified to dig into anything relative to that world. He told them to first study, in detail, the new 3210 S-Rots of Plus-Five history to see if there were any clues. He also asked them to prepare for him a century-by-century summary. He also wanted to know if Plus-Five science advanced to the point where they could manipulate time itself? He doubted it but thought that might be an explanation why their world's time changed and Shonak's did not. He directed they look for any and all documents written by them about time travel. He also wanted them to go through the same time frame of their bot logs to see if they held any clues, too. Bon was very excited by all this and with 32 centuries of development on their higher vibration cousin now available for instant study they at least had somewhere to start putting this puzzle together. Or so he hoped. So, Grand Team Plus-Five quickly expanded into a giant study group, charged with educating Bon and all of Shonak on what has taken place up there all those years and where they are today politically.

Bon was mindful of his mission to establish appropriate relations with modern Plus-Five, now "Earth" and began thinking about the best way to accomplish this. When Bon called OE to provide his first update, OE told Bon that he would be responsible for first contact as Eldest of Plus-Five, and given that he and his team had the most experience with their vast array of cultures. OE pointed out that no other Gold on Shonak has as much Plus-Five time as Bon, and, he added, much of this time was personal and not by subordinates.

Bon was pleased that many of his former colleagues from Plus-Five Base already spoke many of their languages and understand them as of three millennia prior, which at least gives them a departure point for their study of the intervening 3210 S-Rots. This is a challenge they are up to on Shonak and they all admit that this is the most exciting thing to happen on their world since the discovery of phase travel.

Meanwhile, in a completely separate set of Universes, at the time of the temporal event in Plus-Five space, Statyr High Command was confronted with an intense vibrational "storm" that was interfering with its instrumentation on every level. One of their scout ships was intermittently missing, into the bargain. It was present in its assigned position and then it was not, then it was, and then it was not, and back again, while it was trying to communicate. All they were getting was intermittent, garbled contact. Eventually the ship stabilized enough to send in a clear report and it detailed how it had found, quite by accident, another level of existence of some sort. Statyr command was immediately interested in exploring this space and directed the ship to continue trying to "break into" it and send back its findings for analysis. Their ability to do this seemed to be diminishing as the temporal event energy wave dispersed, but they were able to continue for a while.

Concurrently, Teams Plus-Five and Time were eagerly awaiting whatever their various researchers could find out about the temporal event they all just witnessed. Bon was not expecting to be told there was also an alien incursion into Plus-Five space, taking place at the same time as the temporal event, but that's what happened. GT-Exp had noted the sudden appearance of some sort of alien vessel in Plus-Five space but its presence was intermittent and indistinct somehow, in an unexplained way. The craft was alien in origin and also alien in aspect. If that made any sense.

Bon discounted the notion of a coincidence and ordered his teams to pursue both lines of inquiry. What happened on Plus-Five and who are these aliens, where do they come from, and what do they want? And how was this connected to the temporal event? He asked them to coordinate their work with GT Exploration, who was better equipped to monitor this unanticipated alien incursion, and sent a comm summary over to Eldest, Exp.

While his teams were working on answers to his questions Bon was looking for evidence Shonak and Plus-Five had continued open contact with each other over these new historical years, and what the current status of that may be. Eldest of Exploration, his old boss, provided what he needed, some good news for a change. His GT had maintained a small section under a Violet charged with supporting liaison with the people of Plus-Five. There was Shonakian comm equipment on Plus-Five for this purpose, but it had never been used. His records showed that it had been placed with the natives once they became tech savvy but it was not thought by them to be a real thing, only a joke of some sort, sent there by colleagues, as evidenced by the occasional reference to it in that context. They called it "The Cube" and of course it had been and still was live on the receiver side all this time. As a result, they knew a great deal about the people who were and are charged with contact from other planets.

After talking to the Violet Eldest there he learned that over the new-to-Shonak three millennia Plus-Five governments had lost confidence in the existence of extra-terrestrials, even though popular culture continued to keep the notion alive. There had been no direct contact with these people since Bon's last adventure there. Not so long ago but to them but now add 3210 more S-Rots from the perspective of the people of Plus-Five. That said, the mechanism existed for this contact to be re-established and he was passing this team over to Bon for his use as he deemed necessary. Bon thanked his colleague at S&T and told him he would use the equipment to contact them once he felt up to date on their recent history and language. He was relieved he would not need to suddenly appear there in a phase ship in person!

Then Bon got an update on the simultaneous alien incursion and Bon thought, "so much happening at once, what is going on?" The official assessment was that it must be related to the recent temporal event since it happened at the same time. Apparently, whatever caused that event opened some sort of temporary rift between, perhaps, alternate universes? He thanked them for their quick look into that and asked them to monitor Plus-Five space for any recurrence.

He fought hard against the urge to immediately reach out to the native designated point of contact on Plus-Five. He knew far too little about who they were and was painfully aware that his last contact with them was now thousands of S-Rots in their past. No, he would wait and gather as much information as he could before doing anything like calling Plus-Five.

He was also keen to reach out to the aliens showing up in that space so he could begin an assessment of their presence and determine if they were friendly or not.

Bon was formally briefed every 50 portions, with high-value items related as they happened. His time was fully occupied, and he was in his favorite mental zone. His most recent formal brief contained bits and pieces of the modern culture of Plus-Five. Bon was informed that the people of Plus-Five had settled on the name for their planet, "Earth," in world standard English, coming from the word for ground, soil, or dirt, or terrain. They had also settled on a common calendar, using the Universally Accepted Year, or UAY. There was no "year zero", and it began with the historical birth of a religious figure known as Jesus Christ. Earth still had hundreds of religions and languages. There was no universal religion but there was an "official" global language, World Standard English, spoken everywhere, taught everywhere. Traditional languages were taught and spoken at home and around their towns, but everyone was required to learn and speak English. Very much unlike Shonak, the natives had developed a way to inject competition into everything, including games of leisure, personal relations, commerce and finance, armed conflict, and the like. Even their casual conversations were replete with "winner or loser" in arguments, or feats of bravery or sports, etc. There were many different countries but almost all of them voluntarily belonged to a nominal global central government, with its headquarters based in what they call Greater China. It was mostly a coordinating body dealing with trade and economic policy with the members retaining full sovereignty. There was also a global currency, the World Buck, which was used everywhere in addition to local currencies in a few countries. Global population growth had been out of control, but the reality of finite resources made them implement strict birth controls which had been somewhat helpful. Several devastating nuclear wars reduced the population even more. They had achieved sub-light speed space travel within their own solar system, but nothing beyond that. Their short lives made very long trips in space impractical. Life expectancy in most parts of the planet hovered around 95 years, but few wanted to live that long. Voluntary euthanasia was their version of the Shonakian self-termination. Bon was surprised to learn that there was actually an office within the world government with the responsibility for anything relative to "contact with aliens." Their comm cube was in this office. Their files reflected their widespread popular belief in extraterrestrials with much documentation, but there remained no definitive proof. It was noted that the files of this office did have some oral history records of a place called "Shonak." There was disbelief in it by everyone, including the people in the office charged with alien contact. Shonak's efforts over these years had been simply to keep their surveillance devices and bots of all types, including human bots, active, and hidden, providing infotainment feeds for the enjoyment of the people back home. It was noted again that it would be over three thousand of their years since last contact so when they did reach out to them it would be quite a shock. In their mid-twentieth century, UAY the Plus-Five "alien liaison office" had been sent a Shonak comm cube with a letter explaining that it was their channel to the Planet Shonak. This was treated as a joke by the people in the office and by their peers, but the dark plastic cube was pretty nifty, so they put it on a shelf to laugh about from time to time. The letter had been duly framed and was hanging in the office near the shelf where the cube sat. Ignored by the office staff, the cube was perfectly functional, of course. Bon could use it any time he wished. Surveillance and maintenance records showed that the cube had been covertly maintained and even upgraded over the years with Earth none the wiser, since its outward appearance never changed.

During those "additional years" on Earth, the resident major world powers had installed space sensors in various locations in their solar system to detect asteroids or other large bodies with a trajectory that might impact Earth or be a dangerously close fly-by. Immediately after the time shift these sensors began to pick up what appeared to be deliberate, intelligent communications from some unknown source. Bon understood that this was the same alien incursion their own sensors had also noted. Earth analysis by both military and science analysts likened the transmissions to hearing voices through a crack in a door, and then the voices are cut off mid-sentence when the door closes. Of course, Earth's military analysts could not be sure of any of it, but it did seem like non-random radio frequency traffic was suddenly there and just as suddenly wasn't. His own team was still trying to determine the cause and impact to Shonak and Earth of these unknown alien incursions into Plus-Five space. Bon's analysts thought the Earth analogy sounded right. Intelligent communications were suddenly present and just as suddenly gone. There was, however, an odd quality of communications energy detected, which apparently had gone unnoticed by Earth. The Earth analysts also did not have the sophisticated sensors that Shonak had and so had even less information to use in their analysis of this apparent alien incursion. For their part, the Statyr scout ship was attempting additional incursions now that their navigation computers had the "location" of this new space, and while the temporal rift remained open. They did manage to poke through again and Bon's team was there to witness it. As soon as the "door" opened Bon's team sent strong RF transmissions of welcome into the opening which closed immediately, providing a small window of opportunity to learn anything from this incident. Clearly, there was an intelligence behind that "door." The Shonakians could not know, of course, but the immediate closure likely indicated the recipients of their message were startled by the inbound RF signals. This proved correct as the Statyr scout ship captain ordered an immediate withdrawal once the communications were detected. It was indecipherable to them, but it was clearly intelligent and likely targeting them. They notified their high command who ordered them to go back there and collect more data, including the communications.

Bon wanted to be ready if and when this ship appeared again. He asked for the fullest array of sensors and detection equipment at their disposal when it showed up. His team's analysis showed that there was something unusually foreign about this ship. Far from hiding, this energy incursion into their space was glaring in its intensity, drowning out energy readings from most of the universe, and doing so in a very odd spectrum of vibrations, totally foreign to anything in their own universe. These noisy incursions, these so called "door openings" were Shonak's only way to get any additional data. Bon asked if there was any reason to suspect intelligent life behind this and the answer was "yes" this was an inescapable conclusion since the pattern of communications was not random, and it was definitely a ship of some kind. Bon watched the sensor panels waiting for the next occurrence and when it came, he immediately ordered them to phase out of this vibration while monitoring their sensors. He did not want to be seen by this new entity, whatever it was. What they saw then was completely new and Bon opened a live feed to GT-Exp and commed the Our Eldest to watch what was happening. What they were apparently witnessing was a new incursion to Plus-Five by an unknown entity, using similar technology to their own but with a significantly different vibrational signature. The alien phase ship was round, like a sphere, with blisters around its surface in a symmetrical pattern. It appeared in its entirety but did not appear stable or completely there as it remained blurry. It changed color a few times, and it moved a bit up and down but did not seem able to clarify its vibration to precisely match that of Plus-Five. After a few segments it disappeared, presumably back to where it came from. There was no way to know if these people were hostile or what their intentions were, but he was sure the people of Plus-Five would assume they were hostile and act accordingly. Bon thought he would need to reach out to Earth sooner than later to discuss this alien presence and to formulate some sort of mutual coordination to ensure they formed a clear picture of it and possibly a common defense, sooner than later.

Naturally, Earth's response to the incursion was military in nature and assumed the worst; that the unknown entity was hostile. Their simple sensors were also noting these incursions and that led them to begin formulation a military defense. Shonak on the other hand did not and does not default to the worst-case scenario but they did recognize that hostile intent was a possibility, and so kept an open mind, and wanted Earth to know they were not alone should it come to combating a hostile threat. They remembered their own first forays into the various vibrations of the Universe. Because they intend to be the first to make contact with this unknown entity and because they know that Shonak is not psychologically equipped for military action, they want to ask for the help of native Earth gunners to defend against these newcomers should they prove hostile.

An alarm went off on Bon's console. It appeared that Earth space forces had just gone to a high alert as the alien ship was detected. Bon saw that Earth attack ships went there to check it out. His own scout ship was also there, but there was no way the Earth ships could detect it as it was out of phase. In essence, it was "between" Plus-Five and Plus-Four in order to hide from the Earth ships.

The Shonak vessel caught the entire incursion episode on video and their full spectrum analyzers were able to gather large amounts of data, though there were no conclusions yet. Bon reviewed the data coming in and the technicians reviewing it provided their comments in real time. The most striking element of this data was that the vibrational signature of the vessel making the incursion was all wrong. It was different in a very odd way, different in a way that could not even be characterized. Analyst speculation was that whoever or whatever was making this incursion did not see them clearly either because there was no shared phasic frame of reference; no common buzz that could be used to normalize their presence. It was likely they would be unable to totally merge with Plus-Five or even Shonakian space. As a result, they could be detected but could not be connected. For his part, Bon was able to review the data on this new entity for himself. He got an accurate signature reading and he could also see that vibrational signature was not at all normal. It revealed an entirely unknown vibrational quality. They could measure the rate of the vibration, of course, and as it happened it closely but not perfectly matched that of Plus-Five. No surprise there, since they were at Plus-Five space, but it had an entirely new modulation if you could even call it that. He wanted to know its native vibration to get some idea where it was from, but there was no way to do that with so few opportunities for data collection. As it was, this was like finding a fourth primary color, it was that new, and as such could not be compared with anything in their known universe. Was it possible that there was another universe or even more than one other than their own? Like Shonak raising their vibration in a ship to visit Plus-Five, might this new signature represent the same sort of travel but from another universe entirely? Maybe instead of up and down on the resonance spectrum, it was side to side?

Bon shared his findings and his thoughts with Grand Team Exploration Eldest and with OE and awaited instructions. Within a segment, GT-Exp Eldest and GT-S&T Eldest were docking with their phase ship above Plus-Five for a consultation. Oddly enough, they had brought a few gun ships from the newly formed and shared Sub-Grand of both these Super-Grands. It was styled the "Protection" Sub-Team and was a first for placid Shonak. They had never in their long history ever needed either a military or a police force but these were extraordinary times and their sensors had been detecting the very odd signatures popping up in a variety of resonant locations and phases so they did not want to be caught napping, as it were. Extraordinary scientists and technologists, Shonak had developed a wide array of very powerful weapons should they need to protect their planet or their interests anywhere in their known universe.

Bon had never actually seen one of these new security vessels and he wondered how they functioned, and he was even more curious to know about the Shonakians who were assigned to Sub Team Protection. No Shonakian was ever aggressive, so how did this work? He was not long in finding the answer. Our Eldest called a meeting that included the two GT Eldests, Lik, and the Eldest from Protection. He was a Gold, surprisingly enough, but that did underscore the importance given to this new Sub Team. Our Eldest began the meeting with an announcement. He stated that with the extraordinary events just past he was making Protection a Grand Team directly under OE scrutiny and authority.

Our Eldest yielded to the new Eldest of GT Protection, Gold Rin, so he could summarize his findings. His now GT had been reviewing data collected by various sensors over the span of incursions, beginning with the temporal event, and collated evidence of their attempts to gain access to "their" space. He had tried identifying these people with no real luck. This latest sighting off Plus-Five gave them more information. They had been sitting in near Plus-Five orbit and as it happens virtually on top of the alien ship waiting for it to fully synch with Plus-Five space. When it appeared, they noted that the aliens somehow took a sample of the atmosphere of the planet, Plus-Five, then disappeared again. During this time, they were able to attach a sensor to their ship before it phased out. The sensor of course would (and did) return to Shonak space in its time and they had promptly recovered it. He then faced about to view a screen, so they all did as well and there came an indistinct image and a summary of data concerning it. Native Signature unknown and unidentifiable. Origin unknown. Culture unknown. Current Location unknown. Time congruent with recent present. Intentions unknown. Crew status unknown. Weapons unknown. Communications present but unreadable. The Eldest scientist explained, "The minute sample of air they collected was seen to reappear and dissipate as it returned to its native vibration far above the atmosphere it was taken from." The sensors noted, "Duration of presence 4.3 segments, size of vessel similar to Shonakian phase ship, intentions unknown." The one thing they did know is that when taking the sample, the alien craft did not fully materialize in Plus-Five space. Unknown if they were able to, but there was some fundamental difference between their resonance and the resonance of both Plus-Five and Shonak. It was as if it vibrated from side to side instead of up and down. It was simply "off" but in some sort of undefinable way. The briefer said, "We believe we are dealing with a new universe and people from that universe who are exploring this one. The fact that it comes in the timeframe of the recent temporal event may not be a coincidence. In fact, it likely is not. We have not ruled out the possibility that it was their incursion that caused the temporal event, since it was in Plus-Five space that it occurred, and so had the greatest impact there. It is also possible that the temporal event in Plus-Five space lured them there with the rift opening for them at that location. The fact that they did not fully materialize here and only stay briefly tells us that they want their presence to remain unseen, but it also may be that they can't fully synch with us in this Universe. Our own history might be instructive here. When we began our forays into the various vibrations and the solar systems in them, an observer might note similarities. We have been seeing what simple, tentative forays into our space might look like, and we have no evidence of any sinister intent by these people, just as we had no sinister intent during our explorations." He continued, "There are many possible explanations for their behavior, and we remain open minded on this, but of course their behavior can suggest a sinister motive and that is why GT Protection wants to focus on this very closely." Our Eldest then added that the weapons in use by GT Protection were capable of kinetic destruction and also of phase transfer should combat be necessary. That said, there was a search on for Shonakians with any propensity for aggression but have found that this emotion has so far eluded them. They all thought to themselves that aggression was one of the characteristics that would have resulted in the egg or new hatchling being immediately terminated. Good luck, then, finding an aggressive Shonakian adult! For this reason, they wanted to explore the potential for using a Plus-Five native, or natives, all of whom possessed ample aggressive tendencies, for use in their weapons control center.

Meanwhile, the Statyr, the object of Shonak's concerns, were experiencing their own problems. They were surprised that upon arriving in this new dimension they were immediately bombarded with intelligent communications, indicating their presence was known by a dominant and intelligent space faring people. That was a first for them and therefore troubling. Statyr explorers carefully analyzed the air sample they collected from the outer atmosphere of the odd planet with its odd signature. The findings were initially excellent. All the nutrients they required were apparently abundant on this world, but the phase differences were proving troublesome. There were many forms of life in evidence to help sustain them if they could stabilize to their resonance.

Communications signals were dense and across a wide spectrum indicating an intelligent, advanced life form was present on the planet they were witnessing. There was also an odd signature from a small location in the outer atmosphere that indicated something unusual and not indigenous to this planet was hovering overhead. They filed that away for future analysis. Their orders were to avoid revealing themselves so only briefly tried to merge with the vibration of this world in order to collect the sample which of course was not stable once aboard their vessel. Their sensors indicated this was because they were not stable with this space. They only had just enough time to analyze it before it began its reversion trip back to the vibration it came from. The fact that it phased away from them proved they were not fully synched with that space and so the sample went "home" to its own vibration. Statyr had managed to defeat the problem of phase stabilization in their own universe, but here they were unable to do it. In fact, their ongoing analysis of the space they had briefly visited revealed it was more than completely different, it was also completely foreign, unknown, and of a resonance that could not be normalized by their equipment. Chief scientist was of the opinion that it could never be done since it was too foreign, too strange, too vibrationally different in an odd, incontrovertible way. It was almost like it was of another Universe altogether! When advised of their findings Statyr High Commander cancelled the mission and issued a prohibition from entering that space again. Equipment settings for this resonance were ordered to be eliminated. Whatever was there may prove too dangerous to encounter, certainly not worth the risk since they could not even stabilize there. They would not be back. Plenty of places and phases to go to for their needs within their own vibrational arena. Something, the Statyr couldn't say what, made him think this was the correct course of action. Just a feeling . . . .

Itself also somehow knew that the disturbance from "outside" was a one-time thing, and possibly a direct result of his tinkering with the space-time issue just past. He chalked that up to Learning, happy that at his advanced state there were still things to Learn, and that his actions remained Plan Neutral.

Something deep inside Bon also made him think that the odd alien race did not pose a threat after all. This left Bon shaking his head in wonder as he usually did not surrender to "feelings", but he somehow "felt" this was right. In short, if they were correct in their assessment, there would be no threat from these beings because there would be no actual "presence" from them in any real sense. Once these aliens figured this out for themselves, they would not bother to come back. If they were right, of course. And since there was no way to know if they were right, and because the consequences of a hostile incursion by an unknown alien race could be severe, they created GT Protection to deal with any eventuality.

And for the same reason, out of an abundance

of caution, Bon felt contacting Earth directly at this time would be the right thing to do. There may not be a threat at this time but who is to say one will not come in the future? This provides a worthwhile narrative for "coming out" to Earth after all these years of taking advantage of their invasive, global surveillance. Bon did not worry in the least that withholding the information about these aliens, probably not posing a credible threat, was in any way bad or even dishonorable. The existence of a threat of this nature was exactly what was needed to give them a common goal and provide incentive to work together. And, of course, there could be a real threat like this in the future and being ready was far better than to not be ready. He determined to contact them as soon as he felt he knew enough about these modern Earthers and their culture. He therefore spent considerable time reviewing the 3210 S-Rots of data they had collected during the so-called "shift years" that suddenly presented themselves after the unexplained time shift.

Chapter Four

Bon Quietly Introduces Himself

306108//2271// Bon is 1050 It was a normal day in the World Government Center for Studies of the Unexplained and Alien Liaison (WG-CSU-AL), Geneva, State of Switzerland, United Nations of Europe. This two-person team of scholar/scientists perform investigations into reports of unusual activity around the planet, which no government or private organization feels comfortable handling or want to bother with. Its charter also included maintaining contact with extraterrestrials, if there are any, and with a legendary planet called Shonak, if it even exists. Most people dismiss this Shonak out of hand but several ancient myths and legends from across the planet mentioned it and in pretty much the same way, so they are the designated point of contact if it ever comes up again. Nobody really thinks it will. In the 1950s someone decided, as a joke, to put a "communications cube" in the office to illustrate the absurdity of the idea. Nobody knew who put it there, or who wrote the letter from "Shonak" that came with it, and it has just sat there by the framed letter, gathering dust. The cleaning people do it occasionally, as they do all office furniture, otherwise nobody touches it. At present it's just another ignored piece of equipment nobody uses, but sometimes it has been a conversation piece. It's something to laugh about in connection with the office's remit.

A normal day in the life of this small team consists of reading news feeds and reports from universities and governments and hiking clubs and mountain climbers, construction workers and pilots, you name it. This amounts to anyone and everyone who has credibly reported seeing or hearing or feeling something that could not be easily explained and looked either suspicious or interesting. Most episodes of this nature go unreported, but the small percentage that are recorded and reported sometimes end up in this office, where the "unexplained and unimportant" stuff is sent. These days, because of their unique access to multinational databases, most of the work done by this office is answering questions from a variety of investigative agencies around the world. About half of these queries are from people playing games, asking about "men on the moon" or "was the moon really made out of green cheese?" They just hit the delete button on these and block the senders. But occasionally, all over the world, in every country, strange things do happen which have no obvious explanation, and local officials actually want one. This is how the workload of CSU is kept to a small number of requests, small enough for the staff of two people to cope with. Their M.O. is to work with requesting governments willing to share their files and by browsing the various databases they have access to for answers – to explain the unexplained. It amazes them how often pattern-analysis over time and from many different locations can bring a reasonably clear picture together. They have identified more than one serial killer, serial rapist, serial art thief in this manner. While governments are reluctant to allow others direct access to their databases, they have no trouble giving access to this small international team of researchers who freely share their findings with law enforcement, banking, regulators, and the like – without sharing the source data they used. Unless of course in cases where they received permission to share that. Usually, once permission was given on this issue, the parties involved are put in direct contact with each other to pursue leads that would be useful in court, and this office backs out of it.

Helen Manners, the permanent team member from the UK, was scanning a file query from forestry in Germany and saw something that got her attention. She read the file again then said, "John, listen to this. Quite a coincidence. Looks like it happened just over a year ago. One archaeology dig and one construction site being worked at the same time, close to each other but quite independent. "Here's the summary, get this," She read it out loud, "Two ancient sets of bones found in central Germany, very much related to each other. At the dig, one partial skeleton. Clearly that of some sort of chieftain, buried with great ceremonial flair and the accoutrements of his rank. Missing the rib cage, upper spine, and lower jaw." She paused for effect, then read on, "A second partial skeleton, found about a kilometer away from where the chieftain was buried, at the construction site, consists of a ribcage, upper spine, and lower jaw. The two crews happened to visit the same place for lunch and caught each other's conversations, and that put the two sites together." She pushed herself back from her computer and looked at her colleague, then summarized, "The enterprising forensic anthropologist who made the connection gathered the remains from the construction site and when compared with the chieftain at her dig found they were an exact match. The ends of every piece exactly fit, including the lower jaw and all the rest. Subsequent DNA comparison from the marrow confirmed the bones came from the same person. Funny thing is the bone was not cut by anything that would have existed at the time, or even now, come to think. The remains were carbon dated to something like minus 1000 UAY making them around 3200 years old. It does not seem the rib cage bones, or any of the bones, were cut at all. They just separated in some way from the body and then were deposited in another location. Very, very odd." Then, after a pause, and with a smile and a chuckle, said, "Shonak weapon?" This last rhetorical question was just a subconscious throwaway line, but as soon as she said it, she told herself it had to be. Over time anything considered whacko and alien came to be known to them as a "Shonak" item, meaning it was beyond understanding but which needed to be given a label and oh by the way, it could actually be true. Her colleague in the Center, and its nominal chief, permanent member John Marquis, the USNA rep, only half listened to her as she went through that description of the find in the United Nations of Europe State of Germany. Their collaborative network was replete with odd or just interesting finds, but her last comment, or question, got his attention. How odd. He looked up at her then, chuckled, and smiled. "Hey," he said halfheartedly, "Maybe it was." "Can you get more information on that find and please try to contact the team leader from that dig?" "We want a holo-cam report with this report for our files."

For his part, he began a database query on the subject of Shonak weapons to refresh his memory. He also wanted to see if there was any new literature on the subject. He found only legendary entries and no hard evidence that a people calling themselves the Shonakians visited Earth at any time. The legends spoke of people, or gods, with remarkable weapons and technology, flying machines and so forth. Oral histories from the desert southwest of the USNA of all places were the most frequent to mention these things, but the people living there in -1000 UAY had no scientific words to describe any technology. He pulled up the reference, surprising even himself that he would give this even that much credibility, and noted that the report by an early USA federal representative to the

Hopi Indians was intrigued by a story of a historical visitation from people in flying discs who had weapons that could make parts of people disappear, knives that cut without bleeding, arrows that could pass through solid stone. The description of this find from Germany could fit what legend said about the weapon. Apparently, the missing body parts had somehow been transported about a kilometer away from the victim, who would be quite dead of course. He was thinking that if the ancients had known where those missing body parts were, they would have been buried with the body. He guesses that whoever took them out of the body was no friend of the deceased and hid them out of spite? He wondered if the removal had been the cause of death or maybe they were removed postmortem, possibly after digging up the body? He decided to make an entry in his Shonak (i.e. Unexplained) File. He would love to ask the Shonakians for their thoughts on this but there had not been any contact with them for thousands of years so fat chance that will happen, he thinks to himself, good humoredly.

Bon enjoyed watching and listening and was eager to reach out to them but he still was not comfortable enough with his understanding of their newly, to him, modern society and its ways.

His team had been researching Earth history and sociology century by century and Bon was keen to know how they handled information. Could he communicate with John and Helen without also communicating with the whole of the planet? He learned little that surprised him about Earther handling of information over the millennia in question. On the surface, they were very protective of their own privacy but were eager to learn the secrets of everyone else. Their use of social media as they called it was replete with the details of their own lives and also replete with people misusing the Internet as they called it by spying on each other, stealing from each other, abusing each other. Eventually they realized that two fundamental things had to change. First, there had to be an end to the ability to get onto the Internet without being identified. Anonymous presence was what allowed so much misbehavior to take place. The second thing they learned was that by putting everything on a single network there was almost no way to prevent access by unauthorized people, and no way to prevent the migration of one thing into the domain of another. Eventually they created multiple networks that required biometric identification for access and use and everything they did was logged and available to law enforcement, with a warrant, of course. The biometric of choice was the iris of their eyes, which had sufficient detail and sufficient individuality to act as a very accurate and secure method for this purpose. Then with everything on separate, access-controlled networks, like government, health care, entertainment, education, and the military, the ability to misuse these systems and their content was greatly diminished. Laws were enacted that provided for fines and or imprisonment for misbehavior and misuse of information. Every word or sound or image placed on the public Internet was tagged with the author's identity, and people who put lies on the Web or sought to gain illegally by using the Web were caught and severely punished. It took half a decade to wrap all that up and it was hundreds of years in the past so at present, Bon was fairly certain that the files and databases and what went on in their office could be considered secure enough for him to openly contact them when he felt the time was right.

And so, just days after they had discussed "Shonak weapons" in their office, Bon decided he knew enough about them and their language to reach out to his Earth counterparts. These were the people their government had designated as the contact point for extraterrestrial beings. Not that anyone on Earth, Bon knew, thought that would ever actually happen.

Bon summoned the people on his team to provide him background information on John and Helen. They replied that because of their surveillance bots everywhere, they knew quite a bit about them. The Indigo briefing Bon said, "Their Eldest, whom the Earth people termed "Director" of the office, and who is not the oldest member by the way, is named John Marquis. He and his colleague, Helen Manners, one of their years older, are the only two permanent staff and the only two who may believe they have a terminal which links them with the planet Shonak. Other people believe there is a terminal, which there is, but no one else really thinks it has anything to do with an alien planet. It is simply dismissed as another unexplained artifact and probably there as a joke." He continued, "The Bon Watching clubs have been having a field day with this, playing and re-playing you using the phase weapon on that Earther tribal chieftain, and then the recent discovery of both sets of the remains, Helen seeing the report of them put together, and now you are about to make contact with them as they discuss this themselves, there in their office in Geneva. Wonderful streaming!" Bon looked at him with a smile. He had to admit he enjoyed seeing himself and Atsa flying around on Eagle and Dragon bots, breathing fire on the savages below them, and wondered how this next phase would play out. He was confident his first contact was a simple enough matter but given that these were Earthers he was dealing with, and modern ones at that, he determined to remove this from the live streaming feeds of their office for the time being. He told his Indigo to make that happen. He said the removal would be temporary, only until everyone was sure the contact was going well.

Then Bon ensured that he had video by way of his surveillance devices in their office and moved to the terminal's microphone. He studied John and Helen at work for a time, listening, and caught the end of the most recent conversation. He was completely surprised to hear them actually talking about Shonak! His staff assured him this was absolutely a coincidence, as just briefed by the Indigo, but admittedly an interesting one.

They had heard the earlier discussion of the find in Germany and now they were talking about it again. The Indigo gave Bon a summary of their earlier discussion and noted that there had, to date, been only two prior references to a Shonak in their long history of monitoring this office, and neither were part of any serious discussion. In their experience, the word "Shonak" was synonymous with "bull shit" or "hoax" or just "fiddle-faddle" as they might express this thought in World Standard English.

Bon well remembered the first time he spoke to an Earth native, almost a thousand years before they decided to start their former Gregorian calendar. This was certainly different! He was thinking it will now almost be like talking to another Shonakian since this time modern communications devices are in use and his audience is technically savvy. He paused a bit, thinking carefully in his newly acquired World Standard English. He had quickly learned the vocabulary and grammar as well as all the current idioms and usages of their tongue and so without concern he would be misunderstood he touched the transmit button. Neither John nor Helen were looking at it of course, they rarely did, but the view screen of black cube lit up and Bon's image was transmitted to it. "Hello Mr. Marquis, this is Gold Bon speaking from Shonak. Apologies for this sudden message but we wish to reestablish contact with your world." Straight and to the point, like all Shonakian speech.

John and Helen were well aware they had just

been talking about Shonak, and now Shonak was talking to them? No Way! Both of them froze for a moment and then quickly turned to face the "special top-secret alien terminal" they know as The Cube, where the voice was coming from. Somebody was pulling their legs! The office joke-box actually worked?! When they looked over at it they saw there was light coming from the bottom of the cube, and they flipped it over. Since it was a solid, shiny, featureless, black cube, there had been no way to tell which side any screen was on or if there even was one. As they turned it up, then turned it right-side-up, they saw the image of a grey-brown, hairless, almost reptilian figure with big eyes, with a gold dot on his forehead, looking directly at them, showing a mouth full of small, sharp black teeth. He was smiling, but they did not see it as a smile. To them it was kind of scary. The "flat-faced lizard" as they thought of him, appeared to be waiting for their response. They looked at one another, then back to the terminal, and John replied, in a very nervous voice. "Hello, Sir, I'm sorry I didn't catch your name, and greetings from Earth." He paused then, and added " I think." "If this is some kind of elaborate joke, then fine, just don't waste our time with theatrics. You can tell everyone we fell for it and we can all get back to work." He waited for a response and the figure on the screen replied that this was no joke and any discussion of that was a waste of time at this important, historical moment. John was unconvinced and said, "If you are an alien, prove it to me." Bon was taken aback by that.

He did not expect this response but understood why they were not immediate believers in Shonak or its people. Bon said he would get back to them shortly, and the screen went blank. John and Helen started to laugh, and commented on the genius way this hoax was being implemented and proud of themselves to demand "proof" from the "alien."

They went back to their own computer screens to continue reading their incoming reports but within ten minutes the lizard was back on the screen and said, "Please look here." John and Helen looked at each other, smiling, but they did turn to face Bon as requested. Bon said, "On the floor below you, if you will turn around, you will see a jewel." They did and saw a cut and polished gem of some sort, about the size of a lemon, clear like a diamond. Doubts began to creep into their minds when they saw it, knowing it was nothing any of their colleagues could have dreamed up, or their enemies, and they had a few. Nobody had come into their office but there was the jewel as this Bon thing called it, right there on the floor. It certainly had not been there since they sat down at their workstations. No way they would have missed it! Then Bon said, "Helen, please pick it up." John reached for it first, not proud of himself for jumping in like that, and as soon as he touched it, he felt the pure "alienness" of it. It was strangely heavy and made his fingers numb and then his hand as he let it fall into his palm. Helen noted the strange expression on John's face and her face reflected the same feeling when he passed it to her. Helen also felt the odd, very uncomfortable numbing sensation the stone gave off. It was almost like an electrical shock, and it hurt all the way to her elbow. She hastily put it on the table in front of them, next to the comm cube. Both of them knew immediately that this diamond, or whatever it was, was real, and alien, and nobody playing a joke on them from this planet could have made it. Bon then said, "Watch it carefully." They stared at it, and within a few seconds it began to get blurry, then slowly faded from sight and gradually disappeared! They looked at each other, then at the screen to see Bon, then to where the gem had been, then back at each other, then back to Bon, who after a few moments was handed the same gem, or it appeared to be the same, by someone off screen. He held it up for them to see, and Bon said, "You have just seen a demonstration of the Law of Nativity." John paused a moment, looked at Helen, smiled then, and said, looking at the image of Bon on the screen, "OK, I'm fairly convinced, but I'm holding back a little, which I hope you will understand. If this is a trick it's very well done, amazing even, and our congratulations to the people behind it. You should come forward and receive your just accolades and then we can get back to our duties." Then he said, in a more serious tone, "And if you are truly a representative of another planet, please know that we are Doctor John Marquis here along with my colleague, Doctor Helen Manners, sitting next to me. And of course, if you are who you say you are, we are honored to be speaking with you. May I ask, please, because our bosses and everyone else will want to know, what is the occasion for this call after so long a time?" He continued, "If the legends are correct, it is now something like four thousand years since our kind has had direct contact with your kind, and, speaking frankly, we have always thought that you were more myth than reality. This terminal is all the indication we have had that anything like a Shonak exists and even this is swept aside by our governments who prefer that you don't. This black cube has been silent all this time and we have ignored it, pretty much. We do dust it off and examine it every now and then, but other than that it has just been taking up room in our offices. And what is your name again, please?"

Bon smiled and said, without the niceties that a more socially attuned person would have used, "My name is Bon. I am a Gold, by age one thousand and fifty of your years old. I am the Eldest of the Shonakian Team charged with contacting you. We have watched your slow march into technology and we here on Shonak believe that your world has progressed to a point where meaningful relations between our two planets can commence."

Bon added, "Before you know anything more about us you should know that we cannot comfortably exist on each other's worlds, which we will explain later. You just saw, however, a demonstration of the fact that things from our world cannot exist for long on yours. We can, however, at least share matters of mutual interest as they arise. When last we were in contact with you people on what you now call Earth there was no science, no technology, no formal education, no flight or space travel. In fact, there was no agreed upon name for your planet amongst your many peoples, who did not even understand that they were on a planet revolving around its star. Because of these difficulties we did not attempt to explain ourselves or maintain contact. You have come a long way in the last four thousand and more of your years and since you have developed what appears to be a functional world government, we feel it can now be productive to have a dialogue with it. The timing of this contact is related to a matter of mutual interest we need to discuss with your world government leader as soon as possible. We request you set up this meeting as soon as you possibly can." Bon paused briefly then smiled, and said, "I could just appear in what you would call a space ship and ask the first person I see to take me to your leader but that would be a risky public relations move. So, we are content to proceed with a bit more caution and work through the office which has been designated by your World Government as the correct point of contact.

Of course, you will want to know all about us and our planet before the initial meeting. We are very different peoples, yours and ours. By way of formal introduction, we are sending you a written overview of our world to help you understand us better. This is written in your World Standard English, of course.

We have been observing your world for thousands of your years and so need no such summary from you."

Bon added what he considered the most important initial point, "It is imperative that you understand we pose no threat to you. We are fully aware of your automatic reaction to the unknown – shoot first and ask questions later." They saw Bon smile again at that – not a pretty sight. "We on the other hand are a totally benign race with no aggressive agenda towards you or anyone else. We would suggest and appreciate your keeping knowledge of this first contact to just yourselves and the officials we will be talking to until your leader can figure out how to broach the subject with your public without causing distrust or panic. We are appreciative you have maintained our comm cube all these years, which made it much easier for us to make this first contact out of the public eye."

Bon continued, "That gemstone you just handled is of Shonakian origin. I sent it to your office so you could see and touch it before it automatically reverted to Shonak. It exists at our vibration, not yours. If you came to Shonak you would automatically revert back to Earth, but the brief journey would likely kill you. We likewise cannot live on your world. Our summary will explain why this is so, but it is important for you to know, since it means we cannot have any designs on your world and therefore pose no threat to you. You likewise pose no threat to us. This is our first message – we pose no threat to you and come with the best of intentions."

Bon continued, "We want you to establish a meeting with your world president and your world security chief at their earliest convenience" Helen and John looked at each other, then back to Bon, then John said, "I can of course begin the process to set up such a meeting but as we are very low-level functionaries in a vast government with many layers of bureaucracies to navigate before we can arrange it, or even if we can do so without being laughed at. We will need some very compelling reason for such a meeting and since you want us to keep your existence hidden for the time being how would you suggest we approach our leaders?"

Bon said, "Tell your WP's scheduler that you have uncovered some unique and important threat information on the recent near-space anomalies the earth sensor net has discovered. That should do it." John just stared at him blankly since he had heard nothing of the sort. As he was not in the military or space arms of the world government, he would not hear of such a thing unless he saw it on some network news feed.

Bon ignored that and went on to say, "Please know that you are on one of six versions of the same world, as are we here on Shonak. These six worlds are in six individual and completely separate universes, separated by their different, inherent resonance, or vibration, or frequency of existence, if you prefer." He let that sink in then continued, "Shonak has the slowest of the six different resonances of physical existence, that is, we have the slowest natural physical vibration. In fact, there is none slower. Your world, and indeed your entire universe, occupies the highest of these six physical vibrations. Above you the vibration is so rapid that physical matter loses its cohesiveness and flies apart. In other words, there is nothing 'physical' up there. There are additional worlds and universes in between us and only the bottom two and yours at the top have what we might call intelligent life. At least so far as we have determined. Ours and yours are well developed and the world just above us, we call Plus-One, has a newly emerged intelligence that is no more at this time than a small, interesting quadruped, living in the forests and eating insects in the area you call Europe on your world. We call your planet Plus-Five because it is five planetary bandwidths above our own, which is at what we call the Prime vibration."

John sat listening to this in shock. He was flushed, he was breathing heavily, he was thinking that if true, there should be choirs of angels singing to give this the weight it deserved. Instead all he heard was Helen's breathing, and his own, and the hiss of the air conditioning. His vocal cords betrayed his nervous energy as he managed to croak the reply that he appreciated Bon's understanding that the news of this contact and everything else would and will come as a huge shock to Earth. He said he and Helen would indeed begin the process of setting up a meeting with the World President and his security director. Bon then again requested that John and Helen please refrain from notifying their own governments and their world government chain of supervision because he did not want this first-contact to be caught up in hysterical political thinking and one-upmanship that would surely result from people who want to be the "first" to bring this information public. Bon said he was not after headlines or controversy – just action on a potential threat to their planets.

John and Helen both nodded assent to Bon's request for secrecy and then John thanked Bon for his contact and expressed great interest in the promised written summary of Shonak life and culture. Bon then bid them farewell, and the screen went blank.

John and Helen stared at each other in silence for a long moment, each of them racing mentally to take it all in and to plot a course for "what next." John said out loud, almost to himself, that he wished they could see that again and instantly it began to play back from the beginning. They watched it through from beginning to end four more times before Helen asked, overly loud, "What the fuck?!" For an answer he just stared at her blankly. John remembered from his army days being in a training simulation where he was presented a nearly impossible situation and then the exercise controller said, "What do you do now, Lieutenant?" He felt exactly the same way he did back then – a few seconds of panic and uncertainty followed by some formulation of what to do next. Helen, also lost in thought, mind running in circles, was thinking of her home government and who she might have approached with this news, not to mention the world governing body. It was wise of Bon to ask them to hold off so he could bring Shonak to the World President first, who would then determine the way forward with the news of contact with another world. "Heavy stuff," she said, thinking out loud. She remembered her last performance review with her new supervisor, a lifetime bureaucrat – he had actually laughed at her job description! What chance did she have to convince them she had been in contact with an alien from another planet? John's thoughts ran along similar lines. After a long additional silence during which each came up with their next recommended course of action, they both started talking at once. Then stopped, then started, then stopped, then John said, "You first."

Helen said, "Are you shitting me? Was that real? How can we be sure?" They both knew that the comms system for Shonak was stand-alone but over the years it must be possible that somebody had tampered with it. Surely this was someone's idea of a sick joke. John, thinking the same thing, reached over to the black box and moved it, then picked it up to see if there had been any wires installed in the bottom or back – and found none. It was just a cube with a screen in the front, now blank and also now invisible. No wires, no holes, no screws, just a solid cube, black and glassy on all sides. No openings for batteries or power cords or data ports. He put a piece of tape where he thought the screen had been so they could keep it facing them. Helen went into their tool room which held their field gear and grabbed her wireless network detection hand-held. She walked to the box and moved her device around and over and under the box and detected nothing emitting or coming in. She said that the next time they spoke with Shonak they needed to have the full array of detection gear up and running.

Then John remarked to Helen that he found it more than passing strange that they should be talking about possible weapons from Shonak when on that very same day, after thousands of years, Shonak reached out to them. "How could that possibly be a coincidence?" he wondered out loud. Helen said, shaking her head, "No way, Jose."

Bon watched all this with some amusement. He did not fault them for believing that his call could be a hoax of some kind. Open-minded, yes, these two were, but it was just their nature to be distrustful. He replayed their earlier discussion of the unusual skeleton and marveled himself at the coincidence. He had not known in advance they had been discussing Shonak, not until he began watching them before his call. Thinking back to their summary of the recent skeletal find in Germany, Bon had no doubt it was the same primitive chieftain he had killed with a phase weapon when he and Atsa were there trying to deliver Atsa's naïve message of love and kindness. He saw clearly that this was just an odd coincidence, an anomaly, but smiled at the thought that John and Helen would never believe that and also at the thought that this would no doubt create in their minds a sort of superior-super-power status for Shonak as a result. He could only speculate about John and Helen's response, but what fun it would be if they ever learned that it was actually him who had fired that weapon so long ago, at least for them. What Bon does not tell Marquis or Manners is that Shonak has total knowledge of what goes on in the S&T arena, planet-wide, and take active measures to thwart any significant advance of one national power over another. Fortunately, the actions of Shonak, visible now in the records, were completely in line with Shonak's cultural norms. For three thousand, two hundred and ten S-Rots Shonak had been true to itself while maintaining the level of infotainment Shonakians expected and indeed demanded. The infotainment effort was so large it had come under a new communications sub-Grand Team called Plus-Five Infotainment. That had recently moved over to his GT Plus-Five, along with every other Plus-Five related team, and there were many. These had been established over time by many of the people who had been assigned to his Plus-Five Base. Their talents and experience and language mastery, and deep understanding of the many cultures there had not been wasted. All the collection bots that Plus-Five Base had created and multiplied were taken over by the Plus-Five Data Collection and Dissemination team as the people of Earth became more technological their level of sophistication was increased. These also now belonged to Bon's GT Plus-Five. He was interested to note that a great deal of new construction crews on Earth, for example, had been augmented by a variety of Plus-Five human bots installing the necessary front-end collectors in every room in every building, ingeniously disguised as building materials, and using frequencies outside those which could be detected by even the most sensitive Earth equipment. Their fleet of Human bots also became more sophisticated with fingerprints and DNA, blood, saliva, etc. There was an entire sub-team which had oversight of the cover stories for all these human bots, which were there in great numbers. This elevated the risk of discovery, but thus far that had been avoided. All the human bots needed family histories that must be in the various files and databases maintained by their supposed countries of origin. Cover maintenance was a real challenge as Earth's governments cared more and more about positive, biometric-based identification of their citizens. The files showed that late in the 21st century UAY a Shonakian bot was arrested by police in the USNA. They thought he had killed a woman, but he only came upon the body accidentally but before he could make the 9-1-1 call someone else did and said he did it. Fortunately, before any biometrics could be taken the bot managed to escape by anti-grav flight. The local police made a report of it and it went into the same category as a UFO sighting. This incident of course ended up in the files John and Helen maintained on unexplained official reports from all over the world. After that Shonak instituted new protocols for the human bot inventory. They were programmed to maintain the secrecy of their Shonakian identity and technology if they were ever captured. Last resort would be a phase-away tactic with subsequent flight to their desert maintenance facility. This might have to be done in full view of their captors so was to be avoided. Better to escape, and they were equipped with sufficient technology to escape any normal criminal confinement facility, they just had to be patient and wait for the right opportunity, so it would look like a clever escape with no super powers in evidence. The first rule of course was to avoid capture in the first place and they were good at that. Keeping a low profile was their standard MO. The "new" files on Earth's missing years also indicated that bot technology was on the list of acceptable tech transfers but as the population of the planet grew it became socially and morally unacceptable to introduce a technology that would put millions of real people out of work. This alone made the very existence of these human bots on Earth a very closely guarded secret and situations which were likely to result in capture were strictly avoided. While autonomous, for the most part, there had been a team on Shonak through all those years which maintained control of the bot population and monitored their every move and mechanical status. When they needed repairs or a new power supply they either flew to the desert maintenance facility or a maintenance team flew to them. Some of their infotainment collection went into the daily infotainment channels, but not all of it. There had always been various categories of material that were not shown to the Shonak public. This was for several reasons, not the least of which is the maintenance of a totally benign, passive, peaceful disposition on the part of all Shonakians. To that end, most outwardly violent scenes were not released, especially the ones which showed the gratuitous violence these creatures were capable of. Repetitive scenes, of people or of nature, were also not ever released. For example, there is no need to squander resources on live coverage of a waterfall. While it may all be recorded there is no productive issue served by constantly showing it or even retaining it. A still photo and a short clip are all that is necessary. It is also very likely the same waterfall exists on Shonak and the thinking is people can go see it in person if they are that interested. Most are not. Shonakians appreciate natural beauty but do not let that get in the way of Mission. Team missions, team success, is everything. Beauty is a nice-to-have but mission focus is a must-have. The single exception to the social norm of "only teamwork is important" is the entertainment derived from watching Plus-Five natives go about their violent, short lives. Shonakians feel there is something instructive about seeing what their polar opposites do to bring pain into their lives. Their social and living conditions are everything Shonakians do not experience. Competition for food, sex, power, money, are all unknown on Shonak and do not fit into the Shonakian psyche at all. No Shonakian has ever gone hungry or been afraid for personal safety. No Shonakian has ever lusted after a neighbor's wife or daughter or husband or son. No Shonakian has ever prayed or been to a church. No Shonakian has ever been arrested by the police – they don't even have any police. No Shonakian has ever been a soldier or participated in battle. No Shonakian has ever been a king or queen or a member of court. No Shonakian has ever been rich or poor. No Shonakian has ever gone hungry or thirsty. No Shonakian has ever died from a disease or watched a family member die. They have no families so do not have that bond with others. So, it is with great interest to watch people who do and have all these things, be they good or evil. Shonakian Elders have always been concerned that so much observation of Plus-Five activity will begin to have some impact on Shonakian way of life, but other than the avid watching, it has never been observed. Evil thoughts words and deeds are prevalent on the daily Plus-Five feeds, but no evil has been seen in Shonakian behavior. Shonakians rarely ever use any word to describe evil and when they do, it is only in discussions about something they have seen on the feeds. In fact, there was no word for it in their language until they needed one to describe Plus-Five behavior. Evil is simply not something ever found in Shonakian behavior, and the Elders are keen to keep it that way. As they have access to every spoken word a Shonakian has ever uttered and everything they have done has been duly recorded, from their hatching to their death, so there is no way any change in behavior would go unnoticed, even if only by a single individual. It does not bother Shonakians to be so scrutinized in this way since they have nothing to hide and, frankly, nothing to lose. Privacy has never been an issue for them, so they do not worry themselves about any moral breach of privacy for the people of Plus-Five. Nakedness, for example, means nothing to them since they never wear clothing and never think about it. There is no sexual tension about that or anything else. It never enters their minds. And, Shonakians will never meet these people, have no vested interest in them, and the outcome of their lives will never have any impact on them. There is, however, some censorship of the infotainment feeds from Plus-Five. Shonakian elders do not consider gratuitous violence to be in anyone's best interest so while violence is allowed, like in a battle, torture and human sacrifice are not considered suitable for viewing. Plus-Five is, then, a reality show much like going to a game preserve and watching animals live, hunt and kill, and eat their prey. The Gold Shonakian who has been Eldest of the Plus-Five Infotainment Grand Team has had the final say on what is released. Bon has delegated that to what is now a new sub-team of his following the guidelines already established. Our Eldest always takes an interest and like all Shonakians is a lifelong devotee of Plus-Five watching. His particular favorite feeds are from the tribes living in various jungles. For whatever reason. Fortunately for him, these cultures did not much change after the time shift.

Shonakians all have their favorites and are very aware that Plus-Five has many different cultures, which is a good part of the allure. There are large numbers of "study groups" around Shonak who watch their favorites and then chat about their latest viewings. It amazes Shonakians how varied the human population is on Plus-Five; different colors, different appearance and clothing, different sizes, different languages, which they are keen to learn, different forms of government and religion, different forms of payment, and in general widely different habits. By contrast, Shonak is a monolithic culture with one language, no government to speak of, not in the sense that Plus-Five has governments, no religion, and is cashless, sexless, and frankly, boring by Plus-Five standards. That said, Shonakians do not see their lives as "boring"; far from it. They don't even have that word for it in their language. Shonakians revere their placid, relatively uneventful daily lives – testament to the success they enjoy as a culture. Since their whole existence has been devoted to solving all their problems, from housing to living standards to food production and distribution, to science and technology, to communications, to everything that touches them, placid living has become their reward. When asked they might admit that there is little left to interest them because as problem-solvers they most cherish a problem to solve. They work hard but do not play hard since they don't play. They are serious about everything and feel a great responsibility for things which need to be fixed in some way. Not so with watching their favorite Plus-Five tribe or family or region, whatever. The greatest soap opera, ever! They are blessed to be able to watch a reality drama play out in so many different ways among so many different peoples, in so many places, none of which has any impact on their own lives. They might witness a culture implode with the deaths of thousands of people, but to them it is just distant drama that they can never actually be confronted with in person. Perfect! All the problems of Plus-Five peoples are just that and with no way to solve them or take ownership of them or meet with them there is no personal involvement. Keen interest without commitment or responsibility. Perfect!

John and Helen heard the uniquely different sounding "beep" that they just learned meant incoming traffic from Shonak and then they saw the promised written summary come up on the screen. They began to read it with fascination and deep interest. They also had no clear plan of action regarding what to do with it. Should they copy it by hand or take a video of it on the screen? Then a soft whirr could be heard in the back of the cube and a long strip of paper emerged from a new opening with the following printed on it.

"Dear Doctors Marquis and Manners. We are once again speaking to you, the World Government appointed contact office, confident we can now begin to enjoy a fruitful and harmonious relationship to the benefit of both our worlds. It only remains to choose the right time

and place for the introduction of Shonak to the people of Earth at large. We look forward to collaborating with your World President on that issue, and the more pressing defense issue we desire to discuss. We are pleased that your office has been maintained all these millennia even without contact and we realize your office has acquired other duties, but it remains a fruitful convenience that you have held onto our comms cube since it was delivered in the year you would know as 1950 under one of your old calendars. What follows is the promised brief overview of Shonak and its culture.

"On behalf of Our Eldest, Gold Nec, 304697.023.65.06 we greet you, people of Earth. It is the year of our culture 306108. I am Gold Bon, 305058.141.61.05.01, Eldest of Grand Team Plus-Five/Earth in Solar Rotation 306,108 since the establishment of our current world order. We have been what you might call "civilized" for well over five hundred thousand of your years, but we number our years since the last major adjustment in our way of organizing our society."

"We call our world Shonak. It occupies the lowest of the six planetary vibrations and as the people who discovered this, we designated our vibration 'Prime'. We call your world, and indeed your entire universe, 'Plus-Five' because it is five planetary/universe vibrations above our own."

"Geographically our planets are twins. They are virtually the same in size and in rotation and in orbits. Where we are different is how plant and animal life

evolved. Our two versions of the same planet developed in completely separate universes, which occupy different vibrational space. These two universes, vast as they are, comprise only two of the six just like it. We are all separated by our unique, inherent, energy vibrations. The vagaries of the random, spontaneous chemical and biological events surrounding the creation of each of our species has yielded two very different life forms who do not look or sound or think or behave alike."

"When last we visited you openly it was with certain individuals on your planet who lived in fragmented, geographically dispersed locations, speaking different languages, believing different things, and having no technology to speak of. Your Earth today is far different, and we think you are now capable of understanding us and working with us."

"We on Shonak are of a single gender and reproduce by developing eggs inside us and regurgitating them when ready, usually in our four hundredth year. We can produce two eggs in our lifetime, but if we choose not to produce the second one, we simply tell our body not to. We live well over fifteen hundred years and have no disease and no illness. When we decide life has nothing more to offer, we self-terminate by telling our body to shut itself down. This is a quick and painless process. Our remains are cremated and used to nourish our crops. We eat very little by your standards and as we have no taste buds, we have no interest in preparing grand meals. Our food comes in edible tubes which contain all the nourishment

and liquid we need in a single planetary rotation, what you call a 'day'. We are short, by your standards, hairless, and thin, roughly one of your meters tall and weighing an average of 7.7 of your kilograms or 17 of your pounds. We are cold-blooded, which means our bodies maintain the temperature of our environment and so we never had the need for clothing. We prefer warmer climates simply because we are more active when we are warm. Evolving on a benign planet, as we did, there was no need to be large or strong to survive. And with no competition for food or a mate or shelter we have had no need for aggression."

"We have no families since we do not know our parent, nor are we raised by anyone connected with them. We also have no friends in the way you would characterize them. We bond over shared projects and ideas but are always cognizant of our age differences and always defer to the older while we instruct, or guide, or mentor the younger around us when it is needed."

"We are highly intelligent, and by your standards, would all be classed as super-geniuses, but we are much smarter than that, even. There is really no way for us to explain the difference between Shonakians and Earthers in this context. Our brains and therefore our minds do not operate under the same circuitry or chemistry or biology yours do. Our language reflects our intelligence in that we speak in quick bursts of words that contain much more information than yours do. A single word for us can be like a paragraph to you. Our conversations, even about very complex topics, are short since we think so much

alike. We do not read minds and we do not have a 'hive mind' on Shonak, far from it, but we function quite a bit as if we did. There is a great deal of individuality in our thinking, but we mostly come to the same conclusions and very quickly, having thought through all the many variations of possibilities on any given subject in an instant. Consequently, we are very efficient in our communications, unlike your people, whose different languages and different perspectives and different goals and objectives and emotions cloud all your conversations and correspondence."

"We are a very industrious race. We get a lot done in a short amount of time. We do not require much sleep or leisure or time to eat, nor do we socialize in the same way your people do, so there is nothing much else to do but work, our chosen activity. We enjoy our work very much. It is what we live for."

"Our science and technology and manufacturing are far superior to yours. We have been a mature culture for over five hundred thousand of your years, what we call Solar Rotations. *In all this time our people have made continuous advances in all fields of science and technology. Solar rotation after solar rotation, what we call S-Rots, we have improved every aspect of our lives and continue to do so to this day."*

"Our days and years are the same length as yours, based on the same rotations, but we divide them up differently. We have no months or weeks or days of the week. Our planet revolves around our star every three

hundred and sixty-five of our planetary rotations. These are numbered one to three hundred sixty-five. We divide these P-Rots, or days, into what you would call a metric system. Each day has 100 portions, roughly fourteen and a half of your minutes each, which are then divided into 100 segments, which are in turn divided into 100 sub-segments. We have no money, no commerce, and no politics because there is no need for any of those things here."

"There are no countries or ethnic divisions here since we are of one species, one world order, and speak one language. Our education is the same throughout the entire planet. We keep our population stable at around 142 million people distributed into 142 regions, or population zones of the world."

"We first visited your world a more than five thousand of your years ago as you reckon time. We have monitored your growth and development ever since as a matter of simple scientific interest and for its entertainment value. Our placid, monoculture with its obsessive work ethic offers far fewer diversions than your more fragmented, conflicted and violent existence. We find watching you to be hugely instructive and entertaining as well as something of a mystery. You are, individually and collectively, at once capable of great violence towards one another as well as great love and tenderness. To people like us, who only know kindness and civil behavior, the dark side of your natures are of high interest and very entertaining."

"Shonak, or Prime, or even Plus-Zero, is and always has been totally benign. This accounts for the evolution of

a much different intelligent life here than on your totally hostile world. Here, the emerging, dominant, intelligent life form never needed to learn survival skills, never needed to compete for anything. We never encountered harmful plants or animals, and we have no insects. We never needed to worry about the battle of the sexes since we are all of the same gender and reproduce independently of one another. We never needed to worry about poisonous or harmful plants for food, so we have needed no taste buds to survive. We are uniform in our appearance, too, almost to the point of being identical."

"To help identify each individual and to document our age, upon which we place so much emphasis, we all have an age tattoo on our right arms. These tattoos give our precise date and time of hatching. This is essential since every social situation and team affiliation we experience is governed by age. We never compete for 'being in charge' because the oldest person in any situation is automatically in charge. We all get along with one another and in the rare case of a voiced difference of opinion, we are able to discuss the matter intelligently and without emotion. In the even more rare case of an unresolved dispute, the older person automatically determines the outcome of any disagreement. Facts are facts, but how those facts are used is what differences of opinion result from. In addition to our age tattoo, we have a color tattoo in the center of our foreheads that signifies our age range. While we are in our Education and Training Centers, we have no dot and are known as 'blankheads', or juveniles with no dots on their

foreheads. When we finish our early formal education and reach adulthood, at age 40 or so, we receive a red dot and a red wrist badge with the insignia of the Grand Team we are assigned to. The red dot signifies we have joined Shonakian society as an adult. After that our age dots change in color following each 142 years of life. The colors match the colors of the rainbow up to our one thousandth birthday and time when we receive a gold dot which does not change again no matter how much longer we live."

"We have no formal government as you would know it, but we do have some necessary planet-wide administration. The one hundred and fifty-five people who occupy these positions of authority are simply the oldest one hundred fifty-five people among us. First there are the 142 Regional Councilors, each overseeing one of the 142 planetary regions, each with very close to one million people. Their main job is population control and to oversee the efficient provision of public utilities and services. Older than them are the Council of Twelve, who mediate the rare disputes between regions and among the Grand Teams. They also keep track of the Grand Teams themselves, what their structures are and who is assigned. Then finally there is the Our Eldest, who is simply the oldest living Shonakian. Our current OE is 1651 S-Rots old, which is about average. All other Golds are either on Teams or, if not, are free to use their leisure as they choose, to include self-termination. This system, now in its 306,108th S-Rot, or what you would call a year, works well for us since we are all of the same mind on pretty much

everything and because we are an intelligent, rational, placid, uncompetitive race."

"The practical management of the planet Shonak comes from the various Grand Teams who keep the planet's infrastructure operating and the people themselves busy. For all Shonakians the main goal in life is to work hard their whole lives and measure their success or failure based on their own performance and on their achievement of missions within their Team environments."

"Teams are what make the planet work and are the reason Shonakians love life. We now average 1550 years of age but also choose to self-terminate when we feel we have no more to accomplish or give, which can be at any age. Currently, the oldest Shonakian on record reached the age of 1781 Solar Rotations and died simply of old age. Very rare for us. He only did it to see how long we might live without self-termination."

"Once we reach adulthood, all Shonakians are assigned to a Grand Team and become focused on the accomplishment of our Team missions. There are many Grand Teams and each of them have many levels of sub-teams and the teams subordinate to them. Exploration and Science and Technology Grand Teams are among the so-called super-grands, with the most famous and ground-breaking missions, but all the teams are vital to the maintenance of the beneficial good order and discipline of Shonakian life. The Age Grand Team puts extraordinary exactitude on the registration and updating of all age-related data for all of Shonak. We all

trust the age tattoo without question since it is applied by the Grand Team devoted to that single task. Public Utilities, Communications, Information Systems, Infotainment, Agriculture and Food, Transportation, Arts, Construction, Electrical Power, Roads and Bridges, and Aviation are all Grand Teams. Our Eldest is the authority for establishing or dis-establishing Grand Teams. Training and Education Grand Team educates the young 'blankheads' to prepare them for life as an adult and member of a Team. They assist the Grand Teams in the selection of new graduates, young adults then, based on the demonstrated aptitude and desires of their students. Most young adults are assigned to their Grand Teams of choice but occasionally they are assigned elsewhere either due to there being a better match for their demonstrated talents and skills or because the team of choice is full."

"The Training and Education GT also monitors the population of Shonak for behavior and advises the Regional Counselors on anomalous behavior. Disruptive, anti-social behavior is antithetical to our way of life and deviations from this are important for us to know about and deal with."

"We are not without humor or a sense of irony and we enjoy natural beauty which is so abundant on our planet, as it is on yours. We also have very talented artists who help to adorn our parks and buildings and who work with our architects to create beautiful structures for residential and office and industrial buildings."

"We do not spend a lot of time in leisurely pursuits

and do not dream of retirement or of "getting away from it all" as you so often do. We never take a vacation. For us, our lives and our work are so pleasant and meaningful there is nothing to escape from. We run to our work, not away from it. We relish a challenge of any kind. They are like puzzles for us to solve. Whenever there is some condition on the planet that displeases us, we simply figure out a way to eliminate that condition. After more than five hundred thousand years of behaving this way there are not many bothersome things left and so we push the boundaries through exploration and through scientific discovery. Finding your world, and the other worlds in between yours and ours, has been the greatest single event in our scientific history. It has given us much more to do and much more to observe. This is especially true of your world as it gives us so much to observe."

"We monitor life on your world continuously which provides us with daily examples of what chaos is like among diverse, competitive populations. By comparison, we find no reason to emulate our more active cousins on 'Earth'. But well aside from emulation, we have an abiding fascination for all things Plus-Five. Consequently, our population visually devours what we observe on your world. Also, since we live well in excess of a thousand stellar rotations (years) we can follow the 'action' on Plus-Five over more than fifty generations of your lives. We have seen empires rise and fall within our own lifetimes. We have seen climate change. We have seen the evolution of your languages and arts and science. We

know your languages and cultures and history likely as well as you do yourselves."

"It is perhaps unfortunate that we can never mingle our populations in their natural state. There can be no occupation of any of our worlds by people from another vibration. The immutable Law of Nativity holds that every physical thing has a vibration that is native to the one in which it was created, the one it was born into. This cannot be changed. No Shonakian can live on your world without the constant maintenance of its natural vibration and so can never leave the phase ship without a phase suit. Also, no person from Earth can live on Shonak without similar protection. We call this temporary protective vibration a 'Zone of Influence' which keeps us alive when visiting other vibrations. We can communicate, however, using radio frequencies, as we are doing now on the device, we provided your planet so long ago. This is a complex process that requires electrons and photons to be altered from one vibration to another. It took us some time to achieve this but is one of our most prized accomplishments. Our ability to travel among the phases is equally prized by us as an exemplary achievement of our ability to find technology solutions for any and all things we want to do."

"All things considered, and certainly from your standpoint, ours is a well-regulated, prosperous, content society. Everyone on Shonak is proud of that and we work hard to keep it that way. We see harmony through individual and team mission achievement as our collective goal and as our chosen way of life."

"Once again, we greet you. When we go public with our presence on your world and on our partnership of sister planets, there will be more time for you all to become more familiar with us and our ways."

"End Text."

After he sent the summary to Earth Bon let OE and Eldest Exploration know that he had re-established discrete, minimal contact with the modern Plus-Five, which the people there now call "Earth" in the dominant language, World English. He said he accomplished this via the existing but inactive liaison apparatus that had remained in place for many S-Rots in spite of the native disbelief in anything like a Shonak. He gave them both a quick summary of the call and said he would keep them informed as the relationship developed.

As he said that his mind was far ahead of events, defining what that meant. While members of his team were experts on various matters concerning the natives of Plus-Five no other living Shonakian had the intimate knowledge of the Earther psyche he had. But that said, even he was unsure how they would react to Shonak in their modern, technologically advanced world. His team had pored over the "new" three thousand-plus S-Rots of Plus-Five's recorded history for any mention of Shonak or alien visitation. There was a great deal of fictional lore about visits from other worlds but nothing much about Shonak, per se, except for a few very obscure oral history notes from what was now North America. It was clear that a sudden demonstration of their presence on Earth would not be in anyone's best interest.

Earth may have modern technology and a fledgling world government, but their behavior has consistently shown that they are as emotionally unstable as ever. Earth science had not progressed to the point where they could change phases of existence like the Shonakians could, and there was not even much fictional speculation on this score. Reviews of all arts and entertainment and literature showed that "alternate" and "parallel" Earths were fairly common fictional themes with little speculative science behind them. Earth natives, Shonakians preferred the shorter term "Earthers," had shown through all their actions that they had quick, agile minds and were very creative. Their recent ability to create computer graphics had resulted in dramatic visual and audio representations of "aliens" of all shapes and types and temperaments; both hostile and benign. While there were some similarities in a few of their computer-generated images to what Shonakians look like, there was nothing close enough to suggest there had been any record made from their previous contact with Earth. It appeared to Bon's team that Earthers had not maintained the comm cube out of some sense of, or belief in, the existence of Shonak or fear of missing out should it ever prove true. Since it did not cost anything to maintain better to be safe than sorry. Plus, it was to them a visual reminder of the impossible, humorous, campy part of their office's mission. At this point in their history, Earthers simply scoffed at the notion of extra-terrestrial life. Until now, that is, for just two of them. If they even believed it, really. Bon guessed that with every passing moment more and more doubt crept into John's and Helen's recollection of his conversation with "Bon of Shonak." John and Helen's belief system must be seen in this light. What a shock it must have been for them! He got it, now.

Bon was confident this new relationship would soon develop into something more public and it was not too soon to begin to formulate policy with regards to such things as knowledge and technology transfer. Clearly Earth should never be given anything that could be weaponized no matter how helpful it would be to them in other applications. Shonak would certainly never transfer phase technology knowledge to Earth even with the protection of the Law of Nativity. Shonakians might freely share many technological things but Bon was confident that the people of Earth could not be trusted with phase shifting or phase weapon technology since they were far too aggressive and defensive and afraid of what they don't understand. Even completely honorable people on Earth will lie, cheat, steal, and worse given sufficient motivation. How many times had he seen it himself during his work there and also during his life on their live feeds? And any nation which had phase technology first would surely use it to try to dominate the ones who did not. It was just their nature. He could easily see where that might go. If an Earther could half-phase away from his reality, which could enable him to walk through walls, and get into a bank vault, phase back in, take whatever, phase away, and make his way back home, they would not have helped the people of Earth one bit. So in spite of the obvious maturity of many of Earth's scientists there were too many people in and out of that community, especially in the military, politics, and finance, not to mention organized crime, who would use phase technology for some unhelpful purpose. So, Bon felt the million-plus Shonakian collection platforms on Earth should maintain a low profile and keep their existence completely hidden from everyone, most especially the public at large. Any technology they shared with Earth would first need to be confirmed as benign, that is, could not be weaponized or misused. If the technology was deemed safe, and then, if transferred, it could be considered by Shonak as payment for the vast entertainment value of their video feeds from Plus-Five over the millennia.

Chapter Five

Shonak "Comes Out" To Earth

Helen Manners and John Marquis had been colleagues for nearly ten years and were best friends who got along wonderfully well. It helped that there was no sexual tension or bonding between them, just professional respect and honest friendship mixed with diligent work, which they did very well even if their remit was not the most demanding, or the most popular. Truth to tell, their own national governments and the new world government too, for that matter, did not want them to discover aliens or the devil or angels or whatever the odd things they looked into might suggest or bring forth. Things that go bump in the night were expected to have logical explanations. The pair was expected to simply do good, solid work, and if it helped solve a police or anthropological matter then wonderful. Extraterrestrials – forget about it.

They knew this full well, of course. They weren't stupid. In fact, they were both brilliant academics and adept, experienced field workers but now that they had what they felt was undeniable extraterrestrial contact, they were left with that stressful question John remembered: "what do you do now, Lieutenant?" They told themselves that their secrecy commitment to Gold Bon, the Shonakian rep, was OK, and fine, for the moment anyway. This is what they agreed was the reason they would give their own governments when they did come forward with this information, as they must, eventually – and soon. But then what? They did understand that their overriding loyalty must be to their own, not some alien. So they were nervous and apprehensive and frankly neither of them was totally comfortable keeping this secret. Fortunately, Bon wanted a meeting with the World President and Security Director so it's not as if they were expected to keep this a secret forever. And equally good for them was that he wanted the meeting "soon." He had not given any guidance on that, just wanted it as soon as they were able to arrange the meeting. They left that conversation with the understanding that, in their minds, it would take some time to discreetly set up this meeting from their position so low on the totem pole. John and Helen agreed that another reason for secrecy was that one percent chance this was all just some elaborate high-tech joke on the so-called "Nutcase-Files" team. How embarrassing would it be to set up a meeting with the World President only to find out it was some hoax! It was not the first time they had faced this sort of humor from other government scientists with nothing better to do. So, days went by and then a week before they decided on a course of action and began the process of setting up a meeting with the World President and the World Security Director. They chose to go around their own supervisory chain and also to avoid their own governments – decisions that could cost them their jobs – but they could not figure out how to go through their supervisory chain or home governments and maintain secrecy or achieve success in getting on the WP's calendar without an endless round of briefings amid gales of laughter leading to disapproval of any such meeting. John had some contacts from various conferences he had attended in the past and he was able to use them to get a call in to the aide to the World President, who he had actually met at a recent conference. Once in contact he requested a meeting to discuss a "near space anomaly" their office had discovered, which understandably they wanted to keep secret. They used the phrase Bon had suggested and it seemed to get results. They also requested confidentiality, noting that they were going directly to them on this as it was too sensitive to share anywhere else. They knew the standard protocol was to ensure that their governments and their supervisors were aware of the issue and approved them coming to see the WP about it. At the very least, normal procedure would have been for some top-level rep from both home governments and their own departments to be present at any meeting at this level. While waiting for an answer, they did their best to get back to a daily routine, but the elephant in the room sat there like the quiet black cube it was. Every now and then, one of them or both would stare at it, wondering if it was still right side up. They knew there was no way to tell and the nightly cleaning team was apt to lay it down any which way since they had no clue there even was a screen, or a printer port, for that matter. It was just a smooth, black, glassy cube about a foot on each side that weighed less than it looked like it should.

After a few days, and still waiting for a response from the WP's office, John suggested they try to contact Shonak just to see if they could. Helen agreed and slid her chair over to the cube across the smooth, hard, shiny, floor of their workspace and said, glibly, with a sarcastic smile aimed at John, "Hey Bon, are you in there?"

To their great surprise, the screen lit up instantly, but the light was in the back, this time, so they quickly turned it to face them. Bon's image was looking at them and he said, "Yes, I am here, in my office, but not in the comm cube of course. What can I do for you? Has there been some development on your end?"

Helen and John looked at each other, then back at Bon, then back at each other. They stared at one another for a moment thinking how hard it would have been for someone to have arranged such an elaborate hoax. Feeling suddenly more confident in this alien contact, she said, "We still have not notified our bosses of your existence, as we agreed, but we risk our jobs and reputations if we sit on this much longer. We did reach out to the World President's office, directly, to arrange a meeting so we could brief them on a "near space anomaly" like you suggested, and requested they be discrete about the meeting, but have heard nothing back from them. Do you have any better ideas for arranging this meeting?" Bon was ready with a reply, since he had already gamed every possible way this could be played.

He didn't tell them that Shonak felt it was essential their renewal of contact be kept from the public at large. At least for now. There were several reasons for this. First, and this was totally self-serving, Shonak did not want to change Earther behavior lest it interrupt the current and entertaining daily routine of the "natives" Shonakians have come to rely on; and follow religiously. The news on Earth of alien contact would immediately dominate every aspect of life on Earth, at every level, and that was not a topic Shonak would enjoy being discussed. Shonakians had no interest in learning about their own existence from the people of Plus-Five! Shonak also did not want their surveillance bot network jeopardized in any way since they were the source of the Shonak live feeds of Plus-Five. The next big reason for keeping their existence secret, at least for now, was because they anticipated robust and immediate demands for Shonak's advanced technologies. These would be coming from government, science, and manufacturing sectors. So until Shonak had workable procedures in place for vetting technology transfer, they did not want to deal with it.

John tried to get Bon to understand how difficult it would be for him to arrange a meeting with the World President on any topic but the need to bypass his own supervisory chain and to keep it secret added a level of complexity that would take some time to work through. To say the least, he said, "The World President and the World Director of Security are busy and highly visible. Their calendars are scrutinized by the press and heads of state and much of the senior bureaucracy. In fact, the calendars of the WP and all his senior staff are made public in advance for reasons of transparency and also so people with a need to attend or add to the topics could arrange to do so. For Helen and I to get on their calendar, given the office we work in, will not only generate a lot of curiosity but also needs to be coordinated through our own department." He paused to gauge Bon's reaction but could not read his alien expression. He continued, "Nominally we are an independent agency reporting to the WG Secretariat once a year. That's where our budget came from, meager as it is, and that is who we should be going through to request this extraordinary meeting." Humorously, he added that they could just simply say they had made contact with an alien race, but that would get them sent to counseling before anything else happened. Bon told them he was in no immediate hurry but urged them to keep at it and rang off.

Not having any bright ideas, they decided to take the rest of the day off and go have a drink. They were silent over their cocktails for a while, lost in thought. There were so many implications for them personally and professionally, and for their countries and for their planet, for that matter. After two hours or so of internal musing and more than a few drinks, they looked at each other and smiled. John winked at Helen and she smiled broader and said, "Keeping this under wraps is smart. I mean, we should be going to our own governments with the news, but that will likely only get us on everyone's shit list." Helen nodded and took another sip. They parted to go home and left it behind them for the night. Bon had been watching and listening the entire time they were in the bar lounge and was pleased that these two people could bury their ego and honor his request for proceeding quietly on this, their foray into interplanetary relations. Bon reflected on how much more complicated it was now to have open contact with Earthers. Before they had any technology or science or geography or even knowledge of each other around the planet, he was free to travel their world with impunity and visit with them openly, if only with a bot or in a phase suit, suitably disguised as something other than a Shonakian – which they would not have understood anyway. If he did something which to the natives appeared at all supernatural or superhuman the natives would invariably put it down as "the gods" doing something.

Bon wanted to be especially careful to hide the checkered history of Shonak's early days on Plus-Five, before OE determined that Earthers were human. Their kidnappings and experiments would not be an easy sell even with an enlightened and intelligent pair of scholars, much less with the general public. Fortunately for Shonak their darker actions on Earth were lost to history with no way for any Earther to retrieve them.

While John and Helen sat in their office the next morning trying to concentrate on their work, and eagerly waiting for some sort of response from the WP's office, Bon, not wanting to wait longer for the meeting to happen, decided to speed things along. He appeared on their Cube and thanked them for their discretion and their ability to keep this whole thing secret, then he told them about the special comm devices he had constructed for them. He said they could expect a courier package momentarily with their own hand-helds which could not be listened to by any device on Earth. He explained that the frequency they use was Shonakian even though the devices were of Earth manufacture. He did not tell them they were made in his Sahara desert facility, which was now safely underground. There was another feature that translated their discussions into Shonakian for transmission and then back again to English so that all the transmissions were further unreadable since there was no way the Shonakian language could be intelligible to any Plus-Five native. At that moment their doorbell rang and they met a courier there who handed them the small package with their comm devices, just like Bon said.

Bon then told them he had been able to arrange the desired meeting with the WP and the Director of Security through his own manipulation of their schedules. The subject on the diary page for them both simply said, "Classified Space Anomaly Brief." John and Helen were listed in the background notes as the briefers, and so was a Stephen Banks, from a private security company, with classified materials and briefing equipment. Bon said he provided the WP's office with the required CV for them all. He explained that Stephen was an employee of his from Earth, who did various jobs for him given the difficulty he had in visiting Earth himself. Bon said he had also managed to get this entered in the Secretariat log as having been approved. To avoid accidental discovery within the bureaucracy, the meeting was scheduled for the next morning, early, their time, and Bon said he had transportation waiting for them on the roof of their building. Now. They did not need to take anything with them, and a change of clothes was waiting for them in their hotel in Beijing.

It was a tremendous leap of faith for both of them but they took the elevator to the top floor and then the emergency stairs to the roof and stood there, in the wind and sunshine, hoping not to be embarrassed, looking around for anything resembling a helicopter but saw nothing. Then this big disc suddenly appeared like from out of a fog bank, but it was sitting on the roof, on its supports, as if it had been there all the time. (Which it had). A door was open, and they quickly went inside, not wanting to be seen, and the door closed behind them and even before they sat down, they were on their way!

They plopped into the seats and felt movement and then they were clearly in motion but without windows there was no visual frame of reference for speed other than the obvious feeling of acceleration and deceleration and changes in direction and altitude. Then Bon appeared in his phase suit and he bid them stay calm and welcomed them aboard his phase ship. This one, he explained, was constructed of Earth materials so it did not require a Zone of Influence to keep it here, or for them to be in it. He was the one who needed the Zone, since he could not exist in Earth's vibration without it. He said they would be at their destination in China shortly, only a short trip from Switzerland, after all, in a Shonakian anti-grav ship. He thanked them for bearing their message and said they would be met in Beijing by his employee there, the aforementioned Stephen, who would take care of their needs and get them to the meeting on time. Stephen would brief them on how the meeting was laid out and then he said goodbye and phased away from them. They were alone in what seemed to be a pilotless aircraft of some sort. Comfortable enough, and John went to the little galley and poured them both a cup of coffee, and grabbed a Danish, while he was at it. If there had been anything stronger to drink, he certainly would have chosen that!

They landed on the top of a building just after sunset. They stepped out of the ship and the instant Helen's trailing foot left the short ramp the ship disappeared! A tall, nicely dressed European man met them on the roof and introduced himself. He was Stephen Banks, saying he was the one working for Bon. He said the meeting they were in Beijing for was in another building, this was their hotel. He led them to a doorway and then to stairs, then to an opulent, carpeted corridor, then an elevator, then to their very nice rooms. On the way, Stephen said a change of clothing was laid out for them both, in their rooms, for the meeting tomorrow morning. Right now, he said, they would go to dinner where he would brief them on the way the meeting would be structured. After a few moments for them to freshen up Stephen led them to the hotel restaurant for what would be lunch for them back in Switzerland, supper here. During the meal, Stephen explained that they would arrive at World Headquarters in the morning around 7:30 AM for their 8 AM meeting. They would go through the security process, get badged, and then would be taken to the waiting rooms outside the President's office. They were expected and their meeting was on the calendar for half an hour, quite a long time for such a hasty meeting with the World President. Bon asked that they relay what happened in their office and give the WP and Security Director copies of the Shonak summary, which he handed to John, in an envelope. At that moment Bon would appear in the office and take the meeting from there. The meal was nice, and they ate it with some pleasure, but neither had any idea what time it was, as their body clocks were still six hours away in Switzerland. John thought he either needed a big coffee or a comfortable bed and chose the bed. Their alarms went off at 5:30 AM and they were in the lobby at seven, following a quick continental breakfast in the hotel restaurant. Stephen led them to a limo outside the hotel for the ride to World Headquarters. When they arrived at the WH a man in sharp uniform bearing the security insignia of the world government introduced himself and asked, in English, that they accompany him through the security process. He said he was to escort them through the security gates without delay. John introduced Bon's man as his aide, Stephen, and said he was to accompany him to the President's office, and the man said he was on the list, and nodded in acceptance. He spoke Chinese into his comm device to alert his team he was enroute with a party of VIPs to see the WP and Marshal Li Ning, the World Security Director. Stephen then said something to the security person, in what sounded like fluent Chinese, who smiled and said something back. After the security checks they were ushered into the President's outer office where an aide to the WP, Horst, a Swede, greeted them and then let the President know the special party had arrived. Horst then led them into the President's private office. Both the President and Marshal Li rose to greet their guests.

John spoke first and thanked the President and Marshal for agreeing to meet at such short notice. John saw that both men were of sharp, expensive, tailored business dress and regal bearing with intelligent faces and quick, analytical eyes. John, Helen, and Stephen were invited to seats on the sofas while the President and Marshal took chairs that faced them. As this was a security matter the Marshal spoke first said they did not have a lot of time but were naturally interested in what they had to say about the "near space anomaly," coming as they did from, and he smiled as he said it, "The Weird Files" office, which should not have access to this information. The Marshal said his concern, and the reason he did not cancel the meeting, was because he thought there might be a leak in their security or military chain of command that John and his party may be able to help them find. John and Helen both smiled nervously at that, and wore curious, concerned expressions. They were used to being treated as something of a joke, an old joke at that, but not security threats. John looked at Helen, smiled nervously, trying to hide his fears that the meeting was going in a different and darker direction than he wanted or expected. He quickly got to the point and said he had come with information about two things they needed to hear, one of which he was about to explain. The other was something he wished to work on with the Marshal and his security apparatus. The Marshal's eyes narrowed, trying to fix a subject to this and failed and his eyes softened.

"Mister President, and Marshal Li," John began, "My office is charged with contacting alien life when we find it." He paused, then said, "In this case, they found us. I have been asked to introduce the world Shonak to you." He paused again for effect, to let that sink in a little, then resumed, "Shonak is a cousin planet, if you like, to this one, that exists at a different natural vibration, in a parallel world of sorts. The planet is nearly identical to this one but the people who evolved there are completely different. We do not need to fear them, and they do not need to fear us because we cannot live or exist even for a moment on each other's worlds. That said, Shonak has a much older civilization which is much more advanced technologically than we are, and we can benefit through exchanges of ideas and information with them. The representative of that world to Earth is a senior official named Bon." He handed them the Shonak summaries, still in their folders, and said, "I'm giving you written information summaries on the Planet and People of Shonak, to read at your leisure, and Gold Bon will visit us now." At this, the real Bon phased into the room from just "outside" and his shimmering suit caught Horst and the Marshal by surprise. Horst immediately pressed the duress button under the arm of his chair, which would bring the security team in, but nothing happened. The Marshal looked at John with anger at being set up, but Bon told Horst the button would not work and there was no need of it. Both the President and the Marshal were on their feet ready to fight or flee, they had not decided yet which, when the apparition Bon raised his hands, palms outward in a universal sign of peace. John then suggested that they sit down and calm themselves so Bon could explain what was going on.

Bon spoke, "Greetings, Mister President and Marshal Ning. I am Gold Bon, the representative of my planet and my people to your planet and your people. We want you to know that we are friends of Earth even though we have kept our existence secret till now. The reason we have chosen this moment to reveal ourselves is because Earth, and our world too, may be threatened by another alien race about which we know nothing. I understand that this information will be something of a shock to you, but I can prove what I say, and will do at the appropriate moment. For now, I just want to introduce myself and let you know that Mr. John Marquis here, his colleague Helen Manners, and my assistant Stephen are currently our chosen representatives on Earth. John and Helen have long, distinguished academic and government careers behind them and are highly intelligent, and very articulate. They can keep an open mind, as I hope you can. As you know, John and Helen are in government, in the office that has been designated as the point of contact with aliens should they ever show up, which is how we made their acquaintance. With this threat from another alien race we on Shonak agreed that the time has come to meet with you openly about this threat and work together to meet it. We have no thought ourselves for "going public" with our existence, although we can discuss this at your leisure. Any decision to go public is entirely up to you, as this is your world, not ours. I will leave you now but John, Helen, and Stephen will brief you on Shonak and more importantly, at least in the short term, on the potential threat we face and how we can help each other to defend against it." Bon then phased out of Earth synch and disappeared. The Marshal and Horst just stared at the spot where Bon had been standing and said nothing. The Marshal took a step forward and ran his hand through the space Bon had just departed. His face showed that he felt nothing, and it was anyone's guess what he expected to feel. Perhaps he just wanted to be sure the "apparition" named Bon was actually gone. John waited in silence to give them time to process what they just saw and heard. After a moment, Stephen then spoke and said,

"Recently Shonak explorers noted a strange vibrational signature at our Earth level of resonance. To Shonak this is Plus-Five space, since we are five universe levels of resonance higher than they are. They are watching for this anomaly now very carefully should it appear again. They noted that our own Earth space force detected it as well. Shonak's detectors revealed that though the alien vessel was only here a few seconds, it collected an outer-atmosphere air sample and then departed. Shonak thinks these people come from an alternate universe set, not just a different vibration of this one. Shonak on the other hand comes from an alternate world but within our own set of six separate universes. The vibrational signature of this new anomaly is just too different to come from our space. Shonak knows next to nothing about them, including what their intentions and capabilities are. They have no idea if these people are friend or foe. The unidentified alien ship is essentially the size of a Shonakian phase ship scout, so there may be some similarities between them physically, but we really have no idea. They can't even be sure there were people on board. Without knowing their intentions, Shonak's worry is that should a military defense be needed Shonak is not equipped emotionally to respond quickly enough to any hostile threat. This is where we here on Earth come in. If Shonak needs to engage them in combat, they are hoping to have earth-human gunners willing to perform that task.

The WP and his Marshal and his aide stared at Stephen in absolute silence, then at each other, then back at Stephen again. They had not expected this and were completely surprised and troubled by it. Horst looked at his watch and called the outer office to say the meeting would be going long, and to ask the next guests to relax and wait.

John spoke then and referenced the Shonak summaries he gave them earlier. He said, "Gold Bon provided you with the written information summaries that explain his culture which we all need to know in order to understand their motives here. The Shonakians are scientists, really, and they see this as a job for the military, not gentle people of science and reason."

The WP, Li Ning and Horst then took over the meeting, filling the room with their anger, concern, fears, doubts, until Stephen raised his hand to silence them. He stared at them long and hard. Stephen then opened his briefcase to show a display screen. A video appeared that showed scenes and provided a narrative concerning the unknown presence detected in Earth's near-space, that is, within their own solar system. The Marshal watched intently, noting how much more information Shonak had on this thing than Earth had. Of course, the big question was, how hostile are these newcomers? What do they want? Where are they from? To form an effective response, they all needed a lot more information and likely also some improved space warfare capability.

Stephen explained that no one had answers yet to all the obvious questions about these aliens but he did add that Shonak had ships in Earth's space collecting on every aspect of these people when they do show up, something they only do briefly. Shonak was doing this to protect Earth but also to protect themselves. No one knew if this new presence posed any danger to either planet, but they were not about to risk it. This for them was an intellectual, rational decision even though it was completely out of character for them. They calculated that it was far better to stop these people "up here at Plus-Five" before they found their way to Prime. Stephen went on to explain that Shonak had been biding its time regarding their announcement to Earth that they existed but the presence of this unknown alien race had led them to choose to show themselves now so they could more openly assist Earth and also get their help. The Marshal raised his eyebrows at this, thinking that Earth was unlikely able to help these technologically superior people. Stephen and John both noticed this in Marshal Li's expression and smiled, but for different reasons. John was thinking much the same thing as the

Marshal, but Stephen knew the truth and offered an explanation. "Marshal Li, the Shonakians tell me that they have a problem that goes back to the very early days of their evolution. There has never been a predator on their world. No animal or human consumes meat or fish, and the planet provides more than enough plant material for their sustenance. As a result, there is no 'fight or flight' instinct in them. At all. Period. They do not feel confident that they can successfully match an alien race with a killer instinct. They do feel, however, that they have ample understanding through a study of Earth history that these instincts are a part of who we all are. We control it well under non-threatening circumstances but at the least hint of danger we are all about shooting first and asking permission later. Shonak feels this killer instinct will be needed in the first confrontations with these aliens. If they prove peaceful so be it and that is a hopeful outcome but if not you will be a welcome ally in the fight."

Marshal Li asked if he could assemble his staff immediately to receive a briefing from them on this threat. He said Earth forces had also detected the anomaly but had not been able to collect any information since it came and went too fast and too far from their sensors. Stephen then took a comm device from his briefcase and gave it to Horst. He told the Marshal that this device gave them direct communications with Shonak's rep, Gold Bon. He also asked them to use their discretion on giving copies of the Shonak summary Bon had given them so their defense staffs can prepare themselves for working with Shonak's team. "Marshal Li," Stephen said, "Please do call Gold Bon using the comm device he gave you. I know he wants to discuss how to acquire Earth native gunners and also to introduce Shonak to Earth's public, if you think that is at all advisable. Thus far only a few Earth natives have been entrusted with this information because there has been no firm concept for breaking this news to the governments or to the billions of people on this planet."

The President thanked Stephen and John and

Helen for their coming forward at this time with these important issues, and he noted that he was also unsure how to break it to the public or even to their various governments. Stephen assured him that to date, no government on Earth had a clue about Shonak. He asked him to please coordinate with Bon before that knowledge left this room. The Marshal made no commitment about that but offered that it might be wise to create a black program regarding the existence of Shonak and for the gunner selection and training, open to others on a strictly need-to-know basis. This would consist of an operation to provide joint, combined defense of their worlds in space. This would deal with the space incursion in what appeared to be an independent Earth operation but with clandestine and covert assistance from Shonak. Stephen smiled at that and said he thought Bon would agree with that as the initial approach. They could leave the full disclosure issue out there should it become either necessary or advisable to do that. Shonak, Stephen added, certainly would never reveal themselves to the public without WG approval or participation. The President nodded and thanked them for that, then reached out his hand to shake all of theirs to end the meeting. Horst showed them out then went back in to see the President and Marshal.

The President looked at them and said he did not know whether to laugh or cry and asked them both for their thoughts. Horst said he knew John Marquis was an honest, smart, successful man who would not be easily fooled. He had never met Stephen before but felt that if John believed it, then he advised that they believe it too. "Fair enough," said the WP. Then he told the Marshal to begin the process of gunner selection and asked him to coordinate their training with Bon using the comm device they were given. He then said he wanted to hold on to that device personally, so when the Marshal was done with it please bring it to him. The Marshal gave a curt bow of assent, took the device, and left for his own office. Then the WP began to formulate his plan to take this alien contact business to the Group of Eight as a first step in the announcement to the public. He knew it would be a tough sell. First of all, they would not believe it because they wouldn't want to. The fact that the World President believed it would, however, give them pause. They were all intelligent, accomplished, powerful men and women who were thinking ahead to the "so what?" aspect of what the WP would be telling them. If it was true, which they would consider a stretch, what would it mean to them, exactly? They would all understood that perception is reality and it would cross all of their minds that their publics needed to be eased into this concept, this perception, if it had any validity, that is, because the reality of Shonak and its people would of course not match their current perception of "space aliens". All governments have forever carefully denied the existence of such creatures or the notion of inhabited planets because it clouded their visions of reality. Better to focus on the world as they know it. Reality was, feed the people, keep them happy, keep them busy, stifle dissent and contradiction while preserving the illusion of freedom. The WP, for his part, was Egyptian, had an unconventional, half-secular and half-religious education, but he was very bright, and his oratorical and political skills, along with a correspondingly huge ego, had landed him in the bi-annually rotating chair of the World President. He had also, early in his rise to power, learned that perception was reality and he struggled to manage the perception piece of this message to this group. "Yes," he would tell them, "Extra-terrestrial life exists and yes, we are in contact with them! I know because I saw one of them, spoke with one of them, myself!"

He continued to muse, "How to sell that to these leaders and then how to sell that to the people of this world - who had enough problems without adding this to the list?"

The day after meeting with Bon, Earther human nature kicked in and the WP was having second thoughts himself. He believed in this character named Bon when he was all in his face, shimmering in his office, but now, not so sure. He had to do something before he met

again with the Group of Eight to push the issue now that he was having second thoughts himself. He called Horst into his office and also Marshal Li. He shared his second thoughts and they admitted to a little bit of that themselves. Li suggested that they arrange some sort of demonstration for the Group of Eight. The WP took out his comm device and asked to speak to Bon, who answered immediately. "What can I do for you, Mister President?" he asked. And the WP laid out his desire for some sort of demonstration. Horst added his two cents, as well, saying, "The President would like a demonstration of some sort to convince them he's not trying to play some sort of elaborate practical joke on them."
Bon said, "Mister President, what would you like to see by way of proof that Shonak is real and desires to establish open communications with Earth?" The President said, thinking it was indeed some sort of joke, "Make the sun go away and then bring it back!" Bon responded that not even they could do that, but he offered to appear in front of them in a group meeting somewhere, just like he appeared to him in his office. The WP said that would be a good start, but he warned Bon that they were all very skeptical and knew that there were plenty of state-of-the-art light shows to rival Bon in his phase suit.

Then the World President paused for a moment, realizing that he had just struck a bargain of sorts with a person from another planet! He had to admit he was finally convinced, himself, recovered a moment, and said, "On behalf of Earth and its world government, I greet you again, Mr. Gold Bon. It has been a dream of our kind that there is life on other planets and now, I believe we can say it's true. Please excuse my earlier doubts during our first meeting. We on Earth live in a dangerous world and people in my position are constant targets for abuse and even assassination. I was momentarily shocked by your appearance and thought it may be some sort of attack, and certainly a trick. I see now that it was not either of those things. With that past between us, how would you suggest we proceed?"

Bon said, "Shonak has no plan for how Earth

should proceed with the issue of going public with their presence but supposed the next step was as they had discussed, a meeting with the Group of Eight Principals." "As for going public, that will be a good topic for discussion during the upcoming Group of Eight meeting. I fully understand how complex both introductions will be, first to the Eight world leaders and then to the global public." He paused then added, "Shonak's Leader is willing to make a grand entrance, befitting the moment, but we want firm assurance that the military would not interfere." Bon explained that they had been watching Earth since before it had any name for itself and understood the aggressive nature of Earth natives. Security Director Li Ning entered the conversation to say that he could make sure there would be no intervention of that sort – he would meet with the military leadership in person to ensure that they will attend but not respond to the visit. He was sure, he said, he could make them understand there was no threat from Shonak for them to worry about.

The WP then spoke up to confirm that he would like to repeat Bon's introductory meeting with first, the Group of Eight leaders and then perhaps with a larger World Government forum. Bon said that would be fine. He would enjoy meeting the group of eight world partners, the heads of state or government from the eight most powerful members of the world government. A private meeting with them would be most helpful in determining how best to go public. Much easier for them to introduce Shonak to the public if they are convinced themselves that Shonak really exists. So, the WP asked Horst and Marshal Ning to arrange the meeting and ensure the subject was kept secret, and the meeting place secure. Horst said he would make the request, and he felt sure that everyone would clear their calendars for this face-to-face meeting with Bon of Shonak at the request of the WP.

As with any meeting of this nature it could not be scheduled immediately, but they did manage to arrange it within two weeks of the request. It was billed as a "necessary in-person summit meeting" to discuss matters of mutual and world interest ahead of the biannual meeting of all world leaders. The site of the meeting was not made public with the initial press announcement under the pretense that it had not been determined. There were matters of transport, logistics, communications, and security to consider so when it was determined where it was to be the people would be informed. This of course led to wild press speculation and conspiracy theorists put forth a litany of odd scenarios, some new some old, but the truth was exactly as stated – the location had simply not been determined. Bon's staff came up with their best suggestion which was immediately adopted: the island of St. Helena in the south Atlantic off the west coast of Africa. Perfect! Confidential transport arrangements were hurriedly made in all G8 countries; USNA, UNE, Greater Russia, Greater China, USSA, Greater India, Indochina, and Pacifica.

On the day, the so-called World Principal Partners began showing up the morning of the meeting, which was scheduled to start at One PM, GMT. There were to be no overnight stays, so they remained in their aircraft doing business and chatting with their staffs instead of checking into any room. The conference would be held in an old Apostolic church on the hill above Jamestown. There was ample space for their long-range helicopters to land nearby and the church would not have been subjected to any scrutiny in advance, wired for sound, etc. Marshal Ning's team did the advance checks anyway, looking for explosives and for electronic snoopers, and found none. Bon's team had long since come and gone, also finding no threats, and the place was now wired for sound and video for the Shonak live feed, and their historical record. They all of course pronounced the church safe and Li's security detail established a secure perimeter, to include air cover. The principals began to enter and greet one another and chat before the WP arrived. He landed at five till one PM and made his grand entrance with all of them there. He lost no opportunity to let them know who "the boss" was, although he was only nominally that, since the World President and the World Government were not independently constituted. That body and its staff, including the WP, derived their power and authority from the cooperation and funding by the member states, the principal 8 of which were present. They greeted him warmly and he motioned them to sit at the conference table, those who were not already seated, that is. His staff had of course put him at the head of the table with the others arranged four to a side on his left and right, in alphabetical order. Shonakians, watching every move now live on their home feeds, never ceased to comment on how silly they thought people of Plus-Five who always defaulted to alphabetical order instead of the more sensible date of birth, with the oldest being first among them. If Earth did it their way, the World President would be the oldest living Earther. Full stop.

The WP opened the meeting on time with his thanks for agreeing to meet at such short notice, and in such a remote location. He said, "My dear friends and Principals, I have asked you here to convey the most astonishing development in the history of Earth." He paused, and he could see that this opening had gotten their attention. "We have been contacted by an alien race from another planet!" He paused again to let that sink in. The group around the table sat stone faced, not immediately grasping what the WP had said. "I say again, we have been contacted by an alien race from another planet." He paused again to see their reaction and saw that he had certainly got their attention, and he continued, "They call their planet Shonak and it is not located in what we would call outer space, but rather it is another version of Earth that exists at another dimension, or vibration, or another frequency of existence. You might call it a parallel world to Earth, but the people there evolved randomly and naturally, as we did here, and as a consequence there are very few similarities between us. They are smaller, hairless bipeds with a peaceful culture that is now over five hundred thousand years old, as compared to ours which is just a few thousands of years old. My staff is now handing out a copy of their fact sheet which explains something of their history and culture. But before you read that I want to delay no further in introducing you to Gold Bon of Shonak! Bon appeared suddenly directly on the conference table in front of the Principals. He was standing up but elevated above the table, facing the WP. He did this so he could be seen by all of them equally well. He had been slightly off-phase but listening to every word and when introduced he phased in to Plus-Five's vibration which made him visible to them.

Bon slowly rotated in his suit, raised his hands, palms out, in a gesture of greeting and said, in the somewhat tinny voice through his phase suit, "On behalf of Our Eldest of Shonak, I want to extend to you here on Earth our warmest greeting and wish for good relations between our peoples. My planet is simply another version of your own, but it is situated at a different physical vibration of existence. This vibrational difference requires me to appear before you in this special suit, which maintains me at my native vibration."

He continued with this explanation, "People from different vibrations, in fact all physical matter, cannot exist at another than its native vibration without a special mechanism that maintains them at their native frequency. Thousands of your years ago we developed a technology that allows us to travel between the various versions of this planet. Unfortunately, we have not figured out how to stabilize ourselves at any of them. We are quite sure we will never be able to do so and call this the Law of Nativity. That is, everything vibrates at the resonance it was created or born into and this may not be changed. For this reason, I appear to you in this protective suit. The very air you breathe is toxic to me. Were I to leave the protection of my phase suit, I would begin to choke on your atmosphere and die. My body would then disappear as it returned to Shonak, its natural vibration. You would face the same issue were you to visit my world. We cannot live on each other's worlds in the open air or even in a contained space without the special mechanism that maintains our native vibration. There is, therefore, no way for us to meet or interact in person.

From your perspective you may rest assured we would never invade your world or try to even live on it. To begin with, we have no need to do that since our planet is maintained at a population of 142 million. We have no need for living space on another world, or additional natural resources. Although even if we did, we could not use anything from Earth because it would not survive on our world. So, we pose no threat to each other. Given your tendency for distrust, I simply want you to know that up front." He paused to look at them carefully, to see how they were receiving this message. OE commed into his ear that he thought Bon was doing a wonderful job.

Bon then continued, "We on Shonak are people of few words so I will get to the point of my visit here today without further delay. Recently we have witnessed a potential threat to our planets by an unknown, alien culture. We were fortunate to capture sufficient data on their last incursion in "our" space to determine that they will not pose a threat to either Earth or to Shonak at this time and possibly never. The information we have that allows us to make that assessment is beyond your present understanding, but I can assure you it is accurate. That said, this episode has caused our leader, whom we call Our Eldest, to create a special Grand Team devoted to the protection of our worlds. But while we have the technology that will provide protection against any possible threat, we do not have the right attitude or any instinct towards combat. We simply do not have the killer instinct so vital to defensive warfare, but we know that you here on Earth are born with it. There has never been a predator on Shonak, so we simply never needed to develop and maintain a fight-or-flight mechanism in our brains. Freed from that burden and preoccupation we have been able to devote our mental energies to things other than survival, and as a consequence, we have developed a technically adept culture far beyond your own. We propose a marriage of our technology with your gift for combat in order to defend ourselves against any threat to us from outside our planets."

He continued, "With that introduction I will be happy to entertain your questions after you have read the fact sheet on Shonak. I will return when the World President thinks you are ready; and he phased away from them. He could tell from their faces that several of them did not fully believe he was an alien from another planet. There was initially a great deal of discussion amongst themselves, but it grew silent as they read the fact sheet. When they all looked ready, the WP called Bon on his phone and he reappeared above their table. The Principal of the USNA asked the first question, arrogantly and a bit angrily, "Mr. Bon, if that's how you are to be addressed, how do I know I can trust you?" "How do I know you aren't the aliens who have appeared recently?" How do we know you aren't just some fancy holographic projection?" Bon replied, "You don't know you can trust me or anyone on Shonak but I can tell you that we have been here, visiting your world, for over four thousand of your years and we have not done you any harm in all that time. Remember, we have no incentive to do anything more than observe you since we cannot interact with you without difficulty and then only through electronic communications. Simply stated, no object from your world can exist on ours and vice versa. Do you want an example of our good intentions? We have the ability to take all the gold from your planet, but we couldn't do anything with it so why would we? And even if we could, ours is a cashless society in which gold is simply another metal for our industrial and artistic use. We are hoping that our friendly and benign history of observing your world over so great a time would convince you that we can be trusted. If you decide not to ally yourselves with us in the defense of our worlds, we will proceed on our own but we think you will want to participate in your own defense – which we admit will be more effective with you than without you. I think you should also be ready to admit that our defense will also be better with us than without us. And now, as important as our mutual defense is, we think we have an even larger issue to discuss today than that. This larger issue is to determine how much of our involvement do you want your public to know about? People on Earth have been speculating about extraterrestrials for thousands of years, but now the truth be known. Do you want to keep us a secret or do you want to go public with us? We are content to do it any way you like but defer to you since it is your planet and your people, not ours. We do not face this decision on Shonak since our people have been aware of you for millennia.

The room erupted with conversations and gesticulations and proposals, and the WP finally stood and slammed his hand on the table to restore order. They gradually quieted down, but it was clear there was no consensus on either issue. Bon remained with them and listened to them carefully. He asked at one point if there were any further questions for him and the WP said there surely would be, but they were still working on their own issues. Bon said he would leave them now to discuss this among themselves and noted that when they were ready for additional discussion, he could be contacted immediately via the WP's office. He phased out then much to the amazement of the world leaders gathered there. After a portion and a half he got a call on the special comm device asking him to return. He phased back to their resonance and became visible again. The WP stood and informed him that they had agreed to participate in the defense of their planets.

They assigned Marshal Li Ning as his official Point of Contact. Bon said he was pleased to welcome them to their historic new alliance. He also told them that Shonak would be constructing special spacecraft for this defensive mission with propulsion and weapon systems far superior to anything available on Earth. These craft would be captained by Shonak personnel with the gunners provided by Earth volunteers to be trained by Shonak. He said he would send a delegate to work with the Marshal on the details of selection and training and deployment of the Earth gunners. The WP then said that for now, the involvement of an alien race in the defense of their world would not be released to the public. This was an issue that required further study and planning. He felt confident that the public would be informed at some point in the future, maybe even the near future, such time to be determined by a vote of the Council of Eight and then the WG members.

Then things changed. Stories of possible alien contact by world leaders began to appear in the rumor mill and then there was the inevitable headline in the New York Times, WE ARE NOT ALONE, along with a complete copy of the Shonak summary the WP had given to the Group of Eight leaders. Too many staff had access to too many of the pieces of this puzzle and it all came out quickly. This was way too hot a story to keep out of the press.

The WP and the Group of Eight and the rest of the nations hastily conferred and agreed the explanation was that they wanted to first verify it and then formalize the relationship before introducing Shonak to the world. A date for the formal introduction was coordinated with Bon and agreed to by the OE of the moment, and so it was set for Shonak to reveal itself to the public of Earth.

Bon could have named the staffers who leaked it all, of course, quite a few of them, actually, from most of the nations present, but that would have been too much an indicator of the extent to which Shonak had visibility on Earth and its inhabitants. So Bon kept that to himself. He told the WP he was pleased they could now proceed openly, which greatly facilitated the selection and training of the gunners for the space protection patrols.

After much deliberation, and with advance announcements by world and national leaders, the big day finally arrived. The people of Earth had been given the official news that they were "not alone" during a joint session of world governments with the World President actually breaking the official story. He said that the world named Shonak had approached them peacefully and requested a formal, friendly relationship between their peoples. He also noted that there was no way the peoples of these planets could meet in person but that they could still enjoy the sharing of technology for the betterment of everyone from both worlds.

On the day of the formal introduction of Shonak and its world leader to the people of Earth, and broadcasting live across the entire planet, the Earth World President stepped forward and extended his hand in greeting, which was met by the current Our Eldest of Shonak, Gold Lik, in his phase suit. The suit came across in the vids as a shimmering, colorful cloak that helped to enhance his image even though he was only about half as tall as the Earth President, and far thinner. Their handshake was just a touch, in fact, a fist bump, since the Shonakian's phase suit was difficult for an Earther to contact comfortably, but it looked great on vid stream. The crowd assembled in Tiananmen Square in Beijing, site of the world government President and bureaucracy, was record-setting and the worldwide viewership was as well, with more than 90% of the population of Earth witnessing this historic event. The World President greeted Our Eldest warmly and was pleased with all the advance preparations. The WP announced to the people of Earth that they were not alone after all. It was also noted that the people of Shonak were also viewing the event live, as it happened. Even though it had been leaked almost a month earlier, the WP then pushed a ceremonial button that released the slightly tweaked official Shonak fact sheet to all news outlets around the world to help people of Earth understand the world and people of Shonak they were now partners with. They learned that Shonak had been a silent partner of Earth for thousands of years during which time they protected the planet while it matured technologically to the point where now Shonak felt Earth could be an active partner in their own defense and in the defense of Shonak too.

Security was tight at the site of the Shonak introduction, but the crowds were the largest ever seen anywhere at one time in Earth history, which inherently brought security concerns. Marshal Li Ning orchestrated a massive security force composed mostly of Chinese police and Army. As the host country it fell to China to guarantee the security of everyone at the event. Of course, there were protesters, since even now, with a real Shonakian here in front of them, there were those on Earth who thought them a myth or some kind of government trick for some unspecified sinister plot against the people.

The event was also being broadcast live on Shonak, distributed to everyone both at work and at home and at any leisure spot with news feeds. This was a big day for Shonak, too. The World President addressed them directly with a warm welcome to the new family of planets. Our Eldest, resplendent in his very dramatic Phase Suit, waved and addressed the people of Earth as Cousins, which he was told would be a very good way to address them. He knew the definition of a cousin but since Shonakians have no families and never even know who their parent was; the concept was only academic to OE. He saw from the crowd's reaction that it was well accepted and the people of Earth began referring to Shonak and Shonakians as their cousins, too. The WP addressed the multitude of both planets to say he would be meeting with delegates from the appropriate governments and academics to discuss the best ways to move forward in an open way with their Shonakian cousins and said it would of course be a matter for approval by a majority of the world's member nations. In the meantime, he said they could all sleep safe knowing that their countrymen and women as well as Shonakians were building a defense in space that would always be watching over them. The WP and OE then marched together ceremoniously into the World HQ building for meetings with the many governments present and their militaries. The militaries, especially, were interested in determining for themselves if these Shonakians constituted any kind of threat to the current world order on Earth. Military people are by nature risk-averse and take a lot of convincing that something does not and will not constitute a threat.

Once assembled in the conference hall, away from the noisy throng outside, OE took in the people gathered there, which of course was also being beamed back to Shonak. He was joined by Bon and a few of his team who phased in quietly while they were walking to the dignitary's platform in the hall. There were easily two thousand delegates there in a large amphitheater room that reminded him of his Education and Training Center, although this was on a much bigger scale. Much like the people themselves, he thought. Over the waves of euphoria and good wishes proclaimed publicly, Bon reminded himself that they were by nature big, brash, hostile, suspicious people who often shot first and asked questions after. This will make them great gunners, he thought, but what kind of partners will they be?

OE stood when he was ready to begin and before any of the others did, and he elevated himself above the dais to emphasize his importance, and his technology, too, he would have to admit. Privately, he thought, he was addressing children who needed to be reminded who the parent was. This was a kind and loving mental picture, but he was the leader of a world, after all, and one which is hundreds of thousands of years more advanced. He very much wanted to control the dialogue here, so he fought his natural passive nature in favor of aggressive assertiveness. There had been a great deal of noise as the delegates all talked among themselves, but they fell silent as he stood up and elevated himself. Suspended in air, as he was, and shimmering in his suit, he was every bit the impressive sight he had desired to be. He could see that his image was being transmitted to large screens on the four walls of the conference hall so those in the back of the room could see him as well as those in the front row. He raised his right hand in greeting, palm outward, and thanked them for their willingness to at last go public with the partnership they had struck in secret some months earlier. He introduced himself by stating his full name and date of birth, then said this was his one thousand, six hundred and twenty-first Planetary Rotations, or Years, of life. The crowd fell silent at that. To make that even more meaningful, he added that he was born in the Earth year 644 UAY. They had all read the summaries, so they all knew, intellectually, that Shonakians were long lived, but it was something else to actually meet someone who was old on that scale. The silence continued as they took that in. Then OE introduced a Shonakian he said was their considered expert on all things Plus-Five, or Earth, and he would now address them, and he affirmed that he spoke for the OE and for Shonak. The OE stepped off the raised dais and took a seat and Bon strode up there, in his phase suit, plain when compared to the grand one that had been specially constructed for OE. He had a gold dot on his suit, on his forehead, like the OE, but only a few of the closer delegates noticed, not that it really mattered to them. Bon raised himself above the dais as had the OE and introduced himself in the formal way, as the OE did, giving his age as one thousand, fifty years, meaning, he said, he was born the year the Magna Carta was signed, in 1215 UAY. He let them know that for many years he was the leader of the base Shonak had above Plus-Five to protect them. This, he reasoned, would give him what they would call "street cred" for what was to come next. Bon then talked about their goals for the joint defense of the planets and also goals for the partnership and inter-planetary relations they were all forging right now, in real time. He said that he was in charge of what amounted to a treaty working group on Shonak and he would like to work with a similar group on Earth so they could formalize their new partnership. It was essential that this be a true partnership, with shared operational commitments of personnel and other resources. Bon said he knew that it would take the member states and the world government some time to put this treaty working group together and Bon noted that Shonakians were a patient people, as they might expect from people who lived well over a thousand years! He got some laughter out of that, a little at first, then pretty much everyone joined in. He wanted to leave them on a light hearted note and that was likely as good as it would get so he said that Shonak's official party would be taking their leave now and he would await a comm from Marshal Li Ning when they were ready to negotiate the formal agreement on joint defense and their long-term working relationship. He said he would leave his employee, Yusuf, an Earth native, there to serve as a liaison officer between them.

He did not tell them Yusuf was a Shonakian bot. He did tell them that Yusuf had been in their employ as an Earth advisor for some several years and that Yusuf had taught Bon to speak World Standard English. He also added that it was Yusuf who would train the Gunners, along with Shonakians from his team. Yusuf, he said, was very familiar with Shonak and their leadership and would be able to answer many of their questions and could do so from the comfort of his native vibration, unlike the Shonakians who needed to remain in their phase suits or phase ships when on Earth.

Once back in his office, about a portion, or just over fourteen Earth minutes later, he was interested to observe the dynamic of the delegates he had just addressed. He had full visibility of the interior of the amphitheater where he spoke and where the delegates were and was content to watch how their discussion was going. Yusuf was having some trouble getting them to quiet down and he could see that the North Americas, the North Europes, and the North Asias were all trying to dominate the entire group and upstage each other. He heard demands to end contact with Shonak altogether, as well as calls to blast them to "kingdom come" wherever that was. The World President's aide, Horst, stepped in quickly enough to bring order to the crowd before things got out of hand. He noticed several groups were gathering their coats and briefcases and he wanted to keep everyone there since it was too hard to get a group like this together-ever. He looked over his shoulder at his boss who thought it best to engage them all personally. He was definitely prepared to bring some control to a meeting consisting of world leaders and their top aides. Space Command, Ground Command, Global Security Command, Intelligence Command, and heads of state were all there, as was the current World President. At Present, the Principal Secretary of Egypt was the World President, and it was he who had met the OE of Shonak and who at this point stood up and thanked Marshal Ning and his staff for their assistance and then he took control. The other world member delegates deferred to him now, standing on the dais. As they quieted down, he said, "Marshal Li, and Mr. Bon, if you can hear me, please accept our gratitude for arranging this meeting, which we know is like herding cats." He paused for effect and to give people the time to settle down even further. He noted with some satisfaction that the people who were in the process of leaving were now re-taking their seats. "I have the chair but of course it is you, the principal members of the world government, who have all the resources and the power to forge this new relationship with our Shonakian cousins. He also thanked the Emperor of Greater Asia for hosting this unprecedented meeting. He emphasized that they were now faced with the task of formalizing Earth's relationship with Shonak. There must be rules, policies, and perhaps even laws to outline and enforce the details of their partnership. He acknowledged that there was already a plan for the shared defense of their planets which, out of necessity, had preceded any formal document or even the introduction they had today. Their task now was to develop the larger goals and implementation documents this grand alliance would require. He then paraphrased the Shonakian leader by saying that unlike them, the people in this room, with the much shorter Earth lifespan, needed to get cracking if they were to see this thing settled in their short lifetimes! This also brought some laughs. "It is unlikely we will reach any sort of consensus on this while you are here for this first meeting with Shonak so I suggest you return to your own capitals to come up with your draft partnership documents that we can take to the international treaty team for their hard work in negotiating away any conflicts before we address the Shonakians with it. Your meeting handouts have Yusuf's contact information. He will provide you all with whatever background information about Shonak you feel you need in order to proceed with the creation of your draft agreements. We will take all the drafts before a special working group to achieve consensus then let the Shonakians know we are ready to have our formal talks on these matters." He added, "On the face of it their offer seems simple enough. They want to improve and formalize their contact with us. As World President I am charging you with coming up with some courses of action for us to choose and I would like to see your proposals in 30 days. And with that we will let you go. Go safely and with great care. All of our lives have now changed." He paused for effect. "We have the opportunity to chart a historical course for our entire planet in its relationship with another world. Let us be equal to the task, and let history remember us kindly for what we do with this historical opportunity!"

When he got back to his office, the WP asked to see Marshal Ning. Ning arrived shortly after being summoned, and the President took him into his private office. He felt the large, ceremonial office, with its large conference table, was not suited to this conversation. He just wanted honesty. He asked Ning for his impressions about the day and Ning could only reply that the entire thing was unprecedented and wasn't it fortunate that these aliens were proving to be people of their word, honest, with no apparent hidden agenda. He thought it was unfortunate Earth knew less about them than they seemed to know about Earth but given the benign nature of their interest in Earth, it did not seriously bother him that much. The President nodded throughout the conversation signaling he agreed with Ning on these points. After a few more pleasantries Ning was ushered out of the office and the WP pursued his day.

Chapter Six

Gunner Selection, Training, Deployment

While Earth leaders and their staffs were conferencing on the details of a treaty with Shonak, Bon met in conference-comm with Shonak's leadership and GT-Exp and Protection Eldests and commented that the Earth gunners would all need a phase suit for the Plus-Fivers to live in their own vibration aboard any Shonak vessel and Plus-Five stable rooms for them to live in either on ship or on Shonak, for the duration. OE informed him this had all been arranged and now all they needed was a suitable set of Earth native candidates to volunteer. Bon recommended that he proceed to recruit twenty qualified volunteers from which pool Gold Bik, Eldest Protection, could make his selection. Bik said that was agreeable and handed Bon a set of desired characteristics, training, and experiences. Bon was told by Our Eldest that he expected the first volunteers to be on board the GT Protection gunship, mission-ready within thirty P-Rots. With that they all dropped the comm link leaving Bon and his team to make it happen. Bon told Gold Bik offline that the bot Yusuf would transfer to his GT along with the gunners. Bon would coordinate with his Earther-bot, Stephen, for additional gunner candidates. Bik agreed to all that.

Bon immediately commed Marshal Li Ning asking for a personal meeting as soon as possible. He was agreeable and Bon phased down to the Marshal's office immediately.

Bon presented himself in Ning's office without going through the protocols of security staff or working with Horst or the Executive Secretary "gate keeper." The Marshal jumped up sharply when Bon materialized in his blurry phase suit but quickly calmed himself and welcomed Bon to Earth once again. Bon told Ning of recent developments and asked for his assistance in finding twenty candidates who met the qualifications on the paper he handed to him. He scanned the document and said there was something missing. Bon asked what that was, and the Marshal said, "Three things are missing, actually. First, we need to ensure social/political/religious compatibility and the second is gender equality. Third, we need to know how long these candidates will be away from their families. It also occurs to me that you need to tell us if you have any objection to gay, female or trans-gender candidates?" Bon shook his head and mentally agreed that these considerations were missing in their requirements document. Bon knew of these gender technicalities but had no idea how they might impact operational readiness for Earth humans in close contact in close ship quarters for up to a year at a time. Eldest protection's list for the candidates simply said "excellent health, high intelligence, quick reaction time." Of a single gender, it does not naturally occur to a Shonakian that there must be some consideration for gender balance and relations and privacy, not to mention different toilet facilities. There is also no political thought on Shonak so political compatibility does not occur to them in spite of the thousands of years they have been watching the activities of Plus-Five natives. Lastly, Shonakians have no families and it simply does not occur to any of them that family is an important planning consideration. Bon responded that he would defer to the Marshal on these issues since they were beyond his experience. He said he simply expected to provide twenty candidates that he himself would be happy to serve with, himself. He told the Marshal that his OE expected this to be operational within 30 of their days. The Marshal raised his eyebrows and said this was likely unrealistic, but he would do everything he could to have the twenty candidates ready for transport within seven days, much sooner if possible. Bon noted that this marked the beginning of a true defensive alliance between Earth and Shonak. Ning nodded that he understood the historical significance of what they were starting there in his office.

Ning was true to his word, and then some. He commed Bon five days later to say he had his twenty candidates ready for transport. Bon thanked him and asked that they all be present in a warehouse at an address in Beijing he provided as soon as he could get them there. He would brief them himself and their transport vehicle would be there ready for boarding and transport to Shonak. Ning smiled and shook his head and thanked the gods Shonakians were not hostile. How could they fight such people?

Since all the candidates were in Beijing for their final interviews Ning had all of them in the warehouse within the hour and notified Bon they were assembled. The only other people present were Ning and Horst, Stephen, and Yusuf. Yusuf had introduced himself to them as the candidates arrived, telling them he worked for Bon, just like Stephen. Ning told them Yusuf would be the person training them for this mission. Everyone greeted Yusuf with handshakes and kind words, then they took their seats.

All the gunners were then provided the special documents that swore them into the program and to secrecy and all of their personal communications equipment was confiscated, to be returned at a later date to be determined by events. They all signed the documents and then were given the Shonak summaries to read, even if they said they had already read the public feeds on this. They were excited to be a part of this first ever interplanetary space force and eager to get started.

They were all seated in the chairs provided, Ning and Horst off to one side, along with Stephen. Bon phased-in to face them, standing on a raised dais so they could all see him in his phase suit. "Greetings, gunner candidates. I am Gold Bon, Eldest of the Shonak team responsible for relations with your world. The operation you are candidates for is under Grand Team Protection at the special request of our planet's leader. Yusuf here has been working with me but has just transferred to that GT as our manager and supervisor for your orientation and training. You are the vanguard of a cooperative effort to protect our planets from hostile invaders from elsewhere. Time is short so we will be transporting you all to Shonak in a few minutes. You can expect to be absent from Earth for one Solar Rotation, what you call a year. You need bring nothing as everything is provided. "My assistant, Yusuf," Bon continued, "Is to us what you would call a contractor and has been working for us for many years so he knows most things about us that you will be interested in learning. Whatever you need, ask him. Whatever your questions, ask him. During your trip to my world I urge you to read and re-read the short summary of Shonak we've given you. You have all read it before but it is important that you are familiar with us and that you believe what is written on those pages."

Two large sliding doors then opened silently, and there was a real, live spaceship! There was a ramp up to an open door and they could see seats inside. Bon directed them to enter and sit down as they were about to depart. Bon turned to Ning and Horst and Stephen, thanked them for their assistance, and moved with the group and saw them all aboard, including Yusuf. The door closed then, and the ship suddenly disappeared! Marshal Ning and his Dutch aide looked at each other and both shook their heads in wonder. Horst was also thinking it was a good thing these people were friendly!

The trip was made artificially long as all twenty candidates, ten males and ten females, were guided through their written summary on the history of Shonak and the history of Shonak on Earth. Yusuf took them through that step by step. They were also told what Shonak was hoping these volunteers could bring to the effort to protect the six planets. While it was an awful lot for them to take in these were exceptional people, highly trained and both mentally and physically fit, not to mention highly intelligent. They were also opinionated, vocal, with leader-oriented personalities and habits. Ning had recruited them well, if hurriedly, from the various military and security agencies of the Group of 8. He had gone to their security chiefs personally and asked for their best young operational people for a vital, year-long mission with Shonak they would be briefed on later. Their heads of state had all agreed to cooperate in this effort, so these people were all on board. They were eager to provide candidates, and because of the visibility of this effort, they chose only the best. The other incentive to participate is that unless they did, they would be excluded from the program. He did not specify a minimum number but did limit it to five each, and they all provided five. That gave him forty to choose from, and he and Horst did this personally. The twenty not chosen were thanked for their time and sent home, with the comment that should more be needed they would be on the list for re-interview. All of that took the five days before Bon met them and took them to Shonak.

They sat in their seats aboard the phase ship and it did not take the candidates long to re-read the summaries of Shonak and its Earth involvement. They read it with much more interest and attention, however, since now they were actually working with these aliens! After the tutorial on Shonak Yusuf told them where the toilets were and also the food and drink. They would be on Shonak in an hour and they should have gone to the toilet and eaten by the time they arrived. In actuality they were already on Shonak, but Bon wanted time to acclimate them before introducing them to the planet. The volunteer trainees all gravitated to the food and toilets, which were in adjoining cabins on the phase ship. This ship had been built of Earth-stable materials and outfitted with phase shifting equipment that could match Shonak's resonance. The pilots were Shonakian and in phase suits. When they were all fed and had voided what they needed to Yusuf began the first of their many briefings.

He said, "You will shortly find yourselves on Shonak. It is a cousin of Earth, but it is totally hostile to your bodies. You are of Earth's resonance and cannot exist on Shonak. If you were to step out of this ship, your first breath of air would almost kill you. To emphasize this point, we are going to put you through the same exposure they give any Shonakian who is to spend any time on what they call Plus-Five and we call Earth. Each of you will be asked to take in a small breath of Shonak air and then deal with it. I will also be doing this. I'm advised that it will not kill us, but we will be incapacitated for a time. As no Earth native has had this experience, they cannot say for sure how long we will be off our feet, nor can they say how long it will take us to fully regain our mental and physical abilities. When we are all back here and suitably recovered, we will transfer to our living quarters. After a nap, which I'm told we will all need, we will have our first operational briefing." He paused then said, "Right now, I want you to go to your assigned cabins, names on the doors, along with your student number, and get settled. Be back here in fifteen minutes, that's just a little more than a portion in Shonak time."

When they reassembled, Yusuf could hear comments they were sharing about their cabins. They found them odd even though built to Earth size standards of Earth materials. Strange colors, strange odors, nothing unpleasant but still odd. Clearly an alien influence there. One of the trainees joked that his room looked like a cheap motel room seen in old black and white movies from the 20th century! They all laughed at that.

The bot Yusuf overheard the remark and thought the design was a wise idea, intended to make them think Shonak did not know much about

Earthers and how they live today. Their rooms would not raise any suspicions regarding the extent of their surveillance back home. Shonak could have duplicated their sleeping rooms from their own homes if they had wanted to, but there was no way to explain that without full disclosure about the Shonakian surveillance operation on Plus-Five. That was a forbidden topic.

Yusuf addressed them when they settled down, "We are now on Shonak. We don't have time for the niceties of protocol and lengthy speeches by various Shonak Elders here to welcome you. We all know this is a historic partnership between our two planets, the first of its kind for both worlds. If you manage to graduate from this training, your names will go down in history, and you can be proud of that. I will caution you however that the details of our security partnership is still sensitive and not for public dissemination. Your world government is controlling what your public knows about it, so we must respect that. We all signed security clearance agreements that told us to keep this secret or face severe consequences. This is and will remain a compartmented program until we are told otherwise. That means the details of our mission and our weapons and our ships and our patrol scheduled is only to be shared with people who have an absolute and verified need to know. Please follow those rules. To help in this regard Shonak has ensured that communications between you and your families and governments will not happen while you are here. This will help you keep your security promise, but it also enables focused concentration on your training.

Simply stated, what you are here for is to be the trigger-pullers for the defense of our planets. There are six versions of Earth to be protected. They all exist at different vibrations and the top and bottom of them, Earth's and Shonak's to be precise, have the priority for the moment. Eventually all of them will be afforded some level of gunship protection. You may wonder why a civilization as advanced as Shonak's needs any assistance from Earth. The truth is Shonak has the guns but not the will to use them. They know they can automate their gunnery but do not want to do that for fear of shooting a friendly alien visitor. They remember when they were alien visitors to a new world and had nothing but peaceful intentions. They assume, therefore, that others may also be peaceful. There is a split-second, what they call a split-sub-segment, where a human brain needs to determine friend or foe and if foe, then shoot first before being shot. It is an exercise in risk management. Risk harming a peaceful, alien culture or risk being harmed by a hostile one. There will be little time to decide and precious little intelligence upon which to base your decision. That is our task here. You will be trained on the Shonak weapons and then deployed to stand your watch in their gunship fire control centers in Shonak space and in Earth space. As I said earlier, eventually the other four planets will be afforded this same protection. It will simply take time to build the ships and train the crews. Now, if you will follow me, we will proceed to the phase-lock for your first, and hopefully last, breath of Shonak air."

They were lined up in numerical order, that is, the order of the candidate number they were each given upon arrival at the training center on Shonak. They were each given a jacket to be worn at all times during training. This jacket had their trainee number on the front and on the back, in large white numerals. There was a smaller squiggle of some sort below the numerals which Yusuf explained was the Shonakian equivalent of that number.

One at a time Yusuf helped them to a single, small breath of Shonak air. Yusuf was wearing a mask, he said to protect him from breathing the air himself, but actually it just protected his identity as a Shonakian bot. Shonak had not seen what this does to an Earth native since the early days of Shonak's exploration of Plus-Five. At that time, out of scientific curiosity but with no compassion for another human, they kidnapped Earth natives and brought them to Shonak for examination. This was before the OE ruled they were "human" and these kidnappings ceased. Those people all died from the exposure to Shonak's atmosphere, which began as soon as they entered the Shonakian vessel and its Zone of Influence with its Shonak air. Then their bodies disappeared as they migrated back to Plus-Five space. Shonak knew it was dangerous for them to have this one small bit of Shonak air but thought that a single small inhale would not kill any of these people. They were right, but they were shocked at how ill it made them all.

As it happened, their gunner trainees were out of commission for a full P-Rot after their single-breath experience. Every one of them collapsed in agony after about an Earth second. Just as they thought it wasn't so bad, after all, they felt pain like a train hitting their chest and then collapsed as the air fought its way out of their bodies on its journey back to Shonak. Fortunately, the ones taking the breath were not visible to the others behind them, so panic was avoided among those who waited their turn. Yusuf took them one at a time to the door-lock, which closed behind them. The candidates each took their breath, then shortly began to writhe in pain, and lost consciousness. Yusuf dragged them into the recovery room off to the side. He got them all into the room, but barely, since it was not really large enough for all their unconscious bodies. He then carried them individually to their own private rooms for a more comfortable recovery. Bon watched the video of their reactions to the air in real time and he mused that this would convince even the most skeptical among them of the dangers of leaving their Zone of Influence. Most of these people were of the type to need to experience things for themselves before they believed it. If this didn't do it, then nothing would. He well remembered his single puff of Plus-Five air and did not envy these brave Earther volunteers their ordeal. He wondered if being physically bigger meant even more pain. Nothing to be done about it but regretful, if true.

The next day, with the twenty mostly fully recovered, Bon greeted them in his shimmering suit and told them how sorry he was for their suffering. To protect his bot status, Yusuf also acted as if he were a suffering trainee. Bon told them that it had to be done since he knew that sooner or later one of them would decide to try it anyway, thinking Shonak was overstating the reaction they would have. Now they all understood in the most painful way how dangerous the planets were to each other. The Law of Nativity was immutable and testing that law, they now knew only too well, could be painful and even fatal.

The next thing Bon did was show them what happens to a Plus-Five thing that finds itself on Shonak without a Zone of Influence. The video showed a Shonakian in phase suit taking a coffee cup from their own cafeteria, going outside with it, and placing it on the Shonakian ground next to their Plus-Five Zone. Within half a minute it was visibly fading from view, and then it disappeared! They were all remarking on that when their vid screen showed a Shonakian in phase suit, with the Eiffel Tower in the background, looking around him for something. The data bar at the bottom of the video showed elapsed time was seven minutes. Pretty soon he seemed to spot something in the air, then it dropped to the ground. It was their coffee cup! Bon explained that everything returns automatically to its native vibration, but since the planets are not in perfect synch it can appear pretty much anywhere. In this case, the Shonakian was standing in the precise spot on Earth that their facility was on Shonak, so when the cup appeared it was close to where he was standing, but not exactly the same spot. He explained that they had developed the math behind the various locations of the six planets at any given time so they could very closely determine where an object will appear on its return to its own resonance. They had experienced equipment failures in the past that saw whole scout ships reappearing on Shonak and this had proved dangerous when the object suddenly reappeared in a populated area. They saw the cup materialized some twenty feet in the air and some ten feet north of their location. Bon told them that the same thing would happen to them should their Zone of Influence at the Plus-Five vibration fail. He also told them they would likely not survive the trip. They would reappear briefly on each of the in-between worlds before finding themselves back on Earth. Given the current state of secrecy concerning their presence on Shonak there would be no way to explain the event when their body reappeared there. If it reappeared inside a hill or in the ocean, it may be lost forever.

He then reminded them of the brief Yusuf provided them about being the gunners for the shared defense of their planets. He gave them an overview of the recent incursion into their space both on Prime and Plus-Five space. The goal of both planets was to be ready should these incursions prove a threat to any or all of them. Bon underscored the point made in their Shonak summaries. No Shonakian could be relied on to shoot first since at their cores they are a benign, peace-loving people devoted to intellectual pursuits, not physical or competitive pursuits unlike their Earth cousins. Although they can do it, it is simply not in the nature of any Shonakian to cause physical harm to anyone or anything. He noted ruefully that sociopathic people from Earth sometimes do that simply out of boredom. They all felt insulted but knew he was absolutely right, and their feelings of insult quickly gave way to embarrassment and shame.

The next phase of their training was to introduce them to their phase suits, which were to be their homes for the duration of their 12-hour shifts on Shonak gunships until the Plus-Five made ships were ready. Yusuf explained that while this training facility was ready for them at their native resonance, there were plans to build the gunships using Earth materials, on Earth, but this had yet to be accomplished. For the time being, they would be assigned to Shonak vessels. There would be quarters on each at their resonance so when off shift they could rest comfortably. He said, "While we were recuperating from our breaths of Shonak air our bodies were measured and suits constructed for us of Earth materials but with phase shifting capabilities so we can move from our facility at Earth resonance to their planet and their ships at Shonak's resonance. Our suits are also equipped with anti-grav so we can 'fly' in them." They were all very excited by that! He did not tell them they could fly home if they wanted to since he did not quite trust them yet. Also, inter-phase travel could be tricky, and he did not want to lose any of them.

Phase suit training continued to be accelerated to meet OE's desire that the defense be on station and fully mission capable within 30 p-rots/days. So far they were at the beginning of P-Rot nine, having lost a full day in recovery from their breath of Shonak air. Even after all this time, two of them were still a bit groggy from the experience. Bon had no idea how adept they would be with or even comfortable in their phase suits since no Plus-Five native had ever used one. Immediately after breakfast, and it never ceased to amaze Bon that these people expected to eat massive quantities of food three times in a single P-Rot, they were taken to their training room and issued their individual phase suits. Most of them were SCUBA trained and there were quite a few comments about how similar their suits were to the wet suits they were familiar with. But unlike with SCUBA, they were not told how they work since it would be like, to quote an Earth expression, "explaining a wristwatch to a pig." In this, thought Bon, they were little advanced from Atsa back in minus 1000 UAY. They were able to put them on without assistance, which was good since these suits were large and bulky and difficult for a Shonakian in a phase suit to finesse. And as strong as Shonakians are, it would still be difficult for one of them to help an Earth native put on their suit.

The candidates were instructed to keep the headpieces off for the moment while Yusuf showed them the arm controls for the suit. He was also suited up. The trainees did not know he was a bot, but that was not the issue. He had been constructed on Plus-Five with native materials and as such was just as "Earther" as they were, and just as affected by the Law of Nativity. Yusuf explained that the touchpad flight controls were simply an up, down, forward, backward, left, right thing. He said the Shonakians apologized that there was no mind link in these suits since these were the first suits made for Earthers and so they had to proceed with a bare-bones approach in order to meet the thirty-day operational timeline. Subsequent suits would enable hands-free operation, if that is, Earthers could be mind-linked. This was something still to be tested. Speed of movement was a function of the pressure applied to each directional command so be careful, he said, because only a light touch would take them quickly in whatever direction they chose. There was a comm button they were asked to try out, and they were all successful in talking to one another and to Yusuf and to Ops Control. Their phase device was activated by a large red button on their chest plate. They were asked to only activate that function when instructed at the phase lock of their facility. One push would put them at Shonak's vibration and one more push would return them to the Plus-Five resonance. They were then told to put on their head pieces and to follow him. When they got to the phase lock they were asked to step out the door onto the ground and as their foot hit the ground to activate their suits phase capability which would take them to Prime. Of course, they were on Shonak, at the Prime vibration, but in their facility, they were vibrating at Plus-Five. Stepping outside required they quickly go to Prime. When they did this, they would be able to stabilize on the Planet Shonak – the first Earthers to voluntarily visit their world. This was an easy thing to do and trainee Number One did it easily, thus becoming the first of them to visit their world. It went quickly and all of them were successfully transitioned from the Plus-Five vibration to Prime the instant they hit their chest buttons as their foot hit the ground All but trainee number twenty, the last out the door. She hesitated for some reason in hitting her button and actually got both feet onto the ground on Shonak and still had not hit the activation button on her chest. When she did finally hit the button, the phase lock was active as the transition to Earth's Plus-Five vibration had begun. This locked the phase device inside the suit, and it would not activate. Yusuf got to her a second too late and grabbed her bodily and threw her back into the phase lock so she would be back at the Plus-Five resonance. He shut the door and commed the team to wait for him while he attended the trainee. He got the trainee out of the suit and onto the floor of the hallway by the phase lock and stayed with her till he was sure the woman would be OK. She began to revive but was in a confused state, so Yusuf told her to stay put. Once she was fully recovered, they would be back for her. Bon was watching the whole thing and told Yusuf to leave her there and get back with the team. He was also told to deactivate the trainee's suit so she would not be tempted to follow later. She would miss her chance at history because she did not follow directions.

Yusuf did as he was instructed and rejoined the nineteen trainees who were excited at the prospect of exploring this world in flying suits! What a high! Yusuf took them through the up/down, left/right, forward/backward controls and it took a while for them to get used to how sensitive these things were. The suits were not bulky, and the hands were only covered with a thin, pliable, but remarkably tough membrane. Yusuf told them not to worry about how thin it was. It was so strong they could not hammer a nail through it, even. He also told them they had about half a day's worth of Earth air in their suits so there was plenty of time for their training and also for some free time. Be careful, he warned, not to overstay their air. This brought back the horrible memory of their one puff and they all made a note to watch their air gauge carefully.

Their training objective was to become proficient enough with their suits to safely fly where they wanted or needed to be. To prove their proficiency, each one had to demonstrate that they could raise themselves off the ground and hover, motionless. They had to show they could confidently and accurately move up and down, forward, backward, left, then right. One of them remarked that it was like learning how to use one of those upright, two-wheeled transports back home.

Easy to get the hang of and even be proficient in quick time!

When they were all able to show him proficiency in their controls, he took them up to what to them would be a thousand feet. He put them through some drills where they formed a circle and flew around him as if he were the hub of a wheel. Then he arranged them as spokes to the wheel and had them rotate as spokes, keeping their lines straight – not an easy task. This took some time. Once that was done to Yusuf's satisfaction, he told them they were free to explore the planet for the next two hours, along with their Shonakian guides, all Greens, as it happened, who appeared suddenly out of nowhere, and who spoke Earth Standard English. So off they went, in all directions, sometimes in pairs or groups of three or four. Almost everyone wanted to see the place on Shonak where their hometown was on Earth, to see the difference. With only two hours to explore some of them lived too far away to make the round trip so had to settle for other places to visit. For those close enough to make the trip they found that in almost all cases the land where their homes were on Earth were, on Shonak, open land or forest with no habitation. It began to dawn on the trainees that keeping the population of Shonak to 142 million across the whole of the planet allowed for the amazing difference from their world of some 15 billion people. They all realized there was no way Earth could exercise such population discipline but could see the advantages! It was raining in some places and very windy in others, and the trainees remarked at how warm and dry and stable their suits were in spite of the weather. One of those in the high winds was a pilot on Earth and noted that if he were in a plane it would be bouncing all over the place!

At the appointed time they were all back in a group, still excited by their experience, but ready for lunch! Bon was watching them and thought to himself, again, how odd and even burdensome to require so much food . . . . Their large, powerful bodies required so much more energy than Shonakians, but to what advantage? Perhaps in their early days of survival against other animals and people, going hand to hand or hand to claw and fang it was all so necessary, but now? The cost to them of feeding them all on their planet was extraordinary. Perhaps this was another avenue of effort for Shonak to help the people of Earth? They had already helped them with freshwater production and more efficient food production and handling, reducing waste by a huge percentage, but maybe there was more to be done on the consumption side? He filed that for later.

After lunch the trainees did some more exploring, this time with the last of the candidates, who was taken through the suit drills while the others were out on their morning jaunts.

The following day Yusuf assembled the trainees after breakfast and began his lecture on the weapons they would have at their disposal. The first weapon was essentially a kinetic device that fired a hard projectile at the target. In space it would cause a rupture in the skin of the vessel resulting in rapid depressurization and physical damage due to the passage of the dart it fired. They anticipate each dart passing completely through most any vessel. The speed of the dart and its composition were known only to Shonak (Yusuf said he didn't even know these things) and were sufficient to defeat any conceivable type of hull. In the vacuum of space, with no consequential gravity and virtually no friction, the dart would continue to travel through space forever, or until it impacted a planet or a star or a large asteroid. Interestingly, unless they used darts from the resonance of their targets, the darts would repatriate to Prime space and continue their journey there, at speed, until stopped by something large like a sun. The second munition, fired from the same gun as the dart, had an explosive component that caused damage or destruction by way of explosive pressure and fragmentation. This was similar to weapons they were used to on Earth. The shells were designed to penetrate the target and explode inside.

The third weapon was something completely foreign to Earthers. It was a phase cannon that sent a chunk of the target to another phase of existence. He explained that the chunk would eventually return to its native resonance following the Law of Nativity but not to the specific place it was phased away from. The wider the beam the weaker it was, but anything within 100 kilometers would be effectively incapacitated, especially if it was subject to multiple hits. Because it was safer to stay as far away from their target as possible, it was most probable that they would be using the kinetic weapons in rapid, multiple bursts of fire. The pilots would also be moving the gunship in a random, evasive pattern to avoid themselves being effectively targeted. The guns were aware of the pattern and would not be drawn off target by these maneuvers. One hundred kilometers was considered the optimal safe distance for firing all the weapons, but they could be fired from any distance to include point bank.

Yusuf reiterated again and again how important it was for the trainees to become familiar with these weapons and to become acclimated to the notion that they were to shoot at anything they were reasonably certain was hostile. Shonak and Earth were not, they were told, interested in doing harm to any friendly strangers from outside the solar system or outside the native resonance. However, all things being equal, the priority for firing decisions was the defense of their six planets. The difference between a Shonakian gunner and an Earth gunner was thought to be the split sub-segment faster the Earth gunner would determine if it was friend or foe, and take the shot if determined to be foe. The weapons computer would determine which weapons would fire, thus relieving the gunners of that decision. The gunner would simply determine if and when to shoot at alive target. They were also told that they could turn off the automatic function and choose the weapon type themselves.

They spent the rest of the day in a simulator

where different firing and non-firing scenarios were presented, and Bon thought they were very good at what they were being asked to do. By way of contrast and comparison, and unbeknownst to the Earther gunners, Shonak put their own native gunners through the same simulations and drills in separate simulators. They found that to a person, they all hesitated before firing because, they all said, they were more interested in examining the targets out of scientific curiosity than in destroying them. They inherently wanted to study the targets first. A natural outcome, thought Bon, of hundreds of millennia of lives with no threats to their persons, just scientific inquiry and hatchling selection of those predisposed to that kind of thinking. Of course, if those targets were capable of shooting first, this hesitation could prove fatal and open the way for invasion. The Earther gunners, also to a person, reported that their priority was safety for themselves and their planet and so were more prone to see targets as hostile in cases where no information was available. The final training objective for Day Eleven was familiarization with space invasion. They were repeatedly shown the video of the last alien incursion so they would see for themselves what a potential target might look like and how it might act as it approached or entered their space.

After reviewing the results of the gunner drills, OE said he was convinced their decision to use Earther gunners was the right one, albeit a lot more complicated on every possible level. On the plus side, in addition to their gunners, was the rationale it gave them for establishing open contact with the now modern Plus-Five. OE thought this was the most favorable way to look at this issue.

Day Twelve saw them in space firing at a variety of drones and asteroids with all three weapons getting steadily more efficient with every shot. The gunners all remarked that it was exactly like the video games they grew up playing. Bon and Eldest Protection could see that these aggressive and talented Earthers would constitute a formidable defense. Add to that the Shonak capability to quickly find any intruder and get the gunners in range they would be hard to beat. Bon had Yusuf take them through four more days of simulator and drone training. He could see that their decision times and firing times improved every day until the last day when they levelled off. Some were better than others, but they were all extremely proficient. Bon sent Marshal Ning a quick note of thanks along with his training status report. At this point Bon was sure they were ready to do what was required of them. The Gold Eldest of GT Protection was pleased to see how proficient they were and thanked Bon and his team for their work. He would be taking control of these teams once they were deployed.

One unintended aspect of this adventure with Earther gunners was the accommodation of two different resonant frequencies in a confined space - a phase ship. The amazing engineers in the joint teams of S&T with Manufacturing were able to sort out the details and modified a Shonakian phase ship to be one of the new gunships under this program. The problem had never been the generation of the frequencies themselves, but rather the boundary between the two. That area of dissonance had, Bon well remembered from his Eldest Plus-Five days, resulted in the loss of the island where Plus-Five base had been for hundreds of S-Rots. The island in what is now called the Atlantic Ocean on Earth completely sheared off at that discontinuity layer between Prime and Plus-Five vibrations. The top of the island, where the Prime Zone of Influence was maintained, was simply pushed aside by the constant pressure of wind, waves and strong ocean currents. How then to keep this sort of thing from tearing a phase ship apart, one part resonant at Prime and the other part at Plus-Five? They achieved this miracle of modern Shonakian science by simply alternating the resonance at the place these two different vibrations met. This was done many times a second, so the structure of the ship essentially remained the same, a sort of blend between the two frequencies. It worked well in their math models and in their simulations, and then worked equally well when they put it to the ultimate test. The trick was to make the device small and light weight, which they managed to achieve, thinking that future iterations, once they had more time, would be even smaller and lighter.

Because of their size, the Earthers would have the largest space on the ship resonating at Plus-Five and the two Shonakian crew would be in what they considered adequate space, given their much less complicated space requirements. Unlike the Earthers, the Shonakians needed no kitchen, no showers, no laundry, no break room. They were focused on flight and navigation and communications. Maintenance was done back on Shonak, so they did not even need tools. As a result of these advances, the gunships for this program would be livable for the year-long deployments the Earthers had signed up for. Shuttles would bring food and water out to the ships when supplies ran low. Shipping containers capable of generating the appropriate resonance were produced in case they were ever needed and the shuttles themselves were, like the new gunships, made with multiple phase capability, so regardless of the phase needed, Prime through Plus-Five, they could transport it. Both OE and Marshal Ning were pleased and approved the final operations plan.

On Day Seventeen Bon briefed OE and the various GT-Es that the gunners were ready for deployment. Bon relayed their approval to the Earth World President and Marshal Ning and then awaited final instructions to deploy them. Shonak made it clear that they were ready to go, so it now only rested with the WG and its members to give the final approval to launch. All twenty gunners had passed their exams and what remained was to determine where they would station their gun ships and who would be on what shift. Those decisions would need to be taken following the final deployment order that indicated which resonances would receive what number of ships. Bon was proud that all the ships would be multi-phased so the gunners would have sufficient comfort in their down time as would the Shonak crew.

Days Seventeen and Eighteen passed with no guidance from Earth or Shonak on where to deploy their ships. While the gunners were idle awaiting their deployment order, Yusuf's duties remained extensive and it helped that he never needed sleep. Not only did he train the candidates, he also saw to their needs and spied on them at the same time. Bon's Plus-Five team also spied on them, but in a more distant way. While they were on Shonak their supposedly clandestine communications implants would not reach Earth, but Bon noted robust exchanges between the candidates and their home countries back before they left for Prime. Good that they did not know at that point what their mission would be or where! He did not know yet if Marshal Ning knew that their home countries had outfitted their candidates with all manner of tracking and communications means, but he doubted Ning would be surprised by that. Of course, the countries which were intending on spying on the Shonakian training of their gunners did not officially complain that their communications devices were not working. These countries had agreed to trust the process and this, of course, was not a trusting move. For his part, Bon did not care much to what or who their loyalties lie, as long as the people did their jobs. He had been watching Earthers closely for millennia now, and he understood that they were just naturally a suspicious and duplicitous lot. He knew that the gunners did not have access to any information on their weapons so Earth could not duplicate them. Same for the phase shifting machinery. He did, however, borrow a play from their own playbook. He came up with a plan whereby he could ascertain what they had learned or thought they had learned while undergoing training. He told Yusuf to take them back to Plus-Five space for a round of gunnery training while they were waiting for deployment orders. Sure enough, as soon as they were back in "home" space the data began to flow in earnest. It was all intercepted and not delivered, of course, in order to protect the program details from leaking outside official channels. Not all of the gunners played spy, of course, but 17 of the 20 were passing anything and everything to their home handlers. The content, while encrypted, was easy for Bon to read. Most of the transmissions began with confirmation that they were working with the Shonak aliens and had actually visited their planet! They were boastful regarding their success in training and they all told of their horrible experience breathing Shonak air. They were also eager to share basic details about their gunnery training, blasting small asteroids in space! They were amazed by their phase suits which were also anti-grav fliers. They described Shonak, or at least those parts of Shonak they had seen, and reiterated the Law of Nativity demonstration they endured. It was clear they were convinced by it. There could be no true intercourse between Shonak and Earth. Period. End of story. Bon was relieved that they clearly believed in the Law of Nativity. Their firm belief in this would go a long way towards convincing others. Those gunners who were intelligence operatives and not really pilots or soldiers told their people they were not too keen on spending a year defending the planets against who knows what threat – but would of course do so until replaced.

Bon and Yusuf both noted the message traffic between their candidate gunners and their home countries was not something to be overly concerned about, but both of them understood this was something to watch carefully. They well understood that Earthers never fully trust anyone, so why should Shonak fully trust them?

Day fifteen came and went and still no word from OE or anyone else on deploying the teams. This was becoming more of a political decision on Earth than operational. That part was cocked and ready. Day sixteen looked much the same and Bon kept them in Plus-Five space so he could see what these gunners were trying to relay to their governments. He was pleased to note that Marshal Ning's communications with them showed a thoroughly dedicated security person with no hidden agenda.

On Day Nineteen the deployment order for the ships finally came. The ten ships would each have two Earther gunners and would take their defensive stations on the following day. There was no choice with this deployment for all ships to be on 12-hour shifts, one gunner per shift. The turnover briefs between one shift and another would be necessarily brief so the outgoing gunner could go rest and the new guy could begin the shift. Indeed, if no threat was detected during any shift, the turnover brief would simply be an equipment status summary and on a Shonakian vessel things did not malfunction.

Since they had one more day to wait and since it was well understood that with humans, Yusuf called everyone to the training room for a pre-deployment session. After a few moments of operational talk, concerning what phase they would be assigned to and shift schedules, a space gunner (which is what they were now called, having passed all their training) raised his hand and asked if he could learn more about Shonakians. What were they like, really? Yusuf listened and thought this would be a good use of their time. He asked them what they wanted to know. The same gunner then asked, "When do they shit?" "Or do they?" "And when do they sleep or eat or go have a beer, or just take time off from the job?" The other gunners all smiled, nodded, a few laughed, and Yusuf began to answer. "Shonakians", he began, "Do urinate and defecate but less frequently than humans and with much less, gusto, can we call it?" They laughed at that. "Rabbit droppings are the best comparison." He continued, "They only weigh, like, seventeen pounds dripping wet, so as you might imagine their digestion is more like a small pet on Earth. They eat one edible tube of vegetable matter a day and then eat the tube. Their bodies are nearly one hundred percent efficient with the food and water contained in their meals, so there is little to eliminate. Shonakians are always amazed to learn that Earth humans eat three times a day, and huge meals, at that. (Some laughter among the group) We Earth humans eliminate a large percentage of what we eat by being much less efficient users of the calories we consume. Roy over there," He pointed to Roy, by far the largest of all the gunners, "Probably shits more in a day than a Shonakian weighs!" This was met by hearty laughter from the group, including Roy. "Also, they have no taste buds, so food is only fuel to them, not something to enjoy or wrap a family around. And they have no families to sit around and talk with, anyway. They do not think about sex, like we do all the time, (more laughter) since they only have one sex on the whole planet and they self-procreate by regurgitating an egg when they are 400 years old, or so. They do sleep, but not all that often and not for long. When really busy with their team mission they can go a few days without sleep and when sleeping on a regular schedule they need only maybe an hour out of every forty-eight. They can also go a few days without eating a food tube but might sip some water. Their minds are unbelievably sharp and their memories are computer-like. Their vision is excellent, much sharper than ours, as is their hearing, but they don't have much of a sense of smell. Odor is not something that concerns them, so a week's worth of sweat in a phase suit will not be as disgusting to them as it is to us! (More laughter) They have a cashless society and do not acquire 'things' like we do on Earth. They have no commerce, as such, but they have extensive logistics infrastructure, great roads, wonderful modes of transport, and excellent communications as you may have noticed." He looked out at their attentive faces and wondered when the obvious question would come up. He did not have to wait long. "Yusuf," asked one of the female gunners, "How do you know so much about Shonakians? Aren't we the first Earth humans to have dealings with them? If you know so much, you must have known them longer than we have." Yusuf laughed, then, as warmly as he could, then said, "You are to be the public face of contact with this alien race. Those few of us who have been working for them for years prefer it that way. Before Earth knew about Shonak we had to keep that completely secret, of course, but even now that Earth knows I, for one, will continue to keep that relationship to myself as much as I can. The truth is, they've been travelling to Earth for over four thousand years. They have actually watched us grow up! People like me are contractors for them since they can't exist at our vibration. Most of us have no clue who we work for, just the owner of a warehouse, for example, or the boss of a shipping company. They have many businesses on Earth and the people they hire work for those businesses. Everything is normal and law abiding, and they even pay their taxes! (More laughter.) For some reason they took me aside a few years ago and introduced themselves and asked if I would be willing to act as a go-between for them with certain Earth people, some common, some in government. We are not to tell them about Shonak or Shonakians, but it helps if we know. So, there are a few people like me who know about Shonak and its people. They took me to Shonak and showed me around and I met some of their teams, but only so I would understand my own tasks a little better. As you will admit, to be honest, we as a people, on Earth, are suspicious and even hostile towards people we don't know but to my knowledge, with four thousand years of visitation to Earth behind them, and with all the resources at their disposal, they have no history of violence towards us. If this isn't proof of good intentions, I don't know what is. Add to that the fact that they can't live on Earth without their Zones of Influence, so they might as well stay on Shonak where they can enjoy the fruits and beauty of their home planet, so similar to ours."

They were sitting still, taking it in, when another gunner, a male this time, asked about their age seniority system. Yusuf said, "It's a simple system, and almost elegantly so. You all read the summary they provided but, in a nutshell, the oldest person in any group is the leader, whose say is final, on anything. Period. So, Johnson, since you are the oldest gunner, with student ID number one, your word would always be the final word on any subject." The gunners all looked at each other, and they could now see that their student numbers reflected their ages. They had wondered about that since the numbers were not alphabetically related. Yusuf continued talking, "And since there are no hidden agendas, no competition for anything, no ego, nothing but a strong desire to be a successful member of their team, the younger Shonakians have nothing to be suspicious about or fear from any older person's decisions. Consequently, there are no arguments, at least not any that we would give that name to." He continued, "They can have honest disagreement, and hold contrary opinions, but the decisions of the Eldest is accepted as the final decision. Among Golds, even, there are some intellectual disputes but again, the oldest Gold is always right. There are times, when disagreeing over candidates for key senior team positions, two Grand Team Eldests will ask for arbitration from an older Shonakian since they both believe strongly in their own rational arguments for taking the new person on their team. Once again whatever the older person decides is what happens. Usually the Grand Team Eldests will go to their Regional Counselor if they have the same one or if not, they will go to the Council of Twelve. It has never happened but if the Council can't decide, then Our Eldest will make the decision which is final because there is no higher authority on Shonak."

"Sounds like they lead a fairly boring social life!" chimed in one of the gunners and there was plenty of agreeable comment coming from the rest of them. Then Yusuf said, "Well, yes, they do, by Earth standards, but not by theirs. And for the last several thousand years we have provided them with the best entertainment any Shonakian could wish for -- life on Earth." He paused for effect, then added, "They have been watching people on Earth as a matter of information and entertainment for at least three thousand years. They have their favorites, of course, like you have your favorite shows and sports teams. They live long enough to watch climate change, governments rise and fall, wars, not just battles, growth of science and technology. And they have no agenda other than information and entertainment, so the violation of privacy we naturally feel is benign in the strictest sense of the word." This got their attention. "What?!" They pretty much all said it at once. "You mean they watch us all the time?" "Who does this, all Shonakians or just their government?" Yusuf waited till all their questions were shouted out, then answered them. "To begin with, they have no government, only teams and a few elders who see that the teams have the resources to do their jobs. All Shonakians have access to the publicly released views which do not include excessive violence or politics or warfare except in general clips." And now, at Bon's private urging, Yusuf began to lie. "They do not have access to private homes or to private moments among you. They don't go into your bathrooms or bedrooms, to be sure, mostly because they have no interest in that, especially sex which they have no understanding for or urges to explore." This calmed them down a bit, if their body language was any indicator, but they still remained somewhat on edge for, perhaps, what revelation would come next. But none did, because at that moment an alarm tone sounded, and Bon appeared in front of them all in a hologram comm. Bon could see where this discussion was going, so he took action to change the subject. "Gunners of Earth, I greet you. Congratulations on your completion of the training you need to do your jobs, which begin tomorrow. You are no longer trainees; you are Space Gunners! You will deploy in a short while, so you can finally take your posts. The actual start time for the defense of our six planets and their space begins first thing tomorrow morning. Your twelve-hour shifts begin at zero six hundred, as you would call it. We have one more task to perform before you leave. Since you will be working with Shonakians we will put red dots on your phase suits so they will feel comfortable that you are all at least adults. Please do not take offense, but people who are say, three hundred Planetary Rotations, or years old, want to feel that their teammates are capable, even if inexperienced. If you will allow it, we also want to put red dots on your actual foreheads and put red wrist badges on you with the logo of the Protection Grand Team, our newest Grand Team on Shonak. We are not going to make this a requirement, but Yusuf has suggested to me that these will make amazing proofs that you have worked directly with Shonakians in defense of the Planets. These tattoos are permanent so do not take the decision lightly. We have some members of the Age Team suited up in Plus-Five suits who can administer the tattoos. I think there is no need to have your age on your arms, but that can also be done if you wish. In fact, it occurs to me we should use your Shonakian age, not your Earth age. We live on average now sixteen hundred years and you live about one hundred or so. We will therefore multiply your Earth age by sixteen and give you a color commensurate with your Shonakian equivalent." He then turned it over to Yusuf to make it happen. Yusuf looked at the gunner in front of him and said, "Parker, you're 41 years old." He took out his calculator, not that he needed it, but he wanted to appear human, and said, "That would be 656 years on Shonak which makes you a," more tapping, "Blue!" We will put a blue dot on your suit and on your forehead and backdate your Shonakian age to 615 years for your tattoo if you want one." Parker beamed, and said, "Lay it on me Bro, lay it on me. This is the best historical marker or souvenir I can have in my entire life. What a story for the grand kids! Not to mention my girlfriends!" The rest of the team laughed at that, knowing that he was married with children, and then they began to roll up their sleeves. Yusuf and the Age Team got ready with their calculations. Their ages were 25 to 52 on Earth and 400 to 832 on Shonak and so ran from Yellow all the way to Indigo. They were so proud of themselves and were rightly eager to get started in their new roles as protectors of the planets. Yusuf said, "All those who want tattoos please move to the left of the room, by our Age Team rep, who will guide you through it." Then Yusuf said, "In fact, I think I'll join you in this little operation. I'm 38 this year so that makes me 608 and a Blue, I think." Bon commed them when Yusuf reported the markings were done and he said he was well pleased with this last part of the graduation and said it would continue with all future classes as a graduation "certificate". And then he smiled, not a common occurrence. It took less than ten portions to administer all the tattoos. Everyone elected to have their color dot and the age tattoo on their arms, even the ones who were initially skeptical. They got caught up in the euphoria of something new on a planetary level and did not want to miss out. (They also knew that a dermatologist back home could remove it if they wanted to, so no big deal). The Age Team rep told everyone it took some doing to make ink in the Plus-Five frequency so they need not worry it will disappear on them. Everyone was issued their Protection Team wrist badge, again, in their appropriate color, and one was also affixed to their phase suits.

Bon appeared on their room screen then and spoke to them, "You are now going to be transferred to your gunships. You are the first gunners in the protection team effort to defend our planets and can be duly proud of your achievements and your responsibility. I am designating you space gunners as Atsa Force. Your team is named after a proto-Hopi tribal chief of great courage and conviction that peace, not war, was the finest condition of your people. He was courageous and fierce when the situation called for it but otherwise, he was a gentle, intellectual leader of exceptional accomplishment and I want to honor him by giving your team his name." He ended his comments to them with, "Good luck and safe travels, Gunners of Atsa Force."

With that his image disappeared and Yusuf was motioning them to line up in the order they had been given ever since they arrived. It dawned on many of them, for the second time that day, that they were arranged in order from oldest in the front to the youngest in the back. How beautifully Shonakian! Before this last ceremony, their ages really never mattered to them. On Earth such military trainees were arranged in alphabetical order. Here and as long as they were part of a Shonakian effort, it was strictly by birth order.

When the last of them had gone Bon ordered Yusuf to report to Gold Rin, his new Eldest, and thanked him for all his help. Gold Rin was on comm then and told Yusuf to visit Marshal Ning immediately, who was arranging for more candidates to join the ranks of gunners. He would bring them to the training facility and put them through the same program as those who just left. He was pleased Yusuf decided to make the age dot and arm tattoo ceremony a part of their graduation recognition, so important to the Earth psyche. These gunners needed something unique, and this certainly was that! Yusuf replied that he agreed it was an excellent idea and offered another.

He thought that they should have a logo which can be put on their shirts, jackets, and even coffee cups. That was the Earther way! Rin smiled and shook his head and watched Yusuf fade out on his way up to Plus-Five to see Marshal Ning.

Yusuf landed at the desert manufacturing facility, changed into business attire, and flew himself to Beijing. Off-phase, he made his way to the local hotel they had permanent rooms in, phased into his Plus-Five room, and called room service for a meal, just to maintain his human cover. He flushed it down the toilet. When he met with the Marshal the next morning, the Marshal reacted with some surprise at Yusuf's forehead tattoo. Yusuf smiled and rolled up his sleeve to show him his age tattoo as well. He also showed Ning his Protection Team wrist badge. Ning said he was impressed and asked if the space gunners were also tattooed and Yusuf said they were, voluntarily, and were extremely jazzed by the whole thing. They were operational as of this morning, defending the planets as they were trained to do. Yusuf briefed Ning on the details of the training class and some stories from their training, especially the first few moments in their anti-grav suits. That brought a smile to Ning's face. Yusuf thanked him for the new class of recruits and said he would be taking them to the training center on Shonak in the morning. They were to be assembled by zero-nine-hundred hours for immediate departure. These next gunners would round out the operational requirement. Working with the Earth Space Defense

Force, they had decided it was sufficient to use sensors around the planets at vibrations Plus-Two, Three, and Four. There was nothing much there to protect so the effort would be focused on preventing any colonization. That could be done by a gunner reaction force on standby stationed on Earth and/or Shonak who would be picked up by the Shonak gunship and taken to the threat. Plus-One, with an emerging intelligent life form, needed a permanent presence, as did the current contingents on Plus-Five space and Prime. These would be augmented to allow for six-hour shifts with a scheduled day off. Yusuf said he may ask for an additional twenty to forty to compose a contingency force should they be needed. To keep them sharp, they would be rotated into and out of the existing force once or twice a year, allowing for month-long home leave for the teams. He also told him of Bon's decision to name the space gunners unit Atsa Force after a historical Earth figure who was special to Bon for whatever reason. Marshal Ning had no objection to that and admitted that the Earth defense reps had been unable to give them a name due to a lack of consensus from the Group of 8. He commented that the Shonakian age dot and arm tattoo were great ideas for troop morale. It clearly marks them as participants in a special, inter-planetary security force and would be the envy of every warfighter on Earth.

Chapter Seven

"Safe" Technology Transfer

Immediately after the Beijing introduction ceremonies, and while the gunner training was getting started, Bon returned to other matter concerning their new, open relationship with Earth. During the next morning's mission update, Bon's staff informed him that there was something of a deluge of requests for technology solutions to many of Earth's problems. These were being forwarded from John and Helen's office and ranged from military to medical to engineering to social. They were coming from everyone who had access to the Web, so it was everything from governments to businesses to private citizens. Some seemed frivolous, and some were thoughtful, and Bon's team wanted guidance on how to proceed. John Manners also wanted guidance on how much pre-screening was desired and were there any limits to these requests at all?

The process Bon had established was for these to be taken for consideration by their tech transfer sub-team, in coordination with the various Grands who touched on those issues. Anything deemed feasible using Earth materials would go to the inter-Grand vetting team where it was put through their use models to see if the tech or process could be abused in any way. Bon had not anticipated an avalanche of requests from people with no concern for the scientific feasibility of the subject, nor was it to be a quick process and Earthers at every level were of course expecting immediate help. Bon and the OE for that matter, had two major concerns with tech transfer. First, they did not want to give Earthers some technology that could be used for any military or political purpose since that would simply act to destabilize an already (in their view) unstable global structure given the disparity between individual countries, and regions. Second, they did not want their technology to be taken from Shonak and then resold on Earth. Anything they gave to Earth would be to benefit the planet and not certain individuals or companies. While many of the requests were for transitory techs, long-lived Shonakians take a longer view, preferring that any tech given to Earth be of lasting benefit. The Violet briefer that morning asked Bon for his thoughts but before yielding suggested that it would be prudent to have a non-governmental process for knowledge and tech transfer that would be beneficial to Earth humans and their planet without getting bogged down in the confused, jumbled politics of national or world government bodies, all concerned about budgets and competition and power projection and their many other Earther idiosyncrasies. That made them great fun to watch on their video feeds but, as they were finding, made them difficult people to deal with. Bon instantly saw the wisdom of this approach and said he would follow their advice. Shonak wanted to assist Earth with its technology and Earth was eager to receive it but the clamor of requests from governments down to private companies to charities to private individuals has been understandable but unworkable. The WP had recently asked Bon at one point when they would "turn the spigot on" in granting Earth the benefit of their advanced ways of getting things done and improving the lives of their people. Bon's response, endorsed by OE, was that this would come, eventually, once their formal agreement had been coordinated and signed, and once they were sure the alliance was working in space on the gunner teams.

Bon did, however, recognize that there were some ways Shonak could help sooner than later and his immediate solution to the tech transfer issue was to launder their technology through commercial enterprises they already had on the planet and with the help of John and Helen. But not where they currently worked.

To bring this plan to fruition, Bon was in their office when John and Helen got back from Beijing where they attended the "coming out" ceremony and several parties thrown by various government departments and private companies. They were happy to have a prominent role in the opening of relations and were feted around the town and of course the press was after them for "inside" looks at how it all went down. They had then taken a few days to see the sights, since neither had been to China before. When they came into their office on their first day back, Bon was sitting in John's chair, looking all blurry in his phase suit, and something like a child in a seat for grownups. They stopped in surprise and stared at him and then in typical, blunt, no lead-in Shonakian he said he wanted them to resign, after giving the required and expected notice. If they agreed, he would be employing them to work for the benefit of Earth but supported by Shonak. They would operate in a private capacity with their own companies, funded, at least initially, by Shonak. When they became profitable, they would also be a source of Earth-currency revenue for their Shonak business partner, as they were always short of Earth currencies. (This part of the story was not true, but Bon knew it would make perfect sense to them. Shonak had long ago learned how to generate wealth and cash while on Earth. Their bots had become quite good at it.) Their Earth employees like Stephen, Bon explained, always needed operating capital and another legitimate source was always welcome. Bon went on to outline his plan. The goal would be to transfer knowledge and technology from Shonak to Earth in an unobtrusive way. To do this with John and Helen's assistance, they would both establish themselves in business related to their expertise, their training, their professional contacts and their solid reputations. Helen's company would run a historical research bureau, using "new" search algorithms that provided much more accurate if not more believable accounts of historical events on Earth whenever captured by the Shonakian's own research teams and surveillance apparatus. Bon's teams would provide her with actual accounts of historical events, replete with audio and video which Helen could use as a primary source for her reports. She would claim that her depictions were fictional composites from multiple sources and "likely" information to fill any voids. To cite one small example, she would, eventually, become "the" source for accurate depictions of local and regional clothing from around the world from any time period from perhaps minus 2500 UAY to present.

John would run a private company that also

uses "unique, new" search algorithms to merge existing technologies on Earth and create new scientific and technical theories to solve problems and come up with new technologies for Earth without disclosing their Shonak origins. It would be widely rumored, and believed, that John would be using his Shonakian connection to acquire his new products, which of course would make his company wildly popular and profitable. He would of course maintain that this was not the case, but he would allow that from time to time he might consult with Shonakian contacts to examine his work and make suggestions. Bon told them he would slowly provide Shonakian technology through official channels, but this would be painfully slow by Earth standards. This would help John's cover story about not using their technology directly, just a little "help" now and then.

Bon also told them he would provide the necessary funds and administrative support for these enterprises without telling them how, exactly that would be achieved. He said he had access to lawyers and accountants and banks on Earth who would provide them with the help they needed and he told them not to worry about funding or their own personal finances as both of them would be paid handsomely. He felt no need to tell them how he would make this happen.

Bon earlier learned to his great satisfaction

that an Infotainment Team had introduced bots to play roles on Earth to stimulate and/or follow situations the Shonakians would find interesting. One of these families put down its "roots" in Florence and in Milan in their thirteenth century, and this bot family had since spread to more parts of Italy and several other countries in Europe. In this way Shonak employed bots to portray a prosperous and successful family over a span of many generations. While not intended, this provided them with historical bona fides of long standing, very useful to Bon. They had aged the bots appropriately and had children appropriately and did appropriate things, all the while being controlled by the team that ran this mission. Bon had been following this as a matter of both entertainment and professional interest and he queried the Violet who ran the team to see where all the family had spread to outside of what was now Italy. The Violet responded quickly to Gold Bon that there were branches of this successful, well-connected family all over Europe and the USNA. Bon asked if there was a lawyer in the USNA and another in the UK who could draw up papers of incorporation other administrative necessities along those lines. The Violet did have such bots and gave Bon the details. Bon responded that he would like to take control of these two lawyer bots and their families and the Violet quickly agreed, even though Bon demanded that the activities of those bots and their "families" and of his own colleagues on Earth would not be available for the infotainment feeds on Shonak. The Violet knew that there was plenty of other feeds to keep people interested.

Bon set to work with the bots and the Shonakians who operated them to establish the funding and other mechanisms needed to create cover organizations to sponsor the enterprises that John and Helen would run. On the surface these two enterprises would be legitimate and do legitimate business. The Shonakian connection would be kept from everyone but the bots, of course, and the two principal parties in the operation. Bon felt this was a better solution than involving any government functionaries whose motives would always be suspect and who were inherently incapable of keeping a secret of this magnitude. Given the sophistication of identity databases on Earth at this point in their history it was pleasing to him that the pre-renaissance family was traceable back to ancient times and were fully documented moving forward, with actual school attendance, "illness," birth and death records, etc. They had long ago figured out the DNA and other forensic issues needed to overcome modern ID verification, and that was a huge relief to him. Maybe someday he would talk to John and Helen about this, but not now.

True to his word, John and Helen received new small comm devices that looked like the electronic keys to their personal vehicles, and indeed they did function that way, too. John asked Bon what they should do with the comm cube and Bon answered that he would use it to communicate with the people who replaced them and said to leave it where it was. He gave them the contact information for their new legal advisors so there would be an auditable trail of contact for two government officials striking it out on their own to go into private business. They told Bon they had officially informed their respective bosses, both national and in the world governing body, that they were retiring to pursue opportunities in the private sector. They were now famous after their well-documented role in bringing Shonak to their world and they said they wanted to seize the moment for the benefit of their families. Their bosses considered this perfectly reasonable since it is exactly what they would do in the same situation. "Lucky them" one thought, after years of derision, to now be on top of the world. They also explained that the role they had played in introducing Shonak to Earth had been quite overwhelming and they wanted to escape into a quieter place than they were, constantly being pestered by the press and paparazzi. Also, understandable. They managed to extricate themselves from government and gradually immersed themselves in their new lives, ostensibly translating their government and academic research experience into private businesses at home.

With seed money provided by Bon's Earth agents, through appropriate commercial banks, John settled on offices in Research Triangle Park, North Carolina, USNA and Helen chose London, England, UNE, to start her venture. They found comfortable homes to live in and began their new lives with lots of start-up work but no financial worries. Bon's bot teams set to work on the appropriate construction permits and other building and office renovation details so Shonak could be comfortable with the security in each facility and secured a team from the Security Grand Team to monitor their offices and communications for any signs of compromise. After their lawyers arranged confidential financing Both Helen and John hired staff to take care of the overt side of their business leaving them free to concentrate on the covert side of things. They were enjoying their newfound freedom and wealth but were not flaunting it. There was no more interesting thing on their minds than pursuing liaison with Shonak on behalf of their entire planet! Both John and Helen hired private assistants to handle the administrative trivia neither of them wanted to deal with personally. They were not aware that both candidates they hired were Shonakian bots. Bon felt that these bots would ensure the security of their relationship with Shonak and would augment the eyes and ears planted all around the offices and their homes. Since both of them had bought expensive homes on their business accounts, as their attorneys suggested, Bon had his security teams go over them carefully installing advanced security systems as they did so, as well as the full component of surveillance devices. If there was ever a hint that someone was trying to steal from them or highlight this special relationship, Bon would move instantly to shut down the compromised aspect of this mission.

Helen's friends in the academic world of history and anthropology and sociology were all interested in her new venture and wished her well. None of the stigma of her former job and contact with Shonakians attached to her, probably because the popular conception of Shonak was that it was a techno-geek culture with no interest in Earth history.

For her part, Helen thought it was a good start, but she wanted to be busy, not just sit around waiting for Bon to call. And what would he call her about anyway?

One of her friends was the academic advisor to a young history PhD candidate writing her thesis and who was looking for validation of her approach. Helen was given her contact information and called her that day. The candidate's name was Ginger Brooks, and she was working on the history of commercial footwear. She was attempting to find the first example of ready-to-wear shoes; in various sizes and with left and right design. Helen told Ginger she would look into it and get back to her within a few days. Bon and his team were witness to this entire exchange and one of Bon's team told Helen he would search for the scene when at the exact moment the first pair of commercially available left and right shoes in many sizes was made; when and where and by whom. Helen thanked the young Yellow and was hopeful they could help her. She knew Shonakian surveillance was extensive but had no idea how much they really covered. As it happened one of their bots actually caught the moment in question. They did not have it on video, but they did have a conversation about it. The Yellow called Helen and told her the incident they were looking for was in Philadelphia in the year 1818 UAY. Unsure who is speaking, but the gist of the conversation was that this had been discussed in the industry for years. Custom-made shoes had been doing this since before they could remember but for the ready-to-wear industry it had been considered an expensive complication for the equipment line needed to mass produce shoes with these size and right-left differences for men and women. The speaker felt this was an overdue solution to the traditional trade-off in either breaking in new shoes or old feet. With the boot or shoe conforming to the foot more accurately there would be less foot pain and fewer blisters while breaking them in and better overall comfort over the life of the footwear. Of course, this eventually became the commercial standard, but it took years for general acceptance in the industry even though the customers were ready for it instantly. During the civil war in the United States the Union Army needed tens of thousands of boots for their soldiers and that provided the impetus for investment in the machinery and manpower that would turn out left and right boots in many sizes and in very large quantities. The civilian application of this capability was quickly capitalized on as well.

Helen called Ms. Brooks with the news and was thanked for her quick response. Brooks then asked for the full source citations and Helen gulped. She should have thought of that before calling Brooks. She said she had another call and would call her back directly. Then she asked her history contact, the unnamed Yellow, for the reference and was given a local newspaper account of the event, which was duly passed on to Brooks, who was happy to pay for the service. This proved to be a valuable sales event since Ms. Brooks told her friends about the quick turnaround on a research question for her dissertation and that gave rise to others with similar requests on a wide variety of topics. From there it gradually snowballed into a "thing" among PhD candidates the world over and "Ask Helen" became an industry standard for these requests. While normal computer search engines were excellent, they could only uncover information that was available somewhere online. Helen's Shonak resources were able to provide things no database had hold of. Over time, she more than established herself as a legitimate business while maintaining a close relationship with Bon's team.

John's high-tech consultancy was even more successful than Helen's, based on the money it generated and the amount of good it did for the world. Several of Shonak's gifts to Earth through John were patentable and John did that, with the help of his in-house counsel who filed all the necessary papers. The first one was a new, more efficient, less costly way to extract high quantities of drinking and irrigation water from the oceans. This not only helped to alleviate the water problems around the world, but an indirect consequence of this was another patent that provided a cost-effective way to clean the oceans and great lakes and recycle the materials extracted from them.

The heavy metals and rare earths alone paid for the investment in machinery and vessels and crew. In his mind, and with the press, John Marquis saw his name alongside Edison, Bell, Gates, and the like as one whose inventions had made the world a better place for all its inhabitants. John knew, of course, that this was all just a sideshow before his more significant working relationship with Shonak.

Both John and Helen kept busy. Helen was still dealing with the fallout from the most controversial historical expose she had ever published; actual footage of the crucifixion of Jesus Christ. She claimed it was a simulation created from her research, using her advanced algorithms to merge every image of Christ currently known to exist. It generated a firestorm of outrage and protest from the Christian and atheist communities alike. The Pope condemned her work and forbade Catholics from viewing the images – which of course only increased the viewing by both Catholics and non-Catholics. Most people who viewed it were astounded by what Helen's video made Christ look like, far different than he had been depicted since the early middle ages. Gaunt, dark-skinned, unattractive, crying in pain, surely this could not be the son of any God! Of course, it was an actual video taken by multiple Shonakian surveillance bots just doing their collection jobs without comment, or concern for "how it would look." It was what it was. As it happened, in spite of the enemies she made with her much more believable and accurate portrayals of history, she also attracted adherents to her work with the crucifixion video. Those who did not care for the "beauty" of history and could accept the more honest, "warts and all" approach she gave to it became her biggest fans. Her business continued to thrive under this business model.

Naturally, as her business and fame expanded after the Christ episode, there was also an increase in attempted hacks of her computer systems. People with various agendas, pro and con, wanted to know just how she put her historical depictions together, both still and video. Her results were out there, in spades, but not her methodology, for reasons obvious to her but literally unguessable by the public. If anyone did think there might be a Shonakian connection, for those who even knew about it, they dismissed it out of hand.

People just did not think that Shonak was collecting imagery from hundreds or thousands of years in the past. Too fantastic a thought to give it more than a second of consideration.

She did not post things herself, but rather let her customers post online what they wished to post after buying their research products from her. She sold the rights to these things along with the purchase, and that often did not come cheap, especially those products which held commercial value. And naturally those things the new owners posted were fair game for theft, just like anything online, but her own data remained in her own dedicated servers, most of which were standalone. At least to Earth systems and networks. They were of course constantly accessible from Shonak. Using live historical footage was less of a problem than she had thought because nobody ever even contemplated that these were actual live events from Earth's history. But these things still caused other problems that were not so well anticipated. And since her technology was Shonakian there was no way for any Earth based hack since her actual code was not even binary or in any language Earth could know. She called it "proprietary" and nobody could prove otherwise. This stymied the more determined of her critics, so they resorted to burglary and again, Bon's security team saw that none of these attempts were successful, and the burglars were turned over to the police. Even if they managed to steal something it would do them no good since there was no way for any Earth person, however talented, to reverse engineer or reverse hack her systems. Even an attempt to blow up her studio by religious fanatics claiming "heresy" failed and Bon, tiring of all these attempts, had his bots round up the perps whom he had fully identified with intrusive surveillance and had his bots, covered as private investigators and security agents, took them to the police with sufficient evidence to have them arrested and later convicted. The few who fought their bot captors were injured, of course, and three were killed in the gunfights which erupted. Earth was certainly behaving like "The Law West of the Pecos" and the infotainment feeds on this were all very popular. So, Bon's Earth Liaison Team kept a close watch on all the people who had expressed or shown any interest in harming Helen or her operation, and there were many. Every time she produced an iconoclastic view of some historical event, she created enemies as well as adherents. And every time there was even a hint of interest in harm to Helen or her family or business, Bon made sure this was quashed at its inception. He managed to insert bots into the more focused of her hate groups and they were often able to steer their interests into different directions, much more lucrative directions. All of this provided fascinating viewing for his team, but Bon kept these vids off the Shonak infotainment network.

On the technology side, John's business was far less emotional or controversial and far more lucrative. The manufacturing sectors that made the most use of the Shonakian methods was very pleased at John's company's ability to solve their tech problems with his innovative solutions. And of course, manufacturing and technology are far less emotional or iconoclastic than Helen's often revisionist history. John was able to introduce a number of wonderful innovations that made life just a little easier for the planet. After the seawater treatment tech transfers via his company he focused on providing better, cheaper ways to provide light in homes, power generation for homeowners to get them off the grid, and disease-resistant crops with higher yields to name just a few. He was able to break the so-called iron triangle of "better, faster, cheaper". The thinking was you could have only two of the three but with the introduction of new science and/or technology, he was able to provide all three in many cases. But like Helen's business, he also made enemies when his innovations threatened established industries, or when he resisted offers to buy him out. Bon was able to provide John with the same protections that he gave to Helen, with the same good results. Fortunately, most competitors simply wanted to buy him out and made outrageous offers to do so. They also resorted to hacking and burglary, but this gave them no joy, in the same way and for the same reasons as Helen's enemies. The fact that both John and Helen used the same security company raised no eyebrows since it was known that they had been friends and colleagues for many years as World Government employees and so naturally shared their thoughts and ideas and service contractors.

The success Shonak bots were having in the protection of John and Helen started Bon thinking that this sort of thing might be something Shonak could do for all Earth. This would ease their consciences on Shonak for all the millennia of stealing their privacy and the earlier kidnapping and experimentation on Earth natives. Bon thought it would be good to atone by helping Earth in some way that made all their lives easier. Two thoughts; on the medical front perhaps Shonak can relieve these people of some of their most devastating ailments and on the social front, perhaps they can rid the planet of its rampant criminal activity as well as political and government corruption. Acting on this thought, he scanned the roster of their Earther human bots for one with medical credentials. There were several, as it turned out, and he chose the oldest-appearing of them (no surprise there), a Doctor Singh, to begin a medical research company devoted to the most devastating illnesses facing the people of Earth. Almost overnight this company introduced, for initial trials, effective drugs for the most devastating forms of cancer, as well as diabetes, rabies, several antibiotic resistant bacteria, numerous viruses, and radiation-related ailments since their recent nuclear wars had caused widespread radiation contamination. Privately, through his medical bot network, his doctors began to treat their patients with these maladies to wonderful results! His techniques were freely passed to medical schools, hospitals, and clinics around the world.

The issue of crime prevention and judicial action was tabled for the moment, but Bon put it high on the list for a discussion with Ning and the WP.

Chapter Eight

Operation Purge

In the S-Rot 30610, after the gunners were trained and deployed and after John, Helen, and Dr. Singh were well on their way to the successful provision of Shonak solutions to Earth's pressing problems, Bon responded favorably to a request for a face-to-face meeting from the WP and Security Director. He was eager to do even more. Bon was happy to meet with Ning and the WP in the WPs private office and was pleased that they wanted to meet again in person. Bon thought it would be a lot easier for him if he could send Bon bot to the meeting rather than appear in a phase suit but he did not want Earth to know about their bots, at least not yet, and perhaps not for a long while—if ever. The WP welcomed Bon to the office, which Bon simply appeared in rather than arrive outside and walk through the halls and offices to get there. Bon replied it was his honor to be invited. With those pleasantries done, WP got to the point. "Gold Bon, I would like your thoughts on how wec can use Shonakian technology to help Earth on Earth, not just in space." Bon smiled inwardly, proud of the way they were doing just that via the good offices of John and Helen. The WP continued, "My own opinion is that we face more peril today here, on the ground so to speak, than from space, and I wonder if you have any suggestions?" Bon smiled and told the WP he certainly did have ideas and he acknowledged the hundreds of legitimate requests for technologies from Shonak that might solve a wide range of problems. He reiterated that they were taking the long view and also the cautious view, before they were ready to provide Shonak technology to Earth. To himself he was thinking of how effective his team had been in defusing the many threats to John and Helen as they pursued their businesses with Shonak help. The thieves and people with murderous intent towards them were all neutralized and brought to justice in a most efficient manner. So Bon was ready with what he thought was a terrific idea, something he worked up just before he left Shonak for the meeting.

Bon showed them a holographic video of a group of men building an improvised explosive device in a dilapidated old building. From the low-overhead video in the split-screen image, it appeared to be in a less than fully developed country. Bon said that they had visibility on many such groups but had not taken direct action since this was not their planet and they had no authority to do so. He likened it to the way people on Earth have watched wild animals chase and devour or maim each other without interfering with "life in the wild," Both Ning and the WP were stunned! They were insulted, of course, but fought the impulse to show it or act out in any way. They looked at each other and could see they were both on the same page. It was clear to them the Shonakians considered them to be wild animals? Ning, at least, thought to himself, "Well, maybe we are, certainly to these people." Bon continued, saying that to Shonak, people on Earth were "life in the wild" and were horrified at times by what they saw but still only watched. Bon knew that historically this was not true but did not want to complicate matters by explaining all the times when Shonak's operations had necessitated them taking direct action, not to mention the earlier days when they kidnapped and medically examined Earth natives.

So he glossed over that for the greater good. He also thought it best not to mention that there were thousands of special interest study groups, what on Earth would be called "clubs," that tracked certain things they saw on the vids and reported their findings for all Shonakians to view, if interested. This made Plus-Five Ops job much easier since they only needed to do analytical work on those areas where there were no clubs. Some of the most popular areas dealt with terrorism, violent criminal activity, and public service/ political corruption. For every city and town and village in every country, and in the world government as well, Shonak had study groups with continuous visibility of these illicit activities. Bon did not share all that with these two.

The WP, swallowing his pride for the moment, asked how Bon thought his Team could help. Bon replied that he could have the terrorists they were watching in the viewer rounded up and contained for Earth's criminal justice system within the hour. Both the WP and Ning sat straight up with eyes open wide and replied that a demonstration of that capability would be an excellent selling point to the various governments who would need to be on board with this sort of thing, to say nothing of the various national and world courts in all their various jurisdictions. Bon said some things into his comm in Shonakian, the first time they had heard this language, which sounded to them like so many hums and clicks and hisses. Neither of them could distinguish anything that sounded like a word, even. Bon then invited them to watch. On the holographic images in front of them sitting there in comfort on the couches they could see a phase ship materialize outside the bomb factory Bon mentioned and the methodical way the Shonakian team – mercenaries apparently for they were not in phase suits – were able to enter the facility and capture the people involved. They also rendered the bomb device safe, using some sort of tool or weapon. A few of the men fought their captors and parts of them simply disappeared, which killed them instantly and with no blood loss, in spite of what happened to their bodies. Bon asked Ning what he wanted Bon's team to do with those captured and he replied that he wanted them brought here for his jailers to take custody of. Within 30 minutes all of them were in cells in the basement of Ning's security headquarters, being interrogated by his security team. Ning explained to Bon, who already knew this, that Ning was not only the Security Director of the World Government but also the Chief Law Enforcement Officer. While these things were not the same, they had tremendous overlap and it was simply more efficient to conjoin the two disciplines under one office. That said, because law enforcement and security are sovereign issues, Ning's role was law and policy development and compliance, mutual support, database integration, not direct action. This arrest and detention of terrorists was outside his authority, but he anticipated no pushback from the local police or courts given the evidence he would provide them. In due course, he would of course transfer the prisoners to the country they were arrested in. The dead were left where they were for the local police and coroners to deal with and Ning ensured that they were notified and he also thanked them for their cooperation. The body parts that would be returning to Earth somewhere nearby would need to be located and removed. Bon told Ning his people would see to it.

This was all very well received by the WP and especially by Marshal Ning. Personally, Ning, a lifelong policeman, was perpetually chafing at his policy role and was hoping that this sort of operation could be regularized at the world level under his command. His thoughts leaped far ahead as he envisioned using Shonak's Earth-native mercenaries, and the permission of the WG and its members, to improve the safety and security of the planet while bringing criminals of all sorts to justice. When the WP asked Bon if he had information on additional dangerous groups on Earth Bon replied that he did. Ning then cautiously asked how many people might be on the list and he was told it ran into the millions, depending on the severity of the malfeasance that might land them on any list.

For the most serious violent crimes, Bon assured them it was well over five hundred thousand. Bon urged the WP and Ning to coordinate with member nation police forces and send him a list of the offenses Earth wanted people arrested for under this special program. Ning, in a purely Earth gesture, told Bon and the WP they would call this Operation Purge. Both the WP and Security Director raised the practical issue that there was not enough police, or prison space on the planet nor were there sufficient court rooms or prosecutors, or even judges. Bon suggested that Earth create special police and special courts to handle those captured under the Operation Purge program; special Purge police, prosecutors, and Courts. The Special World Police who performed the work of making the arrests were recruited from all nation-members of the WG. To qualify they first had to be trained and sworn police officers in their own countries, must come recommended by their most senior law enforcement official, and must pass an additional background check. That check went through the normal Earth databases for review but unbeknownst to the candidates or the public they were also vetted against Shonakian information. As a result, a noticeable number of them were rejected because the Shonakians knew far more about people on Earth than they could possibly guess, and far more than what was in their official records. The cops who were rejected, most without criminal histories of record, wondered why they did not "make the cut" to join the WP.

All the recruiters could do is shake their head and tell them they were not acceptable, thanked for volunteering, and sent home. Few made a fuss rather than invite a deeper look into their past. It seemed likely to Bon's team that number of police had committed offenses that were covered up by other police and so never became matters of record.

Some few of the rejected officers did lodge formal complaints and request for another review, which were of course looked into. Some small number of them were able to make it through after consultation with Bon's surrogates but those few were told they would be on probation and watched carefully. This was sufficient to keep them on the straight and narrow. These were not hardened criminals, after all. It did cause Shonak control and the WGSP to come to terms on what personal and professional behavior was acceptable or unacceptable and once that was ironed out fewer candidates were rejected. Shonak's own bots, described as paid mercenaries and thought quite human, were also sworn in as World Government Special Police and were instrumental in the take-down of the more difficult and dangerous groups of criminals. Bon gave strict instruction to program all the human bots on Earth to avoid any observable display of superhuman abilities. Their internal sensors could accurately determine when they could get away with these abilities and when they couldn't. This was essential to maintaining the secret of their existence.

Those candidates for WGSP who made it through suitability vetting, plus all the medical and mental testing, were duly sworn and sent to school to learn the do's and don'ts of Operation Purge, and to learn how to use the Shonakian designed equipment used in the raids and captures. They were then assigned to squads to make arrests pursuant to the warrants issued by the special Purge prosecutors and judges. The Chief of the WGSPreported directly to the WG head of Public Safety and Security. Unbeknownst to him, this officer was a Shonakian Bot, deeply covered with a family history of law enforcement going back a century. Using him ensured he was uncorruptible, and to ensure his own safety he was equipped with amazing surveillance radars, communications, phase technology, anti-grav, and enormous strength. He needed no sleep and did not need to eat, although he could and did do both rather than draw suspicion. Everyone knew he liked cognac on the rare occasions when he drank any alcohol at all. Since Shonak would be providing video and audio evidence that unequivocally proved the guilt of those arrested there need not be any fear of lengthy evidence gathering or trials. Bon knew very well the legal tangles they would have to navigate. Unlike Shonak, with a single government, here there were many legal jurisdictions involve. Even within a single city there were often multiple jurisdictions from local up through provincial to state to federal, depending on the crime. For this reason, special Operation Purge courts seemed the answer. They all understood that doing this right would take decades just to untangle the jurisdictional issues involved. The WP said he would press for World Government authority to make arrests anywhere in any member country and try the cases in their own special Purge court system. They also addressed the issue of those countries who had refused to join the world government. They would be a natural safe haven for the word's criminals if something was not done to include them in the program. The WP said he would begin the bureaucratic process of establishing temporary authority to begin a "Purge" of criminals around the world, regardless of country. He said he would go after dangerous terrorism and organized crime first so the politicians would have less trouble in approving this new judicial authority. He suspected the last thing politicians wanted was an efficient system to root out political corruption so would not mention that Operation Purge would be going after bent cops and politicians and government officials after the violent criminals were rounded up. To make the idea more palatable he would ask for the system to be authorized for just two years, renewable of course, until there seemed no more need for it. In the short term it was not thought likely that any local laws needed to be changed as the evidence provided with each arrest would fit nicely within current legal jurisdictions and evidentiary rules. The WP also knew the official process would take at least a year to push through the member nations and the WG so he authorized Ning to begin the Purge immediately, thinking it would be far better to ask for forgiveness than to ask for permission. He would rather have that tied up in courts with the perps locked up somewhere than to give the bad guys years of notice while the program languished in sometimes corrupt, or at least conflicted, national legislatures.

He asked Bon if he had any ideas where this number of prisoners could be taken, and Bon was ready with the answer. He replied, "Prince Patrick Island, in the Arctic Ocean north of the Western Canadian Mainland, of the United States of North America, is uninhabited. It is a bleak, barren, polar desert that offers nothing so much as isolation.

The nearest land is some eight miles away over frigid arctic water and that is simply another uninhabited polar desert island. Although the island has a harsh climate" Bon continued, "Shonak will provide heated shelters, fresh water and food for however many criminals accumulate there." He continued to say that at some six thousand square miles, it was large enough to hold any anticipated prison population. He said that if the population were as many as five million, that would still only be 833 prisoners per square mile. He further noted that what wildlife was left there after the ravages of two nuclear wars in the northern hemisphere was minimal. Any remaining animals and birds would either coexist with them or could be moved to nearby islands. Under Bon's plan, he explained, was that these prisoners would be physically separated from the society of honest, hard-working people with no possibility of escape. They would have no possessions aside from the clothes they were given. They would be taken there and dropped off. The island would be guarded from offshore against attempts to free any of them. The prisoners would be fed by air drop, using indestructible, edible food tubes like on Shonak, but each with sufficient calories and proper nutrients for an Earth human for a day. There would be desalination facilities around the island for drinking water. In addition, potable water is available from snow melt throughout the island. Shonak would provide shelter kits and the criminals would be expected to build their own shelters.

Tools and tie-downs and other necessary materials would be supplied with each kit. Lights and heat for the insulated shelters would be from solar panels and a wind turbine on the roof. The only furniture were the cots they slept on. Each hut would have a chemical toilet sufficient for the number of people in the huts and there would be an outside wash basin for where snow could be put to melt for water to wash clothes or themselves with. There would be no jailers or guards on the island. Bon told them the place would be open for business in as little as four months once it had been secured from the USNA, and the few scientists and their support staff there had been relocated. Then, he explained, they needed to first get the logistics in place so the prisoners could begin to live there. The shelters would be fabricated in advance, and staged for delivery and this would take time. And, he explained, it was very important for Shonak to know what offenses they were intending people to be arrested for – so he needed the prioritized list before they could proceed in an orderly fashion. Bon said the localities where the arrests were made would need to house their own prisoners until CRIMISLE was open for business or if he preferred, the WP that is, Bon could wait on the arrests until everything was ready on CRIMISLE. He finished with the promise that videos of their crimes, as well as documentary evidence, would be provided for each prisoner. The prisoners would all be tagged with a non-removable bracelet containing their case number and case history for easy reference. Shonak would provide special readers so officials could play the history contained in each bracelet. And, as independent backup, each Purge court would separately have every prisoner's entire file for use during their trials and for their records.

The WP, thinking fast at what Bon was offering, told Bon to begin the operation immediately with top priority to violent terrorists and that Ning would determine the lesser priorities for arrest, and provide that to Bon within the day. Clearly those people who had committed violent crimes should be arrested first, before the white-collar criminals, corrupt politicians, or government officials.

Bon's team had been listening to the entire conversation, thinking ahead to create the process whereby the vid-watcher clubs would provide the necessary intelligence to identify arrest targets, along with the visual and documentary evidence against them.

Bon's Purge team would match crimes to the list of crimes Ning listed as qualifying for Operation Purge arrest, prioritize them based on their potential for additional death or injury or destruction, and issue the arrest teams their coordinates and identities, as well as their Purge court warrants.

Using funds supplied by Shonak, the WG hastily purchased rights to the Island from the USNA. The few scientists and support staff in residence there were relocated to places of their choosing with a generous cash stipend for their relocation expenses. Shonak provided transport for all of them to the destinations of their choice, along with their belongings. They were government employees and worked for universities and simply returned to their permanent jobs. They were happy to move quickly given the very generous "inconvenience" payment to them and their employers, courtesy of Shonak, but laundered through the WP's office.

This remote, inhospitable place in the Arctic Ocean was an appropriate location for the world's criminal population. Each prisoner would be given two sets of warm clothing to include boots and gloves and told to fend for him or herself. Tools would be provided for them to build their shelters as they needed them. There would be minimal electrical power from the solar panels and windmill on each hut, sufficient for lights in the hut and heat. There were no electrical outlets and no way to tap into the hut's power supply.

Food was air delivered once a day. Shonak hastily put together food preparation facilities in the USNA to make the special food tubes and provide jobs which made the government there happy. The building materials were procured from numerous countries too, further adding to the positive reception in those economies. The promised desalination facilities, Shonakian in design but provided by John Marquis' company, were installed and the water distributed via a heated pipeline system with taps dispersed around the island. The island was under continuous aerial drone and undersea surveillance to spot anyone who may build a boat and try to leave the place or to spot any escape boats or submarines coming in. Fishing was allowed from shore, but no boats or subs were allowed near the island. They would have no weapons so any hunting they did would be done however they could manage. The only predators to threaten them were occasional prowling polar bears and they would simply have to deal with them, rare though they were. The surveillance system would spot any bears swimming over to the island and they could be intercepted and turned away if this became a problem. There was no communications infrastructure for access to the global information networks and no one was allowed to possess any communications devices. The solar and wind powered call boxes on the island were linked only to Operation Purge Control, a police liaison entity staffed by bot "contractors." The call box could not be modified to any Earth frequency so it could not be used to contact family or friends or anyone else no matter how clever the criminal. It was the way they asked for supplies or reported problems, period. There was also no video or audio entertainment. It was essentially a pre-historic environment with no guards or walls or fences. No one lived there because there was nothing to live there for. Six thousand square miles of polar desert, consisting of frigid, wind-swept rock with gullies and snow and ice, surrounded by an ocean that was frozen much of the year. The only people there would be the criminals sent there of both sexes and all those minors convicted as adults. Not all the prisoners would have a life sentence, but the living conditions would be the same for everyone. Convicted juveniles not tried as adults were to be detained in their countries of conviction until their majority and either released or transferred to CRIMISLE as the courts ordered.

Bon was pleased that the minimal infrastructure needed on the islands was in place and fully functional in just forty-seven P-Rots/days. Ning was also pleased that they had been able to push through the bureaucratic and legal requirements in the World Court system to establish Purge Courts and the special World Police agencies were able to create Purge Teams to make the arrests.

Bon provided phase ships to the WGSP with his own mercenaries (all human bots, of course) to assist the

WGSP arrest teams with "tip of the spear" manpower and technology. Once the island was declared officially open the Purge prisoners in national or local custody began their trips to the Island and so began, in earnest, the cleansing of Earth's criminal population. The ones with nuclear and biological weapons were taken first, along with their weapons, then kinetic weapons like bombs and guns, then physical crimes against persons, followed by cyber weapons and malicious code and then political corruption, government official corruption, fraud, employee theft, and so on down the line. The population of the island grew rapidly. Ning's logistical team did a remarkable job in keeping up with the needed deliveries of shelter kits, food, first aid supplies, and the like. All of this with Bon's Shonakian-assisted manufacturing and transport, of course.

Sentences for all those arrested under the Purge were determined by the severity of eac crime. Sentencing guidelines were given to all Purge courts and judges. Because the intent was to rid Earth of serious criminal activity, and its perpetrators, a good many of the crimes came with life sentences on CRIMISLE. This resulted in roughly three quarters of the convict population going there for life. The minimum sentence for CRIMISLE was five years, with local incarceration for those sentenced to fewer than that.

Only a small fraction of the total population of CRIMISLE was there for that, however, due to the nature of the crimes that qualified for Purge arrests. The average non-life sentence was twenty years. Soon, however, even young, fit prisoners with anything more than ten years soon realized they would never see freedom again given the harsh conditions and the brutality of the population there. The public also came to that same conclusion. Those few serving the minimum sentence of five years quickly drew the conclusion that their primary goal was to survive until the day of their release. Many of these people formed their own camps and defended them with complete ferocity. The reality was that since conditions were so harsh on the island, most people considered being sent to CRIMISLE to be a life sentence. The extreme cold, along with high winds, and isolation from modern society, made for dismal living with no hope for conditions to improve. They were warm enough and had food and water enough to survive unless they ran afoul of people who were a threat to them.

One interesting development was that after a few months of well-publicized arrests under this program, many who had committed crimes lined up at local police stations to confess in the hopes that there would be some leniency, and they could be confined in local jails and prisons. Those were often tried in local courts and not the Purge Courts to the advantage of the criminals who came forward. All those captured by the Purge forces were automatically "enrolled" in the Purge system and sent to CRIMISLE to await trial, in absentia.

The world press was having a field day over the perceived violations of human rights, privacy, and due process. The Purge Court system and its process for a speedy trial came under tremendous public pressure. That lasted until the media were supplied with documentary evidence and video and audio of the crimes these people committed or were planning to commit. At that point the outcry shifted away from the process and onto the criminals themselves. Public opinion swayed quickly to support what was going on. Every time a prominent citizen was taken there were outcries, of course, first that they were arrested without due process, and then the outcry was about what they had done once that was made public after the judicial process was over. The civil and political disruption caused by all this was enormous, not to mention the human cost as families and friends reacted to the shock of what people were being arrested for. The World President pointed out time and again that the greater good was being served thanks to their new friends from Shonak. The world's criminal community, both organized and individual, shrank quickly after thousands of arrests and hundreds of deaths on their side, all killed while resisting arrest, or by their own hand rather than be arrested. This did not go unnoticed by the criminal community. Bad guys tried to suddenly turn good to avoid arres, but their criminal past always caught up to them. There was simply no escape from their criminal activity, be it a one-off or a lifetime of such behavior. Within a year Earth had fewer criminals running the streets and far fewer people committing crimes, and far fewer politicians and cops taking bribes to assist their criminal paymasters. The press was having a great time publicizing the arrest of corrupt police.

In some cases, entire police forces were rounded up and taken to The Island. Very often they found themselves there with their corrupt city officials. The population of CRIMILSE grew at ever increasing rates as arrests and convictions increased. Because the evidence in each case was so compelling and so accurate it became standard practice for those arrested under this program to be taken straight to CRIMISLE while awaiting their trials. One or two were found innocent which of course prompted Bon's research staff to look for jury tampering and it was always the case when hard, incontrovertible evidence was presented and yet the jury found for the defendant. Corrupted jurors soon found themselves on CRIMISLE along with the people who threatened them or paid them off. It was not long before it became nearly impossible to bribe a juror, or a judge, or a prosecutor. For a while, in the early days of the Purge, jury trials were even suspended in some countries because it was too hard to find juries who would or could do the right thing. As things got rolling with this program, as the powers that be bent to the will of hard evidence, instead of their desire to stay out of trouble with powerful crime families, there was a kind of panic amongst the crime lords and their kin. They tried to run and hide but Bon's surveillance capability, backed by the civilian groups on Shonak who followed them religiously and knew all their secrets, always found them and they were swept up by the Purge arrest teams.

The new residents of CRIMISLE lived in a way that had not been seen on Earth for thousands of years. Men, women and even a few children convicted as adults were forced to revert to a basic way of living and survival. They did have modern shelter and heat and guaranteed food, but any and all activities were stone age in aspect, with handmade tools from materials found to in their harsh polar desert landscape. And few of these people had any of the skills they needed to survive, much less the desire to learn them.

For many, a climb to the top of nearby cliffs and a quick fall to the rocky bottom proved the preferred alternative. Harsh as it seemed to the people on the outside this actually made life easier on the Island for the convicts since the complainers took the easy way out or they were sometimes helped on their way by people tired of their constant whining.

The snow melt runoff was mostly effective in cleansing the gullies and waves and currents were usually effective in washing bodies off the beaches and out to sea so at least there was almost no need for burial details. Some bodies, hung up on the cliffs or caught in ravines, were left to rot and feed the birds, or what few rodents lived there. Never a place with abundant wildlife, the aftereffects of two nuclear wars in the northern hemisphere effectively killed off the former native species. They were making a gradual comeback in some places, but not CRIMISLE or any other of the polar desert islands. This large, foreign population of humans was the dramatic change to the ecology of the area, but this was considered a price worth paying given the benefits elsewhere. The seeds of survival were there, of course, for those willing to shoulder the burden of living in these harsh conditions with no possibility of escape. Those with less than life sentences had at least something to live for and they did their best to stay out of trouble and not gain any notice by the more violent human predators on the island with far less to live for. There was a kind of self-policing of the population by people wanting to sleep at night without fear, but this was not sufficient to stop this number of hardened criminals with literally nothing to lose. Vigilantes provided the rough frontier justice which existed there.

People were of course killed for their clothing and any surplus was used to buy such things as extra food stolen from one or another, or sex, or some craft work. After the arrests tapered off around the world the population of the island was seen to decrease as people died from exposure, suicide, and murder. The concept had since the beginning been to provide an escape-proof place for Purge criminals to live completely separate from the law-abiding citizens of the world. It was not considered by the authorities to be an automatic death sentence, at least not for the ones who were not sentenced to life there.

So, when certain prisoners turned to wholesale murder, they were quickly culled by Bon's forces. Murder was accepted as a matter of course on the Island but not random, wholesale slaughter of people who were not causing any problems for anyone. Marshal Ning was keen to ensure that however bad the place was, there were still some rules of civilization expected of those living there. Video from CRIMISLE was available to the WP on a constant, streaming basis and some of this video was given to the press to keep them happy. A year into the incarcerations there the WP issued a status report which painted a grim picture: it was a horrendous place which was intended as both punishment and deterrent. For crimes of passion, anger and mental illness, no deterrent will work, but deterrence does work for most other crimes. While all humans are capable of criminal activity, it was hoped/thought that CRIMISLE visibility would be a good deterrent and so the public was shown imagery of life there from time to time. They also let people know the WP had instituted a program of policing the worst of the assaults on the island. After this policy began the random, violent murder and otherwise harsh, unprovoked treatment of people was greatly diminished. Those who acted otherwise were found to be hanging by their necks with their bodies banging against the rocks of a cliff and being eaten by birds. The Purge Police and Bon's forces stayed busy feeding and monitoring the people there but the world turned its back on them. There was no visitation and no communications, and Shonak's "mercenary" bots kept the place completely off limits. No officials went there lest they and their vessel or helicopter be surrounded by desperate people trying to escape. Shonak kept perfect visibility on the place and provided Ning's office and operations center with live streaming video from everywhere on the island. And of course, the public on Shonak was provided live feeds of the entire island all the time, and received with great interest.

It was clear that Operation Purge was working as intended. Gradually, criminal activity all over Earth fell to unheard of lows. The population of CRIMISLE increased rapidly, and the potential for overpopulation was real. This required constant monitoring and support from Shonak and WG assets. Bon calculated that four million was about the most they could reasonably sustain and his natural default to population order and control caused him some discomfort over the Earther tendency to let things take care of themselves - how inefficient was that?! Shonakians abhor inefficiency, but he conceded hat this was Earth's program – he was just doing them the favor of making it happen. To the relief of everyone concerned, the population never exceeded three million. Ning was heard to remark that CRIMISLE had more people than some countries on Earth! It was often noted by those in charge of the program and by the press that there were many more arrested than survived long on the Island. This was helpful in keeping the number of prisoners in the "manageable" range.

Bon knew, from watching so many generations of Earth behavior during his long life, that Earthers would continue to try to manipulate, steal, kill others because something in the native psyche told them the strong should prey on the weak. He knew enough to know that crime on Earth would never become extinct but at least it could be controlled and honest people were now more able to live their lives without the fear that criminal predation brings. The WG, which had seen significant changes in its leadership after the political corruption purges, approved the Purge mandate indefinitely, to include the automatic incarceration on CRIMISLE with speedy, no-jury trials in special Purge courts.

So as people with criminal habits sought to fill the vacuum created by the Purge, they continued to be taken to CRIMISLE to remove the threat they posed to peaceful society. During the initial year of the purges, almost immediately after they began on a large scale, the biggest, most entrenched criminal enterprises on Earth fought back, as did more than a few of the independent players. The larger organizations had up to tens of thousands of people, widely dispersed over many different nations, and connected to their politicians and law enforcement. They were like armies, really, and were the most violently opposed to the Purge. Feeling invincible, they began a series of high-profile kidnappings and intimidations, to include threats to Marshal Ning, the WP, and all the Purge prosecutors and judges. They tried all the methods in their arsenal of contempt for authority which had been working for them for centuries. To their chagrin, these tactics were unsuccessful. With Shonakian surveillance and early warning detection at their disposal, the honest cops and their Shonakian "contractors" knew their intentions in advance, or as soon as they started something. The WP arrest teams would swoop in off phase, suddenly appear in their midst, and capture or kill them using overwhelming force, without advance notice from corrupt cops or politicians. That rendered their successful, centuries-old tactics useless. Not a single hostage was killed and only a few harmed while none of those criminals escaped. Their crime families were rounded up root and branch and taken directly to CRIMISLE to sort themselves out while awaiting trial. Of course, with no weapons on Prince Patrick Island they resorted to fists and stones and wooden clubs and of course the more violent gangs, with the most people, tended to prevail. Then what? What had they won, really, other than a date with the hangman and swinging from the cliffs? And at the end of the day, there was nothing on CRIMISLE but scared, cold, tired, miserable people accustomed to all the luxuries their wealth and privilege could buy. They were also used to getting their way and getting plenty of "respect." There was a growing number of politicians on the Island, too, but all of them were in the same boat, so there were no "get out of jail free" cards to pay corrupted officials for. There was no wealth to steal or offshore banks to hide their money in even if they could. There was food to steal, true, and clothing to take from weaker people. Some folks were killed for the nice hut they had decorated for themselves.

Others were killed or beaten for wood and stone tools they had made. The criminals who were used to using muscle quickly dominated those less violent criminals, but again, what did they gain for themselves, really? The bottom line was that everyone quickly found that they were essentially cast down from their high places to the lowest and there was no way out, no way to live comfortably ever again. Ever. No one was coming to their rescue, and no one was escaping. No sharp lawyers for them either, even though there were plenty on the island. No one had any real power regardless of their past. There were no crooked cops to bail them out. There were plenty of former cops on the island, but none of them had any more "juice" than anyone else. The anger and frustration and resulting violence that took hold was the only effective check on potential overcrowding. Bon's Earth agents were delivering shelter kits as fast as they could be made and packaged for delivery but arrivals were always at risk for sleeping rough until they could put the huts together. A team of enterprising prisoners specialized in hut construction in exchange for sex or boots or food tubes, whatever counted as "wealth" on the island. Some who wandered off to seek safety away from the crowds died of exposure, injury, or suicide.

Suicide was easy. Jumping off cliffs was a quick, relatively painless and therefore popular way to bring their sentence to an end. The formerly rich and powerful all had made private arrangements for escape, in advance, and a good number of their paid mercenaries tried, in the early days anyway, to get them off the island. None of them succeeded. When it became known that the crews of these air and sea and even under sea craft were captured and themselves interred on CRIMISLE the number of people willing to risk their lives to free someone from the island, at any price, dwindled to zero. Shonak and Ning's people kept a close eye on the population and adjusted the food drops accordingly. With the dispersion of various camps they had to monitor the migrations and keep an accurate census so there was enough food distributed to the convicts on the ground. Various gangs tried to take over the food distribution system but with the scattered drops it was not very successful. Food did not come to a central point for distribution but rather was air dropped directly onto the various settlements scattered around the island. Aerial drones, disguised as sea birds, kept a continuous watch on people and the analysts in Plus-Five Ops know what the headcount was everywhere. Because they are simply dropped from the air over concentrations of people they add another ten percent just to make sure seagulls don't make off with essential food tubes before the people scoop them up. Initially, these were of four types. Two vegan recipes and two with animal protein, both of them being Kosher and Halal. The problem with that approach soon became clear as people were beaten or illed for the more desirable recipes. So after a period of riotous behavior over food the menu was changed to a single, vegan recipe containing everything needed to sustain a healthy life. To further put some discipline on food distribution, in answer to the public outcry from the riots they saw on the non-public vid feeds, Ning's forces went in and culled a gang trying to control the food. The resulting public hangings sent a clear message. Same thing happened with clothing and building supplies. It did not take long before the convicts realized they were being watched and that they paid a heavy price for interfering with the intended distribution and use of essentials on CRIMISLE. Ning was pleased that these gangs turned to other pursuits.

Something to do during the day was pretty much top of the list of things to do and there was plenty of time for foraging, gathering to talk over old times, plotting their escape attempts, and the like. Monotony came easy for those who allowed it, but there were many whose personal industry brought them some little bit of pleasure. Little villages sprang up in various parts of the island, but of course given the nature of the population there, these villagers could find little peace. The better their village looked, the more it became a target. Raids by people seeking a better place to live but who did not want to work for it were common and the smart villages formed defensive squads to protect their hard work. Watchers on Shonak were very entertained and the WP who monitored it all were aware of but unsympathetic for the constant struggle of the villages to stay safe from the marauders. For those who craved human company and grew up in cities there was the main camp which looked a bit like a military base given that the only buildings were the long pre-fabs provided by the WP.

Marshal Ning had no compassion for anyone on the island knowing full well what they did to get there but his human instincts told him that the separate villages, away from the shelter city they had constructed, were a positive thing, especially for those who were not sentenced to life there. He was mindful that people tend to find others like themselves. These groups of people with social simpatico formed their own camps in various areas of the island. They pushed and dragged their hut kits as far as they needed to so they could achieve distance from people they did not get along with in order to form villages of like-minded people. They began using the phone box to request a shelter or two or three or ten at a spot they had chosen for their village. This resulted in dispersion around the entire Island, which was excellent for those who wanted nothing to do with the more violent criminal classes in the "Capital." Life there was harsh because of all the violence, but it made excellent viewing on Shonak. Over the first year a variety of camps or outposts sprung up that followed language, national or regional origin, personality types, etc. New arrivals quickly sorted themselves out and were led to camps which could accept them for who or what they were. The social dynamics there were, Ning admitted, fascinating. The world government assigned teams of social scientists to monitor and report on what was going on there in their great experiment in crime reduction on the planet. Every now and then, an adult was repatriated by the special appeals court process if the evidence showed they were only peripherally involved in the actions of their family or crime gang. These people often served the remainder of their sentences in local jails or prisons. Of course, these people were heavily interviewed and filmed by the world press and the tales they told of life on CRIMISLE went a long way towards the deterrence the WG was hoping for.

The government's long-term plan was to simply keep the island under wraps until a hundred years after the last known living convict died. As long as people committed crimes on the approved list for CRIMISLE there would be people sent there and the longer it would remain in operation. The efficiency of the Shonakian-led anti-crime task force and the prospect of a life on CRIMISLE served as a powerful deterrent to criminal activity everywhere on Earth. But of course, nothing can change human behavior in the macro sense, and crime was part and parcel of the human condition.

Bon was amazed that it was taking so long to sink in with people that criminal activity was impossible to hide or hide from. He thought the survival instinct that came with being an Earther led them to do all sorts of wrong-headed things. He noted that there was plenty of love and compassion, too, but even for him, with so much time spent with and watching these people, all these emotions were all so foreign. He was pleased with the way Ning was solving the crime and corruption problem on Earth, with Shonak's help, of course, and continued to support Ning's purges with his one hundred go-teams of bot "mercenaries" and phase ships. With the aid of Shonak technology they created a seamless process of detection, identification, arrest, transportation, conviction, and incarceration for people committing the crimes on the approved list of Purge-qualifying infractions of the law. Ning was very appreciative of course, not the least reason being that the information used in the arrests and convictions was of Shonakian origin. None of it was tainted by corrupted people in the chain of custody and trial.

For all the short and long-term good being done, the Purge also created a tumultuous time for the global economy. Every sector of the economy and of government was impacted as people were arrested under the program. Logistics, finance, communication, local, state, national and even world government all lost their criminal and corrupt populations. It seemed that even corrupt officials were able to perform the legitimate functions of their offices, most of them anyway, and these functions needed to continue after their arrest. This meant doing things with new people trying to coordinate their responsibilities around sudden vacancies on staff. There was also an understandable learning curve before everyone was on board and up to speed. Dissertations were eventually written and college courses were spawned that dealt with the need for continuity of operations plans. They also dealt with the pervasiveness of criminal activity that was so intertwined with their human cultures, in so many countries, and how The Purge impacted everyone's life. And eventually, with corruption no longer consuming such a significant part of community, economy, or government, everything cost less and taxes went down while productivity went up. Happiness also went up once most people lost their fear of being the victim of some criminal activity.

Three years into the Purge, Marshal Ning felt satisfied that "his" Purge program was an enduring success, and he retired. He was by then an international hero, or villain, depending on how your family fared as a result of the Purges. He was replaced by a Canadian of unquestioned integrity (Bon made sure of that) and world peace and freedom ushered in a new "age" of spiritual growth and enlightenment unseen since people had evolved into their uniquely hostile world. It was, with Shonakian help of course, a time when the honest people of the world had every incentive to remain so. While happy at the success of ridding the world of the worst crime and corruption, it was all too obvious to everyone that Shonak had at one time or another (or continuously) invaded every life on the planet with their pervasive surveillance. The WG and the various nations and the population at large turned a blind eye to that while the Purge was ridding them of the evil stench of crime and corruption but when the worst of that was over the subject of the pervasiveness of Shonakian surveillance of Earth and its people began to become a favorite cause for more and more of them at every level of public and private life. The perfect intelligence of the criminal dossiers provided were seen to be double-edged swords. Questioned repeatedly by the press and by public officials, Shonak reps were purposefully vague about the nature and extent of their surveillance, for obvious reasons. They were however specific and adamant that there was no hidden agenda behind their criminal disclosures. Earth wanted to rid themselves of the terrible condition of rampant crime, and Shonak had promised to help them do it. WG did, however, convene a special, high-level commission devoted to understanding and containing, if possible, the monitoring of their lives by Shonak. Clearly, it was said more and more often, and more and more loudly, by more and more public officials, and the public at large, that most Earth human activity was not criminal in nature and it appeared, just as clearly, that all of it was under Shonakian scrutiny anyway. It was particularly galling to many on Earth that Earth had no such visibility on Shonak. OE at the time agreed that did not seem fair and so Shonak installed surveillance gear in the major public places on Shonak and in some teamwork areas, like food production, building maintenance, etc. so Earth could see Shonakians going about their days in much the same way Shonakians watched the people of Earth. This went some distance to placate the more vocal of the opponents of Shonakian "presence" on Earth although most everyone admitted that the "Purge" was worth the loss of privacy needed to make it happen – at the time. But what about now? Earth also was shown the daily activities of CRIMISLE, heavily edited by the world ministry of information and education.

The special commission report on Shonakian surveillance was released to great fanfare. After just over a year of bureaucratic discussion and investigation by more than one committee, followed by more discussion on how to merge their findings into a single report. In the end the result surprised no one. Their findings were obvious. Shonakian surveillance of Earth and its people was too extensive and too intrusive. The recommendations were just as simple. Chief among the recommendations was that Shonak focus its surveillance of Earth on criminal activity as requested by the World courts. They approved this surveillance as it directly benefitted the planet by helping them purge themselves of criminal activity and corruption. Secondly, they recognized that Shonak derived a great deal of pleasure through the information and entertainment of live views of Earth's population, but wanted this surveillance activity to be limited to public areas and public activities; no more collection in private homes or offices. Finally, surveillance of military and other sensitive places and activities was to be stopped entirely, and immediately, and forever. After much public display and discussion, the World President brought these findings and recommendations and demands to Bon and the OE for some official response.

Bon conferred with the OE on this and they both thought it naïve of Earth to make these demands, and how ungrateful, as well, given the resources Shonak had expended in cleansing their world of evildoers and evil doing. They were of course aware that the public face of the Purge was mostly Shonakian and very intrusive, so OE directed Bon to let the WP know that they would immediately curtail their surveillance in accordance with the commission's recommendations. He also told Bon to change nothing. Bon knew full well that the OE would take this decision as he would have done the same. Nothing would change regarding their collection and distribution of infotainment as before, but Earthers would not know things had not changed. Bon sent a note to the Eldest of GT Protection to ensure the Earther gunners never got access to the open, live feeds of Plus-Five. Those gunners were the only Earthers who could ever learn the truth, since they were working on Shonakian gunships, where there were live feeds for the Shonakian crew. They lived in different sections of the ships, in their native resonances, but Bon wanted to preclude any accidental crossover of this information, especially from a Shonakian crew member talking about their continued access to Earth within earshot of an Earther gunner. The gunners were on the distribution list for live feeds of Shonak of course, which was another avenue of inadvertent disclosure, so he ordered that those feeds be edited to ensure nothing of their Earth views made it into those feeds. And so the Shonakians went on as before, and Earthers felt they had achieved a great victory for their privacy and individual rights.

Chapter Nine

CRIMISLE

Bon was very much aware that Shonak's assistance to help Earth rid itself of its criminal and corrupt classes was likely the most significant interaction Shonak is likely to ever have with their cousins at Plus-Five. Shonak is doing nothing less than reforming the culture of Earth, planet wide. He understands very well that they are not changing human nature, but they are working on the worst of it, which of course is to their benefit. Shonak is also aware that they are providing a more stable social environment, which impacts everyone in a positive way. What that means, Bon accepts regretfully, that without any change in their deep-seated behavior, the reduction of crime on Earth will be temporary. Without the constant support of Bon's Purge teams, it is doubtful Earth can even sustain the program. As he sits at his screens, working all the action on Plus-Five, he is also very much aware that his name is irrevocably linked to this effort.

In reviewing the history of Operation Purge and CRIMISLE it was clear to Bon that it has been an absolute success. He also saw what the most troubling episode was, the one event which had the potential for damaging the good relationship Shonak enjoyed with the people of Earth and their leadership. He asked his team for a detailed write-up with some analysis of that event. He wanted it to be viewed as a Lesson Learned for use in the education and training centers. It would not be a standalone lesson, but certainly an important part of all the lessons they are learning about planet reformation.

This is the report he received.

> *Report for Gold Bon, 305058.141.61.05.01, Eldest, GT Plus-Five. Subject: Bot incident on CRIMISLE, 306111.71.17.90. Background information, analysis, and details of the incident are provided by the vid-watch club on Shonak that specialized in watching DiMonte's activities. The author of this report, Unassigned Gold Din, 304785.220.31.30.03, wrote the following "Earther-style" at the request of the club's members, proud of how well they understand the culture there, its language and various idioms.*
> *Begin text:*
> *Operation Purge incident on CRIMISLE involving a bot and convicted Purge criminal Salvatore Luigi DiMonte.*
> *Background: Three months into the Purges and the opening of CRIMISLE the World Government was focused on the task of cleaning up the planet by exercising police jurisdiction for criminal cases involving serious,*

World Court listed Purge crimes as uncovered and reported by Shonakian surveillance. By this time in the program a good start had been made against the world's most violent terrorists and criminals and were beginning to move against corrupt politicians linked to their illegal activities. An impressive number were already on CRIMISLE *but there were still many vicious criminals at large and the operations continued to round them up everywhere the WG was recognized, and elsewhere, too, as determined by Marshal Li Ning, the WG Director of Public Safety and Security.*

Operation Purge had come as a great shock to the criminal classes who had always and often prevailed against law and order. Few were better at violent crime against persons than Luigi Salvatore DiMonte, age twenty-one years at time of arrest. He was a resident of Naples, Italy, UNE. As he reached adulthood as reckoned on Earth, he had already proven himself to be exemplary, within the strict confines of what his Naples crime family considered exemplary. He was absolutely without conscience in his dealings with the people he was stealing from or beating or murdering. He was careful to pay off the politicians and the local police, stayed away from the wives and sweethearts of same, but otherwise was a ruthless enforcer of his crime boss' agenda. He was doing fine until his arrest, which went typically well. A World Cop suddenly appeared in front of him and used his Shonak-supplied steel mesh to render him helpless. Even before he could react the net was drawn tight, preventing him from moving or even breathing heavily. His trial took less than an hour but would have taken days had every one of his crimes been shown to the special Purge Court of Justice in Naples. The prosecutor only selected the most serious of his more serious crimes. The rest of them would have been gratuitous. Within 24 hours Luigi found himself on CRIMISLE, with a life sentence. He was accompanied during transport by twenty-nine convicts from his same Purge trial court, so he knew most of them, but there was not a great deal of conversation. Videos from the inside of the transport are uneventful. All of them were scared, hungry, and angry, and trying to put the best possible "tough guy" face on all of it. CRIMISLE was still a new concept and not much was known about it other than what the press had revealed; it was cold, isolated, and you were almost always there for life and there was no escape. Of course, Luigi Salvatore DiMonte believed none of that. We know from what he said to the man next to him during transport, a member of the same crime family, that they may have been sentenced to life on "The Island" but they would not be there more than, he reckoned, 24 hours. Their crime boss told all of his lieutenants and soldiers that they would be immune from arrest by local police and if nabbed by the new World Government Specials, they would be immediately busted out of whatever prison they landed in, including CRIMISLE. He did note that it was troubling that they did not spend any time in the regular jail in Naples, where they could have expected quick release, but concluded that their boss was biding his time to get them out of Purge custody. As soon as they arrived at the unofficial "capitol" of the Island, they started looking for their family's designated island contact person to organize his escape. There were crude signs at the drop-off point that directed new convicts to various groups, like "Italians" or "Irish" or "USNA/

USA," etc. People tended to gravitate to groups where they felt comfortable and where there may even be people they knew. He and his colleague followed the "Italian" signs which soon branched out into camps for "IT Nord" or "Roma" or "Campania," and the like. They found a few of their family members when they reached Campania and, to their disappointment, they also found some of the local Naples police they knew were on his boss' payroll, along with several court clerks he knew. Their high hopes sank immediately, and Luigi told his friend that he preferred to go it alone, to figure it out. He walked away from the Italian camps to see what he could find. He finally settled in "New York" which he thought would be better since no one there would know him or even, probably, of him. He reacted with great concern some days later when new prisoners from Naples told him his crime boss had killed himself and his family rather than be arrested. He spent the next year doing everything he could to survive, still looking for a way off the island, but not with any confidence. He and everyone else there wanted to leave but the only way out was a final cliff dive onto a rocky beach or a fatal fight with somebody who decides he wants your shoes more than he wants you to live.

Luigi was keen to learn, and he took pains to befriend the various players and power brokers in the New York settlement, such as they were. CRIMISLE was a lawless, ungoverned but largely uneventful place, where people were cold, unhappy, and bored.

195

Most of the convicts were men and the few women on the Island were "claimed" and protected. A few had returned to the prostitution they practiced early in their criminal careers, while they still had the looks and the energy to pursue that lifestyle. With no guards on the island, there was only the strongest and loudest and most daring to determine the fate of those around them. Food was the principle commodity, but it was plentiful enough, and while it was not delicious, it at least kept everyone alive. Rumors floated around that someone had managed to produce some alcohol from collected tubes, but he had yet to see any, much less try it. Everyone had enough clothing and those who combed the beaches for suicides managed to collect substantial amounts of it, but found it had little value in a place where everyone had what they needed. People who managed to make things, like furniture or cooking utensils were able to trade their wares for more food or a better fitting pair of boots, etc. Other than that, there was no commerce to speak of anywhere on the Island. Treeless and with very little vegetation of any kind there was no industry, nothing much, even, for the artistic to create with. Luigi was fond of saying, "They don't call this a Polar Desert for nothing."

His chosen home on CRIMISLE, New York, was growing. The many criminals from that city and state were naturally attracted to it and there was much socializing. They converted several shelters into club houses where they could play games and talk about better times. They all talked about escaping, but nobody had any way to make that happen. Who could beat Shonakian surveillance? They remember their CRIMISLE briefing before boarding the transport – the island is watched day and night, above ground and under water. There is no escape. Don't waste your time. So naturally it was something they all spent hours talking through the various things they would do if they escaped. Then someone would say they needed to cross a thousand miles of frozen tundra, bears, wolves, and last but not least, Shonakians, before they could be "free" and even then, the Shonakians would find them and kill them. Many people simply accepted that it should be called "suicide by escape."

He had been thinking of how to get off the island since he landed there and now more than a year later, he came up with his course of action for escape. He had recently seen a repatriation. Someone whose sentence was up, apparently, he never knew really why they were taken, but as he watched, a World Cop suddenly appeared on the ground and grabbed a person who clearly did not see it coming. The cop, holding the person tightly, stepped back into a doorway, likely part of a Shonakian phase ship, and then disappeared! He knew that for such a thing to work, the people on that ship needed to know precisely where the person they wanted was, and then wait for a time when they could get close enough to make the snatch and grab. For that to happen he reasoned that they had precise intelligence on where everyone was at all times. Or at least where the non-lifers were. He had no clue how this was achieved but he knew it had to be true. It was the only way. And the only way he could think of for that to happen, was to have informants among them, with communications. He knew that had to be true, but he had not seen anything even remotely like a radio or telephone in the hands of anyone. The WP comm device bolted to a pole outside the desalination plant was the only way he could think of for the passage of information on some prisoner's whereabouts but how could that work? By the *time an informant walked to the comm box, who knows where the person would be?*

197

Luigi was correct, of course in his assessment of informants on the Island. There was continuous Shonakian surveillance, but he had no idea it was human-appearing robots, not human informants, doing the watching and listening. Luigi could not know they were mostly there taking infotainment video, but this also served to keep tabs on the convict's whereabouts. In spite of what he didn't know, Luigi knew he could not make his move until he figured out how the cops did this. Then he needed to figure out how to become one of the people snatched up. One unlikely scenario piled on top of another. But, what choice did he have?

He was careful to leave people alone who were not there for life, but he was also careful to watch them closely. He relocated to a camp for non-lifers, in spite of the fact he was not one of them. His first few attempts resulted in being unceremoniously ejected by groups of these people until he found one that was more inclusive, and it was predominantly Italian, which helped. He was happy to be among his own people and also happy to be in a much less intense environment. Over in the lifer camps it was always dangerous to go to sleep for fear of what might happen to you by people with literally nothing to lose. If your cot looked more comfortable, or if your food looked tastier or if your comments were not to someone's liking it was all too common to have to defend yourself against some sort of assault. As tough as he was, Luigi wanted to survive this Island. In the lifer camps it was only just a matter of time.....

He told no one in his new camp about his desire to escape and did not have a plan yet, anyway. There weren't many options. People who were there at the time, including Luigi, remembered the armada of heavy-duty helicopters descending on the newly established CRIMISLE to whisk away the people whose relatives had paid handsomely

198

to get them back home. There was no way to get a message in to the island to let them know they were coming so they just figured on showing up, landing, and putting out the call for their chosen people. There were no guards on the island so they did not have to hurry, after all, right? The sixty-one helicopters landed wherever they could find a flat space and were quickly swarmed by people desperate to escape. The pilots ran out of ammunition quickly when they shot the people clamoring onto the choppers who were not on their list. These pilots would have been killed themselves except they were needed to fly them out of there. Promises of huge rewards were offered to pilots to take them away. In a few cases pilots who refused were thrown to the ground and people jumped aboard with pilots of their own to whisk them away. There were a number of helicopter pilots on the island, after all. Then it was a giant free for all but finally, one at a time, the choppers left on their own when too full or the pilots too scared to remain. Unfortunately for them, a WGSP gunship appeared in their midst and blew them all out of the sky. All of them. One at a time, with the people on the Island as witness and also the Shonak live feed, and it was sent to the world media for them so see as well. When the gunship phased away and disappeared, those on the island who survived by not getting on a chopper were glad, for the first time since landing there, that they were alive on the Island. Luigi was also pleased that someone had knocked him over the head in the mad scramble and he missed his chopper. So Luigi knew that approach was not going to work, even if he could somehow call for airlift or sealift or even a submarine to get him out of there. So he decided on escaping on his own, completely by himself, since he knew he could not trust anyone to help him without them reaching out to others who would also reach out to their friends, etc. Pretty soon he would be trying to escape with the entire island.

199

Biding his time, watching for a break of some sort, some insights into the informant networks, he witnessed a fight that opened his eyes. Nothing more dangerous than clubs were being used during this fight over whose village back home had the most beautiful women. One man, trying to move away from it, was smacked on the head with a club with such force, Luigi expected to see bone and brain matter sprayed all over the shelter. Instead, the blow made a kind of hollow ringing sound and while the man went down he did not have the injury Luigi expected. He watched as the main antagonists took the fight outside. Everyone else followed to watch. Alone with the unconscious man, he began to go through his pockets, looking for whatever he might be able to steal when the man began to fade away and sink into the floor! In just a few seconds, he was gone! When people began filtering in after the fight, they asked where the hurt guy was and Luigi said he had gotten up and left. They all looked at each other thinking they must have seen him but had to accept that since there was no other way out of the shelter. While they were all chatting *about the fight and the missing man, Luigi sat there realizing that Shonakians had infiltrated the island with informants. So that was how it was done! He knew this would be his answer for an escape once he sorted out the details.*

CRIMISLE Section, Plus-Five Bot control, was of course aware of the entire incident and when the bot phased away for its trip back to the desert maintenance facility, Eldest Bon was immediately informed (as he would no doubt recall). He was told one of the CRIMISLE bots had sustained a blow to the head and knocked unconscious, momentarily. When he was in Luigi's tent the departure program kicked in and Luigi

200

was the only witness to it. Bon said it was dangerous for Luigi to know about their human bots. Fortunately, there were no communications from the island to the mainland but there were people being repatriated and one of them might learn of it and might talk so Bon ordered the elimination of the threat posed by Luigi's newly acquired knowledge. The next morning Luigi was found barely conscious and unable to speak. The village had a doctor, also a convict, who examined him and said he had suffered a stroke. His prognosis was that he would not recover. The villagers then did what they always do with the terminally ill. Luigi was carried to a distant ravine, downwind, and thrown into the deepest part for nature to dispose of. One of them was heard to remark that what the birds didn't eat the summer snow melt would wash away.

End Report.

Bon filed the report away and went on with his

missions. He wondered when the next episode with bots would arise and considered briefing Ning on their presence. Just to get his reaction. Then he thought this was not the time. There had never been "the right time" to do this.

Chapter Ten

A Shadow Falls

For the people of Earth, CRIMISLE was a painful reminder of the ever-present potential for any one of them to turn bad. It evoked the sordid side of the human condition and they were mindful of their nuclear and conventional wars, inquisitions, holocausts; all manifestations of the worst they had to offer. They also reflected on their family or acquaintances or neighbors who had been caught and shipped to The Island. It was a place of and for raw emotions and the news images from time to time as released by the WP simply added to their overall angst about the place. When they were being honest, Earthers could always see something of themselves in the convicts there and it was painful for them. Generally, though, and socially, it was a place better not spoken of and best forgotten. Every night various news feeds were allowed to present no more than sixty seconds of "news" from that cold, distant place but after a while, with nothing ever changing, it received only passing attention and the people of the world were able to turn their backs on it.

For placid Shonakians, on the other hand, with no emotional ties to these convicts or what happened to them, this condensed version of Earth's depravity was much more interesting than the now less interesting, law-abiding Earth population, as a whole. Some CRIMISLE scenes were censored, of course, since there was still concern that at some point there might come a change in the demeanor of the Shonak population from watching Earther behavior and violence. So far, this had not happened. OE wanted to keep it that way, of course, so they continued to cull the more violent scenes from the feed. To facilitate this censorship, live streaming from CRIMISLE to the Shonak public was simply not allowed. The vid-watch clubs that sprung up on Shonak for the dedicated observation of allowable CRIMISLE feeds were no different than the other clubs, all over Shonak, that focused on certain peoples or things or places on Earth. They learned the various languages of their favorite groups, their dress, their religions, their jobs, their family ties, their romances, their successes and their failures. Great viewing for all concerned. Bon knew this, of course, and reflected that Shonak seemed to be getting more from the relationship with Earth than Earth was getting in return. Yes, they had helped rid the planet of rampant crime. They had also provided wonderful technologies for cheap, potable water from their oceans. They helped clean up their oceans, too, and they improved food production and distribution. They also helped fight numerous diseases which had plagued them for millennia. But for all that good, and more, Earth people's lives were still being exploited for their entertainment value without any recognition or, to Bon's non-commercial point of view, commensurate return from Shonak.

During one of their periodic chats via comm link the new World Security Director, a Brazilian named Jorge, told Bon that he was totally happy with the way anti-crime program had been working but he was concerned as well about the effort to combat any threat from hostile space aliens. That program had been in full swing now for several years and there had been no sightings of the alien presence that caused this force to be established in the first place. He asked Bon for his thoughts as his masters in the WG were growing restless over the continued expense in manpower with nothing to show for it. Bon said he understood the problem and likened the issue to one of an 18th century lighthouse keeper on Earth. When the light is successful at keeping ships from sinking or getting damaged on a rocky coast, nothing happens. For the bean counters of the world, concerned about cost-benefit relationships, "nothing happened" is a hard sell to keep the lighthouse fully funded.

The defenders of the lighthouse concept needed another metric to justify their existence, when the obvious logic of the mission is not enough. In this case Bon suggested that he try the tactic that the very visible presence, in space, of a credible deterrent, was the probable reason they had not seen any recurrence of the alien ship "peeking" into their space. In Bon's view they had little to worry about from inter-stellar aliens, the distances were just too great but if some did show up there was an effective defense force in place. Then there was the real threat from wandering asteroids that might impact their planets, and the space force was an effective defense against that threat. In fact, they could go and hunt them down, at least the ones that had the potential to interfere with Earth's satellites or Earth itself. Another potential use for the space force, Bon offered, was in reaction to rogue combat forces on Earth, like the long-continuing issue of pirates on the high seas. The WG grew stronger every year in relation to the member states, and surely the space force could be integrated into the defense of peace and prosperity at home. "Just a thought," said Bon. And to Jorge, what a thought it was! Within the year all the legal and political hurdles were overcome, easier now that political and corporate corruption was largely a thing of the past, and the space defense force was successfully integrated into the World Defense Force. They had numerous successful operations behind them in just the first few months, leading to even more "bad actors" dead or on CRIMISLE. The fact that the space force had Shonakian participation with Shonakian weapons was a huge force multiplier. In fact, one Shonakian gunship with Earth human gunners had more maneuverability and firepower than any ten dozen gunships with Earth-only weapons and personnel. A phase ship can travel invisibly off-phase and suddenly appear on target, engage and destroy, and disappear again in the amount of time it takes to blink two or three times. Earth ground forces, close at hand in advance of these coordinated responses, then swoop in and count the dead, capture or kill any survivors who resist or fire on them, and in general take over on the ground with humanitarian assistance, infrastructure building, and general peacekeeping and nation-building activities as needed. Often it is the simple introduction of food and shelter and electricity generation and employment that reintroduces these patches of outlaw societies into their nation and the world community. With most local warlords and gangsters gone people just want to pursue peaceful lives raising their families. The men who remain after these raids are put to work building their communities and those who don't sooner or later find themselves permanent residents of CRIMISLE.

And so good relations continued for more than one hundred years. Bon worked with many

World Presidents and Security directors in that time and he was always eager to keep their relations cordial.

It was the S-Rot 306210 on Shonak and the year 2373 UAY on Earth, and Bon was 1152 S-Rots of age. Bon was thinking how pleasant it had been for his team that relations with Earth were so harmonious. So very many years of peace and prosperity on Earth and good relations between their two very different planetary cultures. Actually, he mused, Earthers had begun to finally establish a global culture which simply added to their tranquility. Given their temperament they were bound to continue to find reasons to disagree with each other, but it was less and less likely that these disagreements would lead to warfare or even hostility. They had finally adopted a culture-fair legal system for the entire planet, which also helped a great deal. There had been backlash, of course, by people with vested interests, either financial or dogmatic, but they were a minority and their voice was not influential. In the past this would have led to violence to force their message out there but with the threat of CRIMISLE looming for these expressions such actions were few and far between and dealt with swiftly. Bon was thinking he would take a trip "up there" to refresh his image with people of the current generation and inspect his desert bot facility while he was at it. No sooner had that thought entered his mind than his comm panel lit up with several emergency notices. They were all about the same subject. One of their Earth-human bots had been found "dead" in his apartment in the USNA and during an autopsy they discovered it was a machine. The preliminary x-ray triggered its self-defense mechanism, which made it disappear. The bots always did that since they were programmed to half-phase away from Plus-Five's vibration, if they were able, and go to their maintenance facility out in the Sahara, then phase back into Plus-Five so they could be fixed. If their propulsion system was inoperative, they remained half-phased out and could simply remain there until retrieved with no one on Earth aware of it.

Of course, the medical examiner assumed this was some sort of Shonak thing but without a "body" they had nothing to examine and could not prove anything. Fortunately for her they always video their autopsies and its disappearance is clearly shown on the vid. The police were called immediately, and it quickly boiled up to the WG where the WP and the Chief of the World Police were calling Bon about it. They were as curious as they were angry because naturally this called into question Earth's relationship with Shonak and Shonak's relationship with Earth. To the Earth authorities looking into this suspicious death, they thought, here is a guy, living alone in his apartment, some sort of sales rep, who apparently died from something or other. His landlord, not having seen him for a couple of days, went in and found him, apparently dead. He called 9-1-1, and the ambulance took him to the morgue. During the check by the medical examiner, he just disappeared right there on the table. What up with that? Clearly this was some sort of Shonakian surrogate since there was no Earth science to produce this result. A body disappearing on an exam table – or anywhere else – just is not going to happen. So why did this happen? What possible benefit could Shonak be deriving from a lowly sales rep machine on Earth? What possible purpose could it have and oh, by the way, how many more were there? And where were they, and what were they doing? So the World President, trying to get ahead of this story and knowing it was too late for that, immediately commed Bon, with his police chief at his side, with all the above questions, demanding to know what was going on.

Bon took a second to review the summaries before he took the WP's call. The Bot apparently suffered a primary power failure in its apartment and a recovery team got there too late to prevent the body from being taken away. When its power began to fail why didn't it immediately go to the maintenance facility as programmed; likely something to do with its power problem? Bon also learned that the medical examiner took an x-ray before the thing disappeared, but what was it doing there in the first place? And the entire thing was on a video already being broadcast around the planet.

Bon answered the President's call, "Hello Mr. President, what can we do for you?" He tried to sound casual, as if he knew nothing of what the call was about and succeeded, but inside he was bracing himself for the President's response. The WP was cordial, and Bon was thankful for that, but of course, after telling Bon what happened, he demanded to know how and why these things existed on Earth at all. He also demanded to know how many more of these machines were on Earth and where all these "people" were right now, thank you very much, along with an explanation for what they were doing on Earth in the first place?

While still on the vid call, Bon commed over to Bot control and the recovery people to have them track down that x-ray and all file copies and destroy them if they contained any information about the construction of the bot. Too late to grab the video. The WP, hearing Shonakian for the first time, simply thought Bon "coughed" as he gave those instructions to his team. That's what condensed Shonakian speech would sound like to an Earther. Then Bon told the WP that he would arrive in his office shortly, in person, to explain the entire program. When he got there in his phase suit, the Security Director was also in the room along with the Military Defense Director and a few dozen other staffers. "Hello, Your Excellency," Bon said. "I regret this incident terribly as it will no doubt cloud our friendly relationship, for no purpose, really, but I do understand your outrage. What can I do and what can Shonak do to make this right?" The honorable Benjamin Colon, From Panama, the current rotational World President, was curt and just a little angry when he said, "You can tell me why Shonak has machines impersonating Earth humans. We are friends, are we not? Why do you feel the need to infiltrate our society like this? You know how we are. We are not happy with intrusive, undignified, illegal corruption of our values, our privacy, and our laws."

Bon received an earpiece message from his team about the X-Ray. On review it did not show anything of their technology. In fact, it did not show much of anything and there was no need to destroy it. He nodded in assent, which they could see clearly.

"Mr. President," said Bon, " I understand your concerns and I can say that we were going to tell you about them but there never seemed like the right moment." Bon continued, "I can assure you that these bots, as we call them, have been with you since minus 1945 UAY as you reckon time. So, for thousands of years they have been your companions to do all manner of things for you. It will interest you to know that our bots were the major players in the arrest and transport of the most dangerous criminals during the first few years of the great Purge. This saved the lives of many of your courageous human police who would surely have been killed in these dangerous and deadly confrontations."

The WP responded, "Well, we're grateful for that, of course, but you never thought to tell us before now? And why, pray tell, have you kept them here knowing that we now have the technology and stability to not need their 'help' anymore?"

Bon replied, "You are right, of course. We will withdraw them immediately. But please know that they are doctors, agriculture specialists, manufacturing geniuses, artists, friends, benefactors, to make life a little easier for you and to help us understand you better. You would not be feeding your 15 billion people today without our help, which we are happy to provide, by the way, at no cost to you. I know your people don't want to hear, that but there it is. These bots perform tasks we would perform for you ourselves if we could live comfortably on your world. And of course, that is why we never felt truly motivated to deactivate them. They are very useful. And as I mentioned, let's not forget the operations to rid your planet of rampant organized crime and political corruption.

Our bots were key to the collection of the

airtight evidence and identification of the guilty parties and in rounding them up for transport to CRIMISLE. Thanks to bot-assisted law enforcement, Earth is a much more wonderful planet for you to live on and raise your children." He continued, "However, I want you to know, Mr. World President, they will be gone within 48 of your hours. I would like to tell you they can be gone immediately but it will take time to extract them from your presence. Please allow us to do this intelligently. We can of course cause them all to simply disappear but there are issues I'm sure you can understand. A heart surgeon should be allowed to finish the operation before departing your world, for example, and a pilot should land the plane first."

WP paused at that, thinking he would spin this to the people of Earth, that he demanded immediate withdrawal and they complied. He will minimize their numbers in his public statement, and trust Bon to get them off Earth over the next 48 hours.

Bon told the WP he would call him back as soon as they were all recovered and out of their society and then phased away and returned to his office.

When he got back to Shonak Bon requested an emergency comm meeting with the Eldests of Exploration, S&T, Manufacturing, and Infotainment, and OE if he could make it. When these Senior Golds were all assembled, he briefed them on the situation and told them he had no intention of removing every bot. He said they were just too useful to them, and to Earth, in so many ways. He reflected that this catastrophe was predictable and the bot population on Earth was, indeed, far too large anyway. It had, he admitted, just gotten out of hand. Every time one of their Earther vid-watch clubs requested a bot to cover some sort of location or group or whatever, they simply complied. That is how the population had grown to just over two million of them scattered all over Earth, guiding activity that provided maximum entertainment value to their own planet of devoted Plus-Five followers on the infotainment networks.

The bot who "died" simply failed for some mechanical reason, poor maintenance or poor QC on the components. First time this had happened in thousands of S-Rots. He considered Shonak fortunate this had not happened sooner or more often. Bon told S&T and Exploration he was very disappointed in the fielding of that bot. On the bot removal issue Bon said the ones remaining in active status must be the ones with the deepest cover stories and full bona fides as humans. That meant longevity for the family line, full blood and DNA profiles, fingerprints, iris scans, every aspect of identity verification in use on Earth. The maintenance of these machines needed to be absolutely perfect. They should also be stable in the most important of their access requirements. This meant keeping tabs on Earth S&T, military development and plans, space operations, and high-level government access. When they all decided amongst themselves which human bots were to remain, he wanted the list, which should not be greater than fifty thousand. This meant the loss of a great many surveillance assets meeting vid-watch requests, but that could not be helped. He prepared an announcement for the general public to let them know some of their favorite collectors would be deactivated within two P-Rots. He also directed the Plus-Five team that the bots that were not remaining needed to be out of their normal posts within two P-Rots since that is what he promised the World President. He acknowledged that disposing of that many bots would be a challenge, but the newest, best, and brightest should be deactivated and stored in their Earth maintenance facility. The remainder should be melted down and put in containers and flown into the sun. He had insisted that this mission be totally bot-run with no Shonakians involved. He wanted no confrontation with Earth defense outfits. Bon asked for a final report giving the number of bots collected and destroyed, and how many were placed in storage. The final list would be of those remaining in place, living their lives, as before, again, not to exceed fifty thousand. If staff could not decide which to keep, he would help them make those decisions. He said he would personally tell the WP when this task was completed. He also told everyone that he had directed his team to survey the desert storage and maintenance facility for detectable signatures and to fix any that were leaking out. He considered that facility to be key to Shonak presence on Plus-Five. He suggested that there would be an all too human response to the bots, but that this would fade over time once they realized how helpful they really are. He knew the emotions of the people of Earth and that they would be outraged that Shonak infotainment collection reduced Earth to some giant theme park or zoo for their amusement. It didn't matter what good was done by them, no matter how beneficial, the infotainment feeds would be the lead story and the emotional straw that broke the camel's back as they would say up there. When memory fades on this, generations from now, perhaps they can be reintroduced if Earth wants them. His mind was already fast-forwarding to that time and it would be a good touch to finally add the bot issue to their formal, written treaty that spelled out what Shonak could and could not do on Earth.

Bon then viewed news on Earth, which was focused on the "enemy within." Clearly this would be a multi-news-cycle story. Exposes were emerging from all over the planet about roving bands of people looking for the "aliens" who had taken their jobs and unfortunately innocent, real people were being falsely accused of being "Shonakian bots" and assaulted. Quite a number were being asked to prove they were human and some crowds were going so far as drawing blood, chopping off hands, and even killing those they suspected of being an "alien robot scum." This made for great viewing on Shonak but was not beneficial for their relations with Earth. And of course, those people committing these criminal acts soon found themselves on CRIMISLE. How ironic, Bon thought.

Then the WP took an unexpected step in calling all his space gunners home. This was a popular move among his constituents, and the WP was of course lauded for it. The military was not so pleased, but of course Shonak complied, taking them all to Earth military bases to drop them off. They were unfairly treated in some places as traitors to Earth and the ones with tattoos, who had worn them proudly, could not show themselves in many locales. They remained on military installations away from the public while their age tattoos and dots were surgically removed. The gunships returned to their stations with the guns now on fully automatic mode. Should any alien ship return, the guns will now simply fire automatically, given pre-programmed instructions that were designed to give that slight edge to the potential bad guys in the hopes that they aren't.

A dangerous but unavoidable consequence of the removal of the human gunners.

For the next one hundred-plus days a wave of emotional frenzy overtook Earth, and the Earthers were ill-equipped to deal with it. The people of Earth had not known how many incorruptible bots were in law enforcement positions but found out quickly enough when they did not show up for their shifts. Key operational supervisors were suddenly not there. Key defenders were suddenly not there. Key air support was suddenly not available. Key communications were suddenly not working. Information networks began to break down. The people left holding the bag were actually not angry with Shonak. Rather, they were angry with the irrational response of mob mentality that did not care about the benefits of these bots. They did no harm and did a lot of good. Didn't matter. Following the public sentiment, irrational as it was, the WP forbade any contact with Shonak until further notice. This frustrated the scientific community, especially, since they had continuous, daily communication with Shonakian counterparts working on a host of projects that would benefit Earth. Didn't matter. It was high time, they thought, to develop these solutions on their own. Independence became the watchword, key word, first word on anyone's list over this transition to Earther self-dependence.

Slowly, from all over Earth, a picture emerged

of what it was going to be like for them without the bots, or any Shonak assistance. So many people in key positions who were needed to provide for 15 billion people living there were suddenly not there. Few wanted to admit that they had relied so heavily on "aliens" for getting the job done. And Bon actually agreed with this sentiment. He had spoiled his Earth cousins and in so doing had let them down. Earth governments slowly took stock of their situations and began to work on solutions while others preferred to think about getting bots back onto the planet. The thinkers among them realized humanity had a choice: buckle down and get better at taking care of themselves or suffer the consequences. This was hard to do with food shortages just around the corner, but necessary to their long-term survival. If they did not do this, the thinkers among the leadership thought, they may as well just accept their status as "entertaining pets" of the Shonakians. Perhaps there was some way to get themselves weaned off bot support while learning from them what they were doing to help Earth? Unfortunately, it was not possible to ask for any continuity information since all contact with Shonak was forbidden, and the bots were gone. Not even the Shonak Liaison Office, cut to one person to deal with emergencies, was allowed to talk with them without WP approval.

All of this was of course providing wonderful entertainment for Shonak vid-watchers. They took pride in their historic assistance to Earth but found the results of Earth's frenzied, emotional overreaction over the loss of their bots to be highly entertaining. Riots in the streets on Earth, accusations reminiscent of the witch hunts and trials in Earth's distant past, it all came boiling to the surface. Suddenly Shonak was a dirty word regardless of all the good things Shonak had done for the planet at no cost to them (other than a loss of privacy, of course, which no Shonakian was emotionally attached to.) Shonakian lives were an open book for anyone to see and had been since they were hatched. Every word spoken and every word written by them was recorded should it ever be needed.

To be in synch with the World President's desires, Bon decided to completely cease all direct contact with Earthers of any category or status. This included support for the Purge and CRIMISLE. Let the Earthers feed their own on that bleak prison island He instructed the remaining bots on Earth to lie low and just live their lives without any resort to their bot-powers of phasing and flight or super speed and strength. Reserve that for situations which were life threatening and when used, harm no one in the process, and jeopardize no bot identities, especially their own. In fact, if a lifesaving action was likely to compromise a bot, Bon ordered the bots not to involve themselves. He was especially interested to keep the long-standing bot families going because when Shonak was invited back, and they agreed to return, those bots would prove to be extremely useful. It was Solar Rotation 306210.

For the next fifty years, which was nothing to Shonak, but half a lifetime on Earth, there was no unnecessary bot activity on the planet and no communications between Earthers and Shonakians at any level. The human bots who remained were artificially aged and died. They had appointments with duly certified bot doctors and were given autopsies after death, if necessary, by bot coroners. The ones who were to "die" in places where there were no bot operations to preserve their identities, ensured they died in situations where no bodies would be found. Children were introduced, and they were replaced gradually by successively older bots until they matured. At that point they aged more slowly, "married" other bots of the outwardly appearing opposite sex, went through pregnancy, birth, all of the natural cycle-of-life events, and went about their lives without calling attention to themselves. They did well in business and fitness activities but did not overdo it. They did not get involved in professional sports where it may be hard to hide their superior physical abilities. They also wanted to avoid injuries that would bring them in front of Earth native doctors. In all that time none of them were discovered.

Earth, meanwhile, saw a great deal of

trauma. Gradually increasing over the century following cutting off ties with Shonak the scarcity of food and water gave rise to black markets and other criminal behavior which in turn saw a rise in all kinds of criminal activity. Political corruption gradually returned as well as it was another all too human response to trying to make everyone happy, beginning with the family at home, friends, constituents, etc. Civil unrest that boiled up into civil war in some places strained the military and police who were at least initially inadequate to the task of such large-scale operations. The world government was stretched to the breaking point, but it held together in spite of the fact that it would have been easier to just give up and give in to the pressures resulting from overpopulation and lack of food. Strict birth control measures were put in place all over the world but were hard to enforce. They did manage to reduce the global population by a third, to ten billion, but that was largely achieved by voluntary birth control and by attrition through unfortunate starvation and euthanasia. With fewer assets in the military and law enforcement violent behavior began to show up once again which contributed to the much needed but tragic population decline. Bon marveled at how Nature on Earth had a way of "thinning the herd" in times of adversity. Truth be told, the sense of safety and security provided by Shonak had made Earth soft and it was a hard lesson for them to learn to become self-sufficient again, even if modestly so.

When a hundred of their years had passed, Bon thought this was sufficient time to have healed the wounded pride on Earth. It was now Shonakian S-Rot 306310 and Earth year 2473 UAY. There was hardly anyone alive who remembered the bot fiasco and there had been the usual sine waves of reaction to it over this century. Fear, witch hunts, hatred, loss, hard work and more hard work and now Earth had attained a full measure of self-sufficiency, because they had no choice. Because he judged they were ready, Bon reckoned it was time to contact the sitting World President to see if they were really ready, emotionally and politically, for the reestablishment of good relations between their worlds. So he made the call to the special phone, knowing full well it was in the top left-hand drawer of the World President's desk. It took a while for the President to figure out what was ringing and where it was, but she managed to retrieve it and answer it. She said, "This is World President Alice Palma-Chambers, who am I speaking to?" Bon identified himself and bid her a pleasant day. That was as much salutary banter as any Shonakian could abide, so got right into it. "Madam President, we were wondering if Earth would agree to reestablish a formal relationship with Shonak." He continued, "It has been one hundred years now and from our viewpoint this is perhaps sufficient time for old wounds to have healed." He paused to wait for her response. Uncharacteristically, she was at a momentary loss for words, so Bon filled the void. "We are thinking that we should modify our formal relationship with some sort of treaty update setting boundaries that both worlds can live with." He paused again, thinking that this President was just completing the first year of her now three-year rotation as WP. She was 56 years old and only knew about Shonak from lessons in school and stories told about the aftermath of their abrupt departure. Her specialty was agriculture before she went into politics and so was a bit different from her predecessors, who tended to have had the more devious mindset of career politicians and lawyers. The WP finally responded, "Mr. Bon, what an unexpected pleasure. I have always thought we acted a bit too hastily when we discovered your robots but after a great deal of trouble here, it was actually a good thing for us to go through that period of separation. We needed to become more self-sufficient, and we have done so, clearly, since today there is no help from Shonak, and we are alive and well. World government is stronger now than you would remember it, which likely makes it easier for us to deal with Shonak as a consolidated planet instead of a collection of squabbling equals. I agree that the time is good for us to have this discussion but let me get with our Executive Council to sound them out. You probably remember this as The Group of Eight, but it is now much more collegial and all-inclusive, not just something the major donor nations provide. How will I contact you when we're ready?" Bon said she merely needed to pick up the handset she currently held, squeeze it, and speak into it. What Bon didn't tell her was that the handset was not the primary device, or that it was on all the time. Her office was wired for audio and video from Shonak as part of their Infotainment feed so not only Bon would hear her, but so could all of Shonak!

President Palma-Chambers immediately opened a conference call with the EXCON. She briefed them on Bon's call and request, and initially most of them were negative about renewed contact. She thought, from their voices, that this was more a result of the surprise of it, rather than any deep thought about it. More than one opined that there could be some tech transfer benefits. Earth could certainly use some help in the production and distribution of food and potable water. The mood of the people was impossible to assess, but they could begin to raise the issue to see how the public felt about it. And so they did, and in the days that followed the response was almost universally favorable. The "Shonak Period" of Earth history that lasted just two hundred and two years was taught in school but no longer a part of active memory, more of a legend, really, like La

Belle Epoque, or the Renaissance, or World War IV, so why not? Strictly regulated by mutually beneficial treaty, of course. Palma-Chambers said she would be asking for delegates from them for a treaty convention that would draw up the terms for any future relationship. There would not be any tourism of course since no one could visit Shonak but perhaps it would be "cool" to have Shonak back in their lives in some way.

Some thirty P-Rot after Bon's initial call, the WP called Bon directly. "Mr. Gold Bon, thank you for this device, and thank you for asking if we are ready and willing to reestablish contact with your world. The consensus here is that yes, we are, under the right treaty terms, ready to proceed. We want to prevent any renewed dependence on your assistance and prevent the wholesale violations of our privacy that was evident when you were expelled. We also want to guarantee that you will not flood our planet with your surrogates, your bots. While we may find uses for some types of them we are not prepared to allow the sort of numbers that were here previously. In addition, we want your bots here to be less human in appearance, so we can clearly see that it is a machine and not a person performing some task or other." Bon thought this reasonable and indeed this would keep these bots from being "discovered" by accident as was the case before. Of course the bots who had remained all this time would continue as before but completely under cover. He told the WP that the "new" bots would be clearly identified as machines; different in appearance from humans but humanoid in aspect since the bipedal shape was the most useful for locomotion and for using tools, etc. He said he would send her depictions of the design they came up with for her approval. Bon also suggested that all the bots color-coded by function. For example, a medical bot would be white with a red cross and crescent, if that was OK with her. He also suggested that a traffic control bot be safety yellow for visibility. That is the sort of thing he would ask his team to come up with for her approval. He did not tell her that everything the bots did and everything they witnessed would be part of Shonak's infotainment feed. No reason to burden her with that. The WP agreed this could work and said she was eager to see the proposed bot designs. Bon added that they would accommodate any suggestion they had relative to bot appearance and also that each placement would be by mutual agreement. He also said that they could discuss the price of these bots during their treaty negotiations. She said this surprised her, because Shonak was a cashless society. Bon explained that without cost the requests would likely get out of hand and he did not want to create machines that put Earth humans out of work. He only wanted to send bots to do things humans could not do safely or would not do for whatever reason. He offered to donate the revenue of all bot sales to Earther charities designated by the WG, or to fund the operation of the WG itself. Bon said that was all up to them. Bon asked if they were willing to accept his personal bot as a negotiator for a treaty discussion. He said it would be an exact replica of his own body. The WP said she would allow it but preferred to deal with a real Shonak human and not a machine. She did acknowledge however that a Shonakian in a phase suit would be a bit off-putting, but they all would like to see one, "once" so suggested that Bon come in a phase suit to introduce his personal surrogate bot, then he could leave the bot in his place. Bon thought this was a fine idea. She also said that at least at some point in their talks and of course for any formal signing ceremony she would expect a delegation with their world leader and senior staff in addition to Bon. Bon agreed to that and they signed off with the promise that she would contact Bon when they had chosen their own negotiators and had established a date and place for the talks. The WP then went on the news feeds with all of this information, to mostly positive reviews and commentary. When she was finished with her broadcast Bon visited her in her office in his phase suit. To her credit she did not panic, but she did let out a little scream but recovered quickly. The first thing she could think of to say was, "Are you Bon?" Bon said he was and also said he wanted her to see a Shonakian in a phase suit before anyone else by way of honoring her position and also to get her opinion on how Shonakians should visit them. He then phased in his bot so she could see the difference and saw the advantage to the bot immediately. First of all it did not look at all human, so could never pass for one, not an Earth human anyway, and second, the phase suit made her uncomfortable. The odd sensation of the phase differential when she moved close to Bon in his suit made her nauseous and asked him to leave, with all due respect. The real Bon phased back to Shonak, and the Bot asked her if there was anything else they should discuss before he went back to Shonak. She offered "Bon" a seat, asked her assistant for a cup of tea, and they sat down to get acquainted. The WP asked her staff to come in to meet Bon so she could gauge their reaction and it was all positive. They spent the better part of an hour asking Bon questions about Shonak and their culture. When Bon's bot departed, he bid them a good day and said he thought they were off to a great new beginning.

Bon let all the Golds and most especially the OE know of the latest developments with Plus-Five. He cautioned that as Eldest, Plus-Five he would be adamant against jeopardizing the upcoming talks and treaty implementation negotiations. Bon would negotiate the treaty personally with the WP. He also said it was absolutely essential that in any dealings with Earthers by Shonakians that no mention be made of the use of bot-generated information on their live feeds. He informed them that the woman who held the position of World President, their OE equivalent, was from Sweden in the UNE and would not rotate out of the post for twenty-five of their months, some 750 p-rots from now, and his goal was to finalize the treaty while she was still in the post. When Bon conveyed this message to her she said she concurred, knowing her place in history would therefore be assured. She would not be just another rotational president, but the one who brought Shonak back into their lives on Earth's terms! The WP then asked Bon a curious thing – would the Shonakians be amenable to tourism? She said she understood the Law of Nativity, but perhaps Shonakians could visit Earth with their personal bots and Earther humans could visit Shonak in special phase ships made of Plus-Five materials? Bon thought this was an idea with potential merit, but perhaps there was an easier way for an Earther to visit Shonak. If they could operate a human-appearing bot made with Shonak resonant materials, they could explore Shonak without the discomfort of phase travel. She said that might work and could she try it? Bon asked her to wait for the construction of a bot for her to "pilot" around his world, and then she could give it a try. He asked for a full length 360-degree photo so they could construct a bot in her exact image for the people of Shonak to meet and interact with. What a great experiment!

As his team set to work constructing the WP bot on Shonak and her special viewer and operations suite on Earth Bon reflected that people who lived only a hundred years or so faced a completely differently lifetime dynamic than people on Shonak. She wanted to begin her "tour" immediately while Bon was content to do it right, even if that meant more time to get it right.

It was 306311 and the necessary equipment was ready on both planets in just under ten P-Rots or days. Bon called her to say that the necessary headset and controls had been delivered to her administrative assistant. Instructions on their use were included with the equipment. Her personal bot on Shonak was waiting outside the office of the Shonak Our Eldest for her to walk in and introduce herself. The WP thought this a bit ambitious but said she was ready to try it. Bon's bot phased in and showed her how to use the equipment. He stood on her desk while she sat in her chair as he fitted her headset. Then took it off to explain the controller and then asked her to call Bon to say when she would like to begin. She picked up her little comm device and told Bon to stand by. Then she put on the headset with video and audio, turned the bot "on" and saw what her bot was seeing. She was standing on a bare floor in a bare-walled office facing a door. A mirror had been placed there, as Bon said it would, so she could see her personal bot. It looked exactly like her! She reached out and knocked on the door in front of her – carefully. Her bot simultaneously knocked on the door, which looked like a set from Alice in Wonderland, it was so low. She saw the door open automatically, and she bent over to walk in and stand up. That was not as hard as she thought it would be! She stood facing a Shonakian in a chair, no desk, and the Shonakian smiled as they do. This was not a pretty sight for an Earth human to see, with his black teeth and reptilian face, but the OE looked friendly enough to her, and she approached and held out her hand for a shake. The OE took her hand gently and welcomed her to Shonak. Unbeknownst to her, this was streaming live throughout Shonak to huge audiences. The WP said, formally, "As Earth World President, I greet you, Our Eldest of Shonak, in the name of the Planet Earth. With your amazing technology we can not only renew our friendship but also raise it to a new level of personal visits with surrogate bodies to overcome the Law of Nativity." OE smiled again and said, in perfect World Standard English, "Madame World President, I greet you in the name of all Shonak, and agree that we are at the beginning of a new era of friendship and cooperation." He paused, got up from his chair and said, "Now let me show you our beautiful world, so much like your own but also so different."

They spent the next several hours touring

on the ground and in the air, since her bot was anti-grav equipped, and she was completely in awe of their world and how well they husband it. The OE was a bit surprised at the sheer joy expressed by the WP and of course this is a foreign emotion to Shonakians.

Being brilliant, however, the OE could see that this could quickly get out of hand. He told the WP that these sorts of excursions to Shonak by Earther bots would be very limited, scientific events, and not tourism.

He told Bon that the last thing Shonak wanted was a bunch of Earthers with Shonak bots to be flitting around their sedate, serious, purposeful planet. He did think it would be perfectly OK for this technology to be used on Earth itself so people could flit around on their own planet to their heart's content. He let Bon know and asked him to work it into his tech transfer regime.

When the WP was back in her office, flushed with the experience of a lifetime, Bon appeared in her office, as a bot, and they talked about what she had experienced and where that might lead. He told her that they were not interested in repeating the experience the WP just had. That was for her alone, for now anyway, as thanks for agreeing to renew their open relationship. He did say that Shonak was willing to provide Earth with individual anti-grav suit technology so they could all enjoy personal flight as she did, but here on

Earth. She was overjoyed by that and said it would be a huge advance for them in the area of travel for both business and leisure.

Bon also asked her to consider updating their treaty that spelled out what was permissible for their bots on Earth. In response to this the necessary meetings were had and the Earther delegates' positive tone showed how the mood of the various peoples on Earth had changed about Shonak and their robot "army." Most of the opinions voiced were nostalgic about bots, not critical, and the key argument for them was the Operation Purge successes a century and more prior to the present. CRIMISLE was in fact still being used to incarcerate their most violent criminals. Within a year of Bon reaching out to Earth, the new treaty was signed and a permanent working group established to develop solutions to issues like bots and where they were needed most, what they should look like, who would pay for them, and how much, etc. Bon noted with pleasure that the companies he had started with Helen Manners and John Marquis were still in existence and doing good work. He proposed that all the bots and the anti-grav suits be the property of Shonak but leased through John's company, with a fee to them but the bulk of the proceeds going to the WP general fund.

The anti-grav suits paved the way for anti-grav drive for all their aviation needs. John's original company, founded now centuries in the past, was given exclusive rights to the Shonak anti-grav technology and its manufacture on Earth, became the largest company on the planet, by market cap, and Bon was pleased for them. With the backing of Shonak they were able to ensure that the technology for suits and for aircraft were not abused by one country or another benefitting at the expense of others. It was kept affordable for everyone. The CEO's of the company always controlled the majority of voting shares and were always bots. Odd that the richest person on the planet was of Shonakian origin, if not by body parts. Bon smiled at the thought. This woman was also the world's greatest philanthropist.

On review, a year on Earth later, in 2475 UAY, 306312 on Shonak, he noted with satisfaction that the hundred-year ban had not resulted in any permanent harm to their relationship with Earth.

Chapter Eleven

Bon's Examination Of Time

The S-Rots marched on, and with Earth relations back on track for now five of their generations, Bon found himself busy with all the many Plus-Five things that were ongoing but thinking more and more about the unsolved mystery of the time-shift. It had never been understood, much less solved, and so in the S-Rot 306412, at the age of 1354, Bon was lately thinking long and hard about the most significant unsolved mystery in Shonakian history; something his name would forever be attached to. How to explain the sudden temporal shift on Plus-Five? No living Shonakian could think of another single unresolved issue of such magnitude. The Law of Nativity had never been defeated and was accepted as absolute since they had never known a time when it wasn't. This time shift, on the other hand, was something they all had witnessed and still had no clue about. This they could not accept, even after three hundred and five S-Rots of study without any resolution. Not even the wisp of a productive thought had come from a focused collective of the brightest minds among already stellar thinkers!

Shonakians are past masters at getting answers, for nearly everything, and Bon thought himself perhaps the grand master at this game. And yet, nothing . . . .

For Earth of course it was a non-event. They lived through those three thousand two hundred and ten S-Rots/years and so for them there was no time shift. No answers there. And for Shonak, in the three hundred and five S-Rots since that temporal event, no useful theories had been offered, and no answers had been found. The most amazing aspects of the shift were the fact that it did not simply take place as some sort of cosmic clock reset. The time actually happened on Earth but did not happen on Shonak. Or, Bon thought, maybe those years were the ones Shonak lived through and Plus-Five had simply "caught up" to them? And yet, unbelievably, Shonak's sensors recorded those intervening years on Plus-Five, but no living Shonakian had any memory of the events which happened there in their own lifetimes, and none of these years had been taught to them in school, even though Plus-Five history was a popular subject. They needed that in school since it helped them understand their live feeds once they were old enough to have access to them.

None of this made any sense. Nothing any of them on Shonak had ever heard of, read of, or even theorized, allowed for such a thing to happen. Why didn't their brains register these things like their computers did? There had to be an explanation and it seemed likely to Bon that if they ever found it, it would not be one they would understand, which meant they wouldn't accept it.

It was, however, unique in Shonak history for something to be worked on this long, by so many brilliant minds, with no resolution. By now it should have been solved or believed to be unsolvable and taken off their mission task list. Bon privately thought this might mean it was unanswerable. On the face of it however, this was simply too "out there" to ignore. It cried out to all of them for answers, but it had been given to Bon to sort out. He chafed at that. One instant Earth was a backward, undeveloped collection of tribes and city states and the next Earth was modern and space faring! Based on the collective wisdom of five hundred millennia of deep thinking on Shonak about every possible aspect of things, their only firm conclusion on this "thing" was that it was simply not possible. And yet it happened. It therefore had to be some sort of trick, some sort of illusion, some evidence of a "higher power" mocking them? Bon thought that would be a conveniently unscientific and therefore unprovable explanation, but it was also therefore unbelievable so could not be offered on Shonak as any sort of explanation. This may be a way to deal with it? It was its own proof? But proof of what? It certainly happened. For people not living through it was it not like gravity or the Law of Nativity? Just accepted for what it was? Food for thought.

Bon was very much aware that he remained tasked with determining what happened, how, and why. No OE in the intervening S-Rots had taken this task off his "to do" list. His success with the management of the Earth relationship may have pushed the Time Shift into the background but Bon could see that his priorities had now changed with the long-term normalization of relations with their Plus-Five cousins. He did not want his legacy or the legacy of Shonak to be tarnished by this one failure to get an answer.

While he had focused on Earth issues as the Eldest of Plus-Five, his Grand Team Time had continued its work on this task. Thus far, however, they had not come close to developing any new theories. There were plenty of aspects to the changes on Earth, and the other resonant planets, to examine, and they had been, but there was no clue as to how Plus-Five advanced suddenly into their future, much less doing so without Shonak also advancing. Their future remained Shonak's present?! Everyone, including Bon, was simply left shaking their heads. So what happened, how did it happen, and why did it happen? The teams examining the data covering the time shift simply had no answers. Literally one segment they were looking at a primitive civilization and the next it was thriving and highly technological. Like someone spliced a bit of tape from one era to another. That would have been odd enough but for those years to have actually happened on one version of the planet and not another was an unexplained and perhaps an unexplainable phenomenon.

He left his second Eldest, a younger Gold, in charge of Team Plus-Five and began to concentrate on this Time issue which had been neglected for far too long. He gathered his Time team in a conference room and reminded them that they had two answerables: First, explain the time shift and what it meant to Shonak and second, is it possible to travel through time either forward, backward, or both? Then he opened the floor to discussion from all colors. He was hoping for a good idea to emerge that might give them a direction for their inquiries. His own study of the time shift event had produced no "Aha!" moments, so he was eager to hear other approaches from the team. Surprisingly, it was a Red who suggested something that was at least different. His study of Plus-Five and of Prime revealed that at least one aspect of "time" did not happen equally for them. This sounded strange, but it boiled down to the fact that their vibrational difference meant that their planets did not revolve around their star at the same rate. Their orbits were slightly different, with Shonak being slightly farther from its sun than Plus-Five was to theirs. This meant it took Shonak a fraction longer to make a complete circling. The difference was not great, but it added up. He calculated that since the speculated date when the planets formed and established their orbits, assuming they were identical at the time, the difference today would be a little more than three thousand P-Rots, which was very close to the length of the time shift. In fact, and he said he was thinking out loud here, it may be easier to peg the formation of the planet by backward calculation from the 3210 P-Rots which suddenly occurred! The young Red continued, that it should now be a matter of inquiry as to the orbits of Plus-Four, Three, Two, and One to see if there is any consistency to this difference in "time" for them. Bon's eyes widened at this, and his mind raced! Everyone looked at this young Red with thanks for a new insight. It was clear that everyone in the room was mentally calculating the new channels this opened for their inquiry, not the least of whom was Gold Bon. He thanked the Red for his good work and ordered everyone else to get to work using this new lead to some good effect. He asked the Red, also named Bon but 306300.250.20.10, to work with the team as a priority to test his theory and ensure it is an actual fact. Bon then went to his office to ponder.

Assuming there was some intelligence behind the time shift, what was gained by it? What was so wrong, after so many millennia, in the difference in the number of times the planet had gone around its sun? Who cared? Who even knew? Bon sat alone in his office, mulling all that over.

If what the Red said was true, then the planets would not be in the same place relative to their orbits. But when they traveled from one version of Prime to another, they did not pop out in space but rather they came out somewhere in the same vicinity on the higher version than they were on Shonak. Not exactly the same place, but close. So, if one is true, then how could the other be? Perhaps this says something about Time itself? Or is there some gravitational or energetic "connection" between the six versions of this planet that draws them together and draws their phase ships and suits to them when going among them?

Bon was thinking that both Shonakians and Plus-Five natives experience time in measured fragments they have given names to. Shonak has its S-Rots and P-Rots where Earth has its years and days. Shonak has portions and segments where Earth has months, weeks, days, hours and minutes. But surely that that is arbitrary and as such is merely a distraction from what Time really is? The sun, for example, does not know or care what name is given to it by any thinking being. It is what it is regardless of any label put on it. Bon can, however, accept that Time is continuous, irrespective of the artificial fragmentation people may use to measure it. From when, though, did Time start? He knows people on both planets break time up into manageable pieces to help them regulate their lives. But that does not change Time in any way from the continuity it represents. And if that is true, then it is perhaps the resonance differences that matter not the time differences. So when the shift happened it was a matter of vibrational synchronization, not time synchronization. It had an effect on time, but that was not the intent, only a consequence, and likely not one of terrible importance. It also seemed to cause a rift in the fabric of the universe itself, which enabled that alien ship to appear briefly in their universal resonance?

If Shonak had not had visibility on Plus-Five at the instant of the event neither planet would be the wiser and there would not be this terrible conundrum over it. It is only a big deal because they are making it one! Bon shook his head and kept that to himself, pending more work by his team.

After twenty P-Rots Bon's team asked to speak to him personally, as a group, for a thought session on their most recent discussions. What did this time shift event say about Time itself? Did it or would it or even could it help them understand the nature of Time and would this lead to ways to achieve time travel in any meaningful way? It seemed to Bon that a clue to this lay in the fact that Earth actually lived through 3210 years that Shonak did not. During that living, time on Shonak stood still? He rejected that notion as insupportable. Apparently, anyway. If people on Shonak were suddenly frozen in place for two of their generations, why didn't they dry up and blow away? Did everything stop? Including the nuclear reaction in their star? And in the entirety of the universe at Prime? He shook his head as his mind reeled against the facts he was presented with and on the other side, logic and common sense. He did understand that the event itself proved such a thing was possible, but how was it possible and how did it come about? Just because it could happen did not mean it should or would happen. This suggested to Bon that an intelligence of some sort must have been involved. Bon remembered his contact with Plus-Five, Earth that is, and the fact that every one of their cultures believed in and worshipped some sort of supreme being. These Supremes were known by different names and had different characteristics in dress and personality and activities and the demands they made on their worshippers, but they all were believed to possess powers far beyond those of mortal men and women. Bon wondered if perhaps this was somehow relevant to the time shift? He wondered if he should reach out to that god or whatever it was he met not so long ago, his time anyway, for some thoughts?

Of course, Itself heard this as it ran through Bon's brain and knew all the underlying thoughts Bon had and was developing. He did not think it worth any effort to respond. Why did they care so much? Why does Bon care so much, Itself wondered? What was it to Him? No one was hurt and in fact no one on Earth was even aware of it. That the people of Shonak had seen the shift with their surveillance devices also did not hurt anyone. So it was Plan Neutral to Itself and to The Divine. And again, why did they care so much? One of six worlds in a vast set of universes had some visibility over the other five and that seems to have made all the difference to the issue here?! Without that, there would be no issue at all. He was tempted to reach out to Bon to relieve him of the mystery but he was aware that the work he and his team and indeed many others all over Shonak were doing was important to them and he did not want to rob them of that experience and the opportunity for their spirit partners to Learn from it. So, he did not do anything, did not interfere at all, and for Itself right then the matter was pushed back into the category of background "knowing." He also mused that the issue of

Shonakian bots on Earth with near total visibility of their actions was akin to the presence, in every Shonakian, of a spirit partner who had total visibility on what they were doing and even thinking! He wondered what Bon's reaction would be if he were suddenly to find out, like when Earth suddenly found out about the invasive Shonak bots. Itself was well familiar with Bon's spirit partner and resolved to connect about this after Bon's body gave out. No more direct contact with the IPLF Bon. Itself's final thought on the matter was that his effort to synchronize vibrations led to a rift in their existence which another existence had noticed and tried to exploit. He found that far more interesting than the time shift and promised to avoid that sort of thing in future feeling sure that it would definitely not be "Plan Neutral."

Bon was at some level feeling this negative vibe from Itself and thought how difficult it would be to tell others about this line of thinking. How could he bring forth any thoughts or ideas or even solutions to their current questions if they came from a "god" who is known to Earth but not to Shonak. He had to believe in it as an entity because he was there and heard it speak and saw what it could do. He did not have to believe it was a god, however, merely a being from another race with the ability to do what it was doing. That was much easier for him to grasp. But while Shonakians routinely watch their Earth cousins perform religious rites and rituals, and see and hear them pray, they have no such motivation to do this themselves and absolutely no emotional connection to these things. After all the millennia Shonakians have been watching religious practice on Plus-Five there had never been any sort of cult or club or study group formed to look into or emulate religious activity. The inherently slow vibration of Shonak makes it impossible for any Shonakian to communicate with spirits and so no religious or spiritual tradition has ever existed on their planet. Before their contact with Plus-Five they did not even have words in their language for "religion," "god," or "prayer." Conversely, the high vibration of the planet at Plus-Five, at the top of the physical resonance spectrum, allows a fairly universal feeling if not practice among the people there that "higher powers" exist and that prayer actually works to achieve what is prayed for. At least some of the time, that is, depending on the will of the god prayed and/or sacrificed to, or the devotion of the people praying, etc. So, thinking this through, he determined to keep his own counsel on it. He would only come forth with this notion if he could see any benefit from it. And his experience from his past dealings with the entity calling itself, Itself, told him that his thoughts had been heard and went unanswered so he must assume there would be no help from that direction anyway.

Bon spent his efforts in thought over questions like, "what do we make of Time as a concept?" Is it an actual, tangible thing? Was it a noun or a verb or both? How much does it weigh? How big is it? Or how small? If it runs forwards can it also run backwards? What about sideways? Does it have a top and a bottom, and does it have sides? Just what is it? The fact that it is one thing on Shonak and another on Earth seems a good example of how much Shonak does not know about it. There are constants in time, like the time it takes for Shonak to orbit its star. Various atoms had fixed internal activities that were consistent across the entire population of those particular atoms under the same conditions, and in the same native resonance. But what about the same atom at a different resonance? The internal activity of various molecules was also consistent given temperature constants and so forth. So, since time is so pervasive, perhaps it would be helpful to find some situation or thing that does not have time or is not in any way impacted by time? And what might that be? He sent a quick query over to Eldest S&T, then sat back and continued to think. Two basic interrogatives were going 'round and 'round in his mind – how did the time shift happen and why did it happen? The how of it, when answered, would likely also indicate the who of it. They know when it happened, and they know what happened. They also know where it happened, pretty much, and that exhausted the basic interrogatives of who, what, when, where, how, and why. He was still waiting on reports regarding the impact of the time shift on Pluses-One through Four. He suspected the team would tell him that Plus-Four was the second most impacted, down to Plus-One which was the least, after Prime. The key, apparently, and thanks to the young Red on his team for this, was the difference in rotation the six planets made around their suns due, perhaps, to the variations they have in native resonance. But why does that matter? Perhaps that is only a symptom of the issue and not the core of it. Not the reason it happened, just the metric that decided how much it would happen on the various planets, except Shonak. Apparently, following this line of reasoning, Shonak's annual trip around its sun was the baseline, after which the other five must synch. That just simply sounded absurd to him. It must therefore point to a powerful intelligence of some sort behind the shift but there had to be something else to the calculus here. Must be. Right? Bon had spent his entire adult life correcting errors in judgment based on too-little information. He was wary of committing the same analytical sin himself now. There was so much evidence that time exists in many forms but no evidence which helped to solve the puzzle of the time shift and its relevance to Shonak.

This was not the first instance Bon could cite where he had contemplated Time as a thing to be studied and manipulated -- if at all possible. Just as Shonak technology had found a way to manipulate the very vibrations of living and unliving things he thought it was worth their (and his) effort to find a way to bend Time to their will as well. He reviewed again his earlier writing on the subject and found he had tentatively determined some things about it for himself. He figured that future travel, that is, traveling to the future, may be interesting but of no real value. Assuming it could even be accomplished. There are just too many variables. If a person from year one visits the year eleven, for example, that visit will show one of the many futures that are possible ten years hence. All the random causations which resulted in that particular version of the future are not "locked in"; how could they be, since they are linked to random actions? This means that every time you might visit the same time in the future it will be different. It may be similar, but it cannot be expected to be identical in every respect. It would therefore be entertaining to make these visits, but it could not be of any real use to know what some random version of the future will look like. He thought it might be a good topic for the education and training centers. He could illustrate the thought thusly. A person from year x visiting year x-plus eleven can see that a certain Team is working on a variety of projects in furtherance of a continuing mission. He returns to his time of departure and reports that the Team is hard at work on some specific projects. A year later he visits the same Team at the same time in year x-plus eleven only to find that there is a different Eldest in charge and the missions being worked in that Team are completely different. And that is only one situation in year x-plus eleven when of course there are so many, many other situations in play across their population and team structures. An entire planet of human and natural activity means that the whole canvas of movement forward in time is nothing more than a huge number of random variables with untold cause-effect relationships playing out as they will.

Then the next time those variables get a chance to play they likely will behave differently against each other, creating major or minor but certainly exponentially different outcomes. This also means that the farther into the future one looks, the more different it will be since there will be more random causation and effects in the mix. Looking into the future one minute from now will likely be nearly identical but looking a thousand years out will be significantly different.

He also speculated that visiting the past would not be as fruitful as people like to imagine. A person from year one may find himself observing year minus eleven, but he will not be able to interact with anything or anyone in that year since his present self does not exist in that year and there is no known way to make it exist there. He rejected utterly the notion of a time machine that could do this in the same way a phase ship can alter its vibration. He pointed out to a colleague that the analogy falls apart when you consider that the Shonakian inside the phase ship does not change phase, only the ship. So if a time ship were constructed and changed its time stamp it would not change its natural time stamp, the one it was created in. The ship and the person inside would not really exist in the past, and so would the past even be visible? Perhaps, in the same way that a phase ship is visible in another vibration of existence, but it is not there naturally and so cannot achieve anything other than observation? Such a visitor to the past might be able to see a younger version of himself through visual sensors in the ship, but there would be no way to interact with him. It is sort of a twist on the Law of Nativity. You might call it the Law of Time. It would hold that everything created or born at, and therefore into, a certain flow of Time cannot exist at a different one without getting there naturally, and only and always forward, never backward. Through the artifice of a time machine he therefore may be able to witness events, which can be an invaluable historical tool, but there would be no way to interact with the events of history. So, it would be a research tool and nothing more. It would make more sense, in that case, to simply send a camera ship back to view events, or forward if deemed of value, rather than to send a person at all. But this was all just way too "out there" and speculative, based on little more than wild guesses. And none of these thoughts helped move the ball forward on the issue of the Time Shift he was charged with sorting out. He called up the now famous vid of the time change over the place they now know as London, England, UK, UNE. In the first frames it is a village and then in the space of a single frame it is a megalopolis. So, the inescapable conclusion must be that the time shift occurred "instantly." Their scientists have slowed it down as far as they can and the change shows no transition from one frame of London to the next. The change was instantaneous, not just appearing so. The second striking fact is that the 3210 years which "happened" from one image to the next actually happened, as their own surveillance data show. That historical data did not exist in one instant, and then it did. How did it get there? Who put it there? Surely that did not happen over the course of 3210 P-Rots since those P-Rots were unknown to any living Shonakian. The last thousand plus of those years would certainly have been remembered by living Shonakians and yet it wasn't. But the imagery from Earth for that time was there. How could the database have information that Shonakians did not? The word "magic" came to his mind, a word that did not exist in their language till their association with Plus-Five. Magic and faerie tales and ghosts and witches and demons and gods were all the constructs of fertile minds on Earth seeking to explain things or take the blame for things they need excuses for. Without the science to explain their moon, it became a god or goddess watching over them. The Sun became a powerful god in a flaming chariot riding through the day from horizon to horizon. Better not make these gods angry! Shonakians never needed to create such nonsense because even before their science they never had to fear anything so never needed to make up stories to make them feel safe or to explain away things they could not figure out. He knew he was just going around in circles with these thoughts and then he had a flash of brilliance – or what he hoped was brilliance. He commed down to Earth's re-established liaison office and asked them for a favor. He would like to gather a group of perhaps a dozen leading scientists for a chat with his Grand Team Time. He wanted to talk to them about Time and the potential for time travel. If he could link them electronically or get them all in a single place, that would be the easiest way to make that happen. He told them that his proxy there on Earth would handle the transport arrangements and cover all the costs, including rental of a meeting facility and a nice stipend for the people he invited. The liaison officer on the comm said he thought he would be able to find such people through the Nobel committee and places like MIT. Bon thanked him, told him he would reward him handsomely, and asked to be told when they were assembled and ready for a discussion. He said he envisioned a three-day session of discussions, twice a day, with a long lunch in between each session. The morning session would be with everyone and the afternoon session would be in small groups, self-chosen, to discuss the morning session or any new thoughts which arose. He then told his own team of his plan to brainstorm this issue with Earth natives, whose imaginative approach to problem solving may be enhanced by their higher native vibration. He admitted that he could not show any data to support this wild hypothesis, but that it was at least worth a try. He cautioned his team to refrain from any mention of the Time Shift and their Shonak agenda in trying to figure it out, or anything about the live feeds they have, and have had, now or at any time. The conference, he reiterated, will be devoted to an intellectual discussion of Time and the potential for time travel.

On the appointed day, Bon appeared on a large

screen in front of the earth scientists gathered for this extraordinary event. Earth press outlets wanted to carry it live but Bon and the Earth delegates did not want to allow that, but they did allow a press pool delegate to sit and take notes, with no recording devices. None of them wanted public scrutiny as they brainstormed this difficult and somewhat controversial topic.

Like any and all Shonakians, Bon wasted no time in getting to the point but did at least provide some words of kindness out of respect for the protocols on Earth. "Gentlemen," he said, "I thank you for assembling and welcome you to a first for both our planets. Never before in the history of our two worlds has there been such a collaborative event, which I hope will be seen by both worlds as a positive one, and perhaps we can do it again on other topics as we choose. I trust your accommodations and travel have been satisfactory. Please let my man there know of anything we can do to make your stay even more pleasant."

He continued, "I am presently the Eldest of a Shonakian Grand Team that is devoted to an exploration of the concept of Time. Having conquered pretty much every aspect of science we on Shonak want to explore the feasibility of something we have not yet conquered - time travel. We of course have no empirical proof or even suggestion that such a thing is possible, but neither did we before we discovered inter-phase travel. That was discovered by accident during our humble effort to improve transportation on Shonak. With Time, however, we have not yet decided how to begin and hope you may provide us with any insights you may have. Of course, my assumption is that Time is universal and not unique to either Shonak or to Earth. If I'm right, and you can perhaps concur with it or not, this will allow us to arrive at conclusions which apply on both planets. I will now open the floor for general discussion."

The Earth audience sat quietly at first, reluctant to be the first to offer opinions on the subject of time travel! Most men of science on Earth considered such a thing to be very interesting, a dream of people always, but in the end a work of fiction, not science. But this group of learned men felt the subject was actually worth discussing, and they were pleased that this had been put on the table by a legendary Shonakian. He was just as famous on Earth as he was on Shonak.

One of the scientists did stand, eventually, and addressed them all with, "Gold Bon, are you serious, or have Shonakians suddenly developed a sense of humor?" The Earth delegates laughed good-naturedly at this, and the scientist who spoke, a theoretical physicist, sat down, but was looking at Bon on the screen and hoping for an answer. Bon told them that there was no humor intended. He said, "Shonak has decided to look into the feasibility of Time manipulation and thought Earth scientists would have had more of an interest in it than they, on Shonak, and might have some useful thoughts or ideas." Bon said he had researched every Earth paper published on the subject but did not see anything he could use to begin his Time research with. The Earth audience began to comment amongst themselves and Bon sought to get some control of the dialogue. He interrupted and said, "Let us begin with a general discussion on the subject of Time. What is it, exactly? Our own notion is that while we put artificial metrics around it, like your day and our Planetary Rotation, those things do not constitute time. Time, in our view, exists outside our feeble attempts to characterize it with measures we can understand and use. A granite boulder is not changed at all by our determination that it is, say, four billion years old. If we had never lived, the boulder would be there and it would have been there for however long and our giving it a time stamp changes nothing. If I wanted to go back and visit this boulder a thousand years earlier, what would that trip entail? The boulder exists now, but does it also still exist a thousand years previous to now? Is there some record kept of it that can be accessed somehow? If so, how do we get access to it? Where is this record stored? Or does the boulder simultaneously exist in the past, present, and even the future?" He paused, then asked, "What do you say about that?" Another of the scientists rose and said, "Any thought of time travel is, in my view, simply an exercise in theoretical speculation and it is undertaken only because it has been a human fantasy forever. We want to be able to do it. We dream of being able to do it. We develop fancy hypotheses that suggest it can be done. We write popular fiction about it. But at the end of the day, it is not possible for physical matter to move either forward or backward in time outside its normal forward flow. I believe existence proceeds in a linear fashion from history to the present, ever so briefly there, and then into the future. We can observe and report on the history that disappears behind us, we can observe and report on the present which immediately becomes a part of the past, and we can speculate on the future and wait to see if it occurs as we imagined. We can help shape the future by conditioning the present through the actions we take, but we cannot get there before it becomes the present." He paused and then continued, "If I hold a golf ball in my outstretched hand, I have set up a condition whereby the ball will drop to the floor when I release it. When I let the ball go, I have met the conditions necessary to predict the outcome and I can watch as the dropped ball bounces and finally settles somewhere on the floor. I can predict where it might end up but there is no way to know for certain in this case, since I am allowing the ball to bounce and roll on its own. The reason I cannot go to the place the ball settles in advance is because it does not exist there yet and once it does, it is no longer in the future. No amount of theory by learned physicists speculating that time travel might be possible can overcome the reality of the fact that it is not." He stopped talking then and sat down. Bon noted that this physicist had won the Nobel Prize in physics not once, but twice.

Bon thanked his learned colleague for his

studied thoughts and suggested that they all take a break for coffee and refreshments, then reconvene to discuss their thoughts, for the rest of the morning. In the afternoon, after lunch, they would resume talking about the past. Tomorrow he said would be devoted to discussions of the future. His team was also attending via link from Shonak and would be contributing to the discussion as it suited them. There were comm links in the refreshment room to enable discussions on this topic while they had their coffee or tea.

Upon reconvening after lunch there were spirited discussions between the delegates and Bon's team which Bon listened to with interest. He found, however, that while intellectually stimulating they were just going around in circles. He was not at all hopeful that the discussion of the "future" on the following day would offer something better. And he proved to be right. While he was surprised at how far humanity had come intellectually there was seemingly no more help from Earther scientists than he got from his Shonakian colleagues. He had hoped that living so close to the non-physical vibrational spectrum would allow them some additional insights not available on Shonak. Yes, they dreamed, they prayed, they had "faith," they had mediums who communicated with spirits of the departed, they had energy healers, they had all these things but they did not seem to have any special insights into the nature of Time as a "thing" or as anything else. Even if Time were just a construct there was no knowledge of any underlying force or state of being or anything to get your mind around. There were no "handles" on this thing called Time for them to hold onto, to start constructing a math model from. Bon kept seeing the transition from old London to new London with the underlying metadata showing the year stamp going from one number to another one, 3210 years farther along. And the fact that those years were actually experienced by Earth, while Shonak experienced no additional S-Rots, was still mystifying. He was tempted to confess this to the delegates, but he had no confidence they would understand it any better than he did. So, what would be gained?

Itself was bothered by Bon's quandary. He should let it go, Itself thought. Why was this so important to him and to them? It had been a simple "correction" bringing the planets into vibrational synch, while maintaining their differences. Why? There had been no huge reason to do it and of course it could be undone but again, why? There was no impact on the Divine Plan, so it was not an "error" to do this or anything for that matter which was Plan-Neutral. If he had possessed shoulders, he would have shrugged them but as it was, he just closed this off in his mind in favor or more important things to do.

At the end of the conference the formal summary concluded that while nothing was decided about the nature of Time, nothing useful anyway, the delegates from both worlds were very pleased with the ability to interact at this level of intelligence and achievement. They were hopeful it could be done on a regular basis on any one of a number of topics. The delegates made their ways home and the Shonakians got back to work on the issue of Time. It was foreign to their nature to admit defeat in anything technical, so they pressed on. Bon recalled the well documented intellectual agony their science community felt when they finally realized that the Law of Nativity was inviolate. He wondered if this would end up in a similar fashion. Perhaps, but he was not ready to concede that just yet.

Bon struggled to merge his earlier, pre-shift thoughts on the matter of Time with his present thinking about Time. How does the time shift impact his thinking, or does it? When he first decided to take this on "someday" he did considerable research and wrote the following:

"Time in the context of this study isn't a thing in and of itself. It's an artificial construct that allows for the measurement of our lives and our experiences in a linear fashion. A measure of distance, for example, is a construct that allows us to know the length of something physical, like a sidewalk. A measure of duration is a construct that allows us to know the time it takes to walk the length of that sidewalk. Both these measurements are useful, but in themselves are nothing more than arbitrary decisions that have no meaning outside our physical lives. The sidewalk is real, constructed of lime and sand and gravel and water. Which is the real thing, and which is the arbitrary thing? The sidewalk is real enough and the measurements we assign to it are just as real, although arbitrary. One person may use long measures and other short measures; different metrics to deal with the same sidewalk. So that being said, is it possible to discuss time without the measurement of it? "Right now," exists and then it is immediately superseded by the next "right now." It was preceded by the previous "right now." Presumably, "right now" consists of every simultaneous thing throughout all of Creation. All of that exists until it ceases to exist when superseded by the next "right now" throughout all of Creation.

Universally we all feel we need to know how long anything takes to accomplish, so we have invented a metric for duration and we call this Time. It takes so much time for water to come to a boil, from room temperature, at sea level. The time varies based on certain things like the temperature of "room temperature" and how much heat is applied, and the type of container it is in, atmospheric pressure, etc. Knowing that can help us boil water to be ready for some purpose, like making tea. So, time measurement and calculation are handy. But what is time other than this metric? It has no weight, no mass, no color, no odor, no temperature. It is simply this administrative construct, this metric, we created to help understand and measure changes in the world around us. Travel through time is therefore a misnomer. We do not travel through time so much as we travel with it to subsequent instants of reality. How would we achieve actual travel through time to the past or the future? The easy answer is, we wouldn't. Or we can't. Or we won't.

To travel to the past presumes that the previous realities that constitute the past still exist in some fashion and are stored away somewhere and somewhen we can travel to. Since everything continues until it doesn't, where are the past versions of everything all kept? And how do we access them? When we record events in a visual format, we can view them later because we have transferred what we witnessed to some re-usable format. This allows us to have access to them when we want to. We can't change what happened, we can only change the saved image. In the absence of any recording, the changes that constitute the linear, forward movement of events are lost to our view. They can then only be "recovered" through eyewitness accounts or photos or videos. When those eyewitnesses die, or their memory fades, the events are now only recoverable through any audio or video record was made of them. If that has not been done, then the events may become part of an oral tradition which of course is subject to forgetfulness and personal agendas as the years pass. What this means is that all the past "right nows" throughout Creation are lost to us and no machine can go back and find them since they simply do not exist. Their impact still exists, of course, which helps define our "present." Taking that one step further, the present pre-supposes a future reality that will subsequently exist, throughout all Creation. This is the next "right now" and the next, and the next, and the next, and so on. What complicates the future is part and parcel of physical existence. Since random activity is the nature of the Universe, the future must be imprecise. When it arrives as the present, we can see the results of all the deliberate and random activity that shaped it but before that this view is denied to us. Just as water dripping down a windowpane can take many slightly different courses as it follows gravity, grit on the glass, vibrations in the structure, wind, and so on. Where the drop of water winds up at the bottom is difficult to predict with any precision. As we watch it chart its course down the glass, we end up seeing where it lands at the bottom but in advance of the events that direct its downward course there is only a guess as to the result. If we could jump ahead in time to see where it will land then we would see where it landed but we would see only one of the possible, unpredictable outcomes. If time is circular, as some suggest, and not linear, then perhaps it would be possible for us to jump across to the precise spot we are trying to visit but how would that be done exactly? This presupposes that the future events are in the Cosmos somewhere or it presupposes that everything is happening simultaneously, and you can always simply jump to it and watch as it unfolds. Stories of people who travel back in time and join the timeline as a participant in those events is a common enough fictional theme. This could only happen if a physical anything could make the trip without damage or danger to itself. Danger to others might simply become part of the ongoing timeline, which of course would affect the future to some extent. If your time machine landed on someone and killed or maimed them, then the timeline of everyone involved would be altered. This may have no impact on the overall future, or then again it might. Daily, when we decide to stop on a walk to admire the view, we change our own timeline from the one that would have existed had we not stopped. If we stop, we will then encounter totally different situations when we resume walking, however slight or significant. Had I continued walking without stopping I might have looked to the left and seen an old friend and made plans to get together, but had I stopped and then started again, the friend may have been out of sight by then and I would not make those plans or get together. We don't think twice about that, but perhaps we should?"

Reading that now, after all these S-Rots, Bon wonders if he still believes all that and he thinks that, yes, he does.

While Bon was churning all this over in his mind his team was pursuing leads on its own. They knew Bon prized independent thought and action while freely sharing with the team. All of them doing that was not only the Shonakian way, it was the most efficient and effective way to achieve true creative genius. The young Red who had theorized the link to the planet's rotation around their stars, was a perfect example. They all now had that piece of the puzzle and with more hard work and creative thought and analysis any one of them or all of them can achieve additional insights that help move them forward on their quest to provide the answers OE has asked them for. They were all cognizant, of course, that they were breaking new ground here. Nobody had ever solved the riddles posed by Time, but they would not let that stop them from pushing forward. Bon's Team Time had only 24 members at present, and only the one Red. Most were Indigo and Violet. This small team Bon was now counting on to solve the Time questions, was composed of the most independent thinkers he could find – a trait that had stood him well, and so he expected twenty-four of them could do even greater things.

Bon went rummaging at one point in his old Plus-Five kit bag and saw his altered phase suit, with the patch cut out of it at the crown of his head. He remembered the sensation of small pellets cascading onto the skin of his head when he was outside the Zone. He also found it easier to communicate with the gods, such as they were. He wondered if he should try that again. It would have been nice to go visit Atsa, but he was long dead and forgotten. His people, now called the Hopi, had a wonderfully basic way of dealing with the problems nature presented them. They approached their problems with hard work and an open mind, trusting in themselves and their gods, their Kachinas, to help them through the tough times. And for them tough times were a daily reality there on the high, mostly barren desert they called the Fourth World. It had taken them a thousand years to find their home and then they made the best of it. He smiled when he thought of Atsa seeing the ocean for the first time, and use a refrigerator, and behold seeds of corn from a much-improved strain than the weak maize they were planting. He could not leave Atsa at the beach and there was no way to give him a refrigerator, but he was happy to give him the improved corn for his people.

What would Atsa think of his "Earth" now? Bon's thoughts returned to his present situation as the Eldest of Team Time. He refused to give up even though he admitted to himself they needed some sort of breakthrough to advance this question of Time and the Time-Shift any further. Certainly worth additional S-Rots of attention. If they could solve this, they would be making enduring Shonak history – and one with enormous implications for their futures, pasts, etc.

Chapter Twelve

Bon Moves On And Up

Bon and the greatest minds on both planets had worked a total of three hundred and ten years on this issue, but most diligently only in that first year and the last five. In all this time and with all this study they had come up with nothing to explain the how or the what or the why of it. Bon has just achieved his 1359th year in 306417 and it finally came time, in Bon's mind, to bring an end to it. He sent OE a final report that simply said, "After examining every conceivable approach to the matter of Time we have determined nothing new and nothing of use. Time in its essence remains as much a mystery today as it did the day of the great Time Shift. We have not concluded how or why that shift happened and we have not determined how to use it to enable any form of Time travel or manipulation. The value of that shift to Shonak is obviously the fact that we could begin to normalize relations with our cousins on Plus-Five, Earth, since they were suddenly then advanced enough technically, and with a world government, to become knowing partners. Our joint defense of Space to protect our six planets is ongoing and useful should it ever be needed. I request you keep me on as Eldest Plus-Five but disestablish Grand Team Time and abandon any serious effort on it. The Law of Time is as immutable as the Law of Nativity. We don't understand either of these things but must respect their dominance over all things in their respective domains."

He received OE's reply less than a portion later. "Your conclusions and recommendations are approved." There was an unusual addendum to this, for a Shonakian, not to mention an OE, which unexpectedly pleased Bon very much. The addendum from the OE read: "Thank you and your Grand Team for your many S-Rots of devotion and hard work regarding this pressing question and your findings are, actually, as valuable as any other. The matter is closed." As the OE wrote that, he mused that Earth-watching might be rubbing off on him, just a little.

Bon went back to his GT Plus-Five Team to resume his duties, but his mind kept wandering back over the issue of Time. For the first time in his long life he found he could not properly focus on his primary mission. He told himself that the likely reason was that he had no major issues with Plus-Five and had done it all and seen it all before. But, true to his temperament, he continued to work diligently at it until he felt he could no longer do so with great interest. In the S-Rot 306497, at the age of 1439, he resigned from his Plus-Five post and his resignation was accepted by OE. The most senior, the oldest of the golds on Grand Team

Plus-Five, became Team Eldest. Bon wished him well.

And Bon suddenly found himself an unassigned Gold with no official duties. He received an on-screen call from OE who said he wanted to thank Bon for all his good work. As the Eldest of Plus-Five Base, as the first liaison with Earth's Government, as the Eldest of Grand Teams Plus-Five and Time he had proven himself over and over as one of the most accomplished minds and accomplished achievers ever on Shonak. OE asked him what he wanted to do next because surely, he can't be put out to pasture until he is aged into the Regional Council. Bon declined the offer and chose instead to privately review his files, tinkering with Time, until the next chapter of his life would begin. He remained an avid watcher of the vids from Plus-Five, and enjoyed communicating with a variety of the bots there, assisting Eldest Plus-Five in guiding them to best vantage to provide the most interesting surveillance feeds for the worldcast live streams. He stayed away from anything official so as to not usurp the Eldest, GT Plus-Five.

He hardly noticed the passage of time, since he kept busy, and in 306657, at the age of 1599, Gold Bon was notified that he was now the oldest person living in his Region and was therefore the Regional Councilor for Region 12.

Bon knew this day would come eventually, as it did for those Shonakians who had decided to stay alive and active instead of self-terminating when they left their last team assignment. So he threw himself into the job like he had done with all jobs before it. He found it surprisingly interesting to be supervising population control, training and education for his Region. He noted that his population was at just under a million people, so he began to look for ways to bring the numbers up. He decided to do it with a combination of relocations from other, overpopulated regions, with their RC's approval of course, and "second" egg production. He was pleased that there were sufficient volunteers for second eggs to make his numbers. In addition to population control and education he was occupied from time to time with rational differences of opinion between the Grand Team Eldests in his region, mostly over the allocation of resources. These are not rancorous affairs, as they would be on Earth when powerful people disagreed about something. Rational disputes over the same sets of facts, seen from different perspectives, can be very compelling. Resources are not infinite, even on Shonak, and when there are choices to be made on resource allocation for Grand Team projects, the relevant Councilors make the decision when the parties involved cannot. Bon is treated to an unrelenting series of judgement calls and with his experience with his two former Super-Grands, that is, Exploration and Science and Technology, as well as his own Grands, Plus-Five and Time, he finds it interesting to weigh the different arguments and make his decisions. Sometimes the resource in dispute is a particularly gifted or experienced Violet or Gold. Other times it is for priority transportation, reallocation of sub-teams with overlapping missions, acquisition of minerals or metals, or water, or food, or whathaveyou. All in the name of Shonakian quality of life.

In 306668, at the age of 1610, after only eleven years as a Regional Councilor, Bon is aged into the Council of Twelve. He serves what he thinks is a short but interesting forty-six years dealing with matters of great importance for the maintenance of quality of life on Shonak. The Council of Twelve handles all manner of issues that the Regional Councilors find too difficult to agree on, which are not many, but they are of vital importance with planet-wide impact.

Then in 306714 Bon learns of the passing of the OE. Bon is in his 1656th year, and as the oldest member of the Council of Twelve, he was notified by the Eldest of the Age Grand Team that he was now the oldest living Shonakian and would he please go to the OE's office to begin his tenure there. He notes to himself that the short tenures of his predecessors since moving onto the Regional Council has been a bit shorter than usual but Eldest Age tells him when he remarks on it that these things follow cyclical patterns and there is no more to it than that. Yes, he is relatively young for an OE, but it is what it is.

When he gets to his new office, he finds Eldest GT Age there with his OE wrist badge, the last badge he will ever wear. Well, almost. Bon's first official decision was not about himself, but it did affect him as well. He was thinking about Shonakians and how they have been loosely governed since the beginning of this Age, three hundred and six thousand, seven hundred and fourteen years earlier. He had early in his life vowed to tweak the age seniority system if he was ever the OE and had always been somewhat surprised that no OE had addressed it during his lifetime. While it was not possible to argue with the success of their system, it was not perfect, by any means. The two problems they all lived with were, first, the often-rapid turnover in OEs since they are by definition close to the end of their lives and, second, being oldest does not necessarily mean the wisest or most prepared. That said, the absolute authority they have is now especially useful to Bon as he updates the system.

Since the beginning of the current age, all Shonakians have been tattooed with their exact date and time of birth and given dots on their foreheads that correspond to the number of years they have lived. After graduating from school, they receive their Red Dot and on their 142nd birthday, they become Orange. And so it goes every 142 years, through the colors Yellow, Green, Blue, Indigo, and Violet, until they reach their 1000th S-Rot at which time they are given their Gold Dot. This never changes after that, no matter how much longer they live. With advances in the formulation of their universal diet, Shonakians were now living well past fifteen hundred S-Rots. As a result, the growing population of golds has become something of a problem, even though they still fall subject to the age system. There are only so many things for them to do and they can stifle the initiative of junior team members by their mere presence. Many of the Grand Teams complain that it interrupts the nature of team hierarchy to have so many golds to give team assignments to and Grand Team Eldests, all golds, find that managing so many senior Shonakians is too awkward and reduces their ability to promote on merit rather than age. While merit promotions have always been done in one way or another there is no getting around the issue that the oldest is always the Eldest, and always in charge. Their authority is never questioned, but their decisions can be appealed to the next level up. That is up through the chain of Eldests to the Grand Team Eldest. Above them are the regional councilors, the council of twelve, and Our Eldest, the oldest living Shonakian. The easy solution for the overpopulation of golds in the Grand Teams has been to "age them out" to no team at all. A growing issue for everyone, not just these unassigned golds, is what do they do then? A large percentage self-terminate rather than face a long life with nothing meaningful to do. Earth-Watching and all the various vid-watch clubs do manage to absorb a good number of these elders but those who are not interested in that, and do not want to self-terminate, simply exist but find it hard to mingle with others since with their seniority they are always deferred to.

Bon has always thought this was a waste of talent and experience. He determined to create a category called Gold Emeritus which respects their many achievements over their long lives, and so he created an informal Gold Emeritus Council that has branches in every one of the 142 regions and assigned all these unassigned Golds to it. They have a new color dot, gold with a red band around it, and new wrist badges in the same color scheme. Their new job is to provide assistance to their regional councilors; however those councilors decide to use them. For example, Bon was thinking that each region could have an advisory council for population control, another for education, another for training, another for guidance counseling and so on. He also thought that it couldn't hurt for the permanent analysis of Shonakian behavior for signs of intrusion by the constant watching of Plus-Five/Earth culture. That group of Gold Emeritus talent would work for the Council of Twelve and provide them with periodic assessments of the impact of all this Earther watching. This work would require them to perform a great deal of Shonak watching, including every Shonakian's word spoken and every word written. Another change Bon made was to establish that the Regional Councilors and the Council of Twelve and Our Eldest would be Platinum, not Gold. Grand Team Eldests would be known as Senior Golds while in their posts, with platinum rings around their gold dots, and wrist badges to match. A final rule he imposed was that age for these new "ranks" (to use an Earther term) was only relevant within that same designation. If a Senior Gold and an older, plain Gold were in conversation, the Senior Gold would be Elder than the Gold, even if the Gold were chronologically older. This solved a problem Bon noted when he was Eldest of two Grand Teams and found himself in discussion with a Gold who was older than he was. That was a common occurrence since he was relatively young for a Grand Team Eldest. He found it awkward that the older gold would have the final word on the discussion even though he was the one leading a Grand Team. He made this rule apply to all the new designations. When Bon received his new Platinum wrist badge, he determined that the OE's badge and forehead should be unique. He directed that his forehead dot would be emerald with a platinum ring around it and the wrist badge would be a special cut Emerald, set in platinum. And so it was made and so he finally wore the last wrist badge he would ever wear. His final directive on the issue was that this wrist badge always be passed to the new OE upon the death of the current one.

And finally, to end the rapid turnover in positions of authority like the regional councilors, Bon determined that the key planetary administration positions would henceforth be filled by not the oldest people but by the best, most experienced of the oldest golds who were not so close to the end of their lives. They also were required to have stable mental faculties and not be thinking about self-termination. Our Eldest would make these assignments personally and the position of Our Eldest would, after Bon, be filled by the oldest of the Council of Twelve, not simply the oldest living Shonakian. Everyone in leadership positions would serve at least one Stellar Rotation in those posts. While they lived, they could be continued in office by Our Eldest based on recommendations from the Council of Twelve. The Age Team was quick to change the age dots of all those affected and give them their new platinum wrist badges. With these sweeping changes, a new "age" was born for Shonak, but not, ruled Bon, so dramatic as to cause a change in their calendar, designating a new world order. This was just a tweak, at least according to Platinum Bon, and therefore accepted as that by everyone else. Adhering to the authority of OE was, after all, their way of things.

These changes did not cause a great deal of angst among those immediately impacted, or the public at large. The planet and its people had become accustomed to the fact of age seniority, so much so that there was no thought of any other way. There was no need for office politics, no need to "get ahead" of one's rivals for promotion, no animosity when someone else was chosen over you. And by way of example, their lifetimes of watching video feeds from Plus-Five, where all those things were facts of life, showed them how superior their system was over Earth's. For Shonakians, this many hundreds of thousands of S-Rots into their current world order, it was now a part of their social DNA. But of course, the downside was the inevitable turnover that naturally took place as these oldest living people died in office, sometimes just a few planetary rotations into it. They made it work, of course, mostly because of the professional staff that kept things moving along, and because there was so little dissention or disagreement.

Relations with Earth continued to thrive under Bon, and the Grand Team he had started as Eldest, GT Plus-Five, had full control of every Shonakian asset on that planet. All the bots, human and surveillance, were maintained and operated by this Grand Team. All the infotainment feeds were collected, stripped of inappropriate material, and fed to the Shonak networks. All the Earth contacts were handled by this team to include John and Helen's famous and still thriving companies. The new CEOs of both will always be bots, of course, which makes controlling them far easier. The Earther gunners are the only exception to the rule on control of Earth related assets. GT Protection continues to maintain that mission. The selection, training, and employment of the Earth human gunners is run by GT-P as it has since nearly from the start. The Earth WG Director of Defense and Security has the lead on the Earth component of this mission. The Earth-Human gunner program, even with its rocky history, with their Shonakian tattoos, are instant celebrities whose lives when on Earth are made hectic by the paparazzi but they seem to enjoy it. It doesn't matter that there has not been any alien to defend against – it is still like something out of science fiction to the people of Earth. And, of course, they do participate in Earth operations when needed to quell any military aggression that crops up, and they do destroy any asteroid or other space rock that threatens their planet or other space assets.

CRIMISLE still has its uses. Every generation seems destined to produce its own crop of criminals and crooked politicians but when they are found out, as they eventually are under Shonakian surveillance, they are expeditiously shipped off to this remote, inhospitable locale from which there is no escape or return. Many have tried, and all have failed. The surveillance itself is something Shonak is keen on downplaying and so they only provide it upon request through a special liaison section at GT Plus-Five. The Shonakians have nearly as complete a surveillance setup as before the bot scandal, but claim now to Earth officials that they implement it only on their request. Otherwise, their story is, they prefer to not collect against Earthers.

He will always be mentally tied to his former Grand Teams but with things under control on Earth, as much as Earther things can be controlled, and with the Time examination wrapped up, Bon can concentrate his time looking after Shonak itself. In a sense, he muses, he is now the Eldest of Grand Team Shonak! Having created the Emeritus council that looks for the impact of long-term Plus-Five watching by Shonakians, he asked for their initial findings. So far there has been no detectable behavioral change for Shonakians other than the introduction of words to their language to allow for the discussions, in the various vid-watch clubs, of the things they see the

Earthers do or hear them say. Bon is briefed that in this way some 110 words have found their way into the Shonakian language. Some examples show clearly that these words fill gaps in the Shonakian experience. Words like "love" and "hate" and "delicious" and "fragrant" and "religion" show the need for words to express things Earthers do or feel that Shonakians do not. Bon smiled and thought of the many other words that are no doubt on the full list. He wondered how many refer to food and the many ways Earthers enjoy over-eating! Bon was glad that most of the Earther-unique words were spoken in the native language, but those one hundred and ten words listed had been made into the condensed language of Shonak and were therefore now also Shonakian words. He commed the team looking into that to be watchful for behavioral changes to match the language additions.

Chapter Thirteen

Plus-One Heats Up

Earth would always be on Bon's mind but things there were stable and had been for some time, so he was free to look elsewhere. Bon was curious about Plus-One, which he had not paid much attention to, and which he now had time for. The emergence of intelligent life on Plus-One was something he wanted to know more about. These newly discovered and very primitive people, living in underground burrows, were likely thrust forward and into the spotlight as a result of the Time Shift, which propelled them forward in time and therefore in evolution. Bon knew that their presence was missed during Shonak's initial surveys of the planet since they were looking for intelligent life more like their own, with roads, shelters, signs of industry, and the like. One small settlement of these almost black, furry quadrupeds was discovered during a subsequent survey that looked in more detail, for any surface life form that seemed to be of high intelligence. They have now been seen to have discovered fire, tools, very crude shelters, hunting (yes, they are meat eaters like their cousins on Plus-Five), and language. They are capable of walking upright and do so when necessary, but for the most part walk on all fours. They are mammals with two sexes and apparently reproduce via copulation like humans on Earth. They were discovered in a temperate climate zone of forests and large meadows not far from where OE's headquarters is in the corresponding location on Shonak. On Earth this corresponds to Germany, in the United Nations of Europe. GT Exploration has set about doing a census of sorts as well as searching for additional evidence of other possible intelligent life on this, their nearest cousin planet.

There is already a plan to provide live infotainment feeds of these creatures, which are sufficiently evolved to call "people" once the surveillance equipment has been made of native materials. GT Science and Technology and GT Manufacturing are working on the project and hope to have the live feeds within the S-Rot. The OE at the time blessed the venture. Bon sees no reason to go against the tradition of honoring all decisions of previous OE, and in any case, he also approves of the venture on Plus-One. Ever since he was briefed about intelligent life on Plus-One, he has followed developments there with interest. He also wonders what might have been missed on the other versions of their planet that have been dismissed as being of no interest to them. Almost immediately after he became OE, he directed more attention be paid to detailed examinations of the "middle four" planets, He takes very little at face value but he did accept the initial survey results of these planets as true and complete at the time he was reviewing all of GT Exploration's findings. He understands that there were more important issues in play at the time, with things of direct impact to Shonak, but tells himself that this is no excuse for him not posing more probing questions regarding the completeness of those initial surveys. His earlier Indigo period during which he studied all of GT-Exploration's findings revealed that at least ten percent of all work product was flawed across the board. He can't let go of the thought that he let everyone down by not digging further. He comms the Eldest GT-Exp, asking to be kept in the data stream for the new surveys of Plus-One. Bon is grateful for that, at least, and ponders what use this new revelation of life on Plus-One is to them. Perhaps nothing, perhaps of no use, he thinks. But it never hurts to keep an open mind.

It was 306720 and OE Bon received an emergency comm from Eldest, Exploration that a survey crew on Plus-One has been attacked and destroyed. It happened quickly and the unarmed survey vessel's charred remains are repatriating, showing up just off the coast of the Shonakian equivalent of the same area on Plus-One. Bon asked if there were any survivors who could say what happened and he was told there were not. Eldest Exp said, "There are video and audio recordings which I have sent you for review. Please call me back when you have seen them." And the Eldest rang off. Bon looked at the file with great interest. The internal video showed cries of alarm from the crew of three and then what appeared to be an explosion cut them off before any report could be made. The external video shows an extremely bright light and then nothing. Bon sees from his data feed that the bodies and the vessel have been recovered from their watery point of return to Prime. Initial analysis indicates some sort of heat weapon was used but it must have been extremely powerful to achieve the rapid destruction of their survey vessel. GT-Security has a ship on Plus-One near where the attack was made and thus far have seen nothing relevant. He read that the static surveillance devices on the planet were not anywhere near where the attack took place so were of no help. Bon ordered GT-Protection to send gunships to Plus-One to provide cover for GT-Exp survey vessels operating at higher altitudes and hopefully out of range. He asked Eldest Exp if an examination of the destroyed survey ship gives them anything useful concerning the weapon used to destroy their ship and he is told that no, there is nothing yet. Possibly some sort of heat weapon from the melting of items on the destroyed scout ship. They are, of course, all thinking it must be some alien presence there since the small quadrupeds indigenous to Plus-One surely do not have the technology to have destroyed one of their exploration vessels. Eldest GT-Protection reports that nothing has been detected entering Plus-One space or orbit but is pulling ships from Plus-Four and Three to augment and is deploying more static sensors around all their planets.

Bon orders a single explorer member from Shonak be sent there in a phase suit to cover the attack area on foot, as well as close air proximity to the ground. The man landed safely and almost immediately comms with him was lost. Bon asks that a close watch be kept on the location where the destroyed scout ship came through to Prime. Within segments he was told that the body of the man had showed up, quite "dead" and largely burned beyond recognition. "Clearly," Bon said, "There is a hostile power of some dangerous strength, operating on Plus-One and likely in Plus-One space." He added, "Send no more vessels or people or even bots to that location until we have a plan to sort this out. We need answers and we need them quickly, not the least of which is to know if this threat is native to Plus-One or some other place." He then ordered more detection capability to cover Shonak, as well as gunships to guard approached to their home planet. They did not need human gunners; they know this presence is hostile and are ordered to shoot on sight.

GT-Exp sent scouts throughout the solar system of Plus-One to determine if there were other life forms anywhere on any of the habitable planets or moons. They also flooded the planet with scouts looking for any indicators of advanced life, or any intelligent life for that matter, including the quadrupeds they had already discovered. It was not long before they detected significant amounts of CO2 and other atmospheric indicators of combustion and use of manufactured chemicals but did not detect any fires or processing plants. Eldest Exp asked them to look for subterranean sources, volcanic for example, and they soon had a fleet of ships over several locations where these gasses were concentrated. Almost immediately, they came under fire and those that could phased-out of Plus-One Space. Two ships were destroyed by fire with total loss of crews and Shonak went on alert to watch for the returning wreckage somewhere in the vicinity of the earlier attack on Plus-One. Fortunately, they "repatriated" to Shonak in an area with no habitation. Crews from Security and S&T and Exploration converged on the wreckage and a team from Medicine were there to examine the bodies of the crews. Both ships were subjected to intense heat, like the earlier one, heat so intense it melted key components and caused the ships to crash. These were ships that could withstand the cold and vacuum of space, so they were not weak skinned. The mystery was how such heat could have been generated and intelligently aimed while Shonak had no idea there was such an intelligent, advanced technology presence on Plus-One. Space aliens?

GT Protection sent a gunship to the area where the attack had taken place. They had earlier hoped that the first attack was some sort of an anomalous incident with a controllable and understandable explanation. Not now. There was no question that some intelligent agent had deliberately destroyed their ships. These gunships were armed with an array of threat detection sensors and with powerful weapons of their own, stood a better chance of survival and of retaliation. The Earth native gunners were itching to revenge the three ships lost, an emotional response the Shonakians were simply not capable of. Everyone was glad they were on board and ready to shoot.

The gunship made successive fly-bys over the attack area and where the CO2 was the strongest in atmosphere. Their passes were lower with each successive transit. The gunners were ready to shoot, and the pilot was ready to phase-out of Plus-One space instantly. They might even do both at the same time. The gunners chose cannon with explosive shells instead of phase weapons since they suspected there was some sort of weapon installation there to destroy but they could switch to another munition quickly. If they only had time for one shot, it would be with explosive shells via cannon.

It was tense on the bridge of the gunship. Their first time in real combat, for any of them. A few of the Earther gunners were ex-military with experience in small scale ground combat, but nothing like this. Three ships had been utterly destroyed in the blink of an eye by an unknown attacker with an unknown weapon for unknown reasons. Sensors were their only chance at early detection, and they had a probe near the ground with a wide array of detection capability and suddenly that probe lit up like the sun and then faded as it cooled and fell to the ground. The gunners were able to pinpoint the location of the weapon and fired without hesitation, not once but multiple times, firing explosive shells that would eventually revert to their native vibration but in the instant of use were plenty powerful. Huge secondary explosions were seen on the ground, which opened up to expose a vast facility under the surface before it exploded like a volcano erupting, hurtling debris upward towards their gunship. The pilots phased-out instantly and commed GT Protection to report and ask for guidance. They were told to move their position relative to the explosion on the ground, gain altitude, and phase back in to record the damage and gather intelligence.

Their ship was undamaged, so all their sensors were working, and it was a good thing since there was so much to observe on so many levels. There was an enormous crater in the ground, with fires and smoke bellowing out from it. They moved upwind to get better visibility on what lay at the bottom of the crater and it appeared to be a city of some sort, with buildings and roads. They could see crews putting out fires and moving things out of their way, just as they would do themselves. But the most astounding visual was of the people, or what they assumed were people, who were all silvery and shiny and also apparently terribly strong. They streamed their video back to OE and their GT's but these scenes were not put onto the Shonak infotainment networks. Too soon for that. OE Bon was concerned that their confrontation would make it difficult if not impossible to open a conversation with these people, people they had not known even existed. How could their surveys have been so terribly wrong about Plus-One? Of course, the easy course of action would be to simply write Plus-One off and leave them to their own devices. Since they could not exist on each other's worlds, they could simply walk away from this with no further issues. That, however, was not Shonakian, and not Bon. Especially not OE Bon.

Bon told the gunship to move to an extremely high altitude while keeping their eyes on the scene. He ordered another gunship, this one from Plus-Two space, to come and provide cover for the first ship. It was not known if these people had their own flying machines and that must concern them. He placed the remaining gunships from Plus-Three and Plus-Four space on standby. All the while he and the other seniors watched the scene below where their cannon had apparently destroyed the heat weapon threat. GT-Exp ordered probes to get a closer look at the underground city and stream their information back to Shonak. What they saw was astounding to everyone. Here was a robust civilization thriving under the surface of Plus-One, that had been in existence for perhaps many millennia. OE told everyone there was still hope they could open a dialogue with these people once things settled down. Apparently, they did not like direct sunlight since a priority for damage control seemed to be the construction of a netting of some sort to cover the large gap in the ground surface, letting the light in. It could not be to hide the city, since it was obvious that ship had sailed. There were small, rotary wing flyers dragging material over the opening, which must have been as wide as a dozen of their phase ships in every direction. The GT-Exp managed to get a few probes in the crater before the cover was complete and they continued to stream back images of the reconstruction effort. When the cover was completely restored, it was darker in the crater, but the natives did not put on additional light. They seemed to prefer the dark. And then they could see that people were taking off their silver body suits, apparently because now they would not be in the direct light of the sun. Of course, living underground as they did would require extreme night vision and would engender sensitivity to sunlight. Their sensors continued broadcasting until they were discovered, at which time they were destroyed by the people finding them. The pieces of the probes began to make their way back to Prime, having lost their zone of influence.

Shonak scientists also announced a discovery about using explosives in another resonance using out-of-phase munitions. The blasts on Plus-One used Prime explosives which resulted in an "echo" blast of mild intensity on Prime, but which also contained some particulate matter that was returning more rapidly, apparently due to the energy of the blast itself. This was good to know since any terrestrial blast of a Prime weapon on one cousin planet could potentially lead to a sympathetic blast on Prime as well as others as it made its way through on its way back to Prime. Depending on the location of the blast off-Prime, it could impact Shonakian population centers. This had never been experienced because all past use of explosive shells was against asteroids in space, and some target drones, so any repatriating fragments would be in the vastness of space, not any danger to life on any of the planets. They began to formulate a testing program in a remote location on all the planets so they could understand this better and avoid any damage on Prime. They would also temporarily restrict their cannon to kinetic darts and phase guns until they sorted this out. As this location on Prime was uninhabited, the repatriation of a Prime dart would cause no harm on Prime when it reappeared, but they henceforth built this calculus into their firing decisions. This incident on Plus-One had done wonders for their weaponeering! After testing they also came to the conclusion that it would be in all cases better to use projectiles of the same resonance as the target or stick to phase weapons. Circumstances may call for kinetic weapons; i.e. darts or explosives, but in the absence of information for those decisions the first weapon of choice would now be phasic.

Bon was taking it all in and considering the various ramifications of their new discoveries on Plus-One. He determined that after some time elapsed, he would send a single explorer to a spot near the damaged city and await communications with the inhabitants. Until then they would continue to monitor from a safe distance and collect as much information about them as they safely could. How many buried cities are there? Where are they? What are the people like? How do they communicate? Can any radio frequencies be located and collected? And so on.

In the meantime, Bon had a civilization to manage and so he returned to the mundane but no less important job of doing that. The Council had been performing some of his duties in absentia while Bon was preoccupied by the doings on Plus-One and they were pleased to have him back. He ratified all their decisions and then met in session with them to review whatever they considered pressing at the moment. Fortunately, there was nothing major; the only standout issue was the population imbalance between several Regions. He bid them take care of it as they saw fit working with the RCs as they did so.

Bon asked for daily briefings on the progress of Plus-One intelligence gathering, telling them to brief him and the relevant Platinums on their findings twice a P-Rot. The first briefing informed Bon and the other concerned Eldests of their collection of radio frequency energy they believe to be communications. They were looking for patterns that suggested some language was being used, but it was becoming more and more obvious that these communications were between machines and not people. They were also culling the images captured by their probes before they were destroyed. It seems these beings are bipedal who walk erect. They resemble Earth humans more than Shonakians, but their eyes are very large, likely to give them better low-light vision and they may be communicating telepathically. More observation needs to be had before they can be more positive on that score. They wear exo-skeletal suits to perform tasks of great strength, like rebuilding their city. No manned aviation has been detected. Surface roads and buildings have been seen. They appear to be entirely sub-surface dwellers. It is not known what they eat or drink or exactly how they farm or domicile. GT-Exp decides to build non-human bots of native materials so they can begin information collection in earnest. Bon approves of that and urges them to get that done quickly. They are advised by OE to establish a facility on Plus-One similar to the one on Plus-Five if that desert is as empty on Plus-One as on Earth.

One hundred and six P-Rots later, Bon is told the first native surveillance bots have been deployed near the one known subterranean city. They were instructed to find entrance to the city and collect as best they can, streaming everything back to their control on a continuous basis. Their journey was underway, and the live streams were coming in to OE and Platinums and the relevant GTs. Shonak at large was still unaware of this civilization and would be until some better way to describe it were found.

The first burrowing bot to make it into the city provided much-needed information to all the relevant teams, especially those who were constructing bots in the likeness of common things that were found there, living or not. There seemed to be no flying insects or rodents or other pests. No dogs or cats or equivalents. A few of the natives near the bot looked like they were communicating, but there was no sound. It became obvious that they communicated telepathically as was suspected. This would make it difficult to communicate with a bot who had no mind in the biological sense, but it did provide a level of security for their bots, since they had no thoughts to betray their presence. As for appearance, did these people even have ears? It appears they do, which means they can hear the things going on around them, like falling rocks and rushing water, but no speech was detected. Bon asked the pilot of the lowest gunship above them to think thoughts of welcome from Shonak. Maybe the natives will hear them. He thought, "You never know unless you try!"

Shortly thereafter, the Shonakian explorer was ready to deploy, and he was instructed to walk to the covering over the target city, sit down, think kind thoughts, and await the natives. Nothing happened at first, but then the man came under attack by some sort of beam weapon and he phased away before he could be seriously hurt. Bon then instructed the gun ship to drop to the ground, send a thought of welcome, then hastily regain altitude. The response was quick. The ship was fired on, but it was able to stay ahead of their weapon's beam and when it reached a certain altitude, the beam disappeared.

These people mean business! But maybe they fired before they fully understood the non-hostile intent of the gunship? Bon told them to repeat the process but be ready to phase-out as soon as they detected the signature of their weapon, now programmed into their sensors, having gathered that data during previous attacks.

The gunship crew did as they were ordered, dropped nearly to the ground, and the Shonakians and Earth gunners all sent mental greetings and warm wishes. There was no heat cannon this time. In fact, there was nothing. If the natives were sending thoughts back to the gunship, not one of them detected it. Bon told them to phase out and leave the planet, to return to their space patrol within the Plus-One solar system. Bon thought this would provide the natives with a breathing space to digest what was happening. He further ordered the other ship in Plus-One Space to return to its place on Plus-Two patrol and ended the alert posture of the entire fleet, regardless of phase.

Bon then did a curious thing. He recovered his old phase suit from when he was Eldest of Plus-Five Base and asked for the most senior Violet in GT-Exp to visit him in his office. When Violet Dun arrived, Bon greeted him and asked if he would be willing to undertake a potentially dangerous experiment. Dun said that he was and noted that he would be a gold in a matter of P-Rots and hoped to be back for the Age Team ceremony. Bon said he very likely would be but could make no promises and Dun was still willing to go so Bon told him of his efforts to contact a "god" on Plus-Five back in the days when they were trying to reach and exploit Plus-Six space. Violet Dun told Bon that he knew of the effort and had watched the historical vids many times, over and over, thinking it was exactly what an Explorer should do! He showed Dun the phase suit he had modified for the task. Dun was amazed and for an emotionless Shonakian was almost Earther-like in the way he handled the garment, having only seen it in the vids prior to now. He told Bon it was something for the Explorer museum, and Bon admitted he had not thought of that but agreed that is where it should go when they were done with it. He then asked Dun if he would be willing to wear it on Plus-One to try to establish mental contact with the newly discovered advanced race they had found there. Dun said he was eager to do it and so the mission was laid on.

Senior Violet Dun, newly outfitted with a modified suit based on Bon's old suit, found himself seated on a grassy plain somewhere on Plus-One. There was a gunship standing by at altitude above him half-phased out, but ready to return in a sub-segment if there was any threat to Dun. For his part, Dun was ready to anti-grav and phase out of there himself should he feel the need, and in fact, on arrival, he tested his reactions by doing that a few times. But now he was seated on the ground of Plus-One, on a nice, sunny day, and beginning to feel uncomfortable on the top of his head. Like Bon said it would, he felt like tiny pellets were being dropped on his head. It did not hurt, but it was very uncomfortable. Almost immediately, however, he began to hear voices in his head, or at least one voice, which was not speaking words, just emotions. The first was to not be afraid and to relax. Be not afraid he felt, over and over. At first this did make him afraid, but the underlying emotion was so calming he did calm down himself. All of his life signs were beaming back to Shonak and to the gunship in real time and they noted the decrease in heartbeat after the initial excitement and fearful few segments. Dun then felt the question "who are you and where are you from?" He marveled at the fact that their language was not one of words, but rather of emotion, and he needed no translation. He thought back in response, "My name is Dun, and I am from the planet Shonak." He added, "We come as friends." He was then asked about if he was part of the race that had recently tried to destroy their city and he responded that they had only responded to the destruction of their scout ships and the death of their crews. Dun hurriedly thought they intended no hostility but were prepared with that response. Dun pointed out that they fired first on unarmed Shonak scout ships. He then felt a wave of relief and sorrow and friendship and curiosity as to who they were and where was Shonak. Their own planet had no name other than the emotion for "home." Dun thought back that Shonak, his home, is a sister planet of their own but at another vibration of reality. He felt a wave of curiosity at that and no understanding, but also no hostile thoughts. Dun was nearing the end of his tolerance in this suit and sent the emotion for friendship and love and a desire to have a peaceful relationship between their worlds and that he must depart now to rest. He said he would return shortly to continue their conversation. As he phased out and away from Plus-One, he felt a wave of agreement.

On Dun's return to Shonak Bon greeted him and said that when he attained Gold, the very next P-Rot he would be the Eldest of the new Grand Team Plus-One, and as such, a Senior Gold. Bon said he was very satisfied with how he managed that first contact with the people there. He also warned that he should make the next few steps cautious ones, with gunships backing him up in case something in their negotiating went wrong. He warned that this mental communication, through emotions rather than words, was a potential for misunderstanding so to ensure only the most placid of his staff be in direct communication with them. He also told Dun he needed to find a way to convert his thoughts into some sort of Shonak record for their study and to put into the feeds when ready. Bon then sent directives to all GT Eldests of the creation of GT Plus-One and ordered that all assets and personnel currently assigned to Plus-One tasks be shifted to the new GT, except of course for GT-Protection's gunships. He also asked GT-S&T to find a way to make communicating with Plus-One natives easier than cutting a hole in a phase suit, and that he wanted mental communications in some form that could be recorded for their databases.

Chapter Fourteen

Opening Plus-Two

Content for the moment with the direction of their efforts on Plus-One, Bon turned his attention to Plus-Two. It was the S-Rot 306724. He was thinking that if they were so wrong about Plus-One, what could they have gotten wrong up on Plus-Two? He remembered that Plus-Two was the desert planet, with no surface water and no detected life. He wondered at that and wondered why it had not struck him before. Given that all the planets were essentially coexistent with each other why was there no visible water, either on land or in the atmosphere? All the other versions of this planet had an abundance of it, even Plus-Four, essentially one giant volcano and a seething cauldron of molten lava, was shrouded in dense clouds that evidently held most of the planet's water which rained, was heated to steam, went aloft, only to return again as rain. Eventually, he reckoned, when the volcanic activity died down more and more of that water would remain on the ground, assisting in the cooling of the crust.

He asked GT-Exp for their latest assessment of Plus-Two. Their Eldest came on screen immediately and said that based on the fiasco with Plus-One he was conducting new surveys of the remaining three iterations of Shonak which had been written off for too long. He also noted that there were subtle changes in all the worlds and some not so subtle, like on Plus-One, since the Time Shift. He said he was pretty sure that there were more changes than time during the shift event. He said OE Bon would find the latest update on them all on his screen and then signed off.

Bon turned his attention to his vids and saw an aerial survey shot of Plus-Two with metadata bars at the bottom with info on temperature, atmospheric pressure, moisture, wind speed and direction, airborne life signs like airborne plant spores and the like.

To great surprise in the Grand Team but no real surprise to Bon the great oceans of the world were found to be under various thicknesses of crust composed of rock and sand. It was tempting to blast a hole in that crust to see if any of the water would come on the surface and stay, especially in the lower elevations, but Bon asked that they phase into the crust and get to the water, take a sample for life forms while there, using an external probe, then report to him directly. This was done, and they found that the subterranean ocean was full of tiny animal and plant life, but no larger life was detected – but they are still looking. Bon knew he was potentially making life-altering decisions for billions of small life forms but was just too much an explorer to not make an effort here to possibly enable larger sentient life forms to develop if they had not already done so. He ordered the crust opened up with phase weapons to remove small pieces one at a time till the surface was opened and the water was free to come out if it would. He said to find the lowest elevation on the planet first, then find the thinnest crust there and begin the operation. Fifty portions later Bon got an emergency comm telling him that the water came out of the single hole they made with so much pressure it nearly took out the gunship making the hole. The geyser was noted to reach a thousand long measures in height and was creating an enormous lake as the water came back to the surface in a huge torrent. It was also noted that a substantial percentage of the geyser's water was being absorbed by the very dry air on the planet. So much water vapor was trailing away and dissipating downwind that it appeared to be hot water, but it wasn't. It was just dry air!. Bon told them to continue monitoring and let him know of any significant changes. He watched the initial blast of water as it was suddenly freed from the crushing pressure of the rock above it. As an aside, Bon noted that this event on Plus-Two was proving to be one of the most popular shows on the Shonak infotainment feed. Bon asked Eldest GT-Exp to put a gold in charge of a new sub-team under Exp called Plus-Two. If it ever developed sentient life, it should then become a Grand Team in its own right.

Bon felt the responsibility of being OE and

developing the ethics for opening new worlds. He set up a meeting with the Emeritus Golds to discuss the topic. After several P-Rots of conferring with one another and with Bon, it was agreed that OE should approve a binding policy that outlined what actions were and were not permissible when dealing with new worlds and new life forms. He had in a de facto way already written a rule through his precipitous action with the crust removal and wondered if he should tie that off now with a preventive ruling. The drama of the geyser and the rapid changes now occurring on Plus-Two was a great example but surely there could be subtle things to watch for as well. The tiny life in the underground oceans on Plus-Two will now have a different environment to deal with and grow with or possibly even die with, and he did that. Bon did that. No one else. It was not "Shonak" that did it, it was Bon. The Emeritus Council agreed with Bon's assessment and agreed to confer and draft world-opening and world-dealing policies for OE approval.

While Bon awaited the draft policy, he ran this question over and over in his mind: Should he have opened Plus-Two at all and should he have done so in so aggressive a manner?

Bon also reached out to the Council of Twelve for a meeting to discuss the ethics of opening worlds and telling them what the Emeritus Council recommended. He raised the cases of Plus-One, Plus-Two and Plus-Five. Had they handled them properly? Bon told himself and the Council that the breaking of the crust on Plus-Two had been happening from below anyway, through simple erosion, and would have come sooner or later. He had merely helped it along. He could not help but reflect, however, on the things he learned when he was Eldest of Grand Team Time. So many variables all playing out determining from sub-segment to sub-segment how it would unfold. He had just caused a major event to happen earlier than it normally would have and not in the way it would have done. What he did certainly altered that world, but did it really alter the future or just hasten it? No one can say if it was a good thing or a bad thing, at least not yet, and will that be a subjective call anyway? Are they not the agents of time here? Is that what they are doing? They may not be traveling to the future, but they are certainly shaping it. The most intelligent, advanced race on the six planets has, in essence, been acting as the parent of the other five? For good or ill, as parents on Plus-Five they watch every day know, they simply do their best. At some point, the children take control of their own lives from the position the parent has given them? He would never know and perhaps none of them would, ever, even in their long lifetimes, for Plus-Two, but it was worth a thought. Bon began to formulate a directive about this, but the wording was important and touched on so many things he decided to ponder it a bit more and work with the two Councils on it. On the one hand he did not want to inhibit the works of GTs like Exploration and Science and Technology and the GT's devoted to Plus-Five and now Plus-One. On the other hand, he did not want Shonak to be the author of some unique change to create any future timeline other than their own. Or was that even possible? Is this a matter of time or a matter of fact? Once Shonak becomes aware of another world does it not then enter the life of that world; its timeline? Regardless, of course it must tread lightly. Or not? Does it really matter? These are things he asked the Councils to think about and respond when they felt ready to hold a policy review and approval conference.

Bon read the latest report from Plus-Two with interest. Their seismic readings indicated that with the ocean forming above ground after it burst forth the subsurface water levels in that part of the planet were declining, which made sense, of course. Their geologists were of the opinion that the weight of the water will eventually collapse the crusty shell of the planet, or much of it in any event. The crust will settle to the bottom and the water will be on top in an inversion of how it has been with the net result being oceans instead of desert over much of the planet.

The next report dealt with atmospheric changes because of the tremendous release of water to the surface. Humidity had been nearly zero but had risen quickly to two percent near the newly formed lakes and would surely increase considerably as more water formed on the surface. Bon shook his head and asked himself, "What have I done?" He knew that sunlight and seawater could combine to form life and would certainly change the life that was already in the water. He wondered how long before his reports started showing all that in the growing list of changes on the planet? He did this, nobody else. And he felt the weight of the responsibility for that far more than he had anticipated. They really did need to adopt protocols for how to proceed in these cases. He felt that the authority of the OE, which was absolute, needed to be blunted in these situations by a requirement to follow a more collaborative approach. The Council of Twelve might suffice or perhaps even better a council made up of as many as a hundred unassigned golds with diverse backgrounds. They could present various courses of actions to the OE with their recommendations which course they thought best.

Bon turned his attention to reports on Plus-Three, which was under something of a microscope after what was happening on Pluses One and Two. Shonak's scientists had long held that Plus-Three, with its half land, half water profile, had the best chance for the creation and growth of intelligent life. Plant life was lush to the point of overwhelming. Plenty of sunshine and rainfall combined to make an ideal location for such growth. The fact that there was apparently no animal life was perplexing.

Less than a week after what he was calling the "Grand Opening" of Plus-Two reports of the cracks in the surface began to come in and while he watched, the latest video from their stationary drone above the land adjacent to the growing body of water showed huge cracks which were visibly getting bigger! In an instant, a section of barren land of enormous size sank into the ground which then provided a place for water to flow and within segments the lake was a small sea. Bon just shook his head and wondered when this process would stop. How much of Plus-Two's surface would end up under water? Exploration eldest commed him to ask if he had seen the latest from Plus-Two and he noted that he had. The Eldest then reported that their scouts were seeing signs that the land over additional bodies of groundwater was beginning to sag. Apparently, the release of sideward pressure after the collapsing roofs sank away was weakening a greater part of the dome structures than they even knew existed. He said he would keep Bon abreast of significant changes. Humidity in the vicinity of the new oceans was fluctuating wildly with the highs now approaching 20 percent. The water vapor was dissipating rapidly as winds pushed it into dryer parts of the planet. There were still vast tracts of land that remained at near-zero moisture in the air, but he knew this would change. Weather patterns were already shifting with cloud cover beginning to form in the vicinity of the new surface ocean and he expected local rainfall would be inevitable there at some point.

This would be the first rain on that world for how many millions of S-Rots? Bon continued to shake his head with the wonder of it all.

Bon thought they could all benefit from more accurate information from these "middle" worlds and ordered ground-capable, airborne drones be constructed for use on Pluses-Two, Three and Four. He wanted them deployed in under thirty P-Rots and suggested that they build them of native materials. This would require the establishment of ground-based facilities at local resonance that used native materials. The first part was the most difficult – building a native-resonant robotic manufacturing facility that could take over the tasks of phase-suited Shonakians. Once that was achieved all that was needed was to provide the requisite raw materials to the manufacturing facility where bots and other mechanisms would be created.

GT-S&T Eldest, in partnership with Eldest, GT-Fabrication, concurred with that approach and made that their highest priority. The first of the drones were, in the end, deployed in just under ninety P-Rots with the last of 100 being finished and deployed in their favorite number, 142 P-Rots. Shonak's ability to create these things so rapidly stemmed from their experience building Plus-Five and Plus-One facilities of native materials that could then begin producing native resonant items like surveillance drones or whatever else was wanted. That gave GT-Exp twenty-five drones for continuous ground and aerial surveillance up there, as ordered. Eldest of Exploration Team Plus-Two set his drones to explore the bodies of ground water that remained submerged under surface crust. Bon ordered nine hundred more for the effort, split evenly among the planets. He ordered that no precipitous action be taken on information received from the drone exploration effort. All actions on the Middle Four would be determined only after consultation among the Eldests of the GTs involved, and pending a more permanent mechanism, the Platinum Group, consisting of all Platinums on Shonak, would confer before any active measures were taken. Passive information collection was allowed to proceed without further approval. After consultation with all the various working groups, OE would make the final decision as to what to do, when, where, how, and why. He said to all of them that he feels he made a mistake by opening up the crust of Plus-Two. He wanted Shonak to avoid mistakes like that in the future. He went on to note that with all his experience off-world and in auditing the actions of many Grand Teams over his adult life, he still made a fundamental mistake with far-reaching and unpredictable and unintentional consequences for both Plus-Two and Shonak. A collaborative approach to decisions concerning these emerging worlds would help to prevent precipitous decisions with unknown and unintended long-term consequences. He did add that the impact of releasing the oceans on Plus-Two may turn out to be beneficial to Shonak and to that planet itself but that was impossible to know and it is equally true that it can be a negative influence on Shonak so best to avoid mistakes whenever possible. If mistakes are made, he finished, let them be made after full consultation with the senior people of all Shonak.

His comm blinked and beeped and he turned around to look at the screen, which showed rain on

Plus-Two! No doubt this was the first time it had rained there in millions of S-Rots, if ever. He could only shake his head . . . again.

Plus-Three reports were coming in but nothing very important was being discovered. Plant life on land and in the water, but no animal life of any kind. Not even single-cell animal life. He reflected that now in 306727, he was 1669 S-Rots old, but still mentally acute and physically active. He was content with that and smiled again.

Eldest Plus-One commed him early in the morning to say they had made something of a breakthrough with the natives there. He said, "It is becoming easier to communicate with them mentally using Shonakians who are somehow more adept than others at non-verbal, non-physical communications. My Shonakian team is learning more about the natives every day and is telling them about Shonak at the same time. This for that. They need that very much as they are a suspicious lot, unlike Shonakians, and need constant reassurance that Shonak does not have designs on their cities or their planet." Bon said he understood. Eldest Plus-One continued, "It took some time before a common frame of mental reference was achieved but then it became much easier for my team's communicators to achieve clarity in two-way thought. It was still very time consuming in spite of that breakthrough to get them to understand the Law of Nativity. They finally grasped it and it was a huge relief for them to find out that Shonak could not coexist with them on their world." "At that point they communicated to us that there was no need to maintain any gunship in their space and they said they were turning their heat cannon off. Indeed, our sensors did show that the weapon was powered down, but we also heard their thoughts that it could be powered up in an instant. I ordered the gunship to half-phase out for the time being and we think the ship is invisible now to Plus-One minds."

Eldest, Plus-One briefed Bon and GT, Exploration on what his Team had learned thus far. "They call themselves simply 'The People' and they call their world simply 'Home'. They differentiate themselves from all other forms of life on their world and they are aware of the primitive quadrupeds on and near the surface. Every now and then, one is encountered as it burrows in search of food. They are turned around and sent back to the surface. In the early days of discovery, they were killed and eaten like any other meat, but when they encountered one with intelligent, mature thought, they realized that some of them had become too 'human' to kill. They banned the practice of hunting and eating the smart ones and have noted that there is more than one species of these creatures, some with advanced thought and others who still remain in the 'food' category. Now they try to simply coexist with each other. The People themselves are quadrupeds with pure white skin and prefer walking on all fours but can easily walk on their hind legs or on their hands, as the situation dictates. They are highly intelligent, very technical, and very mechanically inclined. They have no central government for the planet, but each city has a leader who is chosen by the people. The incumbent cannot stand for a consecutive term.

They have a cashless society, like Shonak, but have a thriving economy based on trading this for that. If one wants some food, they can trade some labor for it. That sort of thing. They do travel on the surface but only at night unless there is some sort of emergency in which case, they put on their reflective suits to protect against the sun's rays, harmful to them. They reproduce similarly as Plus-Five with two different genders combining to make babies. The young are born live and are cared for in a central creche until ready to communicate non-verbally. Then they are returned to their parents. They live to be something like 100 P-Rots and are small, weighing about two-and-a-half times what the average Shonakian weighs. Their height is somewhere between an Earth human and a Shonakian. They do have verbal speech but rarely use it, considering it a vestigial part of their evolution. They have weapons to defend against the predators they have on their world. Those predators also live underground for the most part or deep in the various forests on the surface. The heat cannon they used to destroy what they thought was an invader was simply a larger version of those smaller weapons. They have found it useful in opening their caverns and in melting tunnels into the rock that separates their cities. They learned a great deal about manufacturing and construction in the effort and considered that justification enough until we showed up with our phase ships doing the more detailed search for intelligent life. They tried to communicate mentally and could not so fired in order not to be fired upon. They are truly sorry. It was their first contact with humans from outside Home and it did not occur to them that they might not communicate mentally."

He continued, "The cities The People have constructed are marvels of engineering and they have a very advanced, mature civilization underground where food and water abound. They cultivate their favorite foods which don't grow in abundance on their own but most nutrients they require are found plentifully in the native plants growing in the many natural caves and caverns that make up their world. They explore for new natural caverns underground to accommodate their expanding population and form new cities as they go. As noted, they use their heat gun to melt away rock and other matter to enlarge these caverns and to make tunnels to connect them."

"There are at present two hundred and thirty-four city-states on the planet, of varying ages and sizes. These cities do not have names but rather use the numerical order in which they were founded. The city state Shonak fought with after it destroyed its phase ships was number one hundred and nineteen. That means it was the one hundred and nineteenth city founded by the People. They love their kinsmen in the other cities and they have a thriving mental network among them. There has been no need to develop radio frequency technology. They have not discovered video and with mental contact they really don't need it since the vision of one person is perfectly transferred to others. To prevent a cacophony of input, their minds can broadcast to selected individuals, like family and neighbors, which is what they mostly do, provided they have met in person and 'felt' their mental signature at least once. During the brief combat phase with Shonak, before they realized Shonak was not invading them with hostile intent, there was a great deal of broad thought sharing which they found very troubling and gave them headaches. Such a need for this much 'wide sharing' had never been encountered and they hoped never would be repeated."

"They have thought it might be possible to send their thoughts to Shonak, even though it's at a different vibration, and are starting to work on that notion. GT Plus-One is assisting. Right now, they are wondering what to make of Shonakians. They know they can't visit Shonak and they know that Shonakians cannot visit their world. So what kind of relationship should they have with us?" For our part, we do not have guidance on what kind of relationship we are to have with them, either."

Bon takes this on board as a legitimate issue for OE to weigh in on but defers to a later time for that decision and tells the Eldest to wait for an answer on that. This is a good issue to be addressed with his new Planet Relations Team, consisting of 100 unassigned golds, chosen because they have experience with every Grand

Team on Shonak. They are working closely with the Platinums and this will ensure the widest possible frame of reference as they ponder the impact of their decisions.

Bon has decreed this is how they will decide to proceed with any new life form, wherever they find it.

Chapter Fifteen

Bon Fesses Up

It was Shonak year 306728 and Bon was in his fourteenth year as OE, at the age of 1670. As Plus-Five/Earth continued to mature as a cohesive world, centrally governed, and morally based, Bon thought it best to update Shonak's stance towards relations with them and sent their World President a note to that effect. The note was received very positively, and informal talks were started with a view towards developing an updated treaty between the two world cultures. The negotiations went smoothly, and Bon went to Earth for a preliminary news conference to celebrate the informal agreement they had come to regarding the various aspects of their new relationship. The key points were shared defense of space, sharing of technical information, and mutual emergency assistance when requested, like defense against threats in space and to include the capture of criminal elements on Earth. Bon found it irrelevant to note how old he was now, but it so fascinated the people of Earth that he allowed it to become a story for them. As much as he understood and respected them, he could only shake his head in wonder . . . and, he mused, they were probably eating while reading the news! How these people could eat!

Only 100 days after the initial letter was opened by the WP the official parties met in Paris to sign the treaty documents. Bon was in a phase suit specially designed to enhance his stature and to provide a stunning visual display of color and motion. The WP was in formal ceremonial robes. There were bands, crowds of cheering people, news outlets, security people everywhere, and of course all the major world leaders were there to witness the historic event and to have their picture taken with the WP and the OE of Shonak. Bon's security detail, half-phased out but watching everything, made a few arrests and had one hostile exchange. Their phase weapon was silent, so the confrontation was achieved without anyone there even becoming aware.

Seven P-Rots later, after all the hoopla had died down, Bon asked the WP what she wanted done with the people they had arrested that day. She was taken aback, but Bon showed her the videos of what the criminals were doing to get arrested, and also of the arrest itself. These people had been detained in Shonak vessels with Plus-Five Zones but now should be handed over to law enforcement in their places of arrest, mostly the area where the treaty was signed. It was noted that at least three of these detainees had drones set to explode over the dais where the treaty was actually signed. These plots were foiled, the treaty document was successfully executed and none the wiser. The WP was stunned but at the same time very grateful. She considered asking there and then for law enforcement support like in the old days but stopped short of it. She would need to follow treaty protocol, which included achieving a consensus among world leaders before acting.

As it turned out, several nations in the WG wanted immediate support for their law enforcement efforts and several did not. It was arranged that there did not need to be a unanimous agreement so the nations wishing the support could request it as they eventually did. Shonak bot-forces of Earth Resonance were taken out of storage at the desert site and put to work, along with law enforcement bots that had not seen action in hundreds of years. Within thirty days CRIMISLE, long since closed, was once again populated by criminals and the Earther press was having a field day. Everyone was happy to see the bad guys taken away from society, but not all were happy with the dependence on Shonak to do it so quickly. Why can't we do this for ourselves? That was a popular theme and indeed, Bon wondered the same thing. Perhaps when there is sufficient dissatisfaction with the situation there would be sufficient motivation to see it addressed. In the meantime, he was happy to perform this service for Earth, as in days past.

In 306741 Bon was actually starting to feel his age. He was 1683 S-Rots old and could see that there would come a day . . . .

He took a hard look at the Council of Twelve, and especially the oldest one. He would do fine as the OE, Bon thought, if still alive when Bon died, but that was hopefully not for a long time yet. He had no plans to self-terminate, ever.

His morning briefing revealed that they were making even more progress in communicating with the intelligent natives of Plus-One. They are an honest, hardworking race who have built a good life for their people. They needed no assistance from Shonak but Shonak stood ready to assist if requested. Plus-Two had continued to transform from desert into a more land/water-balanced planet but there was still no plant or animal life there, except for the traces in the tiny complex plant and animal proteins found in their ocean water. Plus-Three remained a plant-only world.

Plus-Four was so actively volcanic it remained hostile to all forms of life. When it cooled, it might moderate but showed no signs of cooling at present. Even long-lived Shonakians would need many, many generations before they saw any changes on Plus-Four.

So during Bon's lifetime he had witnessed the opening of relations with Plus-Five in a serious, methodical way. He had seen the Time Shift firsthand. He negotiated the first informal partnership with modern Plus-Five in their post-shift configuration and put together a combined space defense effort using Earth gunners and Shonak gunships.

He helped Earth rid itself of its vast criminal

and corrupt population. He renegotiated with Earth following the Great Disaster when Earth went on the warpath over Shonak bots and more recently he updated their treaty documents to reflect the continued progress Plus-Five is making as a world culture. He has opened relations with Plus-One's dominant intelligent life form. He changed the Shonak seniority system at the upper levels to provide a more stable, professional leadership cadre to the benefit of all Shonakians. In his pre-Gold years he developed a reputation for unconventional thinking, detailed research into nearly every report ever written by GT-Exp and was at the time first Gold to be appointed Eldest of two Grand Teams at the same time (Plus-Five and Time).

So what should his legacy be, when he finally dies, he wonders? He is likely the most widely known Shonakian in the history of their world, as well as on Plus-Five, and perhaps even on Plus-One. Relations with these diverse cultures on two different planets has not always been good, but they have lived through periods of distrust and even combat and have come out with cordial working relationships all around. The obsession with Time has been put to rest, with no other resolution than they can't figure it out. Bon does note with some interest the ongoing discussions on Earth by people who just won't let it go. Well, that's for them to work themselves through, he thinks. He shared his findings on the immutability of Time with Earth in the hopes nobody else would waste any more time on it but it remains such a visceral subject for many people there. For Shonak, however, as an issue, it was the end of Time, and people were content to take his word for it. He was the OE, after all.

Bon was also concerned, at the end, with his long relationship with Plus-Five, and the fact that he had never confessed to any of them the real reason behind his obsession with helping them overcome crime, poverty, disease, and the like. It was not purely altruism, as many on Earth assumed. It was also guilt. Most Shonakians preferred to take the academic view of their experiments on Plus-Five natives before they were declared to be human. It was perfectly normal scientific inquiry much like the people on Plus-Five have long done with their own non-human animal population. Bon had always had a contrary opinion on that, as have many of Shonak's Elders, and this fueled their desire to atone for not only that but also for the massive invasion of privacy the people of Plus-Five endure solely for the voyeuristic pleasure of a planet of bored technocrats. (Not to put too fine a point on it.)

He frequently spoke to his counterparts on Plus-Five, that is, the successive World Presidents. They only hold their office briefly, two to five years, as that has changed over time. The current World President was Nils Gustafson from Europe's state of Iceland. WP Gustafson wondered aloud to Bon if Earth were, after all this time, becoming "Shonakian" as a result of their joint peacekeeping and law enforcement efforts. He said there was a definite shift in behavior when measured against what Earth was like when Shonak introduced themselves to the people of Earth 633 years earlier. He remarked to Bon that he was awed by the fact that Bon was actually the same person who led this introduction that long ago and wondered what it might be like to live such a long time. There was a pause in the conversation as both men considered that. The WP then added that to his mind there had been, as a result of their inter-planetary association, social engineering on Earth on a scale unheard of in its long (to them, at least) human history. Bon agreed that Earth had indeed become a more placid place, but to his mind they were a long way from being "Shonakian" in any sense of the word. To himself, Bon felt there was more to Nils' comment than just the surface question and so asked him what he was thinking. WP paused before replying and said, "Look, Emerald Bon, we are grateful for all that Shonak has done for our planet and I am also grateful for the wonderful world we now have as opposed to what we had before. I do wonder, though, if there isn't some agenda on the part of Shonak to reshape us into what you are yourselves." He paused then, waiting for some response from Bon, and Bon paused while he considered his answer.

"My dear Nils", he began in as sincere a tone as a Shonakian can muster, "There is, actually, more to our help for your planet than you know but it has nothing to do with you and everything to do with us."

Bon decided to take the plunge, saying, "Over five thousand of your years ago we first visited your world as explorers. We had visited the other, lower vibration versions of Shonak already, to see what was there and did not find much of interest. We knew that we could not live there since we found out the hard way that the very air on these other vibrations was hostile to us as you know it is to you as well. Of course, we thought we would soon overcome that problem as we have overcome nearly all the challenges we have faced throughout our very long history. But that was not to be, as you know. When we came to Earth, which we called Plus-Five, we found the planet to be hostile in ways beyond the air we could not breathe or water we could not drink. The dominant intelligent life form, you humans, were a hairy, brutish, violent, and cunning lot. You had the basis of civilizations but no technology, no knowledge even that you were on a planet revolving around a sun. No common language, no common societies, no common government, just common, and often violent behavior. People outside your own family or clan were automatically distrusted and even in your own tribes and families there was routine, often deadly violence. Consider how different you must have seemed to us. We at first did not even consider you human, but we were fascinated by you, so we captured a few and took them back here to Shonak to put them on display and to study them further. Of course, the first of them died from exposure to our vibration just as we would if exposed to yours. More died as we dissected them, looking for how their bodies worked, and the work had to be quick because after a short while the physical remains reverted back to your native vibration. We needed to have more bodies, so we took more until we learned how to make a facility on Shonak that was at the Earth vibration. This kept us from visiting them in person, but we could watch them on vid and listen to them. Very much like your zoos, before you closed them. We had to bring them food from Earth and water and even air to sustain them and when we were done with them those still alive were taken back to Earth and deposited in remote locations where they could tell no one of our presence. This went on for perhaps fifty of your years before the Our Eldest at the time declared you were human, and all these things ceased as they were now deemed "mistreatment," which we abhor.

We have borne the shame of that activity ever since and have done things we feel would compensate for our great wrong if possible. This is why we are so protective of you. We want to erase the bad things we did with the good we have done and can continue to do. Of course it is only natural that the definition of "good" we use is utterly Shonakian and since we think our culture is far superior to yours we have modeled our actions on the best social model we know of – ourselves. So, if that makes you nervous, I'm sorry." He finished with the rhetorical question, "What other approach would you have us take?"

Nils had not expected that. He sat there stunned. He was silent for a long time. He was horrified at what he heard but understood at once that it was no different than his own people capturing wild animals in their natural habitat to put them in zoos for people to gawk at, or put them in circuses to perform acts while living in questionable conditions and never living as they were intended. They also had used animals for medical testing, and cosmetics testing, even. When people finally decided that animals had a right to their own way of life in their own natural environments, zoos gradually died out in favor of vids and holos of animals living as they should. Experimentation on animals stopped. He was lost in these thoughts for a while but when he came out of his introspection, and consideration for his position as leader of all Earth humans, he looked at Bon on the screen, and said, "I understand and I forgive you, we forgive you."

Bon was surprised but grateful for the WP's intelligent and thoughtful response. He did not for a segment think this response captured the feeling of the population of Earth as a whole, were they to learn the story of Shonak's early days on Earth. He was, however, content that the two of them, the relevant world leaders, at least had cleared the air on this ancient but sad chapter in Shonak/Plus-Five relations. The WP added that he would not reveal this Shonakian history to anyone on Earth since he knew it would not be favorably interpreted by the general population or governments. The very human default to over-reaction would not be helpful or relevant given the very long history of good works on Earth by Shonak since then. He said he was more interested in how they behaved towards each other now, today, and in the future, than how things were in the past. He added that their own history of mistreatment of their own kind made what Shonak had done pale by comparison. The worst of their nuclear wars had killed three billion people and destroyed or damaged half of the cities on Earth. No, Nils thought, Bon had nothing to be overly concerned about. He told Bon he hoped he could "let it go" and not bother himself about it any longer.

Shonakians do not do sighs of relief, but Bon felt their equivalent. He mentally checked off a mission-related "to do" now that he had formally apologized, as OE, for the long-ago deplorable behavior of his long-dead kinsman scientists. His OE log reflected that this was now officially behind them, as a culture, some thousands of S-Rots after the fact. The recording of that conversation with the Earth WP was of course made a part of the official log on Shonak. This was likely the longest held uncompleted action in their history and he felt a sense of satisfaction that it was he who completed it, especially given his long and close association with the people of Plus-Five/Earth.

Then he issued a directive that henceforth the term Plus-Five would not be used in referring to Earth. He also expanded that to Plus-One, which henceforth would be referred to as "Home." This is what the natives there call it and should therefore be what they call it. It would not cause any confusion on Shonak since they refer to their places of abode as "domiciles" and as unattached individuals with no families or close personal associations, the concept of a "home" has never occurred to them. He smiled at that. He mused about the fascination he has always had with Earth and its natives. So plentiful, diverse, aggressive, and hungry! He chuckled at the thought of them eating three, even four times a day, in addition to snacks whenever they felt like it. Shonakians have no taste buds so have no concept of hedonic eating – eating just for the pleasure of tasting it! And what to him were such enormous meals, and between-meal eating, drove so many of their health problems, cost so much of their money, took so much of their natural resources, contributed so much to their pollution and weather challenges. For all the technology support Shonak had provided them over so many years, their food production and distribution systems were still only just able to cope. He wondered if it would have been better to let them solve these problems on their own, which would have meant millions starving or suffering malnutrition. What's done is done, he thought, all we can do is help them survive. There is no technology that will help them be better than themselves. That comes from within. He also mused that Earthers could be kind and loving one minute and hateful and murderous the next. Hair trigger defense mechanisms were part of their survivor heritage but hardly needed now. Once again, this was something technology could not fix. He sighed, then got back to work supervising his planet and advising another.

His P-Rots and S-Rots marched on with Bon continuing his "activist" profile as the OE. Most of his predecessors were "hands-off" leaders, only getting involved when asked to rule on something. Bon always thought that odd but reflected that many of them had less than a single S-Rot in the job and knew it would be so and determined to go quietly rather than start something they could not finish. Hardly slowing down at the age of 1700, in 306758, Bon preferred to be involved in everything, all the time. He thought that by making final decisions early on he would prevent negative consequences later on, and he was correct about that, but it also stifled initiative for the Senior Golds in their Grand Teams and for all the Platinums. He knew this, of course but he was how he was.

He was at this time in his life particularly interested in the developments on Home and on Plus-Two. These cousin planets fascinated him and he watched them carefully.

The Home natives were becoming more popular on the live feeds and there was a growing fan base for the people watching the transformation of the desert planet at Plus-Two into something much more like Shonak. The absence of recognizable life did not dampen the interest of those who enjoyed watching geology happen in quick time. Most planetary changes in this area happen over enormous spans of time, tens of thousands or even millions of S-Rots, but were now occurring in real-time, as they watched. Bon remembered watching natural things on Earth when he was active with Atsa in his desert home. He and Atsa were having one of their long talks, walking along a dry riverbed. Bon was using his human bot because he could not have become a friend of Atsa in his phase suit. Suddenly, while walking upstream in the dry bed, they stumbled on a remarkable sight. Ahead of them was water, flowing towards them. But before it reached them, it disappeared into the sand. The stream was not wide at that point, perhaps only as wide as Atsa's shoulders. Bon recognized the water had reached the entrance to a below-ground aquifer capable of taking what little water was coming to it. Atsa reacted differently. He stopped at the place and dropped to his knees and prayed to the river Kachina to not drink all the water himself. He asked the god to let the water reach his village downstream, and he promised to be even more faithful to the precepts of his Fourth World as payment. The water continued to disappear into the ground. Bon-bot told him not to worry, that when there was more water it would reach the village (thinking, because it will be more than the aquifer can accept). Right now, Bon-bot said, the world was thirsty and needed to drink.

Bon the OE smiled at that memory, just one of many he had of the time he spent on Plus-Five in the company of Atsa and his tribe, as well as with others over the many years he spent in command of Plus-Five Base. He wished his memories of the advanced people on Plus-One were happier. Shonak only met them after nearly destroying one of their cities, killing many of its citizens. Shonak had also lost ships and crews until they had this situation figured out and could approach these people intelligently and with understanding. Shonak and Home had finally come to understand one another, and relations were good now, but he was not pleased with his decisions as OE in the first segments and portions of their first contact. This led to the establishment of much improved procedures on "first contact" with other biologic entities and intelligent life which Bon was proud of. He was pleased they would not be making the same mistakes in the future.

Such a long road to this point, he mused. In his 1700 S-Rots of life, he had done so much but could see ahead that there was so much more to do . . . .

Chapter Sixteen

Wrapping It Up

In his sleep, Bon quietly passed into Spirit just a few portions after he reached his 1701st birthday. He was expected to live longer but was simply out of time. The Medical Eldest suspected that his activity on Plus-Five in his now famously modified phase suit with the hole in the head cover had something to do with his earlier-than-expected demise. He also noted that by the standards of most Shonakians, who pass in their sixteen-hundreds or earlier, he had lived longer than most. Not that it mattered. When you are out of time, at whatever age, you are out of time, and for all the rest of them, the living life goes on. Bon's new succession plan came into effect when the oldest member of the Council of Twelve assumed the post of OE, who by doing so ratified the concept. The Medical Eldest handed him the now famous OE wrist badge so recently taken off Bon's wrist and the Eldest Age saw to his forehead tattoo.

As a consequence, those few who were older than he was felt it was their duty to self-terminate. What else was there to live for? They were ready and glad to go, having lived very long lives doing good hard work for the furtherance of Shonak's health and welfare. This became a standard for future self-terminations. The age of the oldest member of the Council was informally considered the maximum allowable age for everyone but him. And so, in a de facto sense, the old ways were continued with the OE being the oldest living Shonakian. That just felt "right" to them.

Bon's body was duly cremated and used to feed their agriculture. Itself personally greeted his spirit, his soul, as it were, and ensured the transition from that ultra-slow vibration was a smooth one, difficult as it was after so long a time with the almost standstill resonance at Prime vibration. Atsa also greeted him at the Bridge and they smiled at each other, shook hands, remembering all the times they shared in pursuit of their separate but overlapping life goals. Feeling young again, with memories as fresh as yesterday, no words need be spoken, it was all there in their spirit memories. Had they wished to speak they could easily have thought-created a mouth to do so, complete with recognizable body if they wanted it, but it seemed to Bon so "yesterday" at this point . . . . .

And time marched on. But no longer for Bon, who was above all that now, literally. At last, he understood!

Bon's spirit began the serious transition from Bon's experiences to its own energy self's understanding; of itself and all that had gone before. This led to that period of reflection and Learning so fundamental to its Journey. It could see clearly that the things which mattered to a successful Shonakian were not necessarily the things which should have. There were a great many disappointments among the thousands of people whose lives he impacted directly, both on Shonak and Earth, and especially Earth. His time there with Atsa was productive for Learning life lessons, much more so than his many centuries on Shonak, where nothing much happened in terms of conflicted choices between good and evil, right and wrong, love over hate. While he never hated anything in his life as a Shonakian he did cause people on Earth to hate him, or Atsa, or what they were doing. This he could now regret and apologize for, truly, without the burden of a physical partner's conflicted and clouded view of things. He was keen to apologize for the deaths he caused or helped to cause during his years on Plus-Five as a bot he controlled from the safety of Plus-Five Base. How different it all was now from this perspective! If only he had known . . . .

q His time with modern Earth was no less burdened with these traumas. The assistance he freely gave to Earth's law enforcement to rid their planet of crime and corruption caused huge ripples in the Cosmos as the hate came forth in waves from the people being arrested and whose lives were disrupted and ended, even. He could see now that the social ripples of Operation Purge were immense and spent some significant effort in apologizing, once again, for all the human pain he caused. He knew now that he loved them all but did not recognize it at the time. He was only seeing his mission through to its successful conclusion. To be sure, that overall goal of a more peaceful, law-abiding placid Earth was achieved but at enormous social cost. He could see that indeed; the end does not justify the means. He was no longer blind to the perspective of the criminal class and also no longer tied to the logic of "might makes right," or "It will be worth it in the end." That covered his and everyone else's conscience during those times, but it all seems so pointless, now. All people, on all planets with IPLF, are simply flawed beings who make both good and bad choices. They are all to be Loved even though it is perfectly OK to disapprove of what they do, what choices they make. It is even permissible to punish these people with death, but the thought must always be that the person is loved while what they did was reviled. This, Bon could see, is the great lesson of the Universe. Love over Hate regardless of provocation, as evidenced by every thought, word, and deed.

As the-vibration-most-recently-Bon began its reflection and then research into where and when it would partner with another IPLF, it vowed to remember that important lesson.

Glossary Of Term

Relevant Shonak Measurements

one Solar Rotation (S-Rot) = one Earth Year

one Planetary Rotation (P-Rot) = one Earth Day

Shonak has no weeks or months

Planetary Rotations (Days) are numbered 1 through 365

100 Portions = one Earth Day

1 Portion = 14.4 Earth Minutes

1 Portion has 100 Segments, each equivalent to .144 Earth Minutes

About the Author

Dennis retired from the Army in 2000, after thirty years, and five wars; Vietnam and the First Gulf War, The Cold War, the Global War on Terror, and the peace keeping effort in the Balkans. He is a retired Army Colonel, a combat wounded veteran, and in spite of his first book, A Million Monkeys, not at all religious. The first part of his life was entirely conventional. He grew up in a non-religious Navy family, living around the country and around the world, until his father retired in Phoenix, Arizona. Dennis was in the seventh grade.

After graduation from Arizona State University Dennis went into the Army via the RoTC program and his first tour of duty was in Vietnam where he was wounded by enemy mortar fire. He served for thirty years, more than half of which was overseas, as noted above. In addition, he was the US Army's first "Cyber Cop" and when he retired in 2000, he went to work in the cyber security business. After the tragedy of 9/11, he was hired by the Massachusetts Port Authority to run the security program overseeing three airports and the city's seaports.

As he got older things in his life changed. He married an accomplished artist with a PsyD who was also ordained as a minister in the Church of Spiritualism.

He became a Reiki Master and studied spiritual things while being "coached" through the contents of A Million Monkeys, the Real Story Behind Genesis and The Meaning of Life. It was an odd sensation for this old soldier to channel a Spirit in writing this book. Dennis found the whole thing difficult to accept but finally translated the thoughts he was given into what you can read yourself.

Dennis was more comfortable accepting his role as Narrator of the story, not the originator, and as a result wrote the book in the second person, since it is essentially a lecture to Humanity by a Spirit describing itself only as a "Super-Soul of some magnitude." It may be seen as religious as it covers religious subjects, but it should not be seen as the enemy of established religions. They are what they are and as creations of Mankind, are understandably flawed however well-intentioned. If you are looking for the answers, that is, the actual answers to Genesis and the Meaning of Life, this is the book you need to read.

The second book, The Crown of Happenstance, completes the story from A Million Monkeys but is set in a conventional Science Fiction/Fantasy story. That book relates the interaction of the planet Shonak with that of Earth, around about 1000 BCE. The reader is introduced to the cousin planet Shonak, which is an alternate reality version of Earth. The people who evolved there are totally different from natives of Earth, in pretty much every way that matters. No money, no sex, no politics, no relaxation, no gourmet food, no alcohol, no disease, no anger, no love, no families, no religion—just work.

One of their most accomplished citizens is given

the task of finalizing their mission on Earth, which they call PlusFive, and he sets about it with the help of a proto Hopi named Atsa. Together they constitute a formidable team, each seeking to further their own agenda by finding and exploiting The Crown of Happenstance, which is said to confer god-like powers on whoever wears it.

The Third book, It's About Time, is about that same notable Shonakian, Gold Bon, and his mission to answer nearly imponderable questions about the nature of Time itself. Along the way he develops a strong connection with the now modern Earth, introducing them to Shonak and using Shonak's superior technology to help Earth cope with crime, overpopulation, pollution, and the like. The true, and benign agenda of Shonak on Earth is simply watching Earthers go about their daily lives. Shonakians, whose lives are full but boring, find Earth Watching to be hugely entertaining. To them we are large, hairy, sweaty, violent people who do, say, and think things no Shonakian would ever do, say, or think.

To provide the fullest measure of infotainment feeds from Earth, the Shonakians have put millions of "bots" around the planet, some looking like dogs or cats, eagles, mice, or cockroaches. The most intrusive, however, are the ones that replicate humans in every possible way. Using their vast fleet of surveillance collectors, Shonak has turned Earth into a giant cultural theme park, or zoo, for their amusement. In the end, Bon deals with their complex relationship with Earth and finally makes peace with it.

The fourth book, Bot Diaries, is a compilation of bot collection efforts, thoroughly researched by the various vid-watch clubs on Shonak, to trace some of the more obscure images they have collected. One such "diary" traces the location of the Thirty Pieces of Silver that were paid to Judas Escariot to betray Jesus Christ. Watch for this to come out later in 2020.

About His Books

THE SHONAK SERIES

THE CROWN OF HAPPENSTANCE on its surface this book is about a search for something that may or may not even exist. It is known by many names but the most common is The Crown of Happenstance, and it is rumored to confer god-like powers on whoever wears it. Many rich and powerful rulers on Earth in 1000 BCE are after this Crown for all the obvious reasons, chief of which is to dominate every other ruler who is looking for it. But they are not the only people looking for this Crown. A brilliant race of people from another version of Earth have heard stories of it and what it can do and they also want it. These people, from a very old race of technocrats, already have, through science, what the people of Earth would call god-like powers. They want the Crown for what their science cannot provide—a way of visiting and using the magic of the non-physical parts of Creation. They dream of this Crown giving them the ability to usethoughtcreation to further advance their civilization. These visitors to this Earth are from Shonak, and have established an outpost on Earth to conduct the reconnaissance necessary to find the Crown. During the sixteen hundred years they have been on Earth they have not found it, or even any clues as to where it may be found. Some of their deep thinkers theorize that the short-lived people of Earth have possibly invented stories about this Crown to give people a ray of hope against their decidedly dangerous and difficult lives. Frustrated at their lack of progress in finding it, or anything else of use to Shonak, they have sent their go-to-guy Bon to bring the mission on Earth to successful conclusion. Bon finds young

Atsa, a native of Earth, to help him find the Crown. Atsa lives in a Pueblo village in the Desert Southwest. The joint adventures of Bon and Atsa become legend and at the end of their time together both can claim a measure of success. While they pursue the Crown they are under the constant scrutiny of another race entirely. Not of this Earth, or Shonak, this third party might rightly claim they are children of the Universe. They are alternately called "spirits" or even "souls". They share an interest in the search for the Crown of Happenstance but they see it in a totally different way. And in the end, it is their vision that really matters.

A MILLION MONKEYS

Dennis Treece explains the way this material came to him then narrates the unfolding story of how it all works, how life works, how death works, what human suffering is all about and why it is so common. In the telling, this book provides the answers to life's most fundamental questions Ever wonder what you are here for, what life is all about? Not just your life, but everybody's? How did it all begin and why? Most people accept that they have a soul but what is the nature of the human/soul partnership? What do you get out of it, and what does the soul experience and learn from it? What are souls, anyway? Who are they? Keep reading. You will learn the true nature of Heaven and Hell, what happens when we die, and what the Divine Plan is all about. All that and more. This book is a must-read for everyone who claims a piece of the human condition.

CPSIA information can be obtained
at www.ICGtesting.com
Printed in the USA
JSHW050004210920
8025JS00002B/7

9 781989 942000